Maria Lewis got her start covering police rounds in a news-room as a teenager and has been working as a professional journalist for over a decade. Making the switch from writing about murders to movie stars was not a difficult decision. A former reporter at the *Daily Telegraph*, she also wrote about all things film and entertainment related as the Showbusiness Reporter for the *Daily Mail*. Her work has appeared in the *New York Post*, *Empire* magazine, *Huffington Post*, the *Sunday Mail*, CollegeHumor, Daily Life, Junkee and BuzzFeed, to name but a few.

She's the host and producer of the Eff Yeah Film & Feminism podcast and also presents the Bad Bitches Of History segment on Australia's only gay and lesbian radio station JOY 94.9FM. Maria currently works on nightly news program The Feed at SBS. Based in Sydney, Australia she lives in a house with too many movie posters and just the right amount of humans. She's most likely Idris Elba's future wife. Most likely.

Visit Maria Lewis online:

www.marialewis.com.au/
www.facebook.com/marialewiswriter
www.twitter.com/moviemazz

'It's about time we had another kick-arse werewolf heroine – can't wait to find out what happens next!'

New York Times
bestselling author Keri Arthur

'Gripping, fast-paced and completely unexpected, *Who's Afraid?* has more twists than a tornado. I loved this story! Maria Lewis is definitely one to watch'

New York Times
bestselling author Darynda Jones

'The next *True Blood*'

NW Magazine

'Journalist Maria Lewis grabs the paranormal fiction genre by the scruff of its neck to give it a shake with her debut novel *Who's Afraid?*'

The West Australian

'It's *Underworld* meets *Animal Kingdom*'

ALPHA Reader

'Truly one of the best in the genre I have ever read'
Oscar nominee Lexi Alexander (*Green Street Hooligans*, *Punisher*: *War Zone*, *Arrow*, *Supergirl*)

'Lewis creates an intriguing world that's just begging to be fleshed out in further books'

APN

'If you haven't heard about Maria Lewis's new urban fantasy novel *Who's Afraid?* you must have been living under a rock'
Good Reading Magazine

'Definitely worth reading over and over again, as well as buying multiple copies. Great stocking stuffers, those werewolf books'
Maria Lewis' mum

Also by Maria Lewis

Who's Afraid?

Who's Afraid Too?

Maria Lewis

piatkus

PIATKUS

First published in Great Britain in 2017 by Piatkus
This paperback edition published in 2017 by Piatkus

1 3 5 7 9 10 8 6 4 2

A CIP catalogue record for this book
is available from the British Library.

ISBN 978-0-349-40899-6

Typeset in Sabon by Hewer Text UK Ltd, Edinburgh
Printed and bound in Great Britain by Clays Ltd, St Ives, plc

Papers used by Piatkus are from well-managed forests
and other responsible sources.

MIX
Paper from
responsible sources
FSC® C104740

Piatkus
An imprint of
Little, Brown Book Group
Carmelite House
50 Victoria Embankment
London EC4Y 0DZ

An Hachette UK Company
www.hachette.co.uk

This book is dedicated to Pat O'Keefe: coach, lunatic, legend, boiled egg incarnate.

Thank you for buying *Who's Afraid?* even though 'this werewolf shit' might never have been your chosen glass of Scotch.

R.I.P Patty Cakes.

Chapter 1

It was a peaceful view. The cluster of flats looked down on an old cemetery that was mostly used as a park by local families. The youngest grave dated back to the early 1900s. Many of the tombstones were much, much older. The more beautiful headstones were at the centre of the space, whereas the forgotten ones – the ones falling into disrepair – lined the perimeter where thick foliage attempted to claim them as their own. Vines snaked along the crumbling arms of a grey angel that was resting on a mass of large bushes. Within these bushes sat two men, still and silent.

They were practically invisible as they watched the couple in the flat above go about the tedium of their daily lives. Dressed head-to-toe in black, they seemed to bleed into the darkness of the surrounding night. A bat went to land at the top of the bush and, upon sensing their presence, quickly made for a tree further away.

The nursery was on the second floor of the building and painted in traditional blue. The woman bent down to kiss the baby boy as he squirmed on the mattress. Tiptoeing from the room, she left the door half open so she could come and check on him later.

Another hour passed before the two men in the bushes even began to think about moving. They were waiting for their moment. One moved his head to the side, catching the eye of the other. They nodded in unison. Soundlessly they crept forward and out of cover. There was nothing remarkable about their clothes: black and practical. It was their faces that were more interesting. Both men were relatively pale and the shorter of the two had dark hair cut into a tidy style. As the faint light cast from a distant street lamp crossed his face, two thick scars could be seen running from his temple to his chin. His left eye was white and grey, blind to the world and whatever was happening within it. It didn't seem to affect him though. He moved with more grace and precision than someone else might with four eyes.

The taller man was sporting a heavy beard that acted as a mask, almost completely covering the bottom half of his face. Black, beady eyes peered out from under caterpillar eyebrows and the rest of his hair grew out in trimmed, fuzzy agreement. All it took was for them to reach above their heads and pull themselves up the old brick wall of the cemetery before they were level with the Maentells' balcony. The sliding door was even left slightly ajar. Ignoring it, they craned their necks and looked directly up at the window of the nursery above them. Dropping to a crouch, the men tensed before launching themselves in the air and up the wall. You could barely hear a noise as they scaled the side of the building, pausing only at the window to the nursery as the taller man wedged it open effortlessly.

They slipped into the room and landed with a tiny thump on the carpet next to the cot. The short man walked to the door and listened. Satisfied with what he heard, he returned to the cot. The tall man was leaning on the wooden rail and starring down at the sleeping baby. Both men lost themselves for a moment as they watched the rise and fall of the child's chest. There was no parental pride or longing in the identical stares, only hunger. The tall man shook his head slightly and bent down into the cot, scooping the baby up and wrapping it tightly in the cotton blanket.

He didn't even wake.

The short man went first and shot out of the second-storey window. His companion went about it more carefully, determined not to wake the baby. Not that it would matter now. With the baby cradled in one arm, he used his other to steady himself as he landed perfectly on the edge of the wall and took another small leap down on to the graveyard lawn. With not a glance behind them, the two men walked into the darkness where they'd come from and disappeared into the night.

Chapter 2

What do you do when the people you fight for are dead?

How do you go on when the other is dying?

These were questions I never thought I would have to ask myself. And yet, they were questions I'd had running through my mind over and over again since leaving Dundee.

I kept my eyes shut for a few seconds longer and dwelled in the warmth from the afternoon sunshine that poured through the window. Accepting the inevitable I opened my eyes and let them adjust to the light as I stared at the ceiling. I was only five hours out of Dundee, but I may as well have been in another world.

When I had sped out of town four days ago I'd been possessed by the idea of putting distance between me and the rest of the world. The longer I drove and the longer I had my thoughts to myself, the more I realised where I wanted to go: Wigtown.

The tiny village of just 900 people was known as Scotland's 'official book town' after it decided to rebrand itself in the nineties. Every single shop in the village was a bookshop. Oh, sure, they might sell groceries or food as well but the primary produce was knowledge; there were entire shops dedicated to bizarre subgenres you'd struggle to find a single shelf of in your regular library. I'd gotten lost on my way to Port William during a summer road trip with Joss in my late teens and discovered Wigtown accidentally. It had always been somewhere I intended to revisit, except this time I had a reason.

The sun's cameo appearance was fleeting and I rolled on to my stomach, trying to avoid noticing the shift in temperature as the room got gradually colder. Out of habit I looked at my phone, which was turned off and sitting on my bedside table lest Lorcan be able to track me through it. I wasn't even sure if he knew how to use that kind of technology. The scenario that seemed more accurate in my head was him crouching down on the ground, rubbing dirt between his fingers and looking off into the distance before saying 'she's a hundred and eighty-six degrees southwest from here.' I smiled and scolded myself just as quickly: thoughts of Lorcan soon led to thoughts of Mari and Kane. I didn't want to be left alone with those ghosts right now.

Heaving myself out from under the consuming duvet cover, I skipped the shower and began pulling on the first pair of pants I saw on the floor. I quickly fired up my laptop and checked my emails, replying to one from Joss saying that he had arrived at Mechtilde General in Berlin and when was I getting there.

Shrugging myself into a thick woollen jumper that fell to my knees, and grabbing gloves, a beanie and my shoulder bag, I was soon out of the door and trotting down the stairs of the Glaisnock Guest House. Some of the other lodgers were gathered around the fire in the lounge area and I crept down the hallway quietly to avoid saying hello.

I snatched the bell above the main entry door and held it to stop it ringing as I stepped out on to the street. The mid-afternoon air was crisp and the glimpse of sun hadn't done anything to raise the thermostat. Wiggling my fingers into the gloves, I put my head down and walked the same path I'd been taking for the past three days.

Turning down a residential street off the town centre, I only had to go a few paces before entering an alleyway on my right and following it until a canopy of tree branches blocked out the sky above. The path turned to cobblestones the longer I followed it and then eventually a narrow dirt trail as I neared my destination.

Pushing away a low-hanging branch revealed a dark wooden cottage wedged between the natural surrounds so thoroughly it was difficult to tell where the bush ended and the house began. On my first day in town I did little more than sleep, but by day two I was on a quest to make use of this 'time out' I'd called on my supernatural life.

The deaths of Mari and Kane had left me thinking a lot about my mother, Tilly, who had passed almost a year ago now in a flash flood. Her passing had put me on the path to where I was now: a werewolf whose entire concept of what and who she was had been thrown out the window thanks to one fateful trip to New Zealand. My mother had told me a toxic, dangerous lie to ensure I wouldn't do the one thing she feared most: go searching for my father Jonah Ihi. That lie had caused me a lot of pain in retrospect, more than I thought possible, and I was having trouble reconciling it with the once sunny memories I had of my mother.

I had also been left in a new place: isolated from my

heritage but for the first time actually wanting to learn about it. Wigtown had seemed like the perfect place to do that. With more books than it had people, I had started browsing and asking around the various stores to find somewhere that would have the texts I needed. It was a store that specialised in cartography and selling ancient maps that gave me the first helpful suggestion, although with reluctance. The shop owner had suggested I try The Cavern.

'I wouldn't usually recommend it, especially to tourists,' he'd said at the time, uncomfortably tugging at a thread on his cardigan. 'But if that's what you're looking for I doubt you'll find a better resource for it in Scotland.'

His directions hadn't been precise and I'd ended up using my nose to track the scent of musty old books right to the doorway I was stepping through presently. One of the locals at the town's only tavern had warned me about going here, adding that the owner was a 'nasty old man' who 'hated visitors'. Commerce seemed like the wrong industry to get into for a recluse and I tended to have a way with nasty old men, so I'd disregarded the warning and had set out for The Cavern.

When I'd first entered the cottage, there hadn't been a person in sight. I'd intended to make my presence known when I'd first arrived so that if the owner had wanted to chase me out he had the opportunity at the beginning. Yet there hadn't been an owner to be found. Instead there was row after row of books: they'd started on shelves, but as the space had filled up, columns had been erected on the carpeted floors.

I'd let out an impressed sigh as I'd stepped further into the depths, my fingers trailing along the dusty spines. I'd scanned titles like *Wonder Tales from Scottish Myth and Legend* and *Collected Conspiracies: From Australia to Austria*. I'd picked up the very first book I'd seen with New Zealand in the title – well, had carefully wiggled from the pile like a Jenga block – and before I knew it I had been tucked into the window seat and deeply involved in the historical text. There'd been little about Maori culture or traditions, but there had been an entire chapter on the arrival of Europeans and the ensuing conflicts, treaties and negotiations.

I wasn't sure how long he'd been standing there, but with werewolf senses it was rare that someone was able to sneak up on me. Slowly, I'd lifted my head from the book to meet the penetrating eyes of the diminutive old man staring back at me. I don't know what I'd expected, but I definitely hadn't expected him to be Maori. It was rare for me to see my heritage reflected back at me in Scotland: even rarer in a tiny town that was barely a blip on the radar. Yet there he'd stood, staring right through me as if I'd been bathing in Windex. He'd broken my gaze and had glanced down at the book I'd been reading, then he'd lifted it in my hands to see the title. He'd made a dismissive snorting sound and had snatched it from my hands and stalked off into the maze of books.

'Hey! I was reading that,' I'd said, following his tiny frame as he'd weaved in and out of the row of books. He'd come to an abrupt halt and I'd had to stop myself from walking right into him as he'd bent down and plucked three heavy volumes from a pile.

'Here,' he'd said, turning and handing them to me. 'What you're looking for you won't find in that tourist brochure you were reading. Start with these and then we can talk.'

Open-mouthed, I'd glanced at what he had offloaded to me: *Dreamtime to Maori Deities: Australasian Myths and Legends*, *The Ancient Ways – Polynesian Principles And Understanding* and *Creation Stories of the Maori People*. By the time I'd read the titles he'd disappeared back into the depths of the cottage and had left me to my own devices.

By my third day of coming here, we'd settled into a pattern: I returned whatever books he'd given me the night before and got to work on the new ones he had laid out that day. This time he had a steaming cup of tea made just the way I like it waiting next to the pile of books, as if he'd known the exact moment I was coming. The day before there had been a ham and cheese sandwich. He rarely said a word to me and only occasionally drifted by to see how I was progressing.

I sat at the window seat and moved the books aside, warming my hands on the tea. I sensed his presence before I saw him and I mentally tracked his path to where I sat using my enhanced hearing and scent. He was holding a fat, ginger cat that was purring loudly as he stroked it. This man watched me, always watched me, as if he was moving cautiously in my presence. He moved an old newspaper from an armchair with one hand and sat down to join me. Questions were dancing on my lips, dying to surge forward and take centre stage, but I waited. Somehow I sensed that he had to speak first. And he did.

'This is David.'

'Who is?' I asked.

'The cat.'

'The cat is David?'

'Yes. I thought it was an amusing name.' The way he said the word 'amusing' made the very concept seem foreign and strange, as if he was unsure what amusement was. He gave me a vague smile. 'I'm Chester.'

I raised my eyebrows. 'Tommi.'

'Chester Rangi.'

'Tommi Grayson.'

He nodded.

'When I asked around town about this place, I didn't expect you to be –'

'Polynesian? Like you?'

I shrugged. 'Nice, actually.'

He laughed and the sound was mildly terrifying. Even David was startled, leaping off his master's lap and running for cover.

'Were you, uh, expecting me?' I asked.

'Yes. And no. One should always expect brothers and sisters even when they're not expected.'

Great. Fucking mystical riddles. I wanted to ask him if he had always lived in Scotland because his Kiwi accent was vague, but I didn't want a reply like 'always and never'.

'What have you learned?' he asked, nodding at the books.

'A lot,' I replied with a sigh. 'Although I'm not sure exactly what I'm trying to learn or what I'm looking for ... just a beginning, I guess.'

'You need to tell me your story.'

It wasn't a request: it was a demand. Lorcan's face flashed to my mind and I pushed it away, tracing the scars that encircled my wrist instead. If Chester noticed, I couldn't tell. He just held my gaze until suddenly I was telling him my story. Not the furry version, mind you, the sanitised version. When I finished, he was silent for such a long while I wondered if he had fallen asleep. But then he blinked and shifted in his seat, playing with the faint hair that was growing on the chin of his old, wrinkled face.

'No plurals,' he stated.

'What?'

'No plurals. Pākehā might throw an S on the end of everything, but we are not them. That's not how we speak about our people.'

'Pākehā,' I frowned, recalling the term that I had just read two chapters earlier. 'New Zealanders of European descent.'

'White people,' he corrected. 'You are not that. You're not completely us either, but when you speak of your blood – Tommi Ihi – it's Te Whānau Ihi. No S.'

'Te Whānau Ihi,' I repeated, mimicking his pronunciation before I frowned. 'And it's Tommi Grayson, so we're crystal-bloody-clear.'

He shrugged. 'You feel lost.'

'Aye. And confused.'

'You feel betrayed by your mother.'

'Yes,' I gulped, as he cut right through the bullshit.

'And you think researching Maori history will help?'

'I . . . I don't know. I feel like I'm simultaneously running from and to it. I never had any desire to learn about this side of me before and now after everything, I've realised I'm alone. Truly alone.'

'To live this life is to be alone,' he said. 'That's the reality. You have friends, you have family, you have loved ones. They leave and you lose. People are in your life like seasons. The only way to survive is to become comfortable with the person you're left with when everything else is stripped away.'

I thought about that idea and instinctually found myself tilting my chin upwards, proud. I was a killer. I had killed people to exist here. I was a werewolf and I chose to be bound by no pack. I was Tommi Grayson, lover of art and booze. I was Scottish and I was Maori. Both of my parents were dead and it was only me who could define myself. I was aware of who 'she' was, even if I was uncomfortable with some of the things I had done and some of the things I could do.

'Good,' Chester said. I frowned, thinking not for the first time that he may be able to read my thoughts. 'Now throw away the notion of ever being one of your clan. You may be their blood but you lack the heritage, you lack the years of cultural understanding. No matter how many books you read, you're never going to be able to make up for that.'

'I . . . I know. But what else can I do?'

'Be informed. That is all. Your spiritual ties are severed and they're not the kind of thing that can be sewn back together. Believe me, I know.'

'Huh.'

'You need to become comfortable with being removed, with being *other*.'

I smiled, thinking about just how 'other' I was. 'Alright, I don't think that will be too hard.'

'Now you need to forgive your mother.'

I repressed a growl. 'You're not my shrink.'

'No, but I am right.'

'She lied to me, *for years*. More than that, she let me believe I was the product of a rape.'

'And what was the alternative?' asked Chester. 'Tell you the truth? What would have been more horrific for a child to hear, the lie or the fact that you're a werewolf?'

My instincts were so sharp after weeks of training and transformation with Lorcan that I was on my feet and poised for a fight in less than a second. One of several weapons I had now taken to carrying with me always – in this case, a Scipio dagger – was resting comfortably in my hand with the pointy end towards my target. I liked Chester, I didn't want to hurt him, which is why I had positioned myself in front of the exit. I'd run rather than hurt him if I could, but if he was truly a danger to me I would do what needed to be done. I felt the wolf stir deep down inside me as adrenaline coursed through my veins.

'Okay, no more Mister Nice Old Man. Who the hell are you? Are you Askari?'

Chester blinked at me, seemingly undisturbed by my reaction or the fact that I was armed. Most telling of all, he appeared totally cool about the fact he was chatting to a werewolf. 'You didn't answer the question, Tommi. She was trying to protect you.'

'And to do that she –'

'Oh, boo hoo hoo. Get over it. You're not, are you? You're something else altogether. Your mother is dead; you being mad at her for trying to protect you from being claimed by a pack of werewolves is not going to get you anywhere. If you were in her shoes, tell me, what would you have done? What else would have ensured her inquisitive daughter didn't go probing?'

The tension was thick between us as I tried to focus on his words and any sudden movements he might make.

'Who. Are. You?' I growled through gritted teeth.

He batted a hand at me in a flippant gesture. 'Don't be mad at me, little werewolf girl. If anyone is mad it should be me but I got over that in the first five minutes. Sending a kathurungi to my door, ha!'

'Sent? Nobody sent me,' I hissed.

His dark eyes fixed on me and his mouth twitched with a smile. 'Didn't they?'

'No! And enough with the freakin' riddles and questions within questions, Yoda. It was pure coincidence I ended up here.'

'At this exact time in your life, when you needed answers the most? Sounds like fate. Sounds like someone is pulling your strings.'

I was about ready to stab him out of irritation and seconds away from telling him just that when he broke in.

'I wouldn't, if I were you.'

The hairs on my arms stood up. '*What are you?*'

'You were closer the first time. It's who I am not what I am that should interest you.'

'Who are you then?'

'Chester Rangi,' he grinned.

'ARGH! I give up!' I shouted, spinning on my heels and storming out of the cottage in a blur of motion while his laughter followed behind me down the pathway and echoed off the walls of the alley.

I'd left the books, I'd left my tea, I'd left answers in a bid to be free of the spider web of his words. Although I had decided the old man wasn't an immediate threat to me, my instincts told me he was dangerous. He knew impossible things. He knew about me. A telepath seemed like the only answer but as I walked back to the guest house I felt eyes on me. Someone or something thing was watching me. Yes, Chester Rangi was definitely *more*. Chester Rangi was *other*.

I picked up the pace and didn't fully relax until I was inside and pressed against the door of my room. I let out a breath I didn't know I'd been holding and contemplated leaving town tonight. And go where? Drive right through to London at night and hop on the next plane to Berlin like I was originally supposed to do? If Chester was truly dangerous, I would be dead by now. No one knew I was here besides a few locals who could be taken care of easily enough and he had plenty of opportunities. Instead he had not only helped me – loaned me books, prodded me in the right direction – he'd made me lunch. These were not the actions of someone readying to kill you. He was amused by me, I realised, and for whatever reason this had bought me some kind of leeway that was dangerously close to expiring. Tracking be damned, I turned on my phone and dialled Joss.

'It lives,' croaked a voice from the other end of the phone.

'And you?' I asked. My heart dropped at the hollow sound of his voice.

He laughed lightly. 'I live.'

'The important question, Joss, is do you live large?'

'Aye, I'm living large.'

'All up and down the halls of the oncology ward, I bet.'

'Speaking of large, you should see the games room they've added here. PlayStation, Xbox, air hockey, it's lush.'

'That will keep you occupied. But seriously, the trip was okay?'

'Yeah, you should have seen the hot paramedic I had. She was *fit*. She even came back to visit this morning. I think she wants me.'

'Totally,' I replied with a mock serious tone.

'Where are you?'

'Umm . . .' I peered out from behind the blinds of my room and looked down at the empty street below.

'Tommi?'

'I'm not technically in Berlin yet.'

'What? I thought you were flying out the day after me? Are you trying to swim here?'

I chuckled. 'No, you N.E.D. I'm just taking a few days.'

'I bet. Probably takes a few days to farewell Lorcan with sex from dusk to da–'

'JOSS. No.' As far as my best friend knew, Lorcan was staying behind in Dundee and continuing on with his life since – despite what Joss thought – we definitely were 100 per cent *not* dating. There was no way I would be able to explain away Lorcan being in Berlin with me. It would be too . . . weird. I cleared my throat and ignored the laughter at the other end of the line.

'I'm actually in Wigtown, and there's zero sex involved, I'll have you know.'

'Wigtown? Really?'

'Word.'

'What are you doing there?'

'Taking a few days to myself.'

I could almost hear him nodding through the phone. 'Are you alright? I'd say I don't know if being by yourself after Mari and Kane is the best thing but –'

'I'm a lone wolf?' I supplied.

He howled down the phone at me and paused to address a coughing fit.

'Dude, don't die for the sake of a pun – breathe – that's it. Take a sip of water and settle it down,' I urged. I heard his breathing steady and I felt a surge of relief wash over me. 'That better? You okay?'

'Ergh, yeah. Shit's moving fast this time – I'm wheezing like an old man.'

'Don't say that. And speaking of, I actually met the weirdest old man here. You would hate him. He speaks in riddles.'

'Like Mr Miyagi?'

'Nailed it.'

'Sounds like a bawbag. In all seriousness though, when are you getting here?'

I thought about it carefully. I couldn't risk staying in Wigtown much longer now that Chester knew what I was. It was also clear my best friend needed me and he was one of the only things I had left. To add to that list, I was expected by the Rogues.

'Tomorrow,' I replied at last. 'Tomorrow night. I'll come see you the next day. When are visiting hours?'

'I put you down as family with Ma and Pa so you can come anytime.'

'Clever boy. Do you want me to bring anything?'

'I can't think of anything. You always find stuff I didn't know I needed though.'

True. I was already thinking of grabbing Joss the first few volumes of *The Boys* and a She-Hulk single issue from the comic book store in town. 'Done.'

'So I'll see you in a bit?'
'I'll see you in a bit,' I replied, before hanging up.

I tossed and turned that night, mulling over the risks and the realities before resolving to visit Chester again in the morning – one last time. He had been kind to me, showed me hospitality and in return I had threatened him with a dagger in his own home. Why? Because he scared me. He knew too much and I had told him too little. I had no doubt now that he was a supernatural creature just like me, yet given I was so uneducated with different beings and their ways it seemed only right that I try and fix this, that I try and show a little bit of human courtesy even though the two of us were very far from that. By the time the sun rose I was packing my suitcase and eating porridge downstairs in the dining room with the owners of the place. I told them I would be checking out and they gave me until 6 p.m. that evening to do it, which was gracious.

It was slightly warmer today as I strode to The Cavern in a mini-skirt with a thick pair of aqua tights underneath and knee-high boots. I hadn't bothered to tie up my hair and my long, blue locks trailed behind me as I ducked into the only supermarket in town and bought three types of their most expensive tea and a block of dark chocolate. They were peace offerings. I paused on the dirt path to the cottage, something teasing at my senses. I stilled myself and listened to the quiet surrounds. I jumped at the sound of a deep grunt followed by a crash and glass smashing. Arming myself as I ran, I pushed through the open door and burst into the most unlikely of scenarios.

'CHESTER!' I shouted, thinking that I was running in to rescue the old man.

Lorcan was sprawled on the ground, struggling to get up as blood trickled from the corner of his mouth. Chester was standing over him, face twisted in rage and his eyes . . . I knew I was not mistaken in seeing a glow there. It was fading slowly with every laboured breath he took and his pupils eventually settled back to their usual shade of black. Lorcan stumbled to his feet as he wiped his mouth, looking confused as he pulled his hand away and noticed blood there.

'Tommi, stay back,' he said, waving his hand at me but never once taking his eyes off Chester.

I looked from him to Chester and back again, wondering what I had just walked in on and knowing I was right about the danger the old man presented.

'You know this man?' asked Chester, his eyebrows raised in a question.

'Well, uh, yeah he's –'

'Don't say another word, Tommi,' Lorcan cut in.

'He's my Custodian,' I finished, meeting the angry look Lorcan threw my way. 'Hey, don't be mad at me. I'm not the one who made you bleed your own blood.'

'A Custodian,' Chester whispered in a way that made it sound like a curse.

'You need to stay away from her,' Lorcan snarled.

Chester threw his head back and laughed. 'She came to me, old one. She sought my help.'

'Yo, *men*,' I started. 'Quit talking about me as if I'm not standing here in the room with you while you bicker like toddlers.'

That drew the attention of them both and their heads snapped at me. I lowered the machete I had been holding and tucked it back into the sheath I'd stowed in my shoulder bag. I needed to resolve this situation quickly and quietly, because if Chester could do that to Lorcan I hated to think what he could do to me.

'Lo, I think you should wait outside for a second and let me talk to Chester,' I said softly, imploring him to listen to me and take the high ground. To his credit, he kept his mouth shut and nodded, just once. He cast a wary look at Chester and against his better judgement, turned his back to him and began walking out of The Cavern.

Chester chuckled. 'That's right, run away at the words of the little werewolf girl.'

Lorcan ignored him and paused next to me, lightly touching my arm. 'I'll be waiting for you outside.'

'Give me two secs.' I waited until his footsteps took him beyond the cottage and to the dirt path. I watched Chester visibly relax in the shoulders as Lorcan left, but I wasn't foolish enough to think him the same kooky old man as before. He knew what I had been thinking, I could see it in his eyes, and the way he glanced at where Lorcan had left and back to me again made me think he knew a lot more too.

'What's that?' he asked, gesturing to the bag I held in my hand.

I looked down at the tea and chocolate, feeling feeble in my offering. 'It was a peace gesture.'

'Was?'

'Well, until I came in here to find you throwing around my Custodian.'

Chester smiled at my description. 'He's a lot more than *just* a Custodian and you're a lot more than *just* his ward. How interesting you turned out to be, Tommi Grayson.'

'I could say the same to you but it seems like a grandiose understatement.'

He smiled and gestured for the bag. I slid it across the floor to him, conscious of not getting too close. He inspected its contents and grinned. 'This is a lovely peace gesture. Is it too late to accept?'

'What . . . what are you?' I asked, not for the first time.

'I'm sure he will explain that to you,' Chester replied, nodding at where Lorcan had taken his exit. 'Incorrectly.'

'I'm not asking him, I'm asking you. What kind of man are you? Or creature –'

'I'm not a man.'

'You're transitioning?'

'No, no, what I mean is I'm not a man and I'm not a woman. I'm not human, I'm . . .'

'Other?'

He smiled. 'Other is apt. I'm other. The word for what I am no longer exists.'

'Why did you help me? If you're so dangerous and old and powerful, why did you help me? What do you care for my problems?'

'Ah, that is the question, isn't it? I guess the simple answer is you intrigue me.'

'Um, yay?'

'Yay indeed.'

I shuffled my feet awkwardly, not sure where else this conversation could go. Chester looked around the room at the mess from their scuffle and I noticed David peeking out from behind his legs.

'I've liked it here, but I think I've stayed for long enough. Perhaps it's time to move on.'

'Move on to where?'

He smiled at me, the glow in his eyes returning for a brief instant. 'Wherever takes my fancy.'

I took a step back involuntarily and caught myself, but he had seen the movement. 'I'm not going to see you again, am I?'

'Not like this,' he replied, gesturing to himself. 'No.'

I nodded, unsure of how to proceed. 'Then ... thank you. I don't know what else to say besides that.'

'On your way, little wolf.'

I smiled and turned, before pausing to take one final look at him.

'You know,' he said, 'just because I scare you now doesn't mean the words I said are incorrect. You think about that.'

I waved and left, doing my best not to sprint out of the cottage at full speed. Once outside I increased the pace, keeping my eyes focused in front of me and marching as quickly as I could until I was halfway down the alleyway. My ears registered the slightest scuffle of shoes and I spun, machete in hand and ready to pounce. It was Lorcan and I breathed a deep, shuddering sigh of relief. I let my machete drop to the ground as I stepped forward and hugged him with everything I had. I felt his body relax against mine as he embraced me back and I closed my eyes against his shoulder, breathing in his scent. I was the first to break away, untangling myself before pausing to rest my forehead on Lorcan's chest. Mentally I counted his heart beats, taking note of the thud-thud thud-thud that had been beating there for centuries.

'Who was he?' I whispered, still not opening my eyes.

'I was hoping you could tell me.'

I pulled back to look up at him and saw that he wasn't joking. 'He said his name was Chester Rangi. I thought he might have been one of the immortal guys like you, because even though he was Maori he hardly had a Kiwi accent.'

Lorcan frowned. 'He wasn't a Maori man to me.'

'He . . . what?'

Lorcan pulled back fully and began pacing. 'Maybe he appeared like that to you, because that's what you needed to see at the time.'

'And all of the books I needed that were helpful? You can't just magic them out of thin air. Wait, so you didn't start a fight with old man who served your ass up to you on a platter?'

'No,' he said, shaking his head. 'He was someone else. He was Amos to me.'

'Oh my God.'

'It rattled me. I didn't know how to react. Illusion or not, I had settled with the idea of never seeing Amos on this Earth again then . . . there he was, smirking at me.'

'Lo –'

'I followed you there yesterday,' he said, cutting me off as if he didn't want to dwell on his feelings about Amos any further. 'I went early today to find out what was making you spend so much time there.'

'And you found Amos. The fisticuffs make a lot more sense now. I get losing your mind after seeing your dead best friend in a cottage full of books.'

Lorcan nodded, not meeting my eyes. 'His power was obvious, not at first but the longer I watched him the more it seemed to roll off him in waves. If he, she . . . it is what I think it is then they're practically the embodiment of mischief and mayhem.'

'Alright, if this is the part where you say all I needed to do to stop the fight was whisper "mischief managed" then –'

'No,' said Lorcan, running his hands over his jawline, which was shaved clean of his usual stubble. 'It's closer to a demon or a spirit. Maybe "being" is a better choice of words but it's not dissimilar to The Three.'

'Oh. *Oh*. Shit.'

'Yeah. Nobody has seen it for centuries and here you come, stumbling across what you think is in an old book keeper in Wigtown,' he smirked.

My mind flagged on an earlier comment and I started at him. 'Wait, you followed me yesterday? How long have you been watching me?'

'Only a day. You did a good job at covering your tracks. I'm almost proud.'

'You're not mad that I skipped out?'

His head tilted dangerously and I saw a flash of something cross his face. Oh yeah, he had been mad. He took a step toward me and again I found myself taking one back until I was pressed flush against the alley wall.

'Tommi,' he whispered, shaking his head. 'There's more than –'

He paused, inches from my face and I wondered what had made the words die in his throat. He reached out and touched my face, his hand running over the skin where my ear met jawline and I tried to ignore the goosebumps springing up like measles. He moved forward slowly and I did everything I could in my head to will my body to leap away, to run from this situation, but I was powerless as he moved his lips to meet mine.

'Lo,' I said, breathless as I tried to hit pause on the scenario.

'Mmmm?' He was having none of it.

'*Lo.*' I pushed against his chest more forcefully and he stumbled back, blinking as if I'd thrown water in his face. I kept my back against the wall while trying to lower my heart rate. Lorcan was still staring at me wildly and he took a step closer.

'Na-uh, stay right there,' I said, holding up a hand like a traffic director. 'I don't trust myself if you come any closer.'

He froze and took a step back, then took three more. 'Right,' he muttered, running his hand through his short hair. 'Right.'

'Shit,' I said, looking him over. 'Shit, shit, shit. What happened to hitting time out? Damn it.'

'We survived a mischief demon, that's what happened.'

'Sure, blame the adrenaline.'

I was angry with myself as much as I was him. I was a werewolf, I was supposed to lack self-control right? Immortal warriors turned counsellors should be better at, I dunno, keeping it in their pants after 412 years? I was panicking because my four-day journey of self discovery didn't seem to have made any difference. Neither of us was to blame and yet we both were.

'Okay,' I said, sweeping back the hair that had been covering half my face. 'Let's keep moving shall we?'

He raised an eyebrow at me and I laughed in spite of myself. 'No, not . . . terrible phrasing. You know what I mean.'

'To the guest house.'

'Uh . . .' The thought of being alone in a room with Lorcan right now seemed like a dangerous one, but there weren't really a lot of other options left to me. 'There's a café next door, we can grab lunch there and –'

'Talk?' he said, with a smirk.

'Talk,' I repeated.

'You lead the way,' he gestured, stepping aside with a sweeping gesture.

Chapter 3

'Can I take your orders?' asked a waitress so tiny I did a double take.

'What are you, ten?' I said, looking at the smiling kid in a Gravity Falls T-shirt.

'I'm twelve, thank you very much,' she replied, curtly.

'Slave labour,' I muttered. 'You get paid for this, right?'

'Uh-huh. Mum pays me.'

'Aye, alright. Two steaks please, rare, and a beer.'

She gave me a strange look before replying. 'Two steaks?'

'Two.'

'Um . . .'

I looked at her as she struggled to say what she was thinking. She caught my gaze and I smiled.

'We don't serve alcohol,' she murmured.

'Well, good. That was a test and you passed.' The wee girl smiled at me. 'I'll take a cranberry juice instead. What do you want, Lorcan?'

'The chicken penne please and a glass of water.'

'Coming right up,' squeaked our server and she disappeared, leaving the two of us sitting at a tiny table in the café's empty courtyard. I did my best to try and act normal, to not fidget or appear flustered in any way. I wished the tiny waitress was back so I could make more small talk with her instead of getting down to the nitty gritty with Lo. His eyes hadn't left my face since we sat down and I was finding it difficult to avoid staring into his piercing green eyes.

'You look good,' he said and I let out a breathy laugh.

'Yeah, well, you always look good so returning the compliment feels a bit redundant.' It was true; he did look good. His hair was even shorter than when I'd cut for it him and I gathered that was the way he was going to keep it now. He was clean-shaven and handsome, the bastard, and his defined cheekbones were highlighted as he tried to avoid smiling at me.

'This is not going to be easy, is it?' I inhaled and let out a deep sigh.

'No,' he admitted. 'I don't think it's supposed to be.'

I nodded and appreciated his honesty. 'So I guess the Custodians are a little pissed at me disappearing for a few days?'

'They don't know.'

I looked at him, surprised.

'I didn't tell them.'

'And the Rogues?' I asked.

'I delayed it, said we'd be there by tomorrow at the latest.'

'You just assumed you'd be able to convince me to get back on the road?'

'Yes,' he said, unapologetic. 'As far as the Custodians, the Rogues, the Treize, the Praetorian Guard and anyone else that matters knows, I've taken you away for a few days for a meditation retreat.'

I snorted. 'I hope no one examines that alibi too closely.'

'They have no reason to. How did you explain your absence to Joss?'

'I told him the truth, as much as I could. I said I came to Wigtown to wig out for a bit and I'd see him in Berlin soon.'

'He got there okay?'

I cast a sideways look at Lorcan to see if he was being serious. 'Don't pretend like you care.'

'I do care. Just because I'd save you over your friends doesn't mean I don't care about them either.'

'Friend,' I said. 'Singular. The other two main ones are dead, remember?'

'I haven't forgotten,' he said in a measured response.

As a dark swirl of memories and guilt began to rise to the surface of my consciousness I scrunched up my face. No, no, no, no. It always happened like this. Whenever I would think I was doing okay the images of the people I'd killed would come leering out of the past at me.

Six.

I'd killed six people. Brutally. In self-defence, sure, but my conscience only vaguely registered the difference. I wasn't exactly blame-free in the deaths of my former flatmate and close friend Mari and her partner Kane either. My hair fell over my face as I leaned over the edge of the table and dropped my head into my hands.

'Tommi?' The concern in Lorcan's tone was piercing.

'Get it together, girl,' I muttered before taking a shuddering breath and sitting back up. 'I'm okay. I'm okay.'

'Has . . . has that been happening a lot?' he asked.

'I haven't shifted accidentally if that's what you're implying.'

'It wasn't, but that's good to know as well. You remember with extreme emotions like grief or rage –'

'Or love?' I offered.

There was a long pause. 'No. Love doesn't have that effect on a werewolf's transformation.'

'Huh. Good to know. And so you're up to date with the lies, Joss thinks you stayed in Dundee. I haven't corrected him or said any different because I don't know how I'd explain you being in Berlin with me. He already thought we were dating once.'

'He did?'

'I squashed that quickly,' I said and he nodded.

'He can't leave the hospital so there's no likelihood of you bumping into each other. As long as you don't start moon-lighting as a nurse we'll be fine.'

The kid returned with our food and was well trained enough not to ask anything further about why anyone would want two bloody steaks straight after each other. She left without a word and I savoured the first bite (then the next five, which followed in quick succession). Lorcan seemed to only graze his penne, other thoughts occupying his mind.

'If we leave after this,' he said, 'we can catch the last flight to Berlin out of Heathrow tonight.'

I paused mid-chew before swallowing. 'You've lied enough for me. I'm grateful to get to learn from the Rogues as much as I can. I guess I can't put this off any longer.'

'This isn't goodbye to Scotland forever, you know.'

'Aye, I know. This place is in my blood. I'll be back.'

'My next question then is what are we going to do about us?'

I choked on my mouthful of cranberry juice and spluttered to gain fresh air. 'You tell me. If memory serves you made the first move back there, mischief demon or no.'

His stare was inescapable and his eyes held me for several long moments. 'I don't know if I can stay away from you. And with the way we left things –'

'Aye, I understand,' I replied, watching his face carefully.

He sighed. 'I'm not saying it doesn't happen and that it hasn't happened, but Custodian–ward relationships ... I cannot stress enough what kind of scrutiny this would put us both under.'

I snorted. 'Because it's not like we're rule breakers if we want something badly enough.'

His eyes met my own and he smiled slowly and carefully. 'That's true.'

We sat there for some time, neither of us saying anything and yet saying a lot simultaneously. Yes, I was partially at fault for Mari and Kane's deaths but if I shared that responsibility with anyone it was Lorcan. He'd been trying to help me, undoubtedly, but his actions had led to their deaths. Maybe their end was inevitable, maybe it wasn't, but I couldn't help the way I felt. I was torn: so drawn to him and yet angry, frightened – however illogical, part of me blamed him for everything changing.

'I should get the bill and we can go,' he said, standing up and interrupting my thoughts.

I didn't object as I rose to follow him out. I said nothing as he paid and he was quiet as he followed me into the guest house next door to get my things. There was a deep sadness in my steps as I climbed to my room and I knew Lorcan felt it too. Screw all those poets who wrote romantically about love never running smooth – it sucked. It sucked hard. To have all these feelings and know that he had them too, yet still be frozen in place . . . I wanted to punch something, but I settled for slamming the door behind me instead. My breath escaped in a long expelling of tension as I gently rested my head against the wood of the door and banged once, softly.

When I turned around Lorcan was there, closer than I'd expected. He was within touching distance and I could see the tension buzzing over his body like an electric current. He closed the space between us, cupping my face in his hands. Our lips hovered near each other as we both breathed heavily.

'We –' he started, but I cut him off.

'I know.'

I didn't give him a chance to say anything further as I dug my fingernails into the palm of his hand and kissed him, long and deep and lingering. He responded in earnest and I pushed myself away from the door and into his arms, feeling myself surrounded by his limbs as he held me close. I melted into him as I felt the full extent of what he'd been holding back. The sensation was soft as he kissed me, barely more than light contact at first. The second his tongue met my own it was as if my body's memory was activated and every previous encounter came rushing back in a blur of seconds. I found myself leaning into him as I reacquainted myself with the shape of his lips, the rhythm of his movements.

As soon as I gripped the back of his neck he seemed to lose self-control and his hands were tugging at my shirt and it was pulled over my head in a flash, leaving me standing there in my bra as he tossed his shirt to the floor as well. Skin to skin, our flesh pressed together once more and his kisses moved from my mouth to my jaw and down my neck. All self-control went out the window as I pushed the internal protests out of my head and stopped worrying about what this meant, concentrating instead on how it felt.

We inched our way over the bed in the middle of the room and I fell down on my back, wiggling backwards as I tugged at the belt on his pants. It thrilled me to see his chest rising and falling as quickly as mine. I leaned back as he tugged my boots off one after the other. He took his time rolling down my stockings and the wait was agonising. His eyes burned my body wherever they touched and I longed for the physical connection, feeling the build within my heart as it spread to the rest of me. He lowered himself over my body and I pulled him greedily towards me, done with the play.

'Slowly,' he whispered, his teeth grazing the skin above my breast. I shoved him hard until we were reversed, my legs spread over his chest as I sat on top of him. I unclasped my bra and gasped as he brought his mouth towards my chest.

'Fuck that,' I whispered, the last coherent words out of my lips as our bodies truly combined. Both of us were greedily craving each other, desperate to always be touching. My gasps were met with his own, his moans joined in chorus by mine as I shuddered, feeling the warmth spreading between my legs, growing and glowing in a surge until it broke over me in a wave of pleasure and I screamed. His lips kissed mine furiously as he thrust towards his own climax, his hands holding onto the curves of my body as if it was the only thing tethering him to this moment. He collapsed on top of me and we lay wrapped in each other, shuddering occasionally with the aftershocks of good sex. I was absent-mindedly stroking the back of his head as my other hand stayed linked in his on the headboard. His face was resting in the curve between my shoulder and I closed my eyes, forgetting about everything else for a few blissful moments. As his breathing steadied I think I dozed for nothing more than a minute or two. He rolled himself away carefully and looked at me, our two bodies naked and next to each other. Our eyes met and we both saw the realisation of our actions reflected there.

'Meditation retreat,' I said, my voice sounding distant as I sat up and perched myself on the side of the bed.

'Nobody has to know,' he said, from behind me and I spun to face him.

'You're so romantic, thanks.'

'You know what I mean,' he replied, rising to his feet, the condom wrapper crinkling under his movement. I gulped as I took in his naked form and appreciated the lean combination of muscles and sweet-ass before me. 'This, it can be our farewell to what could have been – the idea of that.'

I nodded, biting my lip as all the reservations and blame came rushing back to the surface of my mind. I huffed internally, noting that they had so conveniently disappeared when presented with the prospect of an orgasm.

'A . . . clean slate,' I said. There were a thousand other things I wanted to say, things that I wanted to bask in. Hell, I wouldn't have been opposed to going another round. Instead what I said was, 'I need to shower.'

*   *   *

One road trip, flight and tram ride later I soon realised twelve hours wasn't enough time for me to get sex with Lorcan off my mind. For the most part I'd had my head buried in two books that had been left for me at reception when I finally checked out of the guest house: a last parting gift left by Chester. It wouldn't have been hard to find out where I was staying, but the fact he had known creeped me out nonetheless.

With the Smashing Pumpkins on repeat in my headphones, Billy Corgan's melodies kept my mind more on track than the literature did (*Haka to Hangi* and *The Modern Maori*). I spent the entirety of the flight staring out the window of the plane and getting lost in the night sky. I partially blamed Lorcan for the death of my best friends, yet I'd still slept with him; what did that say about me? For the most part Lorcan had left me to my own devices: there seemed to be plenty on his mind too. But now we were pulling up to our final destination in the heart of Berlin.

'So this group of lone wolves all just happily live together? Even though they've rejected the pack system?' I asked, hopping out of the taxi and noting the disbelief evident in my voice.

'Yes. That's not to say there aren't prickles, but they make it work.'

'Aye, I look forward to seeing that.'

I checked my distorted appearance in the reflection of the car's paint job and fidgeted with my leather jacket. I was nervous. Nervous and fidgety. We were at the entrance to an alleyway in a district just north of the city centre. The club wasn't far from a major intersection and I watched a group of people waiting at the lights while a U-Bahn rumbled by. The Fernsehturm was patiently blinking far above the city skyline and even in minimal light I marvelled at how much the TV tower looked exactly like a giant olive impaled on a cocktail stick. Sensing Lorcan at my elbow, I turned to find him watching me.

'What?' I asked.

'Nothing,' he smiled, shaking his head.

Hefting my bag on to my shoulder, I followed him down the narrow alley and in the direction of pulsing trap music which got louder and louder as we neared the club. Two large buildings loomed on either side, making me feel like we were escaping down a narrow ravine in an urban canyon. Small groups of smokers were clustered outside and they acted as unofficial landmarks telling me that we were here. Ahead I could see a long line snaking out of a set of double doors as people queued up to get inside one of Berlin's favourite night spots, run unbeknownst to them by a group of rogue were-wolves. I looked up at the name of the club glowing in neon green letters as we passed underneath it; *PHASES*. It was a simple and meaningless name to most. To werewolves like me, it was a winking eye.

'MOVE HÜNDIN!'

The speed of my werewolf reflexes had me stepping out of the way in a blur of movement to avoid a skinny white guy in about six layers of denim too many as he sprinted down the alleyway with reckless abandon. It was less than a second before a huge Latino man dived out of Phases' entrance after him, a wide smile stretched across his face as he took pursuit. I recognised that look. The denim bandit didn't know it yet, but he was nothing more than a rabbit being hunted by a wolf. I was still strides closer than his pursuer and I dropped my bag, dashing a few steps along the alley before sliding my foot forward and swiping the runner's legs out from under him in one swift movement. He landed with an ungracious thud, chin first, and I was comforted by the thought that he had a boy band's worth of fabric to cushion his fall. Skidding to a stop next to me, the man from earlier was laughing in earnest as he loomed over the crumpled figure on the ground.

'*Gracias hermosa*, you robbed me of a jolly chase but it was worth it to watch that mess,' he said with a smirk that complemented his thick Spanish accent.

'You're most welcome.'

'I take it you're Tommi?' he said, extended a hand which I shook.

'The hair give it away?'

'No, it was more Lorcan's presence to be honest,' he replied, offering a nod and a hug to Lo. 'Good to see you again, *pedazo*.'

Lorcan looked only mildly uncomfortable as the hug turned into him being felt up by our new friend. 'You too, Clayton.'

The man removed himself from Lorcan, reluctantly might I add, and returned his attention to the halfwit struggling to sit up on the ground.

Casting a sideways look at Lo, I mouthed the word '*pedazo*'.

'Hunk,' Lorcan replied, blushing slightly.

'Ah, ha! Guy knows what's up," I said, turning back to watch Lo's new admirer delivering a spray in perfectly spoken German.

'– we'll smell you from a mile away, dirty junkie! Be grateful I'm not ripping your throat out. Now get.'

With blood dribbling from his chin, the peroxided skrag started walking backwards towards the main street but he was foolish enough to flip the bird.

Clayton leapt forward in a movement so quick I actually gasped, snarling at the man so he stumbled and landed on his ass again. He didn't take his time getting up however; he struggled to his feet and was sprinting away from us as fast as he could. When Clayton turned around, it was to cheers and clapping from the surrounding onlookers. He took a dramatic bow, using the movement to disguise the wad of cash he tucked into the fanny pack hanging on his hip. His eyes caught mine as I watched the movement and he strutted over to join us, lowering his voice so his words were just for the ears of Lorcan and me.

'Filthy junkie snatched some earnings from one of the tills,' he said, an accent dancing over his English. 'Unfortunately it was manned by a human staff member, not one of us, so they weren't quick enough to catch him. Fortunately we were.'

'If he values his larynx I'm sure he won't be back,' I murmured.

He cast me a look, smiling. 'Your Deutsch must be solid if you were able to pick up that much.'

'Aye, I've spent some months in Berlin before,' I shrugged, 'You kinda need it to get by.'

He slapped his hand on my back so hard I thought my tonsils were going to go flying out of my mouth. I coughed in response and he laughed.

'Ha, this is gonna be great. You tripped him up quick back there too, I have a feeling we're gonna have a lot of fun with you. Not least because of your style, which is fierce *mamacita*, let me tell ya.'

'*Danke*,' I replied, matching his grin.

'You call me Clay, by the way. Everyone does.'

As we walked I had a moment to admire Clay's own personal style, which was *significant*. He dressed like ... well, to be honest, a gay sailor. Bursting out of a tight, white singlet were enormous biceps covered in Americana-style tattoos that ran down his arms and to his knuckles. He had light chocolate skin and glossy black hair that clung to his scalp in tight curls, with further tattoos peeking out of his hairline and running down his neck. He even had a small heart inked black just under his right eye. The only thing missing was a sailor's hat with blue piping. 'Yours is pretty fierce too.'

'Pretty fierce? Bluey, I'm downright delectable.'

'Yes, sir,' I answered, giving him a mock salute, which he cackled at.

'Are the others inside?' Lorcan asked as we began weaving ourselves through the partygoers.

'Yes, papi, Zillia and Yu are in the boardroom and waiting for you. The others are out on the floor or working the circuit, you'll meet them in due time, Tommi.'

'Aight, whatever you say,' I replied, kind of at a loss for words as I took in the interior of the club and the heaving masses of people inside.

'FOLLOW ME!' Clay shouted over the pulsing Presets track, gesturing at us as he carved a way through the crowd.

I spun as we walked, trying to see as much as I could before we reached our destination. There was a decent dance floor that was packed with bodies, all moving up and down like rhythmic pulse as the DJ on the club's small stage commanded their love. He was an Indian guy, lanky, and somehow I felt like his gaze cut through the hundreds of people and right to us. If it wasn't for the flashing lights I could have sworn he winked.

Shaking my head, I took note of the layout: the club was dimly lit, with the brightest light coming from behind the bar directly opposite the stage. The bar spanned one entire side of Phases. My kind of place. Old wooden packing crates had been repurposed into tables and were placed around the drinking area, which was elevated from the remainder of the club by a single step. My eyes followed the path of worn timber steps that led up to a balcony running around the inside of the club, with people pushing and bumping past each other as they made their way through. Phases felt like the bastard child of a town hall and an underground punk club. There was a lot of wood and posters plastered over every spare inch of wall space. The odds of them playing house music in here were slim. I counted that as a small victory. Clay came to a halt in front of a security door, typing in a code and holding it open for us.

'This is where I leave you, I'm moonlighting as security tonight and the patrons are rowdy.'

'Thanks, we'll see you around no doubt,' said Lorcan.

'Indeed,' he replied in what was the verbal equivalent of licking his lips. 'Later, Tommi.'

'*Ciao.*'

Lorcan walked through the door and into a corridor that was so colourful I actually flinched. There was some sort of multi-coloured mural painted on the walls and I promised myself that I would get a better look on the way out. We passed several closed doors, including one I was certain led to a freezer room given the cold air generating from it. Lorcan paused at the final door and gave me a quick smile. I nodded back and stepped with him into the room.

Two women were the only occupants, with one perched on the surface of a long table and taking animatedly to the other who was leaning back in her chair. Conversation immediately ceased as we entered. Lorcan stepped to the side to allow them a full look at me and I held my head a fraction higher defensively. I scanned their faces and gave a tight smile.

'Howdy,' I said.

The woman with ink dark hair who had been sitting on the table jumped up to greet us. 'Tommi,' she said, thick with a German accent. Walking around the table, she grabbed my hands in hers and looked me in the eyes as she said: 'I'm Zillia and welcome.'

'Uh, thanks,' I said, slightly taken aback by the immediate physical contact.

'And Lorcan,' she said, turning to face him. 'How are you? You haven't aged a day dear.' She opened her arms towards Lorcan and he hugged her briefly as she planted two big kisses on either side of his cheek. 'So,' said Zillia, pulling herself away from Lorcan. 'This is our place, welcome to Phases!'

'Thank you, it's quite the joint.'

'We like to think so. This is my colleague and fellow pack member Dolly.'

I nodded at the final person in the room who, truthfully, couldn't have been further from someone who looked like they should be named Dolly. She would have been painfully skinny if it wasn't for the lean muscles I could see flex as she crossed her arms over her chest. Her somewhat angelic facial features were offset by piercings in her lip and eyebrow. I was also betting those were ear tapers. Her hair was bleached and styled into a cool mini-Mohawk that made her look like a heroine in a Swedish crime series.

Zillia herself was a whole other story. She was short, almost tiny in fact. I was guessing 5'1" at most and while I had to look down to her, Lorcan appeared about two steps away from having to bend over entirely. She had a perfectly symmetrical black fringe and the remainder of her hair fell dead straight to her shoulders. I guessed she was in late thirties. A collection of gold bracelets jangled from her wrist as she ushered Lorcan and me to grab a seat.

The one I took was a spinning office chair and I could tell from the look on Dolly's face that she expected me to spin around in it yelling 'weeeeeee'. I resisted the urge.

'Right,' said Zillia. 'I guess I should start by telling you a bit about the rest of the Rogues and what we do here.'

'Aye, go ahead,' I said, smiling politely.

'As I'm sure Lorcan has explained, we were all part of traditional packs at one point or another. There are different reasons why each of us left our packs and if the others would like to tell you their stories at some point that's up to them. For me, it was a personality clash. My family and I never got on and I wanted out of that whole pack system. I moved here and started in hospitality before working my way up to managing a few clubs. That's how I began bumping into these lovely people and dozens of others rogues more and more frequently.'

'Once we established none of us were going to rip each others' heads off,' said Dolly, 'some of us started hanging out, shifting together, becoming friends.'

'Being a lone wolf is a dangerous lifestyle choice,' Zillia added. 'You're going to need training to survive, to prepare yourself from any kind of attack and all different kinds of threats. You're without the protection of a pack and people to watch your back.'

'You're also without the restrictions,' I replied.

Dolly tut-tutted. 'You're vulnerable. You need to know how to keep yourself alive and if you're lucky enough to find others who share your views and can help, you use that.'

Zillia smiled. 'And we became what we are: the Rogues. We bought this place by pooling our money. Dolly, Clay, Gus, Sanjay and myself are all partners in varying degrees. We each have our different roles within the club and together we're making a living. Phases has also become somewhat of an unofficial meeting place for other rogue werewolves in Berlin. We even get pack members in here regularly.'

'Not many,' said Dolly, bouncing slightly as she leaned further back in her chair.

'No,' agreed Zillia, 'but some.'

'Packs don't like their members hanging around other rogues,' Dolly snickered. 'They think we're bad influences.'

'A lot of members of the supernatural community come here,' added Lorcan. 'You could throw a stone and hit a local Askari any night of the week. Treize officials pass through all the time and Phases is known in the underground circles as a safe place for different kinds of creatures to come and relax, exchange information, and generally be amongst their kin.'

'It's not just for supernaturals though, right?' I asked both Lo and those at the table.

'No,' said Zillia. 'The split is about seventy–thirty most nights: seventy per cent everyday civilians and thirty per cent supers. The public is none the wiser. To the authorities and business bodies we're like any other club in Berlin.'

'It all sounds very . . . cosy,' I offered.

Zillia smiled at me with a shrug followed by a little sigh. 'We're an unconventional family, Tommi, but as you'll soon see, we fight like one too. A nightclub of werewolves who happen to live together as well means tensions run high sometimes. I'm sure it's the same with your brothers and sisters.'

My breath caught as I thought of my brothers and sisters. I killed my half-brother, forced my half-sister to run away, and had no idea what had happened to my other half-brother.

'Not really,' I muttered.

Zillia gave me a sharp look, but after a moment's pause carried on. 'How about you tell us what you want to get from staying here?' she said. 'All of us have been werewolves for decades and have mastered different things, but if you're going to be surviving out there in the big, bad world on your own then you've got a way to go.'

'Besides,' Dolly mumbled, 'you won't have a Praetorian Guard-turned-Custodian like Lorcan by your side forever.'

I cast a look at Lo, who had been watching me carefully. 'Aye, you're right. Once the Custodians think I have enough control they'll cut him loose. I guess I'd like to develop some of my periphery senses but the main thing is staying alive. I need to know what you know. The life expectancy for a kathurungi isn't high and what you said is right: I'm vulnerable. I'm also young and inexperienced. Sure, I have power and potential yet I feel like a lot of it is untapped.'

'How old are you Tommi?' Dolly quizzed.

'I'm twenty-three.'

Lorcan's head snapped in my direction and he frowned.

I shrugged. 'It was my birthday two days ago.'

'You're young,' she said. 'Not that we're exactly supernatural senior citizens ourselves but a lot of this will come with time.'

I let out a breathy, nervous laugh. 'Yeah. You also know that time isn't a thing exactly on my side. I'm safe here, for now, but how do I keep on when I'm a real lone wolf out there?'

Zillia clasped her hands together, her wrists acting as instruments as her jewellery clanged together. 'I think there's a lot you can get from your time here, considering you're such a new wolf and developed so late.'

'I don't doubt it,' I said, genuinely thankful for anything the Rogues would offer to teach.

'Passing this stuff on isn't an exact science,' said Dolly. 'Different wolves adapt to things differently and each can have their own set of unique skills and abilities. Some things we try to teach you, you might never pick up. Others will take time.'

'I've got a few moon phases up my sleeve.'

'Great,' said Zillia, clasping her hands together. 'We start tomorrow.'

Chapter 4

Zillia's actions served as a casual dismissal and we headed towards the door.

'Thanks again for taking me in like this,' I said, as she followed Lorcan and me out.

'It's nothing,' she replied, sounding like she meant it. 'This has almost become our unofficial duty. We learn as much from the people who stay with us as we do from them.'

'Stop being modest,' said Lorcan from behind me.

As we made our way towards the main part of the club I started to notice the details of the mural. Tropical leaves and exotic flowers exploded off the wall as tigers, toucans and other stereotypical jungle creatures peered out from behind the collage. Zillia noticed me looking and asked if I liked their 'decorations'.

'It's very George of the Jungle.'

'It's awful, I know.' She laughed. 'We all hated it a lot more when we first took over this place, but now we're used to it. The owners before us had a jungle-themed nightclub. The bar staff had to wear leopard-print outfits. It was atrocious.'

'I take it they went bankrupt?'

'We enjoyed burning the furniture,' she said with a nod.

I pushed through the swinging door and held it out for Lorcan and Zillia to pass through. My ears pinged as I recognised the Bossy Love remix that had the club banging and thrusting through the beat.

'This DJ's great,' I called to Zillia and she beamed.

'That's Sanjay, he's one of us.'

'Huh.' No wonder he had such a good ear for it, I thought.

'And that,' Zillia continued, pointing to a bouncer who looked like a Die Hard villain, 'is Gus. He's not the biggest of talkers, but he's family.'

I was unsure if his werewolf hearing was that good, yet he cast a cursory glance in our direction as Zillia talked. He had little time for me, preferring instead to offer Lorcan the smallest of nods which Lo returned. It was very manly and hetero.

'The others have a few things to do around the club. I was going to show you where you'll be living,' Zillia said.

'Prepare for a hike, Tommi,' Lorcan muttered.

Zillia smiled at him before leading us towards one of the fire exits.

I raised an eyebrow at him and he whispered, 'It's directly across the alley.'

I looked up at the building that loomed in front of us as we stepped out of the club. It was about six or seven storeys high and looked like a standard brick apartment building you could find anywhere in any city. It dwarfed the club next to it and – like so many apartment and office blocks in Berlin – the side of it was covered in graffiti.

'It was a derelict space when my partner bought it two years ago,' Zillia said, craning her neck to get a better look at it in the evening light. 'He's a developer. Besides interior renovations, he's never really had any plans for it. It was a rundown building going cheap. Conveniently it happened to be next to my club, but he says that had nothing to do with it. There's legal mumbo-jumbo they have to go through before the apartments are ready to be sold, so in the meantime, everyone who lives in here is paying a pathetic excuse for rent.'

She entered a series of numbers on a small keypad and with a successful *beep* a roller door began opening to reveal a loading dock with several cars parked inside.

'We've turned this into a make-shift garage,' she said. 'The blue car is mine and the two vans are everyone's. The beat-up Mini is Clay's.'

How the hell Clay managed to fold himself into that tiny car, I had no idea. We ascended a small set of concrete steps and entered the main lobby through a side door after Zillia entered another numerical combination.

'The password for everything is 446437 76277 or if you're looking at the letters it's GINGER SNAPS,' she said, tossing Lorcan a set of keys for the apartment.

'Hold up, Ginger Snaps? Your secret password to werewolf Hogwarts is *Ginger Snaps?* I fucking love you guys.'

She smiled and started up the stairwell. 'Sanjay wanted to go with Lon Chaney Jr but Clay thought it was too obvious. Now, Gus and Dolly have the apartments on the second floor, I live on the third, Clay and Sanjay are on the fourth. We've converted the two apartments on the fifth floor into training rooms. You and Lorcan will be on the sixth floor, which is the top. We like to have at least one apartment on each floor occupied.'

'Your partner doesn't wonder what you need the training rooms for?' I asked.

'He never goes anywhere in the building except my apartment. The place is looked after and that's all he cares about. I honestly don't think this is too high on his priorities list.'

'It's the ideal set-up.'

'You'll meet Kirk sooner or later. He's very easy-going. And we have a foolproof facility under the club for the full moon. There's a ghost wall in the freezer room and below that we have cells which are reinforced and unbreakable.'

'Handy.'

She glanced at us over her shoulder as we continued up the stairs. 'Because of your unique situation and you being a new wolf and all I was told that Lorcan and you would be staying together, so I've put you up in the one apartment.'

I nearly came to a dead stop right there on the stairs, but a subtle push from Lorcan kept me going forward.

'That's perfect, Zillia, thanks,' he said with a straight face.

I gulped and kept my eyes trained ahead.

'Don't *Zillia* me.' She laughed. 'I nearly shifted on the spot when you first told me you were becoming a Custodian. Then we haven't had so much as a peep out of you since, Mr Immortal. Clay's known you for fifteen years and said he never would have guessed it.'

'I'm sorry, things have been –'

'Busy? Complicated? *Verrückt*?' she offered.

'Pick one,' I muttered and she cast me a conspirator's grin.

'Please don't encourage her, Tommi,' Lorcan huffed. 'Zillia and Clay are terrible gossips.'

'I'm just glad you decided to grace us with your ward and presence. And in my defence Dolly is the biggest gossip of us all.'

'Blaming Tank Girl seems risky,' I joked.

'Cute. See you both in the training room at ten o'clock so we can get to know each other with a little morning sparring?'

I grinned. 'Wouldn't miss it.'

Zillia left us at the top of the stairs with instructions on which key was for which and when rent was due at the end of the month. I thanked her and grabbed a case she had carried up the stairs that was full of Lorcan's old things. I could lift it, but I doubted the pre-werewolf Tommi would have been able to.

'Oh ye fooker,' I said as I heaved it through the doorway. 'What's in this?'

'Weapons.'

'Naturally. They couldn't stay in storage until the morning?'

'They're my favourites.'

I laughed. Other people had favourite clothes, favourite books, favourite songs. Lorcan had favourite weapons. And then it hit me: we were going to be living together. *Again.* We were having a hard enough time keeping our hands off each other as it was, so this wasn't going to be a walk in the sexually tempting metaphorical park. I gulped. The apartment was stretched into one long, rectangle shape with the kitchen beginning practically two steps from the doorway. A collection of cooking utensils hung artfully above the kitchen counter and a massive silver fridge hummed in the corner.

'So. Roommates once more,' I said. 'Funny how you never mentioned that.'

'Even if there had been a choice, the apartment across the hall is still being renovated,' said Lorcan. 'And you need to watch what you say and who you say it around.'

I looked at him and he tapped his ear.

'Remember, everyone in this building has your kind of hearing. It doesn't matter floor-to-floor but if someone was standing outside the door –'

'Gotcha. Don't mention someone Lewis and Clarking my body.' I made a zipping motion with my hand and threw an invisible key away from my mouth. With a deep sigh, I shook my head and began walking through the apartment. Every time I began to settle into how I felt about Lorcan, he'd remind me exactly why that was such a dangerous idea. Secrets, half truths, need-to-know onlys ... It was always crumbs with him. I wondered if I'd ever get the full slice of cake.

The entire third side of the space was one long window with arching bars that supported the glass. The view looked down on Phases directly below and on from that you could see Berlin sparkling as it spread out in the distance. Wooden floorboards ran the length of the apartment with no walls or rooms. The only separation was an artful set of stairs made of wood and wire that led up to a mini-level within the apartment. I climbed them carefully and peeked over the top. There was enough room for a bed, a desk and little more. I jumped back down and Lorcan was already placing a few of our cases around the room.

'I'll stay up there,' he said, not looking at me.

I glanced at the other option, which was a massive bed pushed against the exposed brick wall at the end of the area.

Neither option was super private and if I was going to be avoiding temptation and hoping that he'd be doing the same, I was going to need to find some folding screens to get changed behind and build a perimeter. Mark my territory.

'Sure,' I said, making my way over to what was now my bed. 'This place is pretty wow with a capital WTF.'

'You should have seen it before,' Lorcan said, scanning the open plan apartment.

'How much rent are we paying?'

'Six hundred euros a month.'

'That's ridiculous.'

'It's more of a courtesy payment from what I'm told. Kirk didn't even want Zillia or the Rogues to pay rent. He said they were doing him a favour as caretakers.'

'How can this guy be a successful business man with an attitude like that?'

'Many fingers, many pies.'

'Sweeney Todd style,' I said, walking into the middle of the space.

'You like it?' he asked.

'Loathe it.'

Lorcan went off to inspect the bathroom, which was disguised behind a brick wall near the entrance. 'How did you find the Rogues?'

'I'm not sure yet. Dolly and I are clearly going to be BFFs,' I joked. Lorcan laughed and I closed my eyes as the deep, throaty sound bounced off the walls of the vast apartment.

'I should have warned you about Zillia. She can be quite the –'

'Shit stirrer?' I shrugged. 'It's no big. She doesn't mean it maliciously. I think she just likes to know stuff. Mari was like that, but tactful.'

'Mari had a way of getting information from you without you even knowing it.' He smiled. 'She was observant.'

'She was,' I said, my voice dropping as I thought about my murdered friend. I tried to switch the subject as quickly as I could. 'To confirm: this isn't some *Hostel* type deal where a limb is removed fortnightly or something? Are you sure we don't have to sell our bodies to stay here?'

'Not that I'm aware of,' he said slowly and I saw the unintended double entendre in my words.

I sighed. 'You know what you mean.'

He smiled and for the first time he looked as exhausted as I felt. 'I know what you mean.'

We stood there for a while, just taking the place in. Eventually I went in search of the linen I had packed and returned with sheets and pillowcases for the pair of us. A duvet in a matching grey pattern had been folded at the end of my bed and on top of Lorcan's mattress upstairs. I was grateful that I wouldn't have to shiver through the night and collapsed on the bed like a starfish, doing little more than managing to kick my shoes off in the process. I think Lorcan said goodnight to me and I could have sworn I mumbled a reply, yet before I knew I was dreaming. It didn't take much to guess what I was dreaming about.

'You're late,' barked Dolly as I strolled into the training room at 10 a.m. the next morning.

'Sorry, I was trying to find exercise clothes,' I muttered feebly. I felt like a naughty school kid sprung smoking pot behind the shed.

'Heel, all she missed was you glaring at that boxing bag for ten minutes.'

The second voice was Clay's and his mere presence made me feel more positive about what the next few hours would hold. Gus was there too, leaning against a brick wall at the far side of the room, looking nonchalant. Sanjay was stretching his back on an enormous green exercise ball and he bounced up to attention when Clay addressed me. The training room had the same layout as our apartment except here the wooden floor-boards were covered in thin, blue matting that was soft when you stepped on it. A large portion of one wall had been covered in similar matting with various punching dummies and upper-cut bags fitted into it. The remaining part was lined with every kind of weapon you could imagine. To a serial killer, this would have been his or her version of being locked in a toy store over-night. Knives of all shapes and sizes, throwing stars, daggers, axes, fighting poles and more were sitting in holders against a black velvet backing. My eyes caught on a particularly sparkly set of hunga mungas and I felt my fingers itch to hold them.

'As you can see, this is our silverware,' said Clay as he gestured to the wall with a dramatic sweep of his arms. 'All the cases are usually concealed and locked. Zillia said you know the pin. Beneath that we have our artillery.'

'Artillery?' I queried.

'Rifles, Glocks, shotguns. You'll find more guns here than at a Republican brunch.'

My eyes ran over two long sets of drawers as I tried to guesstimate how many guns could be in there.

'From the look on your face you've never used a gun before,' said Zillia, closing the door to the training room behind me. 'I know, I know, I'm late too so cut me some slack, Dolly.'

'We haven't got to guns yet,' said Lorcan. 'The other disciplines are more important.'

He neglected to mention that my reluctance to get trigger-happy had *a lot* to do with not enjoying the experience of being shot in the shoulder a few weeks back.

'They make a better foundation too,' said Sanjay, now up and on the balls of his feet.

'I know you've only been training her for a few months, Lorcan, but this wouldn't have anything to do with your aversion to guns, would it?' Zillia asked with a knowing smile.

'I've seen you use a gun,' I said, confused. 'When we were hunting Steven, Ennis and you were armed. And in the warehouse.'

'I use them if I have to. I prefer not. There are situations when it would be stupid and dangerous not to use them, but just as often I find them stupid and dangerous in and of themselves. If I can avoid it, I do.'

'And you're not that great a shot,' muttered Gus.

'He's a fine shot,' said Zillia, 'Just not a werewolf.'

I opened my mouth to ask what she meant when Lorcan added, 'It's my old way of thinking. Guns still feel like cheating to me.'

'It's all about the hand-to-hand,' said Dolly appreciatively. She looked up at me suddenly and began to make her way into the centre of the room. 'We'll deal with firearms later. Let's get to know each other first and see what he's been teaching you.'

She launched herself at me, sprinting so fast she was a blur of movement and I thanked my superior reflexes for moving me out of her path in time. As soon as she was past me she halted and kicked her leg backwards, a blow I ducked while leaping back. She lunged again with a series of spins and kicks that I recognised as being flashy rather than useful. The group had assembled a rough circle around us with Clay and Sanjay making appreciative *oohs* and *aahs* as I took a few of Dolly's hits and delivered some of my own. Her high-flying kicks were designed to keep me at a distance and after slipping under one, I came up directly in front and palmed her in the face. She grunted but held her stance. I mimicked that sound as I copped two quick jabs to the ribs before I snatched at the hood on the back of her top and used it to yank her to the ground. I leapt down and pressed my knee to her throat.

For a second I thought I had her, but she was a good fighter and somehow she managed to wrestle herself free until it was me pinned underneath her. The position didn't hold me either and soon we were back on our feet and taking, delivering, and blocking blows. She was lightning fast. She also had years of experience on me, but I had learnt from the best. I was stronger, more creative, and had been moulded by a fighter with centuries of skill. A roundhouse kick to Dolly's head ended the fight and I dropped from the air to a crouched position in case she was ready to resume. She wasn't.

She had landed flat on her back and was trying to blink her way into a sitting position. I stayed where I was. This fight had started without any warning and I wasn't about to relent my upper hand because she appeared to be struggling. I felt a thick trickle of blood run from the corner of my mouth as I stayed crouched and ready to attack. Keeping Dolly in my peripheral vision, I looked up at the others.

Sanjay smiled. Zillia and Clay appeared impressed. Gus looked like he wanted to go next. Finally my eyes rested on Lorcan. He was struggling to contain the pride that was spreading across his face. I stood upright and extended a hand to Dolly, who took it and stumbled to a standing position. She nodded in acknowledgment. Was that recognition of defeat? Was I supposed to have learnt something?

'My turn,' said Gus as he lumbered over to fill her place.

Suddenly I was quite certain I was about to get schooled.

Chapter 5

'Get up.'

'Actually, I think I'm comfortable here,' I said in a strained voice.

Clay laughed and dropped down on his stomach on the mat next to me. 'How will I be able to feel good about myself if you're down here refusing to be defeated?'

'Me, lying here bloody and in pain, is hardly a refusal. It's more of a result.'

I groaned as I let him pull me up. The crowd at the daily sessions had filtered down over five days. Now it was just Clay, Lorcan, and me. Clay was the most enthusiastic about working with me and so I had begun my second full day of training one-on-one with him. By 'enthusiastic' I meant 'most willing to continuously beat the shit out of me'. It's funny how deceiving appearances can be. On the surface Dolly and Gus looked the most threatening and to an everyday civilian they would have been. Heck, to a trained fighter and most werewolves they would have been a threat too. For me, they had been stepping-stones to fighting tougher opponents.

My first session with the Rogues saw me face both Dolly and Gus as they rotated between each other. Dolly was fast and flashy, but she was too self-conscious about what she was doing. It was like fighting a demonstration dummy. She ran through moves and drills in an orchestrated way without any flexibility. Gus was all brute strength and force. Although the prospect of going up against someone who resembled a Russian mercenary made me break out in a cold sweat, Gus had been unexpectedly manageable. He was slow, like he looked, and swatted at me like a bear would a fly. His blows were brutal when they connected, yet if I was careful it was easy to dance around him and dart inside to deliver hits when I needed. His powerful frame actually worked against him when we fought. I adapted quickly and stayed out of his range, moving fast. I was curious to see how he would go against someone like Clay, who was closer to his size.

Zillia was unpredictable. Her voluptuous, soft body was a weapon. She was so short I was reluctant to engage with her at first. She insisted we work with daggers and I enjoyed the break from hand-to-hand combat. My enjoyment was short-lived as Zillia was a crafty and intelligent fighter. It took all my concentration and a few tips from Lorcan before I was able to defeat her. Even then it had been close. I had begged her to teach me how to twirl and deliver daggers to a target with the scientific precision she managed to. She agreed, but I felt like it would take forever before I got anywhere close to the level of skill she had with a blade.

'The danger of working with Lorcan for as long as you have,' Zillia said, stabbing in the air with sharp points in a flurry of movement, 'is that you begin to learn how he fights, how he attacks. What happens is that you fall into a routine and that, for a lone wolf, is dangerous.'

She released one of her daggers and it cut across the room, landing in her training dummy with a dull vibration.

'When you're out there living on your own,' she continued, 'threats can come from anywhere. Whether it's a passing supernatural who sees you as easy prey, an unlucky encounter with a ghoul, werewolf hunters or an ambitious pack with their eyes on your ovaries.'

'The fuck?' I hissed.

'It can happen,' Dolly added. 'The werewolf gene carries either way, but there are a lot of packs who want a pure blood-line with two werewolf parents. A lone, breeding female –'

'Imma stop you right there, I can fill in the unsavoury blanks, thank you.'

'The point is,' Zillia pushed, 'it doesn't matter what kind of threat it is, the one thing they'll have in common is that none of them will be alike. You can't fight them all the same way, with the same weapons. You need to be able to adapt your style and become inventive.'

'Which is where we fit in,' Sanjay added, with a grin. 'Think of us as your combat Spice Girls, each driving to teach you something with our own distinct flavour.'

'Except you're *all* Scary Spice,' I huffed.

He laughed at me, but there was motivation behind it. Sanjay was their secret weapon. The way he moved was distinctly inhuman. Lorcan had warned me that if I ever had to fight in public I would have to be cautious of what moves I used and not resort to dramatic manoeuvres. I assumed Sanjay never intended to fight in public. Part gymnast, part spider monkey, he sculpted himself into impossible shapes.

'You're boneless!' I yelled one day as he flowed between two of my offensive moves and appeared behind to grab my throat.

'Sometimes,' he snickered.

'How do you *do* that? You move like a contortionist on fast forward.'

'He was,' shouted Clay who had been drilling with Lorcan at the time.

Sanjay rolled his eyes and clicked his tongue at Clay. 'No, I was never a contortionist.'

'Then how do you do that?'

'You want to see?'

I hovered at the edge of the mat, both curious and cautious of falling for a trick to come closer.

'Truce,' he said. 'Come here and I'll show you.' I grabbed my drink bottle as we took a quick reprieve.

'Watch,' he said, holding his wrist out in front of me. The brown skin of his arm was dotted with beads of sweat and thick black hairs. I heard myself gasp as his wrist began to lengthen and the distinctive crack of a bone rang out through the room.

'You *are* boneless,' I said, gaping in fascinated horror.

'I cannot shift outright without a full moon,' he said quietly, watching his wrist as it stretched. 'What I can do is reach the point in between where the muscles and bones stretch to make the body of a wolf.'

'You shift in part? Or, I guess it's more that you start to shift and then stop it, reset, and begin again.'

'Yes,' he said.

'But you do it quickly. *So* quickly. It looks almost instantaneous when I'm fighting you.'

'Years of practice. And a lot of spare time as a teenager.' He held out his leg and I watched him demonstrate the same process. He looked up at me expectantly. 'Try.'

I tried to stretch my wrist out as Sanjay had done, concentrating on slowing the process down. Yet as soon as I drew on my wolf, the transformation burst through and I was left with a wolf claw from the elbow down. Sanjay leaped back and his eyebrows disappeared under the short fringe of his thick hair. I sighed.

'This is all I can do,' I said, waving my claw in the air like a novelty foam finger.

I shifted my hand back to normal without much strain. My control over partial-transformation was almost complete now. I was working on being able to shift any body part from human to wolf, a significant progression from the days when I was barely able to maintain and manipulate my arm.

'That is no small thing,' said Sanjay, drawing closer. 'Can you shift completely without the moon?'

'No,' I said, hastily. 'Uh, well, I did that one time but that was under intense circumstances.'

'Could you do it now?' he asked with a childlike enthusiasm.

'I . . . I don't know. Maybe. I doubt it. It's not something I want to do again,' I said, meeting Sanjay's stare. 'Ever.'

He nodded solemnly. I ducked then to avoid a swipe from Clay who had taken it upon himself to try and surprise me when I least expected it. The first few times he had got me, but now I was on my guard and had sensed him trying to sneak closer as Sanjay and I talked.

'*Bonito*,' he said, approving of my reaction. 'Sorry to eavesdrop, but I had an idea. What's your night vision like?'

'I assume you mean when I'm not wearing my standard-issue night vision goggles?' I asked.

He grinned at me. 'Of course.'

'Aye, it's good. Normal.'

'When you're in werewolf form what's it like?'

'Like day,' I said instantly. 'It's like how I see everything during the day now.'

'Hmmm.' He looked thoughtful.

'You're thinking of trying to get her to shift her eyes while staying human,' said Lorcan, who had also come over from the bags.

'It's an idea,' said Clay.

'Is that even possible?' I asked.

'With you,' Lorcan said, 'I'm beginning to think anything is.'

'If I can even do it, it will take practice to maintain it long enough to be useful. That's channelling to a very specific place though. The next step is getting me to change just the hairs on my legs.'

'Ew, could you imagine?' said Clay.

'Think how handy it could be,' said Lorcan, hopefully still thinking about the eyes.

'Built-in night vision goggles,' I said. 'Minus the green.'

Green was how I was feeling after four hours of punishment at the hands of Clay. I had eventually learned how to interpret Sanjay's boneless dance and began defeating him as often as he did me. That was when they decided I was ready for Clay. I kind of wished I was back turning ligaments into jelly with Sanjay because Clay was relentless. I always knew Lorcan held back when we trained and although the feminist in me wanted to be furious at him for it, the rational side of me knew I wasn't ready for him full throttle. I struggled to stay afloat with his skill level as it was. He knew exactly what he needed to do to match me, yet stay several steps ahead so that I was challenged. Clay exercised no such courtesy and I bent over to place my head between my knees as I felt my breakfast squirm uncomfortably up my throat. I swallowed it down along with a sharp tang that I recognised as blood.

I need this, I said to myself.

This is making me better.

Tougher.

More inventive.

I kept trying to run these motivational talks through my head as Clay kept knocking me off my feet.

'You okay?' he said.

'It would be easier to be pissed at you if you'd stop being so nice about it,' I spat.

'Just doing this for your own good, Tom. You're the one who wanted to learn.'

'Not learn to die,' I grumbled.

'If we play with the hunga mungas will that make you feel better?'

My eyes lit up. Besides Lorcan and me, Clay was the only member of the Rogues who was proficient with the African fighting tool.

'How about we use your two favourite weapons?'

'Really?'

I didn't wait to hear if he was serious because I was already heading over to pick up my machete. Yes, Lorcan had surprised me with my very own machete two days ago. In reality it was the one we had used at training back in Dundee and Lorcan said I could have it, so it wasn't really a present. Still, I think he felt guilty for forgetting my birthday but I wasn't going to hold it against him – he wasn't the only one, after all. And birthdays made no nevermind to me. He had already given me a set of large knives and my collection was steadily growing as he began separating his arsenal into things I could use. Gripping the handle of the machete I tossed it in the air and relished the slicing sound it made before it landed safely back in my hand.

'Let's not take the Dolly approach to fighting,' said Clay.

I laughed and moved to meet him in the middle of the mat where he held the hunga mungas in a fighting stance.

'All flash and no fire.'

'Now burn baby burn,' he sung to the tune of 'Disco Inferno'.

I took a deep breath and told myself this time I could beat him. This time I wouldn't end up face down on the blue mat.

How wrong I was.

Clay had beaten me with my two favourite weapons and to add insult to injury, it was my first night of phasing in Berlin. Full moon was what it was. Excruciating, always excruciating. Lorcan walked me down to my cell half an hour before it rose in the sky. There was a hidden doorway between one of the shelves in the freezer room that led downstairs to a surprisingly modern set-up. It was all smooth, grey concrete with a long hallway and cells broken up along its length. There were no bars. Each cell could only be entered through a thick, steel door that closed off the room to the world. Lo held the door open as I inspected the interior. There were thick chains hanging from the walls. I picked one up and ran my hand along it.

'I don't think you can find a room more secure than this,' I said.

'Do you want me to chain you up?' he offered.

'You should go,' I said, shaking my head. 'The change won't be far off now and the others don't have as much control as I do. If you get stuck down here . . .'

He nodded and turned to leave before pausing.

'Before I forget,' he reached into his jacket pocket and pulled out a squishy red something inside a plastic bag. I sniffed, pretending to be surprised and delighted. In truth, I'd known what he'd brought the second he walked into our apartment with it. 'It's a T-bone. I thought you might want something to pass the time down here since you're the only one who's alert.'

He placed it on the ground and left, closing the door behind him and leaving me in darkness.

It wasn't long before it started. I could feel the tension building and then all of a sudden it felt like someone grabbed me from the top of my spine and shook me. The sound I made was more of a growl than a scream. Muted cries of agony could be heard through the thickness of the other cells where the rest of the Rogues were.

My knees crashed against the cold concrete and I relished the small pain as every bone in my body began to break, slowly, and then faster and faster. I felt my fingers elongating over the smooth surface and the ends raising as they turned into claws. The natural transformation of the full moon came in waves and it reminded me of the way a pregnant woman had contractions. I huffed and puffed during a brief reprieve.

Gritting my teeth, my back snapped in and then outwards as my body contorted in the final throws of the shift. My teeth pierced through my bottom lip as they extended into long, sharp fangs. Every hair that made up the thick, brown fur of my wolf coat felt like individual needles as it pierced through the skin and I morphed completely into a beast.

When Lorcan came for me in the morning I was dozing against the back wall, clutching a clean, white T-bone in my hand.

'Hey,' I said, sleepily as he wrapped a thick blanket around me.

'Hey back at you.'

He made a move as if he was going to scoop me up in his arms like a child, but stopped himself.

I caught the gesture and watched him carefully from my fetal position A range of emotions played over his face before he extended me a chaste hand to help me up.

'I've got it,' I said, using the wall to slowly inch my way up to standing. I had a fleeting thought about the last time Lorcan had seen me naked and what a different scenario it was.

He stepped to the side to let me out of the cell. I was the first one back to human form out of the Rogues, but I could hear the others stirring.

'You should help these guys,' I suggested. 'I can meet you upstairs.'

I stumbled up into the club without another word, leaving Lorcan and the rest of the Rogues in the 'dungeon'.

Once I was back in the apartment it was shower first, then fall into a coma under a layer of warm blankets. I floated off into a thick, dreamless sleep. It turned out to be sleep I desperately needed: the after-effects of the full moon were never pretty. The days between the full moons usually saw me in a proverbial state of grumpiness. One thing I had discovered was that sugar helped (caffeine didn't do much besides keep me awake). Munching on a constant supply of sugar seemed to fill in the gaps. It almost felt medicinal, like I was ramping my blood sugar back up.

After the second night I needed balance in my life, I needed something so far removed from the gore and the growling that I stumbled out of the apartment just after midday. I caught Lorcan heading up the stairs as I was heading down and he looked surprised to see me moving about.

'Where you off to?' he asked, groceries in one hand.

'The Guggenheim,' I replied, buttoning up a knee-length purple coat as I spoke.

'Is that wise?'

'Well, I guess everyone has their own opinion of Pae White but it made sense to check out her exhibition while it was in town.'

'No, I mean it's just over five hours until the full moon. Are you sure it's wise to go out so close to it, in your condition?'

'Condition?' I said, throwing on the red fedora I was carrying and tilting it to the side. 'I'm not nine months pregnant, I'm just wrecked from transformation. I want some art in my life and I'm gonna get it.'

I lightly brushed past him as I continued down the stairs.

'Hold up,' called a voice from behind me and I turned to see Dolly emerging from her apartment. 'I'm coming with you. That cool?'

I was surprised, as I didn't think Dolly liked me much, but I nodded. 'Yeah, I'd dig the company.'

Lorcan gave me a look that I didn't quite catch, but he proceeded up the stairs. 'Just make sure you're both back with plenty of time before the shift.'

Dolly knew Berlin like the back of her hand having grown up here and it's true that you never wholly experience a city until you do it with a local. She wasn't a big talker and that was cool with me. Full moon days left me exhausted emotionally and physically, so I was quite happy with the time for quiet introspection. En route to the Guggenheim she took me to a dive bar that doubled as a trendy butcher with every type of sausage you could imagine.

'I've gotta eat,' she said by way of explanation and I didn't argue as I followed her down a narrow stairwell and into the dark interior of the joint. It wouldn't have been able to fit more than 80 people inside, but the daytime clientele were spread out around the tiny tables that were illuminated by candles glowing inside reused jars.

'What do you want?' she asked, pausing at the bar.

My eyes scanned the menu as quickly as they could but I was overcome with choices. 'Just order me whatever's good. And a cider.'

We grabbed a table in the corner and I slid her the money for the food and drinks, which I was grateful she accepted. She ran her hands over her face and shook her head slightly. I took a long, satisfying sip of my cider and sighed with relief. To casual observers we would have looked extremely hungover as we sat there downing alcohol and a weird combination of artisan sausages.

'I'm not really an art chick,' Dolly said as she took an impressive bite of the first juicy sausage the waiter dumped on our table. 'But I was all for getting out of there today. If Clay got in my face one more time I would have ended up biting off his perfect nose.'

'Aye, the post-full moon blues are enough to drive anyone to art.'

In saying that, Dolly seemed to really enjoy the gallery. At least I think she did, she was a tricky person to read at the best of times and my senses were not on point in that moment. I enjoyed it deeply. I found myself getting happily lost in one particular piece that featured neon lights woven into an unusual and beautiful pattern.

'Interesting,' said Dolly, slipping up behind me.

'What is? Electricity?'

She laughed. 'No, that you keep coming back to this one. I thought the multi-coloured thing hanging from the roof would be more to your liking.'

With my blue hair and clashing hat, she wasn't far from the mark. 'No, this . . . it's all about the weird use of space. You get a kind of loneliness from it. And you know what I keep thinking about?'

'What?'

'You see, in the far corner? There must be three hundred lights here all interwoven and then metres away there's a cluster of lights – alone – and completely unprotected from the pack.'

'Alone or liberated?' she asked with a smirk.

'Can you be both?'

'I can't answer that for you.'

Dolly left me alone as I pondered that question, still unable to tear my eyes away from the lights hanging on their own. It forced me to think of my friends, Joss, Mari, Kane: alone but shining bright in the dark.

When we returned to Phases that afternoon we had both fallen silent as we felt the impending change inching closer. The one consolation as I locked myself in the cell for the final night was the thought that Dolly and I had real femistry. Maybe I'd even made a new friend. Maybe.

Chapter 6

As a reward for making it through the full moon I was going to visit Joss in the afternoon. Bruises and tiredness aside, I was looking forward to spending time with my best friend – hospital or no. Lorcan had insisted he drive me there and pick me up, and I didn't object to the free ride. It was hard being around him and it was made even harder by the pair of us trying to pretend as if nothing had happened. Yet there was no alternative. As he pulled into the drop off zone, I cast him a sideways glance and cursed myself for doing it. It shouldn't hurt to just look at someone you couldn't have, but there I was. Hurt.

'Call me when you're done,' he said.

'Righto,' I replied and he pulled out into the throng of Berlin traffic. The oncology clinic was on the eastern side of Mechtilde General and I started making my way there. As a general rule hospitals are designed to be a labyrinth. This was my third visit to Joss at his 'new digs' and I was still struggling to get my bearings. I was relieved when I spotted a familiar entranceway and I headed through the electronic doors without hesitation. Hitting the button for the fourth floor I waited patiently at the elevator.

'It's so awful, I can't believe it,' came a hushed voice full of emotion speaking in German.

I was tempted to turn around to see the person it came from, but I realised they might be very far away. It would be strange if I looked over at the exact moment someone began to speak. My werewolf hearing was incredibly sharp and the clarity was natural to me now. I had to frequently remind myself that normal people couldn't hear like this. Normal people couldn't recite word for word what a couple had been saying to each other as you passed their apartment on the street outside. Normal people also couldn't hear a whispered conversation between two nurses standing to the left of what I guessed was a water bubbler from the constant buzz of the cooling system. No, normal people couldn't do that. I could and I was trying very hard to focus on the faded silver of the closed elevator doors. Yet there was something in the nurse's voice – a sense of panic and grief – that sparked my interest. Hospitals were raw places and I didn't want to intrude on her private moment, albeit invisibly. If only this elevator would hurry up I wouldn't have to.

'How could anyone do something like this? And the poor parents.' The nurse paused for a moment as she blew her nose.

'Sweetheart,' came the mature-sounding voice of another nurse, 'it will be okay, the police are very capable. These things never last more than a few hours and I'm sure she'll be found and brought back, right? Safe and sound.'

'It's the work of a devil,' the nurse sniffled while the older one patted her on the shoulder.

'Look, take the rest of the day off. You've been interviewed and the detectives have your number if they need anything else.'

'Yah?'

'Sure. How much busier can it be after this?'

The nurse laughed and sniffed once more. 'Thanks, Bernie, I owe you.'

'Now get out of here. Have Dedrik pick you up.'

'Thanks.'

'And hon? Your mascara is running.'

They exchanged a few more goodbye words before I heard the first nurse move away in the opposite direction while the other came and stood a few paces behind me as she waited for the elevator.

I tried to keep my eyes ahead, but I couldn't help turn around and give the greying woman a warm smile. I had no clue what had happened. What I did know was the effect a friendly face could have on someone – even for a second – in a hospital sometimes full of misery and despair. The lady smiled back at me. We moved forward when the elevator doors slid open with a high-pitched ping.

She hit the button for level three, the nursery, and when she stepped out on her floor I was shocked at what I saw. The pastel-coloured hallway was packed with people, mostly police officers dressed in uniform and the occasional plain-clothed one as well. The doors closed slowly and I marvelled at the scene. What had happened here?

I resolved to ask one of Joss' nurses when I got to his room but I found his bed empty. For serious cases like Joss, where the patient would be staying for a prolonged period, the rooms were nice. More than nice, they were comfortable. Welcoming. Joss' was painted pale green and had been decked out with an array of brightly coloured furniture for the guests that would be spending hours at his bedside.

There was an impressive TV fitted into the wall and I could see a collection of his other gadgets scattered around the place. The aim was to make leaving your room seem less appealing. That clearly wasn't working for Joss.

Backing out of the doorway, I headed for the place I suspected I would find him: the rec room. It was actually just a normal room the same size as all the others but it was equipped with a plasma TV, gaming consoles, air hockey kit and pinball machine. When the juvenile oncology patients were well enough to be out of bed, this is where they came. Sure enough, there was Joss propped in a beanbag in the middle of the room and punching the air with an Xbox controller in his hand.

'I'm not sure if that motion means you've won or lost,' I said, leaning against the doorframe. He was biting his lip and the look of fierce concentration disappeared as he registered my presence with a big smile.

'I was losing,' he said. 'Now that you're here I'm a winner in every way.' He pouted at me as I held my hand to my heart with mock esteem. Joss was the only one in the room, which was strange considering I'd never been in here without at least three or four other patients engaged in some activity.

'Where is everyone?'

'We're in lockdown so they're in their rooms. Gobshites,' he said casually.

'Lockdown? As in, there's a gunman storming the building so everyone should be in lockdown?'

'Pfft. I don't know exactly what happened but it was hours ago and not on our floor.'

'Oh, well, let's start dancing through the hallways then.'

'Don't be so dramatic. One of the nurses will send me back to my room in a second anyway. You may as well come and enjoy the freedom with me.'

'I do love a rebellion,' I said, making my way over to the window seat where a handful of books were scattered. I cleared a space as Joss joined me and started rummaging through my bag.

'What did you bring me?'

'Ebola virus, you greedy wench.'

He laughed and his face lit up. 'HARIBO Star Mix! You rock. Tommi!'

'You're so easy to please,' I said, patting him on the head. 'Oh –'

I let my hand hover inches from his scalp as I familiarised the sensation.

'Yep,' said Joss, downtrodden.

'It's completely gone.'

The last time I'd visited, his rusty hair had thinned considerably but to the unsuspecting viewer it just looked short. Now he was entirely bald.

'It's so . . . smooth,' I said, running my hands over the hard skin there. 'It happened a lot quicker too.'

'I shaved it,' he said.

'Say word?'

'I didn't want it to get all patchy like Gollum. I shaved the rest off.'

Tearing open the packet, Joss shoved an entire handful of gummies in his mouth and tried to force his teeth to chew it. 'You'd be such a good gay man,' I muttered.

'WHKTS?' he said through a mouthful.

'Never mind.' I cringed as drool hit the yellow material of his T-shirt.

We sat there in a comfortable silence for a while and I picked up one of the books lying on the window seat. It was a weathered version of Beauty and The Beast and I found myself frowning at the crude depiction of the monstrous title character. When did I start identifying with the wild animal in this story and not the female protagonist? Sometime around the point I became a werewolf, I guessed. At least there's no way anyone would be able to get me on my hind legs and into a dinner suit on the full moon.

'If only we had some vodka to go with that,' I said, watching Joss pull more sweeties from the bag. He nodded enthusiastically at the mention of an old drinking custom of ours. If Mari, Poc, and I wanted to get wasted in a hurry we would buy a bottle of vodka and a stack of junk food. Once we had a tumbler glass full of vodka we would dump lollies into each glass and drink the reaction. It was delicious. And cheap.

'Do you think about them, like, all the time?' asked Joss, who had been watching my face. My stomach dropped the way it always did at the mention of Mari and Kane.

'Yes.'

'What happened that night?' he abruptly asked.

'I . . .'

I wanted to tell Joss the truth, but I knew I couldn't. I had to live with the fact my actions had led to Mari and Kane's murders. I hadn't delivered the killing blows – that was all Steven – but no matter how strongly people tried to convince me it wasn't my fault I couldn't eradicate that sense of responsibility. At least not so soon after their deaths. I couldn't bear to see my inner accusations reflected on Joss' face.

'I can't, Joss.'

He nodded, eyes full of tears.

'I'm sorry,' I whispered.

'No, I'm sorry,' he said, leaning forward and bringing me into a one-armed hug. 'I just wish . . . I wish I'd been there. That's the way it should it have been, all of us together.'

'What good would that have done? You could've been dead too, Joss.'

'Aye, because I'm the picture of health now.'

'Hey,' I said, lifting my head from his shoulder and roughly grabbing his face. 'You've beaten this before; you can do it again. You can't leave me too.'

He returned my focused stare and I watched his eyes fill with a grief I didn't understand.

'Joss? What are you doing in here?'

Our heads both snapped to the door where one of Joss' doctors, Dr Matthews, was standing with a clipboard. I released Joss' face as Dr Matthews gave me a polite smile.

'Hi Tommi,' he said, 'I'm sorry to interrupt your visit, but Joss should be in his room right now. We're supposed to be in lockdown.'

'Right, sorry, I'm a terrible influence,' I said, getting up from our seat. 'I was just trying to talk him into dyeing his hair blue too.'

Dr Matthews smiled indulgently. 'I don't know if that would suit him.'

'I would own it,' said Joss as I helped him up.

'Honestly, Tommi, I don't how you even got in here,' Dr Matthews muttered.

I shrugged. 'I walked straight in. I didn't even see a police officer until a nurse got out on the maternity floor.'

He shook his head and cursed in German. 'Lisa, could you help Joss back to his room please? I'm going to escort Miss Grayson out so she doesn't get arrested,' he called down the hall.

'Please let her get arrested,' said Joss, walking slowly forward. 'I've got radiation tomorrow, can you come by the next day?'

'Done,' I said, grabbing him in a light hug. We were still hugging when Lisa – Joss' second favourite nurse – came to help him to his room. I bid him farewell and walked with Dr Matthews to the elevator.

'I wanted to talk you when Joss was out of earshot,' he said.

'We could have just spoken Deutsch, his is a little shaky. What is it?'

'He's sick, Tommi.'

'I know, hence the room in the cancer ward.'

'No, he's sicker than we originally suspected. The cancer has moved further along.'

'What are you saying? He's going to die? A few days ago when I was here you said we had a fighting chance.' I tried to keep the panic out of my voice and failed.

'The test results were still coming in then and now that we have a better idea . . . ' he trailed off.

My blood had frozen as the enormity of what he was saying hit home. My forehead pounded in time with my heartbeat. Dr Matthews was a straightforward man, he wouldn't have told me this information if there wasn't a reason.

'What do you want? What can I do?' I asked.

'I was hoping you would give bone marrow.'

I blinked. 'Of course, that's not even a question. Whatever you need.'

'I saw in his files that you were a compatible donor.'

'Yes, it never got to that stage last time but Dr D had his family and close friends tested in case that became an option.'

'You were the only match.'

'I know.'

'A bone marrow transplant is beginning to look like a serious possibility.'

'When do you need to do it? I can have it taken now.'

'Slow down. It's a serious operation, Tommi. It's not like getting your blood taken.'

'I know the specifics.'

'Do you? Because it's a very painful procedure and there can be complications.'

'I don't give a shit about that. Did you ask for my bone marrow or not? Don't try and talk me out of it.'

'I'm not, I just want you to be informed about what you're doing.'

'Consider me textbook savvy,' I replied, keeping my voice firm.

Dr Matthews saw the determination in my eyes and nodded. The elevator doors *pinged* open as it arrived on our floor.

'I want to do another dose of radiation and then the preliminary operation to remove the accessible cancer cells,' he said. I nodded. I knew this.

'I don't think a third round of chemo is going to be an option after the operation. I'm hopeful for its success, but realistically a bone marrow transplant would be the next step.'

'Then let's take it.'

'*Good.*'

I stepped into the elevator and shoved my hand out just before the doors shut behind me.

'Dr Matthews,' I said, 'does Joss know about this?'

'No, only his parents. We'd all prefer it if you didn't say anything until after the operation. We want to keep his spirits up. It's amazing what a patient's positivity can do. He's serious, but stable.'

I smiled at him weakly. 'Sure.'

'You should be fine getting out by the way. I believe most of the police are leaving the premises as we speak. If you do get stopped, direct them to me.'

'Cheers.'

He waved and spun around to make his way hastily down the stark white hall. With the soft thud of the closing doors I felt my back press against the elevator wall. A quick rush of air escaped my lungs and I heard a sob come from my own mouth. I dropped my head into my hands and my knees buckled together. Hot tears began filling up the inside of my hands as I pressed them to my face, lost in my own despair.

'Joss,' I whispered.

Chapter 7

'It doesn't make sense. Any of it!'

I straightened up from my hunched position at the sound of the newest occupant to the elevator. He was peeved, that much was clear, and his German was so thick I could barely decipher it for my own ears. I turned my back to him so I could dab my eyes quickly.

'*No*. NO. I followed the *Spezialeinsatzkommando* unit here first but we were hours too late. The night shift nurse missed it completely. They picked it up on morning rounds. Ya.'

The man looked to be in his late thirties, maybe early forties, and was short with dark features. He was looking at me with curiosity as he spoke into his phone. I tried to avoid his stares. No doubt I looked like a hot mess. I took thanks from the fact this awkward elevator encounter would be over in a matter of seconds. Of course I shouldn't have thought that because the very second I did the lift lurched once, twice, and on third shudder it came to a complete stop. We both steadied ourselves against the wall and tried to regain our balance.

'The fuck?'

'Not again.' The man sighed. 'This is the fourth time today.'

'You don't seem concerned,' I said, switching to Deutsch and trying to envision various *Speed*-esque scenarios where we plummeted to our deaths.

'We're stuck between the first and ground floors,' he said, examining the illuminated floor indicator. 'Worse case we'll land with a soft thud. You from Ireland?'

'Scotland, actually.'

'My apologies, I suppose that's quite offensive.'

'Not at all. The accent becomes jumbled when you're trying to speak someone else's tongue.'

He had dropped his phone on the ground as we came to an abrupt halt and I bent down to pick it up.

'Here,' I said, handing it to him from a crouched position. As he lent forward to retrieve it the flap of his jacket opened and I caught a glimpse of a gun strapped into a holder at his waist. I gasped and recoiled involuntarily. He frowned at my reaction and followed my gaze.

'Oh, I'm a cop,' he said by way of explanation. 'Standard issue.'

'Right,' I said, cursing my natural reaction. I'm sure that wasn't the way 'normal' people reacted to seeing a gun, but most 'normal' people hadn't been shot in the last month.

'Not a fan of guns?' he asked, examining my expression closely.

'Not a fan of what they can do. You here because of the lockdown situation?'

He nodded, cursing as he saw whoever he had been on the phone to had hung up.

'Apparently there was maintenance scheduled for this elevator today but then the abduction happened and there's been more than the usual amount of traffic coming and going to the maternity ward. My forensics team were stuck in here for fifteen minutes this morning. I should have taken the fucking stairs.'

He grabbed the red emergency phone from its holder against the wall and waited for someone to answer.

'Yes, hello, this is Officer Dick Creuzinger from district seven and I'm stuck with a woman in the elevator. What number? Uh ... two. Great, as soon as possible please. I'm supposed to be attending the press conference in the lobby in ten minutes. I understand, thank you.'

He hung the phone up with unnecessary force and leaned back against the wall. He noticed me smiling – or trying not to – and asked what was so funny.

'Officer Dick? Really?' There were a lot of questions playing on my mind about the whole situation, but they were yet to take centre stage the way Joss' ailing health had.

'You wouldn't be the first to be amused,' he said with a tone that implied he had heard the joke a thousand times before.

'It's just, you didn't consider becoming a Private Detective? That way you could have been a Private Dick. Literally.'

He gave a grudging laugh. 'I hadn't considered that.'

'It would take the phallic symbolism of carrying a gun to a whole new level.'

Sliding into a sitting position in the small space, I extended my legs in front of me. I was wearing leather boots with black and purple striped socks that went up to mid-thigh. Fiddling with the top of one of the socks, I could feel Officer Dick's' eyes on me. I knew the question was coming before he asked it.

'You seemed upset when I got in. Are you, uh, okay –'

'I don't want to talk about it,' I interrupted.

'Sure. Sorry.'

An awkward silence hung in the air. I kept fiddling with my sock as the minutes ticked by. 'My best friend is dying,' I said after a long while.

'I . . . I'm really sorry to hear that,' he replied, startled by my sudden response. 'Is he a Scot, like you?'

I nodded. 'Aye. He was treated at the clinic here the first time he got it and when the cancer came back, so did we.'

'Is it bad? Treatable?'

'He has nodular sclerosis which is a form of Hodgkin's lymphoma. It's one of the more common types but every time it comes back –'

'It's harder to fight.'

'Yeah.'

'One of the officers in my unit had a daughter with it. She passed away last year after three good fights.'

'I'm so sorry.'

'She wasn't in a hospital like this though, police wages and all that. This place . . . they're the best.'

I smiled at his attempt to cheer me up. 'I know. Thanks.'

'How old is your friend?'

'Joss? He's twenty.'

'Shit, so young. How old are you?'

'I'm twenty-three.'

'I guess he's doing chemotherapy then?'

'Yup. He's Stage IVA so it's a combination of radiation and chemotherapy at the moment. It's not working as well at they would have hoped. Bone marrow transplant is the next option. His cancer cells are as stubborn as he is, the wee bawbag.'

My nostrils began to tingle, informing me that tears were imminent and I raised my face towards the ceiling in an attempt not to cry in front of this cop *again*. 'Abduction, huh? We thought it was a gunman storming the hallways or something really awful.'

'*Hmph*. It was a newborn that was taken.'

I jerked my head in his direction. His expression was grim. 'That's . . . significantly awful.'

'Second in a fortnight too.'

'From here?'

'You haven't read the papers?'

'I can get by verbally, but reading German has never been my strong suit – much to my old tutor's despair.'

'There was another baby taken from an apartment in the city. No ransom demand yet, which is unusual.'

'Jesus. You don't think someone's after a hundred and one of them to make a coat, do you?'

He almost smiled and then looked like he regretted it. 'I feel this is something else.'

'I'm just sayin', if any of them had babysitters called Cruella I'd be locking on the cuffs.'

He pulled a paper leaflet out of his pocket and unfolded it. 'Does this look like a Cruella to you?'

I scrunched up my face at the police composite. 'Yeesh, his facial hair is certainly cruel. This is the babynapper?'

'One of them, yes.'

'Wait, nappers? Plural? There's more than one person trying to make a baby coat?'

Officer Dick settled next to me on the floor. 'This guy we got off the security camera footage at the hospital. He just strolled in last night, grabbed a baby girl from maternity and walked out of the building.'

'How is that possible? There's security and staff and patients who would have raised an alarm.'

'You would think, but he seems to have got by unseen. The night shift nurse didn't even know the baby was missing. The nurse on morning rounds picked it up. This is just so brazen and completely unlike the first abduction, I'm hesitant to even say they're related.'

'They have to be though, right? It's too much of a coincidence.'

'Maybe. At least we have a visual of the guy. We can get this out all over Germany. Someone has to have seen the man. If only I could get out of this fucking elevator.'

With that he was back on his feet and at the emergency phone again. 'Yes, Officer Creuzinger here again. Funny thing is, we're still stuck in the elevator. Mmm-hmm. You do that. In case you haven't realised it's hard to solve a major crime from inside a lift.' He hung up while muttering curses 'I'm going to miss the press conference.'

As he began speaking to another officer on his phone, I slowly got to my feet. If we were only stuck between the first and ground floors we might be able to climb out. Craning my neck up, I examined the ceiling for a manhole. Uh, there it was. Unfortunately there were no handrails for me to stand on, but if I took a slight running start I could push off from one wall and make a jump for it. There was no doubt I could do it. The doubt was whether I would look human doing so. Fuck it. Officer Dick was still preoccupied on the phone and I took a second to wish I was wearing pants instead of a short black dress. Meh.

'Brown was looking in t – CHRIST! Hold on, I'll call you

back. The woman I'm in the elevator with just climbed through the roof. No, I'm not kidding. Alright, bye.'

Easy, I thought as I hauled myself on to the top of the elevator. I pushed the cover to the side and positioned myself in a crouched position as I looked around the dark elevator shaft.

'How the hell did you get up there?' Officer Dick called.

'Ran. Jumped.'

'You okay?'

'Covered in grease, I suspect, but fine.'

'I don't think this is the best idea. You should come down and we can wait for the maintenance crew.'

'Or,' I said, standing and walking over to a service ladder that ran down the wall, 'you could make it to the last five minutes of your press conference.'

The silence from inside the elevator indicated that Officer Dick preferred option two.

'What was that?' I called.

'Fine. I would like to state that for the record I advised against this.'

'Noted.'

I chose to climb up to level one instead of down to the ground floor because – hello, human jam – and I balanced at the top of the ladder where the two silver doors sat shut tight. I tried prying them open with my fingers to no avail. Taking a glance behind me, I checked the cop was still in the lift and not watching. It took less than a few seconds and I shifted both hands. Elevator doors were much more susceptible to werewolf claws it turns out and I heard the metal groan and creak as I pulled the doors apart. When I felt they were wide enough that we could slip through, I shifted my hands back with a tug of concentration.

'I told him there was no way we were going to his mother's wi – ARGH!' A woman laden with a bunch of flowers shrieked as my face appeared in the open elevator shaft.

'Ello," I said before jumping off the ladder and down on to the roof of the lift. I peered into the manhole to see Office Dick waiting anxiously.

'How'd it go?' he asked, relieved to see me.

'Swimmingly. We can climb up the service ladder to level one and take the stairs back down. The doors are open.'

'Great, but how am I supposed to –'

I cut him off by shoving a normal, human arm down into the elevator.

'Climb. Right. You might be nimble but I don't think you can pull a grown man into an elevator shaft.'

'Of course not, you lazy sod. You'll be doing most of the pulling yourself. I'll just give you a boost.'

He considered me for a moment longer before grabbing my wrist.

'Jump on three. One, two, three!'

He jumped and his other hand got a grip on the inside of the manhole. I tried not to pull him too much due to a) not wanting to overly display my strength and b) wanting to see him struggle after implying a girl couldn't haul his ass up here. After much puffing, swearing and squirming we were both climbing up the ladder and through to the first floor. Officer Dick was definitely worse off than I was, but we both had smears of grime on our clothing and bodies.

'The elevator is out of service, ladies and gents,' he said, displaying an official-looking pass of some sort. 'Best to take the stairs.'

The small crowd that had been watching grumbled with dissent and made for the exit. He turned to me, grinning. 'I'm counting that as my workout for the day.'

'You and me both.'

'If you can hang around for twenty minutes I can give you a lift to wherever you're going. I owe you that at least.'

'Thanks, but my friend is picking me up any sec.' The word friend felt strange on my tongue as a way to describe Lorcan.

'Ah, course,' he said as we followed the flow of people descending the stairs. 'Well, thanks for that. Hopefully I won't see you in the hospital again.'

'If you ever raid Phases, you might find me.'

'Phases? The club near the Rosenthaler Platz U-Bahn stop?'

'The one and the same. I'm staying next door with the people who own it. I'm going to be doing some casual work there a few nights a week.'

'I can't speak for the kind of bands that play there, but Phases has a good rep. We never have any incidents, bashings, overdoses, nothing.'

'Huh. Good to hear.'

We reached the lobby and faced off in the separate directions we were heading. He extended his hand and I shook it.

'It's a been a pleasure – I, uh, I don't even know your name.'

'Tommi Grayson,' I said, returning the handshake.

'Tommi. Unusual. Best of luck to your friend.'

'Thanks, Officer Dick. Good luck with the babies.'

That last comment earned a strange look from a passing elderly man and I smiled, leaving the cop and the hospital as far away from me as possible.

Chapter 8

'How was he?'

It was a simple enough question. Yet as I climbed into the car with Lorcan it was one I found myself struggling to answer. He picked up on my mood and didn't push. We spent the first five minutes of the trip in silence. I was replaying my encounter with Officer Dick Creuzinger in my head when Lorcan couldn't take the quiet any longer.

'Tommi, why are you covered in grease?'

'I got in an elevator with a cop and we had to climb out.'

'And?'

I met his concerned gaze. I'm sure the expression on my face said more than my next words ever could.

'The doctor thinks the next dose of radiation and surgery aren't going to work. Joss needs a bone marrow transplant. As soon as he gets through the op, Dr Matthews wants me prepared to donate. I'm the only match.'

'You can't.'

'What?!'

Lorcan sighed, looking genuinely grieved.

'Look, I know there can be complications and it's supposed to hurt like a mother, but it's a quick and sim –'

'No,' he said interrupting me, 'you can't.'

I picked up on his meaning and my voice wavered. 'What do you mean I *can't*?'

'Your werewolfism is carried in your blood. It's in your genes and in your bones,' he said, keeping his eyes on the road.

'So? You've all said the only way for someone to become a werewolf is to inherit it from a parent. It can't be transmitted by blood or bite.'

'That's true, but it can still be deadly: especially for someone like Joss whose body is weak already. If he received your bone marrow it's more than just a small transmission of blood: it's inserting a large part of you into his body. The werewolf genes would destroy him. A mixing of blood is minor. Something as large as this would kill. His body wouldn't be compatible with what is being given to him. Your genes would obliterate his central nervous system because they're too strong for him to handle. They're too strong for any non-werewolf to handle.'

I felt like all the breath had been sucked out of my body and my chest sunk into itself. Tears welled up in my eyes and all background noise disappeared as blood thudded through my head in time with my heartbeat. 'Pull over,' I said, keeping my voice quiet and firm, even as my hands shook.

Lorcan pulled off the main road and into the car park of a rundown public park without question. He barely had the ignition off before I was unclipping my seat belt and leaping across my seat to him. I grabbed his face with both of my hands and kissed him violently.

He was surprised, I felt his shock and he pulled back as though he was about to question me, but I silently begged him not to. Something flickered in his eyes and he seemed to understand what I needed. He grabbed me firmly, throwing me against the dashboard and steering wheel.

Yanking his T-shirt over his head, I unclipped his seat belt and fumbled at his zipper. He wrapped my legs around his torso and pushed me back into the passenger seat. It was too much. Everything was too much. From one life-shattering tragedy to another, I couldn't mentally take another blow right now. All I wanted to do was funnel my anger, my pain, and my fears into a primal physical act.

Lorcan tore off my underwear and I hitched my black dress up to my waist, not bothering about my boots and not wanting to wait. We had never been this rough with each other before. I relished every thump as it was met by a searing kiss. I gripped the headrest as Lorcan pushed inside me and we coordinated our bodies to work together in the awkward space. As the sound of our animalistic yells filled the jeep I felt nothing but pleasure as I fucked the pain away.

An hour later we were pulling in to the loading dock of the apartments. We both sat in the car for several long minutes, neither one of us wanting to be the first to say something *or* be the first to leave. The small, enclosed space smelled of sex and the tiniest bit of shame. Winding down the window, I let out a deep breath that felt coiled up inside my chest.

'Serious but stable,' I mumbled, looking out the window at the rest of the concrete garage.

'What?'

'Serious but stable, that's what Joss' doctor said. What does that even mean? He's seriously dying at a stable rate?'

'It means that his condition is significant, but not deteriorating just yet. He'd still be cleared for day trips and quarantine-free vis . . .'

His words faded away as I shook my head, sighing.

'I'm sorry, you don't want to talk about this,' he said.

'No,' I replied. 'I really don't. I don't wanna talk about Joss or what just happened back in that car park. I just . . . I just need physical action. Er, a different kind of physical action. I need to get my body moving to keep my head straight.'

Lorcan's hand was reaching out for my own, but I shifted too quickly and out of the car before he could make contact. I adjusted my dress, feeling both uncomfortable and strangely free without my knickers, which were ripped and buried within my shoulder bag.

I was towelling off from a quick shower by the time Lorcan wandered into the apartment. He knocked lightly on the door and I told him to give me a second as I firmly wrapped a towel around my body in the steamy room.

'Come in,' I said, and he gently pushed the door open. He didn't step any further into the room. I took one look at his face and sighed, resting my body against the basin.

'This has to stop,' he said.

I nodded my head while looking at my feet. 'I know. The hornymoon is over.'

'If *we* don't stop it . . .'

I looked up, searching his face for the words he didn't finish, saying, 'Then what?'

'If I can't control myself and you can't get it together, then I'm going to have to put some distance between us, Tommi.'

That's what I thought. 'You do what you have to,' I replied. 'But that was the last time. I needed an outlet and you were it.'

He frowned then, noticing something on my body. 'You got a new tattoo.'

I looked down at my wrist and the shifting crescent moon that was there. 'I did. Before I left Dundee. I'm surprised you only noticed it now.'

'Me too,' he said, moving to the side to let me out of the bathroom.

I heard the shower start up again behind me and I threw an oversized flannel on over a pair of jeans and a tank top. Firing up my laptop, I checked my emails and frowned when I saw one in my personal account from my old boss Alexis Scales. There was another sitting above it from an address I didn't recognise. I opened Alexis' first. It read:

Tommi,

You are missed here at McManus! But alas, I hope Berlin is treating you well. I was getting in touch to let you know that we were contacted by a distant relative of yours who saw your staff details on our website (I really need to update that). I didn't feel comfortable passing on your phone number. I hope it's okay that I gave him an email address, as that's easy enough to ignore if necessary.

Stay safe, Alexis.

I froze for a moment, then with a sense of dread I clicked open the next email and read who it was from: James Ihi.

Kia ora, Tommi, my sister,

I know that term won't sit well with you but that is what you are, my blood. You have every right to dodge our attempts to reach you so far. If space is what you need then Simon and I understand that. We hope that you understand what we were trying to do for you back home, that we wanted to help you through your first transformation and protect you from the full moon. When we learned of what Steven had done, he was dead to us and dead to the Ihi pack forever. In a testament to how bad things had become, my aunties would have killed him if he hadn't fled before . . .

Lorcan stepped out of the bathroom shirtless with a pair of sweatpants hanging loosely off his hips. It was testament to how rapt I was in the contents of the email that I barely noticed his body as he padded over towards me. My eyes were scanning through the contents of James' email at such a rapid rate the words began to blur.

Lo was drying his hair with a towel and paused the motion as he registered my expression. There was something bubbling underneath the surface of my skin and it felt a lot like rage.

'Where is Quaid Ihi?' I asked, struggling to keep my voice flat.

'What?' Lorcan didn't look surprised at the question, rather that I had known to ask it.

'You heard me, Lo. I asked back in Dundee when I was still in hospital what had happened to him. I had a mixed bag of answers, ranging from "you don't know" to "not at liberty to discuss". I didn't think those were evasions at the time –'

'They weren't evasions,' he cut in.

'Then what were they? Because it definitely wasn't the truth.'

'You didn't need to know that.'

'Oh?' My voice raised to an unnaturally high pitch. 'Call me bonkers but I feel like I probably needed to know my half-brother had been *imprisoned* by the Praetorian Guard.'

'Technically he was imprisoned by the Treize.'

'SO VERY NOT THE POINT. He's fourteen, Lo ... fourteen. He got roped into his brother's maniacal schemes and dragged halfway around the world, like his sister, who I'm told never returned home. The Ihi pack are still looking for her, Aruhe.'

Lorcan let out an agitated breath and shook his head. 'His age is irrelevant.'

'Really? Do you remember yourself at fourteen? I mean, I know you were probably en route to the Holy War but when I was fourteen I could barely find my own genitals let alone be held responsible for my actions.'

'You make it sound like he got caught shoplifting,' he replied, throwing the towel down on my bed. 'He took part in two kidnappings that resulted in the deaths of innocent people. Even in a court of law he'd walk away with a double manslaughter charge.'

'The difference is he'd be tried in a juvenile court, not an adult scenario. And did he even get a trial before he got thrown in some supernatural prison or wherever you keep people?'

Lorcan's silence spoke volumes.

'Who gave you this information?' he asked, spinning around my laptop to view the screen.

'I'll tell you who didn't give me this information,' I replied, shooting him a pointed look.

'James Ihi? You really believe he's looking for Quaid and Aruhe out of the kindness of his heart?'

I thought back to my time in New Zealand, when I was their prisoner and the brief encounters I'd had with James. 'Yes,' I said. 'Yes, I do. Family is important to a lot of people and to the descendants of a tribe with supernatural abilities – to whom iwi affiliations are very important – I dare say it's crucial. *Especially* when they're looking to name a new pack leader.'

'They already have: it's Simon Tianne,' he muttered.

It was like I had been slapped. 'You didn't think I needed to know that either?'

'You read some Maori books and now you think you're one of them? Chester Rangi, or whatever he said his name was, wasn't a tribal elder, Tommi.'

'Could you be more condescending right now?'

'Could you be more single-minded?'

'I'm not saying I'm one of them, I know I never will be and I never want to be but that doesn't mean I'm disinterested in the fate of my bloodline,' I huffed. 'Besides that, locking up a fourteen-year-old boy without a trial or contact with his family is plain wrong – regardless of whether he's related to me or not. I don't even wanna think about what happened to bob girl, Aruhe, whatever.'

'Nothing happened to her,' he said. 'We didn't touch her. She's still out there, missing, and if she hasn't gone back to the Ihis it's because she didn't want to.'

'Te whanau Ihi,' I muttered.

A loud knocking broke apart the argument and Lorcan glanced at the door. I ignored it.

'You're not a PG anymore,' I whispered. 'You're supposed to believe in peace and rehabilitation and giving people chances.'

He blinked and looked at me in way that I thought was sad at first, yet turned more towards pity. 'Maybe I've seen too much.'

He turned and walked to the door, obviously welcoming the time out on our *tête-à-tête*.

'What?' he barked as he ripped it open.

'Hey, Lorcan.' It was Sanjay. He shifted his weight uncomfortably from foot to foot as he took in the rage on Lorcan's expression. Little did he know it had nothing to do with him.

'Sanjay,' he said with a breath, calming himself.

'Zill's running around at the club and asked me to come and see if you could do us a favour.'

'What is it?'

'We've had a few of our regular staff call in sick. Since Saturday is our biggest night she wanted to see if you could help out.'

'That's not a problem. What do you need me to do?'

'I can help too,' I said, nodding at Sanjay as I marched to the doorway. He smiled at me and looked at the Run DMC logo on my singlet.

'Nice.'

I shrugged. 'It's tricky to rock a rhyme that's right on time.'

Sanjay laughed. Lorcan looked confused.

'We could really do with another body,' he said. 'And you're supposed to start next week anyway so ...'

Lorcan had worked at the club a few times in the two weeks that we'd been here. My own Saturday evening was suddenly looking very free and I was desperate not to be left alone in the apartment with my anger and no outlet.

'Can you serve drinks?' asked Sanjay.

'Can I serve drinks?' I batted a hand and looked at Lorcan with a 'can you believe this guy?' expression.

'He said "serve" drinks, not consume them at a rapid rate,' said Lo.

'You say rapid, I say impressive. And yes, Sanjay, I can indeed serve. I worked at a bar when I was at university.'

'I didn't know that,' said Lorcan.

'I don't tell you everything,' I replied with a look. 'Plus there's not a lot to know. It was a busy, sweaty, and tiring experience. I made good tips though.'

Sanjay raised an eyebrow at me.

'With my customer service,' I added.

'Of course,' said Sanjay. 'Good. Bar staff is where we're down. Gus can serve drinks as well and you can take over his shift at the door, Lorcan. See you guys in twenty minutes?'

'See you then,' said Lo.

'Bye,' I called after him.

Lorcan shut the door and looked at me, considering.

'What?' I asked. 'If you're going to say we should talk about this later, I'm way ahead of you.'

With that I left to slap on some make-up and get changed into bar-staff appropriate clothes.

Working at Phases was way more fun than I originally thought it would be and I was able to push my anger about Quaid to the back of my mind. For now. It was also surprisingly fascinating. Sure, Gus looked like he would rather bite the customers than take their money, yet he could mix *any* drink. Quickly.

I was good with the basics and thankfully that's what most people wanted. If someone was after something tricky, Gus was the go-to man. The crowd began filtering in slowly from about 8.30 p.m. and by 11 p.m. Dolly and Lorcan had to start turning people away. Phases filled to capacity rapidly and I think a lot of that had to do with Sanjay. The man was incredible on the decks. He had the crowd eating out of his hand as he spliced between well-known remixes and underground beats. I was leaning against the bar and smiling to myself as Sanjay elicited a hand-raising roar from the crowd with his transition from a Lady Leshurr jam to a Hudson Mohawke banger.

'I couldn't get a Corona on the house, could I?'

I looked up to see Lorcan's handsome face smiling warily at me over the bar.

'I'm sorry,' he said, offering a truce. 'You've been going through a lot lately, I didn't want to add something else to your plate.'

I sighed as I got him that beer. 'Lo, my plate's so full I'm afraid to take another spoonful. But you understand why not telling me about it was wrong, right? Even hurtful?'

'Honestly? No. He's not your family. He's practically an enemy.'

'He's a *kid* who got wedged in a really bad situation. I'm not saying I would have made the same choices he did when I was fourteen, but locking him up and throwing away the key is not right, no matter how you look at it.'

'I can't apologise for that as it has nothing to do with me,' he said. 'That's just how it is: those are the consequences for his actions in our world.'

'That worries me,' I replied, handing Lorcan his beer. His fingers lingered on mine for a moment, then his face was momentarily wiped from my vision when a white light made me blink and stumble back.

'Cheese,' said Clay, Phases' sometime photographer. His duties seemed to shift between a managerial role with Zillia and snapping the happy patrons. His time behind the lens also served in an undercover bouncer capacity as he dissolved any fights throughout the club and kept an eye on hot spots. Tonight he was in fine form. In tight designer jeans, he was wearing a silver singlet that looked more like a second layer of skin than actual material. Clinging over that was another singlet, this one made of royal blue mesh. He looked like a back-up dancer for the Vengaboys. I glared at him as my vision returned to normal.

'Don't make me smash your camera,' said Lorcan, his voice laced with annoyance.

'You wouldn't dare,' replied Clay, clutching the camera to his chest in mock sincerity.

'I think we might dare,' I said, rubbing my eyes.

Clay grabbed my wrist to stop me. 'No, Tommi, you'll smudge your liquid eyeliner.'

'Meh.'

'It's the first time I've seen you wear make-up. Don't ruin it for me.'

'Fine.'

'You give good face, Tom. I had to capture the moment.'

'Something as beautiful as that? Me asking for a beer?' mocked Lorcan.

I left them to their conversation as I served four other customers jostling for my attention. I was making a Midori cocktail for one of the palest women I had ever seen in my life when she leaned across the bar to whisper at me conspiratori-ally. 'Tell me you know the name of that bouncer.'

I didn't have to look over my shoulder to know who she was talking about. 'I do,' I replied, smiling as I fixed her a drink and poured myself a shot of Midori.

'Well?'

'His name's Lorcan.'

'Oh,' she said, as if sensing something. 'Are you two –'

'No,' I cut in. 'No, he's actually . . . gay.'

'Really?' she asked. 'Argh, I bet that's his boyfriend he's talking to right now. They're cute.'

'Aye, sorry about that,' I said, doing my best to hide a smirk and stop myself from feeling too bad about feeding this woman a lie. Just because Lorcan and I couldn't date, that didn't mean I wanted a clam jam.

'Everything is ashes.'

She spoke in a slow, almost lazy drawl and glancing again at her alabaster skin I wondered if she was albino. Her waist-length hair was as white as her skin and she almost seemed to glow in the dim light of the club. She could have been a plus-size model and I envied her curves as they winked at me through the blue velvet of her dress, I deposited her money in the till and handed her the drink. As she reached for it I noticed one of her hands was a stump. She caught me looking, if only for a second, and gestured towards her stump dramatically with her other hand.

'Witches,' she said, sounding bored. She threw back the shot. Mine had paused at my lips in shock. She looked at me expectantly.

'Bitches,' I strangled out, downing mine.

Her long face broke into a smile as she laughed. I slid another shot to her across the bar, on the house.

'To the hot bouncer,' she purred, nodding in the opposite direction. 'For being gorgeous and flaming.'

I looked behind me and smiled at Lorcan who was engrossed in conversation with Clay. 'Amen.'

I clinked my glass with hers and we drank. Grabbing a piece of sliced lime, I returned to the lads.

'I see you made friends with Casper over there,' said Clay.

'Don't you think that's a bit rude?' I snapped, frowning.

'No, Tommi, she's called Casper because she's a medium,' explained Lorcan. 'Her real name is Corvossier von Klitzing.'

'If you want to communicate or find any ghost in the world, that's your girl. Rumour has it she can even get spirits to do her bidding if she wants,' said Clay as he absentmindedly looked through the photos on his LCD screen.

'The thing about witches –'

'Happened,' he replied.

'Yeesh. They don't like mediums?'

Lorcan shook his head. 'No, they were interested in her being an albino. Some covens believe the bones of albinos have magical properties and that their blood can make you immortal.'

'Idiots,' Clay interjected.

'Her brother Barastin was killed in the attack,' Lorcan continued. 'I've read the case files. She barely escaped with her life.'

'How did she escape?' I couldn't see her physically fighting off anyone, but appearances can be deceiving.

Lorcan gave me a significant look.

'Ghosts? She fought off a bunch of witches with *ghosts*?'

'Rumour has it,' said Clay, turning his attention back to us. 'The Askari hire Casper out from time to time. She's very talented.'

'Awesome,' I breathed.

Clay left us to find his next victims and Lorcan downed the remainder of his beer.

'Did you notice I'm now drinking your beer of choice?' he asked.

'I did. Have I converted you?'

'Yes. That and they don't serve Guinness here.'

'We're getting an order in,' shouted Zillia as she rushed past us to meet a man at the back of the club. He looked a good ten years older than her and had that whole silver fox thing going on. He was dressed in business-casual clothing which I guess is enough to make you stand out at Phases, but no one seemed to pay him any mind.

'That's Kirk Rennex,' said Lorcan, following my gaze.

'Zillia's fancy boyfriend?'

'Yes. When he's not out of town for business he's here a few nights a week. Speaking of partners, Dolly's girlfriend is here. I said I'd man the door solo for a while, so I better get back.'

I watched his tall frame part the crowd as he relieved Dolly at the door.

It was a few hours later before I met Dolly's girlfriend Yu, an attractive Chinese woman. She ordered two vodkas on the rocks and I assumed they were for her and Dolly until she sat down on a stool at the bar and began drinking the first. I could smell smoke on her and it made me crave a cigarette. Bar traffic had slowed considerably as it drew towards the end of the night and I had time to talk to her.

'You're Dolly's partner, right?'

She looked up at me with an intelligent gaze and nodded. 'And you're Lorcan's ward,' she replied in an accent-less voice.

My mouth gaped open as I registered what this could mean. She watched me as my mental cogs clicked into gear. I'd only ever a met one person whose voice was absent of almost any kind of accent or national dialect: Lorcan. It was unusual and something he had told me occurred when you spent centuries living around the world amongst different voices and tones until your own was practically neutral. I stepped closer to her and dropped my voice.

'Are you part of the Praetorian Guard?'

She looked impressed. 'I'm surprised Lorcan didn't mention it, although we never worked together much. The first time I properly spoke to him was when he stayed here five years ago.'

I didn't say anything. I was still in shock at discovering Dolly's girlfriend was PG. 'Are you based in Berlin?'

She shook her head through a mouthful. 'No, I'm done. I asked to be relieved four years ago.'

I felt my mouth drop open even wider. I'd never met some-one who had asked to be relieved from the Praetorian Guard. Lorcan had told me it happened, but to see a living example was another thing entirely. Not only did you resign yourself from your duties with the Guard, you also resigned your immortality.

'How old are you?'

Without missing a beat she replied, 'Thirty-four.'

'No, I mean, legitimately.'

She smiled at my phrasing. 'Eight hundred and ninety-two.'

'Fuck me,' I said, amazed. I had never got around to asking Lorcan how old Ennis was – the only other Praetorian Guard member I knew. I sensed he wasn't anywhere near as old as Yu or Lo, given he still had an accent. She was undoubtedly the oldest person I had ever spoken to, probably would ever speak to.

'You're more than twice Lorcan's age,' I said feebly.

'If only I had twice his skill level.'

There were so many questions I wanted to ask her.

'I better go,' said Yu, finishing her second vodka.

'Wait,' I said, leaning against the bar as she got off the stool. I didn't know what to say to make her stay and she saw my indecision. She looked behind me quickly and I followed her gaze to where Dolly was emerging from behind the silver door that led to the meeting room.

'Look,' she said, lightly resting her hand on my own, 'I can see there's a lot you want to ask me. I don't have time to talk about it here.'

'Then why did you seek me out? You knew who I was.'

'I did. I wanted to meet you for myself. I wanted to meet the blue werewolf that Lorcan is training. You've become a hot topic.'

I blinked at this revelation. 'I have? With who?'

She looked pointedly around the club. 'All for another time and another place, Tommi. I know your abode, I'll seek you out.'

'I look forward to it.'

She gave me a tight smile and walked off to meet her lover. I served the next several customers in a daze, taking money and pouring drinks without thinking as I ran the things Yu had said through my mind again and again.

I also began paying closer attention to the clientele. It was only once it slowed down that I could *really* look at the people in Phases. The werewolves were easy to spot as they always tended to be in groups of at least three or four. Even rogues seemed to congregate together. I watched Corvossier converse with different people before she found a quiet corner to stand in. I was sure I spotted PG members amongst the crowd – there was a certain lethality and no-bullshit air that they projected. The others . . . there were so many varying hints of the unusual that I could barely keep up with my own different theories. A man's iris that reflected like a snake's here, a trail of smoke following a woman there, and – most disturbingly – an older man who replied to a question I was preparing to ask him before I said it out loud. It reminded me of Chester. I might be *kahuatairingi*, but when it came to the supernatural world I was most definitely not alone.

Once the call for final drinks was well and truly over and the last drunkard shoved out the door, Zillia gave me the nod that the shift was finished. Relieved but still a little amped, I walked to where Lorcan was helping pack up the wooden crate tables.

'I'm gonna head out,' I said, 'take a walk and clear my head. Meet you up in the apartment later on to finish that chat?

'Sure, I was going to stay here for a bit and help with the rest of the clean up.'

'Fine. I'll see you later.' As I was about to turn he grabbed my wrist.

'Can you help me carry up a few kegs from the cooler room?'

I frowned. He could easily do that on his own and I was itching for some space. He knew both of these things, but he asked anyway. 'Sure.'

We left down the jungle-themed hallway and he held the cooler door open for me, closing it after I walked through. Shivering, I was halfway down the stairs when I felt his hand on my shoulder. I spun around and craned my neck upwards to meet his face. He was considerably taller than me anyway, but with him standing a step above he was colossal.

'Lo, wh –'

He placed a finger over my lips and shushed me. Slowly, he leaned forward and swept a strand of hair that had escaped my double buns off my forehead. Even in this darkness, his eyes seemed to penetrate. My breath came out in a cloud of steam and he moved through it to kiss me once, gently, softly on the lips. I was frozen in place, partially from the cold but also because of his actions. This was the opposite of everything we had talked about, everything we had discussed this same very night. Yet it felt different . . . it wasn't full of uncontrollable passion and we weren't ripping each other's clothes off. It felt like goodbye.

'I just wanted to do that,' he said. 'One final time.'

'Right. Before the "never again" part,' I replied, breathless.

'Before that.'

In the darkness we took a while, not kissing, barely touching, but I needed it.

Without another word I stepped up, past him, and out of the cooler. I didn't pause. I worried that if I stopped I might go back and say fuck it all, let's wipe the slate clean tomorrow and have one more night. Yet one more would become two more and then three and we'd be in a worse place than when we started.

I absent-mindedly said goodnight to the Rogues as I walked through the empty club and they muttered responses. My mind wasn't on their replies; it was on Lorcan. Less than twelve hours ago I'd been shouting at him for keeping information from me, vital information. He kept secrets. He was hot and then he was cold. He did not have very big trusticles. He also didn't understand where I was coming from about the whole Ihi thing. Yet despite all that, I was hit by the notion that I was quite possibly in love with him.

I paused, coming to a dead stop at the entrance to the alley as I realised someone was with me. Spinning around, I met the sheepish expression of Sanjay who quickly held up his hands in surrender. My body relaxed and I felt tension leave my shoulders.

'Sorry,' he said. 'Didn't mean to catch you off guard.'

'It's cool, I'm just a bit jumpy tonight.'

'I heard you say that you were going for a walk. Can I join you?'

I nodded, curious at the actual intention behind his company as I sensed a mutual need to get fresh air wasn't it. There was no direction I was set on, so I followed Sanjay's lead as we marched our way out of the city district and along some of the quieter streets.

We passed the Altes Museum and even in the darkness of night, it was still breathtaking to behold. The huge pillars of the coliseum-like structure looked downright menacing as we strolled over the grass parklands that stretch before it. A couple were making out near the fountain, giggling and completely unaware of our presence.

'I can help with that.'

'You what?' I replied, dragging my eyes away from the affectionate pair. 'You're chirpsing if you think I need a kissing tutorial.'

Sanjay laughed, his tiny frame shaking with the effort. 'Not that, ha,' he said, breathless. 'I shouldn't have been able to sneak up on you in the alley.'

'Oh, I was distracted.'

'It shouldn't matter. You haven't had a wolf to hone the senses with you, but you'll need them to survive. A big part of being a rogue is knowing when to fight and when to flee. If you can't sense danger until it's too late, then you won't make it long.'

'You weren't a danger to me,' I argued.

Sanjay rolled his eyes in frustration. 'You can't *sense* intention, but you can sense other supernaturals whether that's a werewolf or something else.'

'Is that why you joined me tonight?'

He shrugged nonchalantly. 'Not really, although now was as good a time as any to talk about your tracking weaknesses. Mostly I just figured it was smart for you to not go out alone.'

As if sensing my incoming protest he again held up his hands. 'You can take care of yourself, I know, but you've been seen at the club now. People know you're working at Phases, living with us, learning from us. The community is talking about the new werewolf in town under the combined guard of the Rogues and the Custodians. It would have been fine for you to walk the night off alone, but it would be *smart* for you to do so with company.'

I smiled, looking up at the cloudless night and attempting to inhale the stars as they sparkled in the sky. 'Thank you for being honest with me.'

'Of course.'

I cast him a sideways glance to see if he was joking. 'That's a rare thing, you know, people being honest with me. Especially men from this world.'

'I'm sorry to hear that's the case,' he replied, meaning it. 'On a completely unrelated note, I do know a 24 hour burger joint that will rock your world.'

'Dude, why didn't you open with that? I am *so* invested in this idea.'

Sanjay was easy company as we made our way to his secret burger spot. He never pushed further than our new acquaintance would deem acceptable and once I got him on the topic of music, he was unstoppable. He'd been angling to have Phases incorporate one live band a night, but he'd built up such an audience with his DJ sets Zillia was reluctant to risk losing any clientele. As for that burger joint, well, it lived up to his hype.

'Burgermeister,' I said, rolling the word over my tongue as we lined up. It didn't matter that it was four in the morning, there were still plenty of patrons crowded around the tiny hut and standing as they dug into their food.

'This used to be a public restroom,' Sanjay said. 'But they sold it off and this place popped up.'

'That's not the best sales pitch.'

'Make sure you get the cheese fries as well,' he added, ignoring me.

The man was right. It was the best bloody burger I'd ever eaten, maybe even the 'best burger in Germany' as I overheard the girl behind me saying. I practically inhaled my cheese-burger before we split the fries between us. Werewolves were a greedy lot and I wished silently that I'd ordered my own.

We took our time finishing our ciders, enjoying the buzz of people milling about and appreciating the after-effects of the carb and cheese double-header. There wasn't a whole lot to say on the stroll home, the rest of the city was quiet as if savouring the last few hours of rest before it would truly begin to wake up. Sanjay held out his arm, stopping me as he gripped my elbow.

'Let's try now,' he said, replying to my inquisitive look. 'The city is sleeping, there's not a whole lot of interference.'

'What am I supposed to track? Plastered people?'

'Do you know where we are?'

I did a quick swivel, spinning around to take my bearings. The Fernsehturm was just visible over the rooftops to the east. 'No, I don't know exactly but on foot I'd guess we're about fifteen minutes away from Phases.'

'Good,' he nodded. 'Try tracking your way back to the club.'

'I will not be blindfolded, mister,' I warned, holding up a stern finger and wagging it.

He chuckled. 'Course not. Use your scent, taste the air, bookmark what's familiar and trace that home.'

'Aight,' I replied, closing my eyes briefly as I centred myself. Digesting Sanjay, I registered his aftershave and the sicken-ingly sweet smell of his e-cigarette as he puffed on it.

Moving outwards, the street swam into view. There was the hot, spicy tang emulating from a pile or rubbish overflowing outside an apartment block. Trees were free of their leaves, their branches stripped of the usual foliage as winter approached and dry bark was overwhelming as we carried on past a park. It was slow going as I tried not to follow the images my eyes were perceiving, but rather the scents and what they were telling my brain. There was a cluster of smells and noises that were all competing for my attention up ahead and I registered it as the main road we needed to cross before we'd be home at Phases.

We were less than a block away and I turned to tell Sanjay this when I paused, sensing something else. I wasn't sure what it was at first, but I was drawn towards it as I took a sharp left and let my nose tug me in the direction of what was intriguing me. There was something familiar yet *wrong* about the scent and soon two sets of footsteps could be heard coming closer and closer towards us. There was a long, brick wall covered in street art before us and I knew the scent was headed around that blind corner even before the two men it belonged to appeared in front of us.

They'd turned the bend so sharp, they must have missed us completely or simply failed to care as they nearly collided with Sanjay and me directly. Lucky we were both very quick, with Sanjay dodging the lads while the other brushed past my shoulder. My body was knocked back only slightly as they walked on, not reacting to us anyway. I was so shocked by their sudden appearance and subsequent rudeness that I said nothing at first, casting only a backwards glance at the two assholes. They were big guys, almost wider than they were tall, and there was something distinctly 'other' about them.

Sanjay was muttering to me what pricks they were when I suddenly came to a halt, pausing as I caught the faintest scent of the something that had drawn me towards them in the first place. I inhaled deeper, willing my body to confirm what I was thinking.

'– complete and utter –'

'Sanjay,' I snapped, holding my hand up. 'Do you smell that?'

'What?' he said, following my gaze back to the two men who were continuing their hasty pace.

'It smells like . . . blood. I can smell blood on them.'

'Are you sure? Let me see . . .'

He mimicked what I had done just two seconds earlier and his eyes snapped open, wide, as he came to the same conclusion.

'Yes,' he nodded, 'I smell it too. Not a lot but enough.'

The men were faint in the distance now, yet it wouldn't take much for Sanjay and me to track them. Any thought of that, however, was cut short as a sirens pierced the night and lights in the surrounding houses began flicking on. Soon two police cars sped down the very street the men had appeared from.

'Come on,' Sanjay said, grabbing my wrist. 'We should get out of here.'

I agreed and the pair of us crossed the street as an ambulance and another police car tore down the road at the kind of pace that screamed something was wrong: very wrong.

The main road was in sight when we heard feet running in our direction. Three plain-clothes officers skidded to a halt in front of us, weapons drawn, and Sanjay and I both threw our arms up above our heads in a flash.

'DON'T MOV – argh, dash. It's clubbers,' cursed one of the officers in German. 'Extend the perime – wait, Tommi?'

My head swivelled in the direction of my name and I squinted, pretending to try and see through the darkness at the man even though I knew who it was.

'Officer Dick, innit? Twice in less than twenty-four hours.'

'What are you doing out here?'

'My friend Sanjay and I grabbed a bite at Burgermeister. We're on our way back to Phases. You?'

'Sir, we can't stay here,' one of the other officers snapped. 'We have to keep going with the search.'

'*Ja, ja*. Let's go,' he replied, making a gesture. The three of them moved off and he paused, frowning slightly as he turned to speak to me. 'You pop up in the weirdest places, Tommi.'

'Ditto.'

He frowned before turning and rushing into the night. Sanjay and I exchanged a glance.

'Let's just get the hell home,' he said.

'With you. Way with you.'

My eyes were sore with fatigue as I stared at the keypad to the apartment block and scrunched up my nose. I hit the incorrect code twice before finally getting it right on the third go.

Having said goodbye to Sanjay on his floor, I trudged up the six flights of stairs and thought greedily about the big, soft bed that was waiting for me.

Closing the apartment door with my back, I glanced at the creeping light coming through the windows as the sun began to rise.

I stiffened, suddenly sensing the presence of someone else. There were two someones, as it turned out. Two women were standing less than a metre in front of me. They ran their eyes quickly over my appearance. They were identical twins. From their harsh and pointed facial features to the shaved heads and trim physiques, I wouldn't have been surprised if every single cell was a perfect match. They were almost wearing matching outfits: black boots, black jeans, black T-shirts, and denim jackets. At least they had different styles of denim jackets. I noticed bulges emerging from strange places under their clothing. Weapons.

Immediately I sunk into a fight stance and backed up towards the kitchen. They looked surprised by this and glanced at each other before mirroring my own movements. Without looking behind me I reached back and drew two butcher's knives from the holder on the counter. Everything about them looked dangerous and if I was going to have any chance of escaping this I needed to act quickly.

'Listen,' one of them started.

I didn't wait to hear the rest of what she said because I hurled a knife at her. My aim was true, but she darted out of its path with cat-like reflexes. I tried to dash for the door. Her sister beat me to it and landed a front kick directly in my chest. I went flying backwards and landed on the bench, smashing the plates we had left there from dinner. The wind was knocked completely out of me. I spun my legs around and made contact with the other twin as she tried to come closer. I flipped off the bench and grabbed a hanging saucepan in the process. Great. I was going to fight these two very skilled strangers with a saucepan and a knife. I was fucked.

One twin jumped up from where I had knocked her down and they came at me together. It was a smart move. Why wait to take someone on one at a time when you could work with the aid of an identical fighter? They operated in perfect unison and whenever I would go to block one punch, there was always another waiting for me from my other adversary.

I thought about trying to shift, but in my current state I was too tired. The saucepan connected with the ribs of one of the twins and she made a painful grimace before the other kicked it out of my hand. I managed to slash her face with the knife before the other jumped on my back and tried to wrestle it free.

I hadn't expected her to recover so quickly and I executed a roundhouse kick on her sister before throwing myself backwards. The twin hit the ground hard as I had thrown all my effort into tossing us backwards. I let gravity do the rest. Her grip loosened significantly and I elbowed her in the stomach to be sure. Making a move to get up, I was knocked back by a palm to the face. I yelled with pain as blood started to gush from my nose. I had no doubt it was broken.

The cut twin jumped on me and pinned both her sister and me with her legs and elbows. A forearm locked around my throat from behind while I felt the knife jab softly at my side, held by the crushed twin. We were all breathing heavily and I relaxed my body. It was clear this fight was over. I had lost. I had nothing to say, never had. These were two strangers who had appeared in our locked – and what I thought was secure – apartment. You don't do that if you want to stop by for a cup of tea. I was certain they were here to harm either Lorcan or me, but I wondered why they halted their attack now. They held me firm and unflinching, making sure there was no way for me to escape. I hoped they would make my death quick if that was what they intended.

When the twin on top of me spoke it was in a soft, feminine voice that couldn't have been more contradictory to her physical appearance.

'My name is Jaira and that is my sister Jakea.'

I said nothing. It was clear they had my attention. Her voice was heavily accented with some sort of European dialect. Her next words abruptly stopped my analysis.

'We're from the Praetorian Guard and we're here to recruit you.'

Chapter 9

Leaning over the side of the kitchen bench, I had my fingers pinching the bridge of my nose. I was trying to staunch the blood flow with a towel. Jaira – the twin with the cut face – brought over a packet of frozen vegetables from our freezer.

She held out the bag to me and I attempted to glare at her. Glaring hurt too much. I sighed and took the bag. Her sister Jakea spoke up.

'You're not going to be able to ice it until we set it back,' she said in a voice that perfectly matched Jakea's.

'No bloody way,' I said.

'We don't set it, it will stay looking like that forever.'

I held up one of the discarded saucepans to my face and although the reflection would have been distorted anyway, I didn't like what I saw there.

'Fine,' I said, dreading the pain but knowing it needed to be done. 'I suppose you've done this a thousand times before?'

'I have,' Jakea said as she stepped forward.

She positioned both hands on either side of my nose and gently prodded with her fingers. I winced.

'Ready?' she asked.

'Aye.'

She snapped my nose back into place with a soft crack and the pain seemed to cut right through my skull. 'MOTHERFUCKING CUNT BASTARD!'

She stepped back as if I was going to hit her again. A final ooze of blood issued from my nose and I wiped it away with the towel, surprised to find it soon stopping. I pressed the frozen veggies to my puss and tried to ignore the stinging throughout my face. Looking up at them, I waited for the twins to get on with whatever they had to say. They glanced at each other and seemed to have a quick wordless conversation. Jakea nodded and Jaira turned to me.

'Recruit away,' I said, waving my free hand at her.

'You have been flagged by the Treize,' she started. 'We're here to offer you a place with the Praetorian Guard.'

They were silent as I let the words take effect. 'How can I have been flagged? The scouts – from what I'm told – scour the world for the best fighters. Yeah, I've practised Muay Thai for over a decade and I'm fit, but I haven't got anything close to the kind of skills Lorcan has.'

'We think you show tremendous promise,' said Jakea.

'Bullshit. I only learnt how to use weapons properly a few months ago.'

'And in that time you killed six extremely dangerous werewolves. From what we've read in the report, some of that was with your bare hands.'

I gulped. I had told the Askari – therefore the Treize and the Guard – that I shifted the night I killed Steven and his lackeys. What Lorcan and I had decided to omit was the fact I had been able to partially shift for several weeks prior to that. He said it would raise unnecessary interest and I trusted his judgement. I was slowly revealing how developed my talents were to the Rogues in a timeline that was more acceptable, but I'd be surprised if that had got back to the Treize so quickly. I had to be careful what I said.

'This is about the people I killed.'

'The Praetorian Guard was very impressed.'

'With murder?'

'Was it pre-meditated?'

'No. Steven was, I guess. The others . . .' I was coming to terms with the consequences of what I'd done, yet my shoulders still tensed as the familiar feeling of guilt crept up my spine. I looked away from their identical questioning gazes.

'You regret it,' said Jaira, surprise lacing her statement.

'Yes and no. Those people shouldn't have had to die. There was no other way. Although I'm stuck with the consequences, I'm beginning to see there wasn't another choice.'

'The end of life is not something to ponder lightly, even if it can be taken easily,' said Jakea. 'The Praetorian Guard understands and respects this.'

'There's medical stuff in the top drawer,' I said, gesturing to the kitchen cabinets. 'For your cheek.'

She touched the blood coming from the wound and frowned at the red substance on her fingers. She held her hand up to Jaira and the twin examined the blood. They both looked at me in unison, a creepy and subconscious gesture.

'We approach all manner of supernatural beings,' said Jakea. 'Werewolves can be especially useful within the Guard. If you were to join us, there are many others of your kind you could learn from.'

'We will teach you to become the best fighter you can be, a lethal force acting as the hand of good and evil,' added Jaira.

After a long moment where I said nothing, she continued: 'We can offer you the gift of eternal life.'

I snorted and regretted the move, wincing as the pain from my nose once again spread through my skull. 'Immortality is not something I covet.'

Given their reactions you would have thought I said I lusted after Ted Bundy. 'Living forever, seeing how the world changes and develops, that's not something you desire?' asked Jakea.

'How much has the world really changed? How much has mankind really learnt from their mistakes? I'm sure there's an alternative version of history that you guys know and I don't that is a lot worse. I'm sure the lives you lead are more exciting and exhilarating than the standard experience, but I don't want to live forever. There's enough good and bad in this life, I wouldn't want to have that drawn out indefinitely. I don't want to be left here when the people I love cease to exist.'

'You have no one left,' said Jaira, still trying to contain her shock. A part of me told myself I should have been offended at that. What she had said was fairly accurate so I let it slide.

'I have my grandparents, and I have Joss.'

'Your grandparents have not much longer, it's inevitable. And your friend will not survive his condition. Deep down, you know this too.'

'Lorcan will live forever,' said Jakea. 'Do you honestly see him continuing as your Custodian as you age?'

'*If* I age. I'm twenty-three and already I've been poised to shuffle off this mortal coil too many times to count. Well, thinking on it I probably could count them. I tend to believe there's only so many brushes with death you get before the scythe drops.'

My mind snagged on a thought and I rapidly chased its origins. 'Immortality is the gift to me, but Lorcan said along with that you offered other things. Financial security for relatives, that kind of stuff.'

Jakea nodded. 'Lorcan has said a lot.'

'Can you save Joss? Could curing him be my price?'

'It cannot,' answered Jaira. 'It's not our place to tamper with nature's path.'

'One of your main duties in the PG is killing. And you're immortal! You're constantly tampering with nature's path,' I said, frustrated.

'I'm sorry. It cannot be done.'

Disappointment and grief washed over me. 'Then I guess there's nothing more to say.'

'There isn't anything else we can offer to persuade you?'

'You gave me a fairly decent beating, so that should get me an easier time at training.'

They looked close to smiling. I got the feeling they didn't do that often. 'We shall be leaving.'

When they didn't make a move to leave I glanced at them, trying to see what they were waiting for.

'Ah, actually,' I said, 'while you're here, I have a fourteen-year-old half-brother in your custody – Quaid Ihi. What are the odds of me getting in to see him, wherever he's being kept?'

They both looked at each other and smiled. Their smile was unnerving. 'We could put in a request.'

'Really? I get that it would have to go higher up the chain, but if you could let someone know that I want in there I'd really appreciate it.'

'Yes,' they replied together. My head was throbbing with the pain from my broken nose. Trying to think too hard about something was undesirable. I opened the door and felt relieved as they stepped outside.

'I'd say it has been nice to meet you both although . . .' I gestured to my face.

'It's a shame,' said Jaira.

I thought she was talking about my nose and I was about to open my mouth in protest when Jakea finished her sister's thought process.

'You would have been a great fit with the Praetorian Guard.'

'I'll get over it,' I mumbled.

'Goodbye, Tommi,' said Jaira.

'Goodbye,' added Jakea.

'Later.'

I closed the door, grateful to have them out of the apartment. They were nice enough, I supposed, besides beating me to a juicy pulp. Technically it was my fault. I was the one who attacked them before waiting to hear what they had to say or finding out why they were there. Yet I had read them correctly: they were lethal. Their clear ability to inflict damage had put me on the defensive. Man, were they incredible fighters. Still, there was something distinctly creepy about them. They were like the twins from *The Shining* all grown up.

I looked at the kitchen and the thought of cleaning it reminded me how exhausted I was. I had been up all day, all night, and now been in a brutal fight. The kitchen was a mess – broken glasses and plates, utensils and saucepans scattered everywhere and blood smeared across it to add to the effect.

Ergh.

My body ached, my mind ached, everything ached. I couldn't bring myself to start cleaning up so I stumbled over to the bed and stripped off my gory clothes, throwing them into a pile on the floor. What I really wanted to do was put on one of Lorcan's T-shirts but I didn't want to bleed on it. I grabbed the baggiest shirt I owned – a tattered *Jem and the Holograms* one – and collapsed on my back. Positioning the frozen veggies on my face, I closed my eyes and tried to think about anything but the pain. I thought about the oddity of the Praetorian Guard trying to recruit me. Was I really that good a fighter? No, I wasn't even the best in this building. I was progressing quickly and maybe they did believe in my potential. It was a tremendous honour to be approached, yet I didn't feel flattered by it. It wasn't that they failed to have anything I wanted – though they had – it was that I believed there was more to it than 'my potential'. The whirlwind of ideas began to lure me to the edge of sleep. My last thought was a hope that I didn't bleed on the pillow.

A light shaking was bringing me to and I tried to grumble at the cause of the movement. The effort caused my face to hurt and I couldn't remember why.

'Tommi, Tommi.'

It was Lorcan's voice, the only sound that could have convinced me to wake up. He was saying my name repeatedly, his words muffled by his lips pressed against my body.

'Yeah, yeah, I'm awake.'

He gripped my shoulders tightly and began to roll me over to face him. It hit me then; he didn't think I would be here when he came home. He thought I was going to accept their offer.

'You have no idea ho–'

His words stopped as soon as he saw my face. I watched the emotions play over his features. There had been joy, followed by shock, realisation, then anger. Lots of anger.

'The twins,' he said through gritted teeth. 'They did this to you?'

Waves of fury were pouring off him, but there was also concern as he examined my broken nose.

'Crap,' I said, imagining what I must look like. 'I don't even want to see how disgusting it looks.'

I closed my eyes and was relieved to find the gesture didn't hurt my face. I was sure every other motion would.

'You've had your nose broken. Badly.'

'It's in place though? Besides being gross to look at it?'

He looked at my nose more carefully and nodded a quick, curt nod. 'Yes. Did you –'

'No, Jakea did it. Or was it Jaira? Uh, Jakea was the one I cut and the one who broke it. She was the one who put it back in to place too. Fuck it hurt.'

'I'm going to kill them,' he said. 'They were supposed to talk to you, not fight you. If I'd known –'

'It's fine,' I said. 'It's brutal to look at, sure, but I can wear one of those tasteful *V for Vendetta* masks for the next few days. It really wasn't their fault.'

'How is this *not* their fault?'

I tried to remember the anger wasn't directed at me, but at

the twins. Jakea specifically. 'I might have slightly attacked them first. Maybe.'

'What?'

'They were already in the apartment and standing there looking all sinister,' I explained. 'It immediately got me on the defensive and before they could explain themselves we got to brawling. They looked dangerous and I assumed the worst. Fighting first, asking questions when they were unconscious later seemed like a good decision.'

He lightly tapped me on the nose and I winced. 'Ow, okay, point made.'

'It's still not your fault. They've recruited before. They know it never ends in blood.'

'And what does it end in?' I asked, struggling to sit up.

'Success. It usually ends in success.'

'You thought I was going to go with them,' I said, trying to keep the disbelief out of my voice.

'No . . . I wasn't sure,' he looked down, somewhat ashamed. He was silent for a moment before meeting my gaze. 'The Praetorian Guard can be very convincing.'

'Not to me,' I said, mentally adding this to an ever-growing list of things he had chosen not to inform me about – things that directly affected me.

'You can't tell me immortality doesn't appeal to you, Tommi?'

'I can. Living this life is hard enough. Knowing there will never be an end, that it goes on indefinitely? That's not something I find attractive.'

'Death –'

'Is final. And scary. And quiet. I'll take my chances with what I have left on the clock.'

Lorcan leaned back and edged off the bed, getting to his feet. 'It's so easy to forget that you've just begun,' he said. 'Sometimes I feel like you have a better grasp of the world than I do and I've spent four hundred and twelve years roaming it. It startles me.'

'I've been a total of three places in my life, Lo,' I laughed, naming them. 'The UK, New Zealand and Germany. I'm the opposite of worldly. It's just with the PG and the Custodians for that matter, it's not like you get immortality and off you trot. It's a reward for servitude and I honestly can't see myself obeying orders for the rest of my life. Lives.'

'No, I can't see that either.' He looked at me again for a long moment, examining every inch of me.

'Hey,' I said, 'I'm still here. I'm not going with them.'

He smiled briefly. 'Come, let me make you breakfast.'

Lorcan pulled me to my feet and held my hand as I negotiated my way off the bed and on to the cool timber floor. 'I could break all of the fasts right now,' I said, my tummy rumbling on cue.

'Whatever you want, it's yours.'

'Really? Eggs Benedict and tomato juice?'

'You got it,' said Lorcan, beaming at my enthusiasm. I padded to the kitchen where my excitement was brought to a shuddering halt.

'Uh . . . right.' I looked over the debris of plates, saucepans and cutlery that had once been our cooking area. Lorcan caught up to me and we stood side by side surveying the mess.

'Look, I would have been disappointed if you had fought the twins and it hadn't ended in a war zone,' he said, trying to keep the amusement out of his voice.

'It looks like a tornado swept through here,' I said. 'Any second Helen Hunt and Bill Pax –'

'I've got it,' interrupted Lorcan.

'You're going to clean *and* cook breakfast for me?'

'Think of it as a reward for taking on two of the Prateorian Guard's most valued henchmen'

'Henchwomen. But they weren't single-mindedly trying to kill me. If so, I think you'd probably be cleaning me up off the floor as well.'

'Technically I am. See that spot of blood over the –'

'Okay, okay, clean away,' I said, laughing.

I showered and as good as hot water felt on the rest of my body, it further antagonised my face. I awkwardly tried to wash around it. Looking at my reflection in the mirror as I cleaned my teeth didn't make me feel any better. The bruising wasn't as bad as it could have been, but it was still pretty bad. A purple and black sausage sat where my nose used to be. The skin under my eyes was puffy and an unnatural colour of light purple.

Huh, there's nothing to be done about it, I thought. Zipping up my denim cut-off shorts, I wiggled my feet into a pair of blue Converse Chuck Taylors that I was particularly fond of (a former flame of mine, Poc, had drawn various figures and slogans over them in permanent marker). In a feat of what had to be supernatural magic, when I returned Lorcan had cleaned the entire kitchen. He was just hanging a saucepan back on the hook when I dragged a stool over to sit at the kitchen bench.

'I think I broke Jakea's rib with that saucepan,' I said, watching him. Lorcan looked at me thoughtfully.

'You were a great candidate. Your ability to go up against both of them proves how right they were about flagging your skills as a fighter.'

I snorted and regretted the movement immediately. 'Right.'

'If I was a recruiter for the Guard and had seen what I've seen you do, I would.'

'That's just the thing, they haven't seen what you have. No one knows my abilities better than you do and you've been keeping them in the dark about most of it.'

'Someone else knows your abilities better than me,' he said.

'Who?'

'You, Tommi.'

I shrugged. 'Sure, but they surprise me as often as I'm in control of them.'

'For now,' he replied, smirking.

I sighed in exasperation and returned his smile. 'How long do you think this will all be?'

'About another ten minutes.'

'Cool. I'm going to duck out and get the papers,' I said, sweeping up the keys.

'The papers? You? You can barely read German.' Lorcan looked like I had just told him I wanted to take up fire twirling in Cambodia. With dwarves. On acid.

'No, but *you* can. There's something I want to see. The cop I was stuck in the elevator with was telling me about this case he was working and it was the weirdest thing when Sanjay and I ran into him – literally – last night. Or, technically this morning, I guess.' Lorcan still looked shocked at my first statement. 'Forget it. I want to see if it's in the paper and I'll show you.'

'Okay,' he said, hushed. 'Stranger things.'

I laughed and headed to the door. Outside it was surprisingly chilly and I could feel the German winter coming on. I took a left out of the alleyway and crossed on to one of the main roads to reach the convenience store. Every paper was covering the kidnappings. Images of the two babies were splashed across all the mastheads and I grabbed a random selection of different ones from the pile in the store. The clerk looked at my battered appearance with knowing concern. I paid and headed back to the apartment, trying to pretend I couldn't feel the stares on me. Walking back inside, my knees nearly went weak at the smell that greeted me. I tried not to spring over to the kitchen bench as my mouth began watering. Sanjay was sitting at the bench helping himself to breakfast and juice.

'Perfect timing,' Lorcan said as he slid a plate over to my position.

'Get in my belly.'

'The toast is a bit burnt. I'm hoping the sauce will make up for it.'

'Isszft de busst snom,' I attempted through a mouthful.

Lorcan laughed as he turned up the volume on an Ella Fitzgerald song playing in the background.

'Sorry,' I said, swallowing. 'What I meant to say was this is amazing. A-freakin-mazing.'

'Good.'

'Lorcan can cook,' agreed Sanjay. 'As soon as I smelt it I came sprinting up the sta –'

Sanjay looked up from his plate for the first time and his words fell limp on his tongue as he registered my face. He looked how I felt.

'Tommi, what . . . what happened?'

'I, er, had an interesting early morning visit from the PG.'

'I take it wasn't a verbal discussion?'

'More a wee misunderstanding on my behalf,' I said, sounding bashful. 'I behaved like an eejit and got my ass handed to me.'

Sanjay was still casting an uneasy glance my way when I added: 'We worked it out.'

Lo pulled up a stool and grabbed his own plate of steaming eggs and bacon stacked on two pieces of thick toast and lathered in hollandaise sauce. I followed suit. I'm not sure if it was because of what I'd been through in the last 24 hours, but it felt like the best breakfast I'd ever eaten. I unfolded the papers and laid them out of the table.

'That cop on the street, Sanjay, this is the case he was working on,' I said.

'The kidnappings?'

'Yeah, I wonder if that's what they were doing out last night?'

'Listen to this,' Sanjay said, pausing me mid-story to read a few lines from one of the articles.

THEY should have been celebrating the birth of their second child, two-day-old Trshyna Croad.

Instead parents Dileep and Samantha Croad are 'terrified' about the fate of their baby girl.

Trshyna was stolen from the prestigious Mechtilde General on Saturday morning in a bold abduction that has stumped police and shocked the close-knit hospital staff.

It's the second baby to disappear in as many weeks after

eight-month-old Seb Maentell was taken from his bedroom at
the family home in Gormannstraße.

A ransom demand has not been made.

Sanjay let out a gush of breath and leaned back on the stool,
shaking his head.

'Isn't that crazy?' I started. 'That's the case he's working on.
It doesn't sound like they have any leads beside the sketchy
sketch of the guy from the hospital.'

A fork was hovering in front of Lorcan's mouth where he had
paused eating as Sanjay began reading. In fact, it looked like he
had stopped breathing altogether. He was frozen in his seat.

'Lo?' He seemed to snap out of it briefly and placed his fork
down on the plate. Picking up one of the other newspapers on
the bench, he spread it flat between us and began re-reading
the piece. I watched him for a moment, but he was engrossed
in the story. Sanjay continued reading.

Police said they are not ready to confirm that the two incidents
are linked, but they have identified a man involved in Trshyna's
kidnapping after reviewing security footage.

"The man we are hoping to speak to is around six foot seven
to six foot eight in height, has pale skin, red hair and a long
beard," said a police spokesman.

'Hmm ... at least he's conspicuous,' added Sanjay.
Silence.

Lorcan looked like he was about to press his nose to paper
if he leaned any closer to the words on the page.

'Lorcan? LORCAN.'

He jumped and turned to me with a mix of disbelief and horror on his face.

'Lo, what is it? You're scaring me.'

'I . . . I'm sorry, it's just . . .'

'What? What did you read?' He was thinking hard about something. I could practically see the process going on behind his eyes.

'I need to do something,' he said, standing up from the stool. He pulled put his phone from his jean pocket and began scrolling for a number.

'Lorcan, what the fuck is going on? You need to t–'

'Clay? Hey, it's Lorcan. Do you think you could move gun work forward? Today?'

I turned to Sanjay. 'I thought we were working on more sensory stuff? It's very obvious after yesterday I *need* the work.'

Sanjay shrugged, glancing at Lorcan with a look I registered as nervous.

'Great, Tommi's ready to go whenever you are. Right. See you soon.' Lorcan had his back to me and as he hung up the phone he turned around to face me. I was fuming.

'What. The. Fuck. Is. Going. On.'

'Tommi,' he started.

'No,' I said, 'you just had a conversation with Clay about me as if I wasn't even in the room. Tell me what's happening?'

'Uh, I'm just going to . . . yeah.' Sanjay awkwardly manoeuvred out of our apartment with his plate of breakfast, eager to be far away from the beginning of a conflict. Neither of us said anything. I was focusing on Lorcan's eyes and a look that was returning there, one I hadn't seen since I first met him. It was a haunted look.

'Lo,' I said, softer.

'There's something going on,' he said.

'That has to do with the article?'

'Possibly. I don't know. I hope not.'

I waited for him to explain further. He didn't.

'I need to make some enquiries. I need to find out if there's more to this,' he said, gesturing to the paper.

'More than missing babies?'

'Yes.'

'What does that have to do with you?'

'I . . . I can't explain that right now, not until I know for sure.'

I blew a loose strand of hair out of my eyes and crossed my arms. Lorcan looked at my posture and could see the frustration.

'Tom, do you trust me?'

I said nothing.

'Do you trust me?'

'Yes. With my life, Lorcan. But you also have a problem with keeping things from me so . . .' I shrugged.

'This has nothing to do with us. I need a day to go digging. I can't explain it to you right now, but I will. Can you trust me to do that?'

'Yes,' I replied, 'but can you trust me to trust me?' His face contorted with confusion and I rolled my eyes at my own miscommunication. 'We're supposed to be a partnership, Lo. You know everything about me. Everything. I tell you everything. I know you have a whole web of lives and stories and secrets that you haven't even begun to tell me and that will take time. Just realise you can trust me.'

'I –'

He was cut short as a swift knock on our front door punctuated the moment.

'The other thing is I need you to go with Clay for the day.'

'Gun work?'

'Yes.'

'Fine. And you're going off to "make enquiries" by yourself?'

'Yes.'

'I don't know what you're doing, but can't you take someone with you? Gus? Dolly?'

He smirked. 'You think I'm going to need back-up?'

'Since you won't tell me what you're doing and I'm getting the vibe that it's somewhat dangerous and important, yes, I'd like you to take someone with you.'

Another series of knocks rang out. 'Coming, Clay,' I shouted over my shoulder. I heard a muffled reply.

'I'm not taking anyone with me, Tommi.'

'Fine. But I don't like it.'

'You don't have to. Hopefully this will all be for nothing.'

I gave him my back and strutted to the door to meet Clay. Dressed in ripped three-quarter denim jeans and a skin-tight white shirt and a tasselled silver scarf, he was looking fabulous as he leaned against our doorframe.

'Yes, I know I look awful and no, I don't want to talk about it,' I said by way of greeting.

'Trouble?' he said with a grin. I ignored the question.

'So . . . we're going to play with guns?'

'You betcha. You ready?' Without a second glimpse at Lorcan I followed after Clay as he began a chorus of '*Tommi's got a gun*'.

Chapter 10

Donna Summer. I was being driven to a shooting range and we were listening to Donna Summer. The queen of disco and lethal weapons just didn't mix.

'Can we put something else on?'

'I like Donna Summer,' said Clay defensively.

'What could you possibly like about Donna Summer?'

'Her music touches me,' he replied, straight-faced.

Picking up the Popeye doll that was resting on his dashboard I leaned toward him. 'Clayton, show me on the doll where her music touched you.'

He laughed, a continuous stream of noise that sounded like Elmo had hit puberty. 'Just because you and Lorcan had a fight don't take it out on me.'

'Hmph.'

I gazed out the window at the buildings moving past us as Clay drove further and further out of Berlin. We'd been driving for about an hour and he said we were almost there. The houses were getting spread out, the road was less busy and there was more country than city bustle. We were going somewhere remote, he said. I guess normal shooting ranges would begin to ask questions if you came in with a dozen different guns that you personally owned. We drove through a small village and turned down a long, dirt road surrounded by thick trees on both sides. Clay pulled up in front of an adorable cottage that looked like it had been plucked straight from a fairytale. There were flowers everywhere. Flowers in the garden, flowers adorning the stone path up to the front door, flowers hanging in pots from the window.

'Dolly's girlfriend lives here.'

'Yu?'

Clay seemed surprised that I knew her name.

'I met her at Phases. She bought some drinks from me.'

'Right. These are her digs. Her and Dolly are off doing whatever it is they do, but she said it was fine for us to use the range.'

I raised my eyebrows in disbelief. 'She has her own shooting range *here*? At Casa de Cute?'

'Course she does. There's nothing normal about former Praetorian Guard members. She actually built the range for Dolly, who likes to shoot. We all come out here and practise.'

I followed Clay to the back of the vehicle and helped unload two suitcases and three sport bags. We made our way to a small shed-like structure that sat off to the left of the cottage and at the start of a vast field. There was a long, wooden table pressed against the inside wall and Clay took to emptying the contents of each bag in ordered piles.

'Welcome to gun work 101,' he said.

I let out an impressed whistle as I gazed over the table. 'Are you planning a *coup d'état*, sir?'

Clay laughed. 'You've never shot a gun before, so I thought we would run through five different weapons, that way you get a basic understanding and begin to know which you prefer.'

'In one day? Clay, I'll be lucky if I know how not to shoot myself in the foot with that Glock over there by the time we're through.'

'See, you already know what it's called.'

I rolled my eyes. 'I've been shot in the shoulder by a Glock 26, I'm unlikely to forget its name.'

'No, you'll see. Gun work is a cinch for us. This is piss-easy compared to sword work or any of the weapons training you've done with Lorcan.'

'Guns are fun. What an American point of view,' I teased.

'Latin American,' he said with a flirtatious wink.

'And what do you mean "easy for us"?'

He shrugged as he began assembling what looked like a machine gun of some type. 'Werewolves make for great shooters.'

'They do?'

'Think about it. Our heightened senses, the improved eyesight and instinctual reactions: these are the essential skills needed when it comes to firing a weapon.'

'I thought it was just point and shoot,' I said, making a finger pistol and shooting a far off imaginary target.

'For your standard close-range guns, like a Glock and a Derringer, it is. Not much skill is needed there. But the more complex machinery ... Tommi, it's no coincidence the best snipers in the world are werewolves.'

'Huh. That's something new.'

I was still tossing the information around in my head when Clay handed me the Glock and said, 'Let's begin.'

* * *

The sensation of shooting a gun is unlike anything else you can experience. Having been shot quite recently, I had a cautious respect for what these weapons could do and the pain they could inflict. That agony was still very clear in my mind. To start with I was using a Glock 26, which Clay said was a good beginner's handgun and easily concealable. It was all about the sneak factor. I was standing in front of the target at the mark Clay had pointed out and he had spent the last twenty minutes teaching me how to load and unload the magazine.

'Now load it up, *mamacita*.'

I did as I was told, no longer fumbling over the mechanics of slipping a magazine in to the Glock. It was the eighth time I'd done it now. It was getting easier. I locked the slide back and did a chamber check to confirm the magazine had gotten in there.

'Ready to go,' I said.

'Good,' he replied, smiling with approval and handing me a pair of earmuffs and putting on his own. I slipped on the protective glasses that were resting on my head. 'Line up the target.'

I took the stance he had taught me: legs grounded and slightly apart, hips straight, shoulders relaxed. 'Grip it like you would a hammer,' he reminded.

I squished the top of my left hand right up into the dovetail and almost cupped my two hands together, loosely interlocking the fingers at the bottom. Letting out a slow breath, I pulled the trigger.

BANG.

I was surprised at how loud it was. Back at the warehouse massacre I hadn't noticed considering everything else that was going on. The screams of other people and my own adrenaline must have drowned it out. I winced and continued to fire off the first round, the noise rattling through my ears and shaking my skull.

'The superior hearing doesn't help,' I said, taking one hand off the gun to rub my left ear under the earmuffs.

Clay's voice broke through the ringing. 'The other werewolf senses certainly do, no?'

I titled my head to look at the target sheet. I don't know why I'd expected a target similar to that of a dartboard with red and black circles within each other.

That wasn't what I got. If I was learning how to shoot a gun it would be to shoot human-shaped targets. One such target was littered with holes. I'd missed the vital areas – the head, the heart – and instead most of my indents were in the lower abdomen range.

'That's because you keep jerking the gun down when it fires,' said Clay, watching my gaze. Walking up to the target he pointed at the bullet holes for emphasis. I'd also hit plenty of the white space surrounding the 'evil' silhouette.

'Aye, I'll get used to it,' I said. 'The movement catches me off guard.'

'Ha. The recoil on these puppies is nothing compared to the earlier models.'

He peeled off the paper sheet with the target on it and hung up another. 'Okay, you've got nine more rounds before you're dry. Let's go again.'

Some two hours later I had hit the heart. Er, where the heart would be if it was on the right side of someone's chest. I let out another breath and fired again, this time edging closer to the medically correct location. Progress. It was a matter of blocking out everything around me and concentrating on where I needed the bullet to be. We were surrounded by the relatively quiet sounds of the countryside, so I briefly marvelled at the amount of skill it would take to hit your target in a room or place surrounded with noise and distraction. Clay must have been happy with my development because we switched guns after that.

'This,' he said, handing me something similar in size to a closed umbrella, 'is a Beretta Xtrema 2.'

'Radical,' I said, getting a feel for the weight and size of the shotgun in my hands. 'It's heavier than the Glock 26, obviously, a touch over three kilos. But it's a hunting rifle so –'

'More powerful.'

'Exactly.'

'I assume that means its got more kick to it?'

'Actually, the recoil on the Xtrema isn't that bad. That's why I like it. It's the smoothest out of any other shotgun I've used and believe me, I've used a lot of shotguns.'

There was a devilish glint in his eyes and I made a nervous laugh. 'Oh, I believe you.'

Clay grinned at me and shrugged. I liked the shape of the shotgun, but overall I think I preferred the Glock as it was easier to manoeuvre. It was also harder to control where you hit. Clay said that wouldn't matter in a real scenario as the point of impact was wider.

'You pretty much just aim for the middle of the target and you'll fuck shit up.'

'I don't doubt,' I replied, bracing myself for the power of the kickback as I fired off another shot.

We passed the first half of the day that way, alternating between the Glock and the Beretta so I'd be confident switching between the two. Clay had me empty and load the guns so many times I was certain I'd be able to do it as easily as painting my nails. The sound of a car coming down the dirt road drew our attention away from examining my latest target sheet – all nearly perfect hits.

I looked at Clay and he returned my puzzled stare. I cocked the shotgun and he nodded, heading into the shed to retrieve his own weapon from inside the bag. Keeping half of my body shielded behind the structure and the barrel of the Beretta raised, I turned to face the approaching car. I couldn't see the figure driving, but Clay must have because I heard him let out a relieved sigh.

'Tommi, it's Yu.'

'Oh, right. We're eejits.' I emptied the weapon and placed it on the table, not wanting to welcome Yu back to her home by sticking a gun in her face. Clay was slipping something back into a suitcase when I froze. 'My God, is that an actual Uzi?'

I had never seen one in real life, but I recognised the compact shape from action movies. He held it out to me the way a man might hold out a new watch for his friends to inspect. 'It's my favourite.'

My fingers hovered over it, not wanting to get too close or touch it. 'This isn't *The Expendables*, Clay. When did you think we would need to use an Uzi?'

'Hey, we're at a firing range. I figured why not bring it? It's not as if I can go fire off a few rounds in the alley at Phases.'

I snorted. 'No, you definitely cannot.'

'Look at you,' came a clipped voice from behind us. 'A few hours shooting guns and you're already coming at a mystery vehicle with a rifle. I'm a little impressed.' Yu certainly looked impressed, giving me a tight but genuine smile.

'I'm sorry about that, we're a bunch of fat grapes. Clay said you weren't coming back for the day and he didn't seem to recognise it was you so . . . I'm a lil' defensive.'

'Careful, Tommi, she likes that in a woman,' added Clay.

Yu gave him a look that managed to be both amused and dangerous.

'Speaking of which,' he added, 'I thought you and Dolly were going to be out romancing all day?'

'So did I,' she said, clearly peeved. 'Apparently she was needed for an errand.'

The way she looked at me when she said that made me certain it was Lorcan who had broken off the couple's plans. What could he possibly need her and not me for? Or even Yu? If it was something dangerous, like I suspected, she was formerly of the Praetorian Guard and more experienced than he was. Plus, she had to be a far better fighter than Dolly. *I* was a better fighter than Dolly. And yet, here I was, off in the country and as far away from whatever Lorcan was doing as possible. Him keeping me in the dark was pissing me off to no end.

'What have you been teaching her?' asked Yu, walking over and examining the weapons we'd laid out.

'Being a virgin to gun warfare I thought I'd be gentle.' Clay winked. 'We've been alternating between the Glock 26 and Beretta Xtrema 2.'

She nodded her approval. 'And?'

'And I'd feel comfortable having her back me up any day.'

I glowed at the compliment.

'How do you feel you've gone?' asked Yu.

'I wouldn't say I'm ready to shoot an apple off his head. I think I've got the basics on each of them down pat.'

Yu studied me for a while, as if deciding on something. 'Since it's your first time, how about we make it special?'

I laughed at the innuendo and looked at Clay, who was beaming. 'Candles and Lionel Richie?' I offered.

'Sniper school,' said Clay, as if to him they were the exact same thing.

Yu, as it turns out, had been a sniper during the Vietnam War. For the PG of course, not the Viet Cong or anything.

'There were evil extremes on both sides,' she said. 'Whenever there's war or a country in turmoil like that it's a playground for the soulless.'

My mind had automatically jumped to Steven as it so often did when the word 'evil' was mentioned. 'I can imagine my half-brother thriving in a situation like that.'

I was following close behind her as we made our way up a steep hill hidden by thick forest. She turned to look back at me before returning her gaze to our path.

'Was he one of the six you killed?'

'Yes,' I replied.

'Good.'

I couldn't disagree. 'Dolly told you?'

'She mentioned it,' Yu confirmed. 'She doesn't know the specifics though.'

'No one does,' I said, ducking underneath a thick tree branch. 'Except Lorcan and the PG.'

'And the Treize.'

'Hmm?'

'The Treize and the Custodians will know the specifics now too. It's protocol. I'd say that's why you were tagged to join the Guard.'

'You know about that as well?'

Yu gave me an indulgent smile. 'You think Praetorian Guard recruiters can be in town and I wouldn't know about that? Especially the twins.'

I laughed. 'Good point. Do you guys all catch up for a reunion each century or something like that?'

'Something like that.'

We were silent for a while as we pushed on through the woods and reached the top of the summit. The trees began to thin out until we were standing in a small clearing overlooking the rifle range. We had circled around the back and I could make out the shed about three kilometres off in the distance. This was an area Yu came often as there were signs of frequent use in the grooves worked into the natural surrounds. A long, flat rock that arched towards the sky even had carvings in it where she had marked the number of hits and misses. She set down the sports bag she had been carrying over her shoulder and began removing various parts that – when constructed – would make up a sniper rifle. I watched her in easy silence as she methodically went through the process.

'Say, how many other people would know the Praetorian Guard came to see me?' I asked.

'Very few,' she said, 'now.'

'What do you mean "now".'

'They keep their selections close to their chest until they've been acquired. Lorcan knew they were in town to recruit you, but I believe that was only a few hours beforehand.'

'You found out after the fact?'

'Yes. I'll tell you this, Tommi: they don't get turned down very often. In fact, I can't think of an example in my lifetime. It's unusual. Word will spread.'

I pondered over that information, not sure if I should be flattered or worried. Yu must have read my expression.

'I wouldn't concern yourself with it,' she said. 'That place leaks like a sieve.'

'The PG don't really strike me as gossips.'

Yu grinned. 'The PG. I like that. PG . . . New members to the PG are significant and eagerly anticipated. For the twins to come back *without* a new recruit, things will need to be explained. Information will spread. Not outside of the main institutions, mind you. People are already curious about the blue-haired werewolf that Lorcan's guarding. Add to that the fact the PG wanted to recruit her after barely four months of being a functioning lycanthrope *and* that she turned them down. Plus, I heard you gave the twins a run for their money.'

'Jaira and Jakea? Look at my face. The only thing that's running is the blood from my nose.'

'Those are honourable wounds. I don't think the twins were expecting such a good fight.'

'Will they get in trouble?' It suddenly occurred to me that there may be consequences for not returning with a coveted item such as a new recruit.

'Why? Are you worried for them?'

I snorted. 'The same way you would be worried about two

sharks in a tank full of tuna,' I said. 'I guess I'm more ... I don't want them to get punished for me not wanting to live a life of immortal servitude.' Then I added, 'No offence,' remembering that Yu had lived that life for over eight centuries.

'None taken. And no, the Guard doesn't work like that. They can't force someone to join as much as they can't control the decision of an individual. The twins will be fine.'

'Did you ever fight with them?'

She shook her head. 'No. I've heard about them though. Everyone has. They worked under Lorcan for a time.'

'He was their commander?'

'Something like that.'

I tried to run that idea through my brain. 'Are they telepathic? Is that possible?'

Yu looked at me sharply then, really looked. 'You don't miss much. Do you?'

'They *are*?'

'No one knows for sure. They're not big sharers. There are a few who suspect. I've watched hours of fight footage of them and there's a way they move that's –'

'Otherworldly.'

'Exactly.'

'It's as if they have a direct link to what the other is thinking.'

Yu nodded. She leaned back on her heels and stood up, wiping her hands on her cargo pants. She was wearing a pair of army green Nike's with a tight T-shirt in the same colour. She was all business: outdoorsy, active business.

'This,' she said, gesturing to the tools beneath her, 'is a CheyTac M200.'

'A CheyTac M200,' I repeated.

'It's fifty-five inches long, weighs twenty-seven pounds, and can kill someone from two and a half kilometres away.'

'Woah.'

'If,' she added, 'you can take the shot. It has a detachable barrel, which is essential, and an integral bipod, and 3.5 LB trigger pull.' Yu told me she had been using the CheyTac for the last four years after upgrading from the .338 Lapua. Her new weapon outclassed the old in every way. Having spent the day learning different calibre and mechanisms of weapons, these numbers weren't as boggling to me as they might have once been. We went through the logistics of the weapon, how to put it together and basic maintenance.

'I'm rushing you through this because I want you to at least have a go at firing before it gets dark,' said Yu, as she made a gesture for me to get in to position. 'As a sniper, you could be forced to hold your position for hours at a time – sometimes days. You have to find one that's not only comfortable but useful. If you can't get to your instruments or your water, then you may as well just shout out your position to the enemy.'

I didn't want to point out that I wouldn't be playing the Jackal with enemies in the Vietnamese wilderness anytime soon. I held my tongue and shifted into position, making sure the rifle was steady. I checked the scope to make sure I could see my far-off target.

'How does that feel?'

'Good,' I told Yu, who had dropped into position next to me.

'Snipers talk in yards,' she said. 'It's an American thing. You'll get used to it, but I'll translate for now. The shot you're about to attempt is five hundred yards, which is just under five hundred metres.'

'Aye. That's easy math.'

'Exactly. For a shot like this you can wing it, especially for your first magazine. Anything over that I recommend using one of these.' She held up what looked like a chunky calculator. 'It's an ABC: Advanced Ballistic Computer. It does the trigonometry for you and tells you how far away you are. It factors in the winds, Coriolis, latitude, barometric pressure, everything, so you can make the necessary adjustments and take the shot.'

'It's so technical,' I said.

'When you shoot from these distances a bullet doesn't go straight like you think it does in the movies. There's an arc to it.' Yu made a motion in the air to demonstrate her point. 'The bullet will fall between thirty to forty feet just because of the range. The arc needs to be calibrated to work out how much it will fall, how much the wind will move it back and forth and how much the curvature of the earth will play into it. Humidity can also be a factor.'

I nodded with grim determination. 'Got it.'

'Now, you think you're ready to take a shot at five hundred yards?'

'Hells yes.'

'Be my guest, Tommi. Read the wind. Stay calm, get inside your bubble.'

I let out a deep breath and tried to run through everything Yu had taught me in this short space of time. I scanned the nearby treetops, which were swaying a lot stronger than they were when we first came up here. North East. 'I can't use the ABC?'

'Not this time.' She smiled. 'Let's try without it first. You don't want to get dependent on it and then be stuck in a situation without it.'

I agreed. I watched the trees again, swaying a message at me. I adjusted my target in the scope slightly, aiming a fraction above and to the left. I exhaled and pulled the trigger. I jerked back ever so slightly with motion before quickly returning my eye to the scope to see where I hit. I couldn't believe it. The head. I had hit the dead centre of the target's head. Yu had binoculars pressed to her face and hooted.

'Werewolves.'

'Beginner's luck,' I added, shyly.

She looked at me, doubtful. 'You'd never shot a gun before today?'

I shook my head. 'Nope. Only been shot by one.'

'Amazing.' She looked through the binoculars again. 'You've got seven rounds in there. Let's go another three on that target.'

I did. All were near-perfect hits in and around the head area. How was I better at this than a close-range target? I stopped analysing my results and decided to just be pleased with them. Yu was beaming like she'd discovered an uncut diamond in her backyard.

'Alright, let's go seven hundred yards.'

I winked and settled in behind the scope. I got my winds. I got my distance. I got my bearing. I exhaled, letting calmness wash over me. By the end of the session, I'd also shot a seven-hundred yard target.

I'll admit it, when Clay and I arrived backed at Phases I had swagger. I'd spent the day learning how to shoot guns and after ten hours I was pretty confident with a handgun and a rifle. I was more than confident with a sniper rifle. I excelled. Yu and I had already arranged to meet up after sensory training with Sanjay tomorrow and go through the same targets I'd been working on today. She also said she'd give me a proper run through of the ABC so I could try something at nine-hundred yards. I was excited. That feeling quickly evaporated when Clay's phone pinged. We had been walking towards the entrance to the apartments when he received a text. He frowned at the screen.

'We're to meet everyone in the boardroom right away,' he said.

'Boardroom?'

'You know, where you first met us all.'

'Oh.'

He smiled. 'I know it's not exactly a boardroom in the corporate sense.'

'No. It's a boardroom in the Tommi-sense.' I liked the place, with its clashing furniture and collage of band posters. 'Righto, let's go.'

We dumped the guns back in Clay's car, which he didn't like. 'I don't understand why there isn't time to put them away first. It's not proper gun security.'

All of their weaponry was kept in the locked training room on the fifth floor. We each knew the pin code, but the guns were kept in separate drawers that could only be accessed by entering two additional pin codes. It made me feel a touch safer knowing how responsible Clay and the others were with the firearms. Actually, maybe responsible wasn't the word for Clay. The man did own an Uzi.

'I wouldn't have minded a shower either,' I muttered, grabbing my water bottle and a packet of aspirin we'd bought on the way home. My head was hurting something chronic: an after-effect of having my nose broken and the shit kicked out of me. Firing guns all day probably didn't help, but Lorcan had achieved his prerogative.

It had distracted me. Now all my fears and nagging anxieties about what was going on came rushing back. Lo had sent me a message after lunch asking how I was and if my head hurt. There was also an apology about keeping me in the dark. I didn't reply. He could explain and apologise to my bruised and swollen face. A text meant nothing to me.

Clay unlocked the side door to the club and we made our way across the floor. When we started down the jungle-painted hallway I heard voices coming from inside the room. We stepped inside and Zillia, Gus and Sanjay greeted us, with Dolly and with a surprised-looking Yu following in behind us. She grunted at me as she passed and Yu gave me a wide-eyed look that showed she had no idea why she was here. She wasn't a werewolf. She wasn't one of the Rogues, but she was involved with us so this must affect her in some way too. Or we needed her skills. I stopped pondering that idea as soon as I heard Lorcan coming. After being caught off guard too many times in too short a period, I was attempting to hone my senses at every opportunity. I could recognise Lorcan by the tread of his steps and the pace he set. Another handy werewolf thing. Or maybe a love thing. He ploughed straight in and walked to the head of the table. He cast a brief look at me before he started.

'As you all may know, I've spent today investigating a very serious matter. Something Tommi brought to my attention and something I hoped couldn't possibly be true. With help from Dolly I've been able to contact some of my old underground sources and . . .'

Lorcan trailed off then. He looked down at the table, one hand flat upon it. He was silent, somewhere else. We waited patiently for him to continue.

'This is something that affects all of us: werewolves, humans, the supernatural community, everyone. I've learned that what I feared is here. One of the greatest evils I've ever encountered and thought long vanquished is very much alive and very much in Berlin.'

He paused, creating an unintentionally dramatic effect as he tried to formulate the words. 'The Laignach Faelad have returned.'

Chapter 11

People began shouting from all corners of the room as Lorcan tried to quell the tide of voices.

'That's impossible!' shouted Zillia.

'There's no . . . there's just no . . .' tried Sanjay.

'Just listen to him!' pleaded Dolly.

'LIES!' bellowed Gus.

'They were all killed, slaughtered centuries ago!' exclaimed Clay.

'Are you sure? I mean, are you absolutely certain?' That was Yu.

The only person who was silent was me. I'd like to say it was because I was the cool, rational one. Frankly, I might have had something to contribute if I knew who the heck the Laignach Faelad were. Lorcan gave up trying to talk over the others and resigned himself to leaning against the wall with his arms folded. He looked like a stern schoolteacher. Our eyes met across the room. He held my gaze for what felt like minutes until I realised the room had fallen silent. Well, not silent exactly. I could hear the dramatically increased heart rates of everyone, pounding and pounding. I winced as the rhythm joined the throbbing of my head. I tried to hide the gesture by scratching my face, but when I looked back up at Lorcan I knew he hadn't missed it. Wanting to get this over with, I asked the obvious.

'For those of us new to the game, can someone please explain to me who the Laignach Faelad are?' Every eye in the room was suddenly on me. It was as if I had said I believed in Santa Claus. And Jesus. Santa Jesus.

'I will,' said Lorcan, breaking the audible tomb. 'They were from Ireland. Back in the early history of the country they were known as a group of fierce warriors. Their enemies would tell stories of men so wild and deadly that they would shift into wolves mid-battle and tear their adversaries apart.'

'Werewolves,' I said.

'Yes, but that's not what we thought at first. Stories like that weren't uncommon and back in those days fantastical tales would spread from village to village very quickly. Mostly they were metaphors. The heroes in the tales could turn into golden lions to overcome whatever evil it was. Vicious fighters would be wolves. Yet after a while we began to realise there was some truth to what people had said the Laignach Faelad were. In the aftermath of battles the signs were unmistakable.'

'What year was this?' I asked. 'You joined the PG in the 1600s. Was this before or after that?'

'Both. Their origins can be traced back to the late twelfth century when the country was in turmoil as ancient kings tried to grab land and power for themselves. They were relentless and would look for any advantage they could get over the scores of other kings trying to do exactly the same thing.'

Yu picked up the thread. 'The Laignach Faelad were soldiers for hire. Even just having them on your side was said to bring good luck and fortune. When they weren't fighting they kept exclusively to themselves in the mountains of what's now known as County Tipperary.'

'They came to the attention of the Guard some forty years after I joined,' Lorcan added.

'Why?' asked Sanjay. 'If they'd existed for all that time why did the Treize only take an interest in them then?'

'Because of their price,' Lo said softly.

I watched a visible shudder go through the room. Zillia turned away with a look of horror and disgust on her face. Clay was softly shaking his head. Looking up at Lorcan, I could only imagine the puzzled expression that must be on my face.

'They didn't fight for money or gold or lands,' he said. 'They were paid with babies.'

I felt my face contort in confusion. 'Babies? What do y –' It suddenly hit me. The missing children. My voice sounded foreign and far-off as I tried to string a sentence together. 'You don't mean . . . *babies*? Living babies?'

'They were paid in the flesh of newborn babies.' His voice was businesslike and clear as day. Yet somehow I couldn't quite grasp the sheer horror of the concept. 'That's what they live off. That's what they fight for. It's a terrible price and one that the king had to pay from within his own community. It wasn't the babes of the enemies that went to the Laignach Faelad. It was the babes of the king's people. If you wanted to hire them you had to be willing to pay that price.'

I felt like I was going to be sick. I stared at Lorcan, willing him to tell me something else, anything else. He just stared back at me, willing me to understand this evil. This evil that had come here.

'They eat live babies,' I said, my voice shaking over the last word. 'Oh my God . . . those two kids. Is it too late? Can we still hunt them down and save them?'

Pain and understanding in Lorcan's eyes met my desperate pleas. He didn't say anything. It was written all over his face. It was too late. The children were dead, torn apart by a pack of ravenous, ancient werewolves. How the fuck was this happening here?

'They're gone,' said Dolly, so quietly I almost thought it was a whisper.

'How is this possible?' Zillia murmured in Deutsch, burying her head in her hands.

'They were wiped out,' said Yu. 'The Guard wiped out the last line.'

'That's what we thought,' said Lorcan. 'Hell, that's what I've thought for almost four hundred years. Until today.' He ran his hand through his hair and took two paces in one direction before turning around and repeating the process. I'd never seen him look so flummoxed. 'We wiped them out. A group of over a hundred members of the Guard tracked them to their base and slaughtered them. We slaughtered the entire village. We made sure there were no survivors. It was the only way to be sure they would never crop up again.'

'And yet,' said Clay.

'Here we are. Here they are. Are these survivors from the original pack or new werewolves? The one comfort in all of this is that their numbers are small.'

'You found them?' I said.

'No,' interjected Dolly. 'But from the amount of children

taken their ranks must be small, otherwise they would have needed more.'

'Needed more babies to eat,' I finished.

I saw Dolly flinch at both my words and the harsh tone in my voice. 'Because only two babies have been murdered we should be relieved that it's just a pocket Laignach Faelad movement?'

'That's not what she means, Tommi,' said Yu, jumping to her girlfriend's defence.

I ignored her. 'How many then? How many baby killers are a manageable amount?'

'I don't know,' said Lorcan. 'It's not more than a dozen, I think.'

'Still double our numbers,' I said.

'Stop talking as if you're just going to run off and fight them, Tom,' Clay mused.

'Aren't we?' I looked around the table and was shocked to be met by resigned expressions. Call me crazy, but I thought the first thing we'd be doing was running out and destroying the baby killers. No one at the table seemed to be thinking the same thing.

'It took a hundred of the Guard to wipe out seventy of them,' said Lorcan.

This halted me. The PG were the best warriors on the planet, hence why they were in the PG. They needed better odds than one on one to overcome the Laignach Faelad. That didn't bode well for us, a group of rogues.

'You need to contact the Treize, the Guard, Custodians, everyone,' said Zillia.

'We have,' replied Dolly. 'Once we were able to determine that it was definitely them, that's the first thing we did.'

'And?' asked Sanjay.

'They're sending the twins back, they're closest and only a few days away. And someone quite high up in the Guard, I think. They'll seek guidance from The Three before they make any other decisions.'

'How did you determine it was the Laignach Faelad?' I asked.

'Lorcan,' Dolly shrugged.

'I read the newspaper reports,' he started. 'I went to the scenes and asked a few local Askari to reach out to their contacts, see if they had anything unusual.'

'You think that was wise?' I asked. 'Turning up to known crime scenes and snooping around? That's a way to get on the police radar.'

'I was covert.'

No doubt. 'And?'

'Nothing concrete. Scary things being scared, odd occurrences being strung together with facts and . . . a feeling.'

'A feeling?'

'Intuition. I've faced a lot, defeated a lot, but there's a certain trace the Laignach Faelad's evil leaves behind. I can't describe it.'

'Tommi.' Sanjay's voice sounded strange and it drew my attention immediately. The look on his face was one of both realisation and horror. 'Those men last night, the cop . . .'

'What abo— oh. Oh my God. You don't think —'

'I do,' Sanjay snapped. 'They smelled of blood, they reeked of it. And something . . . else, something neither of us could place.'

'Wait,' Lorcan started, holding up his hand. 'What men? What cop?'

'Last night we went to Burgermeister after the club closed up,' Sanjay said. 'On the way back I was trying to start her sensory training and she picked up something.'

'Where was this?' Yu asked.

'Back on Dietrich Street, near the lane,' he replied. 'And we physically ran into these two men who were rushing away from something.'

'And you didn't think it weird they were covered in blood?' Clay snarked.

'They weren't,' I said, jumping in. 'There was nothing about them that was unusual and neither of them matched the description of the guy who stole the baby from the hospital. The papers said the known assailants were six foot something and these two were both well under that, stocky even. I had just been pulled in that direction until we met them. I thought I was imagining it at first, but I definitely smelled blood on them. Sanjay confirmed it.'

'It's true,' he added. 'I couldn't even pick up if they were wolves or not, which if they were we should have been able to.'

'It was only a few minutes after that we ran into the same cop I was stuck in the elevator with, the one who's running the case.'

'That can't be a coincidence,' Zillia mused.

'Of course not,' I agreed, 'Not now. Dick and two others were searching for someone in that area, guns drawn and the whole bit.'

'Police cars and an ambulance drove past too,' Sanjay added.

Lorcan began rifling through the newspapers that were scattered across the surface of the table we were gathered around, searching. 'They could have taken another child,' he said, 'but there are only reports of two missing. And there's been nothing on the news about a third victim.'

'We would have heard a child,' Sanjay added. 'We would have seen and smelt it. They had nothing with them, it was just the two men.'

'Do they eat them en route?' Gus asked, speaking up for the first time in a long while.

Yu made a clicking sound with her tongue, sounding frustrated. 'No, they take them back to their base. They all have to share in the spoils, so they would never . . . how did you put it? Eat them en route.'

'Yeesh,' said Zillia, shaking her arms as if bugs were crawling over her skin. 'What were they up to then?'

Lorcan sighed. 'Who knows, maybe they tried and failed? Maybe they were spotted. Maybe they were interrupted.'

Looking around the room at all the tense and tired faces there, I cleared my throat and raised my hand. Gus gave me a strange look, before Lo nodded for me to go ahead.

'This may be an obvious question and I've missed the answer completely, but who hired them? If they only fought for kings who gave them the flesh of newborns before, who's offering up the babies now? An ancient Irish king can't be behind it.'

As soon as I said that last part I regretted it. Never assume anything, Tommi, not in this crazy life that you're living. Confused and curious stares were exchanged.

'I don't know,' said Lorcan. 'I'm still in shock that they're even alive.'

'It's just a coincidence, right? That they're here in the same city as you? They're not after you personally?'

'No,' he replied. I let out an inward sigh of relief. 'That's not in their nature. They don't have personal vendettas. They do what they need to get paid. Plus, there were a hundred of us there that day. The surviving members of the battle are scattered all over the world. My presence isn't why they're here. I think you're right, Tommi. They're here because they're getting paid.'

'Aye, but by what kind of spawny-eyed mutant?' I pondered.

'What do we do now?' Gus asked, tapping his fist on the table for emphasis. 'We don't just sit around until the Treize or the Praetorian Guard decide what they want to do. We're not their disciples.'

'We're all disciples of the Treize in some way,' said Yu, under her breath.

'I agree with Gus' stance on action, but we need a plan,' Zillia affirmed.

'We need to find their base,' said Lorcan. 'That should be priority one. It's going to be more dangerous than any of the other tasks.'

'We can assume they're not living in the mountains now, otherwise they wouldn't be taking babies from within the city,' Clay said.

'Maybe that's what they want you to think,' added Sanjay.

'No,' rebutted Lorcan. 'They're not that smart and they're not that careful. They're not careless per se, but they're bold. They're not used to being challenged and they wouldn't make a great effort to hide themselves.' Turning to Yu, he said suddenly, 'See if you can work your demon contacts. Find out if any of the big players are on the move. Look for a pattern. If there are supernaturals fleeing a specific area then that's where I bet they'd be.' She nodded and an indomitable look passed between her and Dolly.

'Tommi,' he said, 'what I need is to find out who we're dealing with. If these are old faces then we know some of the Laignach Faelad survived. That begs the question of how? Who kept them alive and to what purpose? Why resurface now? If they're new faces that's a different problem altogether.'

'And how can I help with that?'

'What about this detective?'

'What about him?'

'Get in touch, get him close. He's a talker and if he shared that much info with you on your first encounter then I'd bet he's willing to share more. We could use whatever you can get, even anecdotal information.'

'*Pfft*, shouldn't be too hard,' I said, rolling my eyes. 'How am I to "get in touch" with him, Lorcan? It's not as if we move in the same circles. It was pure luck that we were stuck in the same elevator and pure unluck that we bumped into him on the street.'

Lorcan gave me an indulgent look. 'I'm sure if you left a message for him at the station, he'd get in touch with you.'

I raised my eyebrows, not quite sure what he was saying.

Clay banged his head on the table in frustration. 'Gah, use your feminine wiles, Tommi!' He'd practically shouted it at me.

'Huh. *That's* what you want me to do?' I looked at Lo for confirmation. He had the grace to look slightly guilty. Slightly. 'I'll do it,' I said stonily.

'In the meantime what do *we* do?' asked Zillia. 'Keep our eyes and ears open and continue running Phases as if nothing is wrong?'

'Exactly,' said Dolly. 'Until we have more information and a plan of attack, that's what we have to do.'

'What about the babies?' I asked.

'They're dead Tommi, the –'

'No,' I said, cutting Gus off. 'Everything that's been suggested in the last five minutes is defensive strategy: gathering information, learning more about our enemy, locating their base. What about the babies? Isn't there some way we can protect their targets?'

'What do you propose?' asked Lorcan, curious.

'*A dinnieken*.' I shrugged, 'I'm new to supernatural warfare. Maybe we can go out, keep watch or something? Both children were taken when it was dark, so that gives us a window. If we presume they're operating from somewhere in the heart of the city then we could do sweeps of the boroughs. See what they were after on Dietrich Street. Pass by a hospital every now and then.'

Gus wasn't convinced. 'The odds of us actually preventing something that way when we know so little –'

'We have to do something,' I said, determined. 'We have to try and prevent *something*.'

'I'm with you,' said Clay. I smiled at him, grateful for the back-up.

'I don't know if we can spare the bodies at the club the rest of the time,' said Zillia.

'You won't have to,' I said. 'I only work for you guys when you ask. The rest of the time my nights are just that – mine. The nights Clay is doing street sweeps I'll cover his shift.' Clay held out his fist to me from across the table and I bumped it.

'I'll keep watch on my nights off too,' added Sanjay.

Dolly sighed. 'It won't do anything. The chance of you witnessing or being able to sav –'

'Leave it,' said Yu. An unspoken signal must have heralded the end of our meeting because everyone started to get up and make for the door. The contrast between the atmosphere in this room the first time we had met to now was stark.

I pushed my way out of the door first and headed for the club exit without waiting for anyone. I made my way up the apartment stairs in a daze. Babies. Two babies had been eaten alive by a pack of ancient, evil werewolves. It was beyond a nightmare. And worse yet, someone knew the price and was willing to pay it anyway. That thought terrified me the most.

Kirk Rennex was the first person I saw when I walked out of the hallway, the door swinging behind me as the others slowly began to leave the boardroom. He was perched on one of Phases wooden stools at the bar, seemingly unaware of my presence as he tapped away busily on his tablet. Zillia was still a way back and I could hear her talking urgently with Lorcan, trying to determine what extra security measures they should be taking at the club. Clay joined me and cursed as he spotted the billionaire casually sipping a Scotch.

'Shit, this is not a good time,' he grumbled.

'Does he . . .'

'No,' Clay replied, picking up on what I meant. 'He doesn't know about any of us.'

'How do you go about keeping a secret that big in a relationship?'

'When I work out how, I'll let you know. He can't see Zillia right now, she's a mess.'

Glancing up at Clay's face, I couldn't disagree. 'We all are. Want me to handle this? Give her half an hour?'

'Handle this how?' Clay smirked. 'Give him a lap dance?'

'Fuck you, I meant have a conversation or take him out to get coffee or something. Create a *diversion*.'

'Uh. Right. That actually would be really helpful. Go, do your thing – I'll get to Zill.'

'Aye aye, captain.' I sighed, walking slowly towards Kirk until he finally lifted his head at my approach.

'Hi,' he said, a huge grin spreading on his face and revealing a set of sparkling, perfect white teeth. I could almost see the money wedged between his gums with that set of dentures. 'You must be the new recruit, Zillia's told me all about you. What happened to your face?'

I accepted his warm handshake of welcome and smiled gently, trying not to aggravate my headache. 'Aye, that would be me. I'm Tommi Grayson and I'm also terribly clumsy with not a cool story in sight to explain away a broken nose.'

'Kirk Rennex, lovely to meet you, and as someone who once broke their ankle en route to the bathroom in the middle of the night I can relate heartily. I know most of the staff Zillia has here by name, but it's always good to get to know the live-ins properly.'

'You and Z got plans?'

'Dinner and a movie, actually. Very pedestrian, nothing too exciting.'

'That actually sounds like heaven,' I chuckled. 'Listen, she's not going to be much longer. Clay and her are going through stock out the back so maybe another half hour at the most.'

'Ah, good to know,' he said, glancing down at his watch to check the time. 'I'm happy to sit and wait.'

'Clay said you'd say that and I thought that sounded pretty boring.'

'Well, I won't argue it's as exciting as The Rock movie we're going to watch later but it will pass the time.'

'I'm just about to head out to satisfy the major lemon meringue pie craving I have at a café down the road, care to join me?'

'Sure.' He grinned. 'You can tell me all about how a Scottish art lover ended up working in a Berlin nightclub.'

'Geez, you weren't joking when you said Zillia had told you about me.'

'I was not.'

Night had fallen when we stepped out into the alley and I shrugged into the retro baseball jacket I had tied around my waist. I wished desperately for one of the many beanies I knew I had upstairs. Instead I just gritted my teeth as wind swept down the narrow space and blew hair around my face. I muttered to myself as I batted the long, blue strands out of my vision and finally surrendered to winding them back in a loose braid.

'Welcome to Berlin autumn,' he said, still tapping away on his phone as we walked. 'What's a shorter word for expanded?'

'Bigger,' I offered. 'Big, large, mighty as fuck.'

'Yes to all except the last.'

'Are you tweeting?'

'Attempting.' He smirked. 'My PA has been bugging me to "engage with the consumers" for a year now, so she signed me up. I'm struggling to get a grasp on the hundred-and-forty characters limit, to be honest.'

'Tbh.'

'Excuse me?'

'Tbh. You can save yourself three words in "to be honest" and just write "tbh".'

'God, I just feel like giving up.' He laughed. It was a loud, warm laugh that somehow didn't reach all the way to his eyes and I wondered if it had been decided by PR people that this was the most appealing laugh to his client base. Everything about Kirk – from his tailored Tom Ford suit to the scarf knotted at his neck in a casual manner to bring the whole look down to earth – felt very consciously considered. Zillia, in comparison, was an effortless beauty. I wondered what it was about the two of them that clicked together, thinking that maybe it was their differences. To his credit, Kirk seemed comfortable in the grungy café where I had been eyeing up the cakes in the window for the past week. Considering his cufflinks alone would have been worth the waiter's annual wage, he didn't appear hoity-toity as he found us a corner seat and flopped himself down on a communal bean bag.

'Can I get you anything?' I asked. 'Your own slice of lemon meringue pie? Because I do *not* share.'

'A soy cappuccino,' he replied, smiling. 'Please.'

I ended up getting two slices of pie – both for me – and the coffee, before joining Kirk. The beanbag I sat in smelled like incense but the thought was soon pushed from my mind as I swallowed my first mouthful of dessert.

'God dang it, that is fookin' delicious,' I moaned, savouring the sharp tang of the lemon and the gentle crunch of the meringue on top. 'It's as good as it looked.'

'I take it you have a sweet tooth?' he asked.

'It's more like a sweet fang.'

'Zillia too, but it's anything with coconut.'

'Eh, we all have our vices I guess. What's yours?'

'Not food,' he said, with a gentle laugh. 'Probably ambition. If I could've just been happy with the first small business I owned and never driven further than that, things would be a lot less stressful.'

'There aren't many small business owners who can afford Tom Ford though.'

'You have a good eye,' he replied, nodding appreciatively. 'I thought Clay was the only one at Phases who could spot a clean line.'

Half an hour with Kirk passed surprisingly quickly and I learned I had more in common with the savvy entrepreneur than I first thought. Art, for one. It's like an unwritten rule of being a rich asshole that once you make over five million you start collecting art as an investment strategy. And Kirk? He had the bank account but not the best advisor when it came to picking the right pieces. By the time Clay texted me saying that the coast was clear to come back, I was scrawling a list of artists that he should look into on a napkin. Zillia was waiting out the front of Phases when we returned, a huge smile that I recognised as forced plastered on her face. Kirk, he didn't seem to notice at all as I discreetly split off to the side and left the two of them to their date with The Rock.

* * *

I heard Lorcan enter our apartment some ten minutes after me. I had my back to him and was looking out of our broad, glass windows and down at Phases. I didn't say anything. I heard and sensed him as he moved to stand behind me.

He didn't say anything. When I turned to face him I knew tears were swelling in my eyes. It couldn't be helped. The horror of it was so much worse when I was alone, when I wasn't in a room with seven others trying to work out a strategy to combat this or stuffing my face with pie.

'Babies?' I said.

'What do you want me to say, Tommi?' He could tell I needed something from him, some sort of support to help me understand this.

'I . . .' I didn't have a reply. I had only fantasies. 'I want you tell me this isn't happening. I want you to tell me that the survivors of a pack of evil cunts haven't come to Berlin and they aren't abducting babies to *eat*.'

God, that last part was difficult to say. I shook my head in disbelief as Lorcan waited for me to finish.

He moved, hesitated, then pulled me to him.

Safe. I felt safe pressed against his hard chest as his arms secured me to his body like a barnacle to a rock. He was holding me so tight I realised Lorcan needed my proximity right now almost as much as I needed his. I closed my eyes. We stayed like that for what felt like hours, though could only have been a few minutes. Eventually we broke apart.

'I need to know everything,' I said.

'I thought you might.'

Lorcan tried to make two cups of tea, but I dismissed that gestured in favour of hard liquor. He returned to the kitchen with a bag of frozen peas that he tossed to me as I sat on the couch. I pressed them to my face with a winced. They were so cold I wouldn't be surprised if my nose snapped off and dropped into my lap. I removed them for a spot of fresh air.

'Keep them on there,' growled Lorcan. He had his back to me as he poured the whisky into glasses. I hadn't even seen him turn around.

'How do you do that?' I grumbled, putting the bag back to my face. 'It's cold.'

He sat next to me on the couch, handing me a glass. He lifted the peas off to softly touch the bruising. 'Good. It's healing fast. At the werewolf rate I'd say you won't be able to notice anything at all in the next few days.'

'Why babies?' I asked. I took a cautious sip of the amber liquid and sighed with pleasure as it scolded my throat.

'The Laignach Faelad worship the god Crom Cruach. He's an old world god, someone you'd only ever see referenced in historical texts on ancient religions and mythology. Their offerings to Crom Cruach grant them increased strength compared to other werewolves.'

'Those offerings being babies.'

'Yes,' said Lo, swallowing a sip. 'In theory Crom is pure evil. He is everything unnatural and unbalanced in the world. Therefore, he demands a sacrifice of innocence. What's more innocent than a baby? An infant is too young to be tainted by greed or power or lust. It's the purest form of humanity. Devouring it is the ultimate sacrifice. It's also the ultimate destruction of the pack's souls, which is the other offering to Crom Cruach. They just don't know it.'

'You think they're soulless?'

'How can they not be? How can you do what they do and have any remaining concept of what is right or wrong?'

'Sanjay and I . . . are we targets now that we ran into them? We crossed their path. We mightn't have known they were werewolves but I bet they knew we were.'

'No,' said Lo, shaking his head. 'Other werewolves aren't a direct threat and it would have been apparent you didn't know what you'd stumbled across given how you reacted. They're not interested in you.'

Tucking my feet underneath my body I mulled that idea over. 'Tell me about the battle.'

If I didn't know Lorcan so well, didn't know his every tic, I wouldn't have noticed his body tense up. 'I've fought supernatural evil for centuries. *Centuries*. Facing off against the Laignach Faelad was the worst thing I've done, then or since. Just being amongst them . . . It was evil in its most undiluted form. I had no doubt that they had to be completely annihilated. It was the only way to be sure. Or so we thought. It was Jaira and Jakea who first discovered their location and scouted the campsite. I can't imagine the things they saw during the days before the battle, but it's hard to envision anything worse than what we experienced.'

'Bodies? Baby bodies?'

'No. None. They leave nothing behind except the bones. There were mounds of children's bones around the perimeter of the camp. I busted into one cabin in the middle of two wolves finishing off a meal and . . .'

He was silent for a long period. I was glad my stomach was relatively empty. His piercing green eyes met mine. 'I know that you're hurt because I didn't tell you about this.'

Amid the gruesome nature of his revelations I wanted to bat a hand in the air and dismiss him. But it was true. I was hurt. Considerably less so post learning about the Laignach Faelad, but the fact remained. I nodded.

'I've lived four hundred and twelve years, Tommi. There are four centuries worth of events –'

'I know,' I said, cutting him off. 'It's impossible for you to tell me every tale and every misadventure Lo, I know. It's not this one thing you've kept from me, it's all of them – all of the conscious choices to keep me in the dark.'

'You can't know everything and I can't tell you everything. It would betray what we're trying to hide,' he said.

I mulled that over. There were bigger things at play here, but I still wasn't buying this dismissal. 'Fine,' I said, getting up off the couch. 'I'm just sick of having this conversation over and over again.'

I wasn't mad, I was just exhausted deep down in the fibre of my being. I was at the door before Lorcan asked where I was going.

'To the training rooms,' I replied. 'To punch and stab things.'

'Do you want company?'

'No,' I said honestly.

As I let the apartment door close behind me I stood on the landing for a few moments. Lorcan knew how secrets made me feel, yet he continued to keep them. There was always a reason, always some justifiable excuse he could argue – there was never a compromise. Instead I funnelled my frustration into an hour on the treadmill, a few more on fight drills and a satisfying burst with the daggers. Fight the pain away.

* * *

It had been many nights since I had had a nightmare. That had to be a small victory for my mental recovery, I figured. And it wasn't me who woke thrashing and screaming in the bed. I slept through most of Lorcan's night terror, only waking when he started to force the rebellious sheets into submission upstairs. I sighed and got up, getting him a glass of water and taking it up to him. With a jolt he was awake and alert, taking in the surrounds and the fact that I was standing there with a drink. He was shaking.

'It's okay,' I whispered, placing the glass of water next to his bed and leaving without another breath.

My mind caught on the words just as they escaped my lips. They weren't that different to the ones I had uttered the first time Lorcan and I had woken up next to each other, when I had been comforting him from a nightmare then as well. I also realised this time I had lied. This time Lorcan wasn't a thousand miles or a hundred years from his nightmare. This time they were here. And things weren't okay.

Chapter 12

'Hi, yes, I'd like to speak to Officer Dick Creuzinger of the *Landeskriminalamt* Special, er, Children's Victim Unit ... thing.' I had been trying to use my most official voice and soften my accent as much as possible as I spoke down the line. Scrunching my eyes up, I tried not to make myself too aware of how much of an idiot I sounded. I shifted the phone to balance between my shoulder and ear as I tried to spread avocado on a piece of toast.

'I'm sorry, he's away from his desk at the moment.'

'Oh, uh, right,' I said, fumbling to get my mind back on track.

'Can you please leave a message for him saying that Tommi Grayson called?' The woman assured me she would as I left my number and we hung up.

Lorcan had been working on a laptop over on the couch and he lifted his head up when I finished on the phone.

'How long until he calls back, do you think?' I asked as I bit into my toast and deflated with pleasure as the soft, delicious taste entered my mouth.

'Not long,' shrugged Lorcan. 'Even amid an investigation like this one, you leave an impression on people.'

I narrowed my eyes at Lo to ascertain his true meaning. 'When you said "feminine wiles" yesterday –'

Lorcan interrupted me quickly. 'I did *not* say "feminine wiles". That was Clay.'

I took another bite of toast, quietly pleased with how strongly he was opposed to the idea.

'Just get him talking about the case and feel your way from there.' He quickly added, 'Feel with intuition.'

Our plan of attack was simple: we were going to try and learn as much as we could until we heard from the powers that be about a course of action. Neither the Treize or Praetorian Guard had responded with follow-up movements besides the twins' deployment and a representative headed our way.

Lorcan had already spoken to Jakea and Jaira during their travels to keep them abreast of the situation and said they were 'extremely disturbed'. He seemed to be making a point of keeping me updated on every person he called, what they said, who they were and the outcome. I gave feedback and made suggestions, we argued or agreed, and we moved on to the next stages of the plan.

Lorcan and I split up later in the afternoon when I returned to the shooting range with Clay and worked again with the Glock and Beretta, then sniped with Yu.

Dolly and Sanjay were also at Yu's and the five of us practised hand-to-hand combat before I had some one-on-one sensory training. We utilised the surrounding woods and Sanjay had me attempt to track Clay as quickly and quietly as I could. The Laignach Faelad had everyone wanting to step up their game.

I returned home to find Lorcan and Zillia poring over piles and piles of books. Er, not books exactly. Some of them were definitely books. A lot of them were pages held together with a variety of archaic bindings. There were a handful that weren't bound at all and the pages of those looked like they would turn to dust at the merest touch. I thought of Chester Rangi and wondered if there was any way to get him involved without creating a shit storm, then decided against it. We could have definitely used The Cavern's resources.

'What are we reading, kids?' I asked.

Lorcan had barely noticed my entrance until he sniffed and looked at my hands. 'Is that Chinese takeaway?'

'Why, yes it is, and why yes, I am the greatest woman that ever did live.'

I had assumed we'd have company for the evening in the form of a few local Askari helping out. With the sounds of the rest of the Rogues thundering up the stairs, I was glad I had ordered a province worth of spring rolls. After snatching the bags from my hands, Clay began serving out the food on plates and I admired his hospitality. I grabbed a few armloads of cushions from beside my bed and brought them to the coffee table area where the majority of the texts seemed to be placed.

'What in the name of Selena Gomez is this?' shrieked Clay as he took a plate of food and settled into the couch. He was holding up a small book that had tried to uncomfortably wedge itself beneath his buttocks.

'That's mine,' I said. '*The Gashlycrumb Tinies.*'

'By Edward Gorey. It looks like a kids' book,' he muttered as he flipped through the pages.

I nodded. 'Aye, kinda. It's basically an ABC of children dying. After what we learned yesterday I wanted to revisit. It seemed . . . timely.'

'We have enough books on evil in this room. We don't need any more.'

With a triumphant yell he pitched it across the other side of the apartment.

Reaching over, I pulled the nearest book towards myself and began reading from where a green Post-it note had marked.

'The Wolf Men of Tipperary. This refers to them?' I asked Lo.

'Yes,' answered one of the female Askari who was buried in a pile of papers. The tattoo that identified her as legitimate was peeking out from under the sleeve of her coral cardigan. 'An English writer named William Camden referred to them in the fifteen hundreds. He had loose ties to the Custodians so he doesn't go into extensive detail. Most think it's a work of fiction. Still, it paints a picture.'

'Irish monks used to refer to them as the *fianna*,' added Lorcan. 'They condemned them as "sons of death" – a warrior cult.'

The female Askari smiled at him, impressed, and I prevented myself from frowning as he smiled back.

She flicked a strand of her stylish blonde bob back into place and continued. 'There are consistent mentions of a "vow of evil" they undertook, which we think refers to the consumption of babes' meat.'

I mulled that over.

'Music?' asked Sanjay.

'Heck yes,' I murmured.

'My choice?' perked up Clay.

A resounding 'no' from everyone in the room was his reply. He looked mildly annoyed. Sanjay was rifling through the iPod resting on the speaker dock.

It was weird. There I was, in a room of rogue werewolves and supernatural researchers, investigating a pack that ate babies as part of a tribute to an ancient god. Yet, it was *nice*. Simply hanging out, listening to Wanda Jackson and eating takeaway food with furry friends.

Some hours later I was preparing to head out solo on my first attempt at a street sweep. We had waited until it was at least 10 p.m. Given both of the previous abductions had occurred well after midnight that was the window we were working with.

'I don't like this,' said Lorcan, helping me strap a machete into a hold on the outside of my thigh.

'You don't have to,' I said. I'd watched the blonde Askari – Jenica or something – openly flirt with Lo for the past few hours. He hadn't exactly given her the cold shoulder either. I guess the rules for Askari and Custodians were different to those between a Custodian and his ward. Deep down I knew it was smart. It would kill any vague suspicion about us if there was any. You couldn't question 'us' if there he was, making eyes at another woman in front of me. At least I hoped that's what he was doing. I really didn't need the help arming myself, but given the way Lorcan's fingers lingered over the bare skin of my legs I was betting he wasn't doing it for my benefit. I moved my thigh in a test motion, satisfied that I wouldn't be restricted in my movements.

'Feels good,' I said, dropping the material of a long skirt. The black fabric was only tight at my waist before it flowed out and down to my ankles. When I walked it looked like a pool of black liquid *swishing* around me. It also perfectly cloaked what I was hiding underneath: a machete at my thigh, a Glock strapped to my hip and a Scipio dagger tucked into my black combat boots. Although most of the Rogues thought these patrols would amount to nothing, I wasn't taking any chances.

Up top I was wearing a tight Lonewolf T-shirt (an addition I found amusing and Dolly found blatant). My prominent chest kind of warped the red and orange background on the shirt, but the grey wolf was still clear and howling at the moon.

'Right. Where the shite am I going?'

Zillia mentioned she and Lorcan had a few ideas. A spare space of wall in between our kitchen and the apartment doorway now had a massive map of Berlin stuck up on it. The locations of the first two abductions were marked on the map with red dots, as well as where Sanjay and I had run into the two men. From there what looked a 30-kilometre radius had been sectioned off with strings of blue wool.

'We were thinking start on Dietrich Street, try and see what they were looking at. Then expand out into X-Berg.' Lo pointed to an intricate patchwork of streets in between the two locations the Laignach Faelad had already hit.

'Greater Kreuzberg is the focus,' provided Zill. 'There's a patch of land here technically owned by no one. The locals call it "tent city". Gypsies and all kinds of people camp out year round in tents, caravans, shacks, whatever you can imagine.'

'What makes you think they'll strike here?' I asked.

'It's where I'd go,' said Lorcan. 'The families living there are the easiest targets in the city as they have the least protection. It's surprising infants there weren't the first victims.'

'This is all guesswork. We have no idea where they might try to target next given there's no regularity to their movements,' added Zillia. 'Plus there are a lot of residential apartments in that general area you can cover in the same patrol.'

Using everything Sanjay had been trying to teach me in the past few days, I used my sense of smell and wider intuition to track back to where we'd first collided with the Laignach Faelad. Then I went further. It had been days and potentially hundreds of people had passed through the quiet residential street since then, but I drew on my wider werewolf instincts to steer me right.

Even with all the interference, their scent still lingered and something . . . more. It led me right to a discreet garden shed at the back of a duplex. I didn't stay long, conscious of the fact the place might be watched by police and that I needed to remain unseen; I didn't have a good excuse for being here once, let alone twice. The shed was filled entirely with tools needed for outdoor upkeep: a hand mower, clippers, abandoned garden pots and vine lattice. Yet there were clear signs the men had been here – and for some time. The ground had been disturbed: the imprint of their bodies where they had sat crouched was still evident in the dirt. I mimicked the positions, trying to see what they could see and understand why they had been in this spot. The duplex backed on to this location and there was window access not much further than a few clean strides and a leap. With a jolt, I realised what it was about their scent that stood out to me so potently: it was death. They smelled like death. I got out of there quickly after that, jotting down the street address that had been their clear target in my phone.

Tent city was exactly what you would expect from a place named tent city. Wedged between two expensive looking apartment blocks, makeshift accommodations popped up on the grassy space like pimples on the surface of skin. I admired Lorcan's cold calculations: this place was definitely vulnerable. While some people lived in repurposed vans, others were sleeping under nothing more than a propped-up sheet. Anybody could come on to the land and wander through tent city, no questions asked.

As I strolled through the maze of tents and vegetable gardens, it was obvious how much of a target this place was. A cluster of residents were sitting around a bonfire while a guy played a song I didn't recognise on the guitar. I was so busy watching them I nearly stood on a toddler, who was crouched in the dirt playing with a broken plastic truck. He was barefoot and grubby, barely noticing my approach as he immersed himself in his make-believe game.

A massive piece by street artist Blu adorned the side of one of the apartment blocks. It looked down on tent city like a silent guardian. The land opened up on to the Spree and I spent a solid ten minutes sitting on its bank watching the occasional boat pass by and the foot traffic cross Oberbaum Bridge. I used an almost invisible path that ran alongside it to work my way through several suburbs as I scouted for action. The sounds of tent city faded completely as I progressed deeper and deeper into residential areas.

It was quiet, getting quieter, as it ticked past midnight and closer towards dawn. When I crossed back on to actual streets

I caught the occasional person wandering home, but for the most part I was the only soul occupying the empty Berlin streets. The most exciting thing that happened was when I caught a whiff of the mouth-watering smells coming from Burgermeister. I won't lie: I had not one, but two cheeseburgers and my very own side of cheese fries to round out the night. I regret nothing.

Officer Dick Creuzinger came into Phases the last night before the full moon. I was working at the bar covering Clay while he took on the night's patrol.

'Well well, if it isn't no call Nelly,' I hollered.

'How are you, Miss Grayson?'

'Just fine. Can I get you something to drink?'

'Schneider Aventinus. How's your friend at the hospital?'

I had visited Joss that afternoon. His operation was tomorrow morning. He was in relatively good spirits and his parents were putting on a brave front. Realising I had taken too long to reply, I skipped it altogether and asked about the investigation instead. He let out a long, deep sigh and shook his head.

'These aren't by-the-book kidnappings. We would have had ransom calls by now. We keep trying to look for connections between the two families but there's nothing. One family are wealthy British nationals, the other of Indian heritage but born and bred in Berlin. Both worked in different industries. Both have vastly different incomes. There's every chance that neither family had ever been in the same suburb as the other before. There's nothing connecting them.'

'Except the missing kids.'

'Except that.'

He took a long sip from his drink. Lorcan caught my eye from across the bar, where he was manning the door. He was covering Dolly while she and Yu rustled up some supernatural contacts. He was watching my conversation with hawk eyes that I was fairly certain had nothing to do with an objective observation into how my interrogation was going. A jealous Lo – I kind of liked it.

'Did y'all find what you were looking for the other night?'

Dick cast me a brief glance before replying. 'In a manner of speaking. Sorry if we scared you both. There was another group of kids down the road who nearly maced us when we startled them too.'

'Tragically I had left my mace at home,' I joked. 'And no luck with the guy caught on camera at the hospital?'

'Nope. The comfit didn't even generate so much as a whisper. A few calls from old ladies trying to throw every redhead they saw under the bus, but nothing useful. I thought the CCTV footage might shake something loose, someone might recognise his build or the way he moves.'

The despair in his tone was evident. I realised that even when – not *if* – we brought these Laignach Faelad fuckers down Dick was not going to stop looking for answers. The case was going to plague him.

'*Ghosts*,' he said. 'One of my detectives joked that the first kidnapping had been done by ghosts. Considering what we have to go on, I'm beginning to think he wasn't far off.'

The sound of a glass smashing at the end of the bar distracted me. A scuffle was breaking out between two groups of people and I watched a drunken man in knitwear take a swing at an equally plastered gent. My blue-collared companion made a move to get up, but I was already over there and leaping the counter. Placing a hand on the chest of one short yet burly man, I pushed him backwards as he tried to launch himself into the fray. I caught the startled expression on his face as my strength sent him flying into three of his mates. Good. That kept them out of it for a few more seconds while I grabbed a bottle from the hand of the opposing ringleader who was brandishing it at the enemy. Slipping myself in between the two troublemakers, I looked up at them and tried to quell the fire.

'On a Tuesday night, guys? Really?'

They paused for a moment, looking down at me as if they had just realised there was a blue-haired woman standing in front of them. The taller of the two actually leered at me, not hiding the fact he was looking down my singlet and at my bosom. I sensed movement and turned to see a guy throw a punch in my direction. These men were off their tits. I ducked with plenty of time to spare and grabbed the man's arm, pinning it behind his back until he yelled. I held him there, spinning him around the group so they could see the result.

'This is what happens if you don't play nice while blootered at Phases,' I said loudly. 'You get your ass whooped and thrown out on the street.'

Releasing him, I pointed at the members of the two parties and shouted, '*OUT!*'

One last idiot tried to make a run at someone. I stuck out my foot, tripping him, and watched as he landed on his face with a pleasant crunch. The sound of a bottle smashing spun me around to face an angry and obscenely drunk woman – his girlfriend, I assumed. She was swaying on her feet as she raised the jagged glass towards me. I sighed. From behind her a hand wrapped around her wrist and squeezed. She shrieked and dropped the bottle, clutching her wrist. Lorcan looked at the group of people: all silent except for the odd few panting in pain. He glanced at me and I shrugged.

'Gee, I feel useless,' said Officer Dick Creuzinger. He had finally made it over to us and was looking over the strewn figures. He had his police identification in his hand and at the mere presence of it the rat-arsed troublemakers started hustling towards the exit. Lo threw the rest of the stragglers out (ungracefully, might I add).

'What happened?' came the voice of a flustered Zillia. She joined us at the door as we watched the forms of the two parties hulking off to cause trouble somewhere else.

'Nothing Tommi couldn't handle,' said Lo.

'I've never seen a woman handle themselves like that before,' said Dick, looking at me with awe.

'You mustn't have a very high opinion of the women you work with then,' I replied.

'No, it's –'

'You work in bars long enough,' said Zillia flippantly in a bid to cover the moment.

'I thought you used to work in an art gallery?' he asked. I was saved from a reply by the ringing of his mobile phone. I gave Lorcan a relieved glance.

'Hello. What? Where? I'm on my way,' he said, hanging up. '*Fuck.*'

'Not another one?' I asked as Lorcan moved to my side.

'I don't know. This mightn't be related.'

'Dick, this is my friend Lorcan. Lo, Officer Dick Creuzinger,' I said, rushing out the introductions.

'How'd you do?' Dick shook Lorcan's extended hand with a firm grip and nodded.

'Officer,' Lorcan replied, stern. It was all very masculine and tense.

'I've got to be off,' he said, withdrawing his hand. 'I'm sorry, Tommi, I'll catch up with you properly another time.'

'No sweat,' I said, waving as his walk turned into a steady jog. Lo looked down at me.

'Well?'

'Well what?' I retorted, immediately annoyed by his expectant expression. 'You heard the phone conversation, there's a lead you can follow up.'

'There was nothing else?'

'No,' I sighed, looking out into the night where Dick had disappeared. 'They've got nothing. They think they're chasing ghosts.'

Lorcan followed my gaze before replying. 'In a way, they are.'

I spent the next day at the hospital with Joss as he recovered from his operation. The results weren't back yet and until that time we wouldn't know whether he'd definitely need my bone marrow. It was something I couldn't give but I was not looking forward to the conversation when I'd have to formally say no. I didn't have a good excuse yet. I was hoping time would provide me with one. Propped in a chair next to Joss' bed, I was chewing on red licorice and describing the dynamics of Phases to the patient in an animated fashion. Joss loved hearing about the club as it gave him a life – even if it wasn't his – outside of the hospital and his treatments. I enjoyed indulging him and added as much animation to the story as I could with big hand gestures and exaggerated expressions.

'– and by the time the cop ran over I was just standing in the middle of a pile of very sorry looking jugheads.'

'No way.' Joss laughed. 'Fookin' fat grapes.'

'Way,' I confirmed.

Joss squinted at me in examination. 'You look like shit, Tommi.'

I raised my hand to whack Joss playfully on the arm, but reconsidered when I glimpsed his frail condition. He was completely and utterly bald, no shaving about it, and dark purple rings hung under his eyes. He'd lost weight and his cheeks had sunken in. If he was telling me I looked bad, I truly must.

'I slept shite,' I said, lowering my hand. In truth, I was exhausted. Between shifts at Phases, street sweeps and trying to fit in extra learning with the Rogues whenever I could, I was bone-tired.

'Well, *I* had a major operation and I still look ravishing,' Joss said, flipping imaginary hair off his shoulders. I stuck my tongue out at him and settled more comfortably into the chair. Anecdotally the operation had been a success, Dr Matthews informed me. It looked like they had removed most of the cancer, but they were still waiting for the full report. The good part about that, besides the obvious, would be that if everything came back tip-top then I wouldn't have to dodge the issue of a bone marrow transplant. Somehow I wagered neither of us would be that lucky.

When we got back to the club, all of the wolves and Askari were gathered at the bar and waiting for me. I tried not to notice Lorcan and Jenica sitting a little further away from everyone and deep in conversation. The posse was digging into an early dinner laid out along the bar and everyone looked a little worse for wear. That wasn't what alerted me though. It was their faces. And the newspapers. Several newspapers lay scattered across the bar and I met Zillia's stare with a sense of dread.

'Another one?' I asked.

She shook her head sadly. 'Another three.'

Chapter 13

The most overused phrase quickly became 'it's like something out of a horror movie'. I promised the next person who said it that they would end up in the scope of my CheyTac M200.

'It's no coincidence these happened in between the full moons,' I said.

'How do you figure?' asked Gus.

'The days after the full moon we're down, we need a pick me up. I need sugar; they need more of what they need: babies.'

For all the increased hunger, the Laignach Faelad still weren't sloppy. The kidnappings were flawless, if such a word could be used to describe something so sinister in nature. No prints, no witnesses, no trace. One of them had been caught on security footage leaving through the window of an apartment block. The resolution was too low and they were unable to see the face properly. There wasn't even a new artist's impression in the papers. Officer Dick Creuzinger had released the footage to the media and the thirty-second clip was playing on every news update. Lorcan didn't recognise the man as one of the original members of the pack. For me, I intended that every night be filled with street sweeps. Armed to the teeth, I was pulling my hair into a high ponytail when Lorcan joined me.

'I'm coming with you tonight.'

'Are you sure Jenica doesn't need help with her research?' I muttered.

He gave me a look and ignored the comment.

'Besides,' I continued, 'I thought you didn't think these escapades would amount to anything?'

'I was wrong. I think being out there will increase our chances of stopping something. It's better than being cooped up here and arguing over how best to interpret the information.' He strapped a longbow sword into a sheath, which hung across his back. He was agitated.

'Still no word?'

He slammed his hands down on the table where I had the leftover weapons spread out. They jumped at the movement, as if afraid of his rage. 'I don't understand it! This is the very reason the Treize exists! It's the purpose of the Praetorian Guard to wipe out threats like this, so why isn't anyone here yet?'

Lorcan had been on the phone most of the day trying to speak with someone high up at the Treize. He'd conversed with both the Guard and Custodians, the latter who were keen to have a force of PG operatives deployed as soon as possible. Apparently such a force was on their way. As to when they would arrive, where and how many there would be? We were being kept in the dark. We had been given our instructions: find out as much as you can and observe. Do not interfere with the investigation and do not alert them to the fact that they are being watched.

'Basically,' I'd translated, 'do all the groundwork and then stay out of our way?'

'They know what they're doing,' had been Lorcan's reply.

Tonight we were heading back to X-Berg, somewhere Zillia was shocked hadn't had an abduction yet. Judging from Lorcan's expression as we passed through tent city, he shared her belief that these people were in danger. 'They have no protection,' he said to me quietly.

'And what would they usually need protection from? They watch every outsider, there's always someone awake, and they all know each other. That bearded guy had us marked the second we crossed over on to the land. For most situations all of that would be protection enough.'

'They don't know what's out there.'

Of that I didn't disagree. It was a Friday night so the boroughs were full of people heading out to their respective haunts. I envied them a little: blissfully unaware and unburdened with the horror of the current crisis. I tried letting my senses guide us, but there was so much interference I couldn't be sure if I was following my inner wolf or just meandering.

After a few hours on the streets we took to higher ground, scaling several smaller rooftops to negotiate our way on to the flat surface of a four-storey collection of old apartments. It was the tallest building in the surrounding area and it gave us a great 360-degree vantage point.

Lying flat on our stomachs, we faced opposite directions to try and cover as much terrain as possible. It was a clear night but chilly enough for the boots, jeans, turtleneck and beanie – all black – that I had teamed together. Camouflage was key.

We'd been lying still and motionless for almost two hours when something to my right drew my attention downwards. There, in the darkest spot in a narrow alleyway that ran along the back of several houses sat two men. They were dead still and seemed cloaked in the shadows around them. I couldn't make them out clearly, so I put my sessions with Sanjay to use and focused on shifting just my eyes. Slowly my vision changed, adjusting as the scene before me sharpened and my pupils successfully transformed. Yes, without a doubt two members of the Laignach Faelad sat crouched and staring straight ahead at the attic window of one of the homes. I could see a soft glow coming from the room they were looking at. Probably a night light coming from a nursery: their target.

I recognised one of the men as the abductor from the hospital. His thick, matted red hair was unmistakable. They'd done well to keep him out of the public eye.

The other man was, put simply, what nightmares were made of. He was completely bald and seemingly much younger than his 'colleague'. Everything about his features was feline. He was the closest to a cat I had ever seen any human look and considering he was a werewolf that was saying something. His eyes were sharp: like two beady, black coals that pierced the night itself.

The men were so still I wondered what had alerted me to their presence. Another movement, this time slightly higher, gave me my answer. A bird was flying off into the night and I'd bet it had come from the branches of the tree they were hiding under.

So unnatural they scared nature itself. My spine crawled. My nostrils flared as I attempted to inhale the full scent of them. I shifted my foot back to nudge Lorcan, who turned and looked at me with mild curiosity. Nodding downwards with a grim expression, he followed my gaze with binoculars as he shifted his position to lie next to me. I pointed a finger in front of Lorcan's nose to where I knew they waited. At that instant they both stood and slipped silently from the shadows and into the grey light of the alley. They vaulted the back fence like they were stepping over a gutter and within another second the redhead was making his way up the roof towards the window.

'Lorcan,' I hissed.

'I know.'

'We have to do something.'

'I *know.*'

I wasn't waiting for any more confirmation than that. I went to get up when Lorcan yanked me back down. 'What?' I said, through gritted teeth.

He paused, mulling something over in his head. 'We have orders.'

'Fuck their orders.'

'They're not supposed to know we're on to them, Tommi. What happens if we ambush them now, save the baby and they go running back to the rest of the pack? The element of surprise is gone and we risk elevating their spree.'

I let out a stream of curse words and glanced back down at the house. The attic window was open and I could see the bald one waiting on the sill with one foot in and one foot out of the room. Anger was bubbling through my blood, making my skin itch and my muscles twitch with anticipation. Mari and Kane had been killed at the hands of a psychopath and, despite my best efforts, I had been unable to do anything but watch them die. Their families and friends had been ruined because of it. I had been ruined because of it. Now I was being asked to sit still and observe as that happened to someone else's family. I. Could. Not. Do. It.

'All that's necessary for the triumph of evil is that good people do nothing, Lo. We've been hunting these pricks for days trying to do something useful. Here we are! There are two of them and two of us. We have an opportunity to save an innocent life!'

He stared at me, our faces barely separated by space, and I waited impatiently for him to make a decision as the seconds ticked by.

'Alright,' he said. His eyes scanned the alley quickly. 'We need to wait until they're off the roof and out of the yard.'

'I don't like that. It gives them an opportunity t–'

'Tommi.'

'Fine,' I snapped.

'The alleyway passes directly beneath this building and we can drop on the man with the baby from above.'

'What about the second dude?' We crawled on our bellies to the other side of the rooftop in preparation. I glanced behind me and saw the redhead appear at the window with the child. 'Motherfucker,' I muttered.

'Forget him,' Lorcan said. 'If he stays and fights then we'll deal with it. If he runs, two missing pack members would have been cause for alarm anyway.'

I nodded. 'We both take the ranga, then you get the child back into the house as quickly as possible and call the police. Do something to alert enough people so there's too much going on for them to come back.'

Lorcan looked at me, confused as to how the orders were suddenly being dished out to him.

'The baby is our priority,' I explained. 'I'd prefer it if we killed them too, but if they get away then they get away. At least we will have saved a life. You're the better fighter, the kid will be safer with you.'

'Okay.' He looked like he wanted to argue but there was no time.

'Let's make them smell colours,' I growled.

The Laignach Faelad were now in the alleyway and sprinting in our direction at a rapid pace. Baldy was in front and the redhead behind, which worked better for us. Lorcan and I both crouched in unison and silently unsheathed our weapons. The silver of his ancient sword glinted in the night, as if sensing it was about to be put to use. My own weapon of choice was much less impressive but it was razor sharp and I knew how to use it to maximum effect. They were almost directly beneath us when Lo whispered: 'Now.'

It was only after we had launched ourselves from the rooftop that I realised it was eighteen or so metres in the air. It made no difference to little ol' werewolf me as I landed squarely on the back of the baby-eating ginger. The downward pressure had the desired effect and, shocked, he let go of the baby. It went flying in the air like a displaced basketball. Lorcan had timed his fall perfectly and swept the child into his arms mid-descent. His soft landing was a nice contrast to the meaty crunch the redhead made as he hit the concrete face first with me on top of him. The baby must have woken with a jolt as it began to cry. Good, I thought, as the sound grew fainter with Lorcan's departure. That's one way to wake the neighbourhood up.

I leapt off the man's back just as he tried to throw himself – and therefore me – backwards. He spun to face me and I could see his accomplice slowly pacing his way back towards us. Feline McEvil thought we weren't alone and he was glancing above him with every step as he inched closer. His accomplice was not as cautious, staring at me as blood dripped down from several deep cuts in his face. In the light it looked as if he had rivers of his red hair travelling down his face. He snarled and extended his hands in a gesture that looked like he might want to give me a hug if it wasn't for the wolf claws extending at the end of his digits. I had never seen anyone shift on command like that before except, well, me.

Two could play that game. I snarled back at him and felt my teeth elongate as I bared my fangs. He was surprised and I realised that up until that moment he didn't know I was a werewolf. The dog was out of the bag now and he launched himself at me, using his claws in big sweeping motions the same way Freddy Krueger used his knived fingers. The man was huge and I recalled the mention of his six-foot-seven frame in the papers. I had to throw myself backwards each time he struck out to avoid his range. He was on the offensive. After a dozen or so attempts at trying to slash me to ribbons I took advantage of that by stepping forward instead of backwards. I moved in a graceful swirling motion bringing the blade of my machete with me. Just as easily as I stepped into his range I used my lack of height to duck under his armpit and out the other side. Not wasting any time, I brought the blade down on his back and felt a spray of warm blood splatter across my face.

I swivelled quickly to check the location of the other werewolf. Good thing I did, as he was racing directly at me. The redhead was screaming in the background and I was disappointed to learn that none of my blows had been fatal (only painful). Maybe they would have killed a normal human, or even a normal werewolf, but these two were neither. I was trapped between the pair of brutes and I had a second to decide a course of action, which was to propel myself into the air and let the two of them collide with each other. Flipping, I landed on the pavement in a crouched position only to find both sparing no time and – after picking themselves up – coming at me as a united front. Great idea Tommi, great idea.

Their immense body mass blocked the entire width of the alleyway. There was no escape. I hurled my machete at baldy and it lodged in the space between his shoulder and heart. Damn. Reaching for the Glock tucked into my waistband I had barely raised it to the face of the redhead when he knocked me and my gun against the brick wall of the alley. I saw stars momentarily as I slumped down on to the ground. A swift kick was delivered to my face and I was thrown over on to my side, which put me nearer to where my gun had landed. I felt a hand extend around my foot and I just had time to grab the Glock as the redhead started dragging me towards him. Ignoring the gravel rash I flipped from my stomach to my back and pointed the gun directly up at him.

I had the perfect shot at his head. I didn't even think about it as I pulled the trigger. The bullet hit just inside of his left eye and his brains exploded into the air around us. There wasn't a second to relax as his body was pushed aside to reveal an entirely different man altogether. If cat-face was from nightmares, than this fellow was from the nightmares of nightmares. He had two thick scars running from the tip of his temple and down the entire side of his face, making his mouth lop-sided. One of his eyes was grey with blindness. I saw nothing but pure evil radiating from his remaining iris. He was holding an enormous spiked mallet – an actual *fucking* mallet – and he swung it down towards me. I screamed and rolled to the side, missing the impact by less than a few centimetres. Using my body like a croquet ball he shifted the mallet to the side and whacked me so hard I flew off the ground and into the opposite alley wall.

A cut above my eyebrow had opened up and blood was spilling over one of my eyes and clouding my vision. Frustrated, I brushed enough fluid out of the way to block a punch from baldy just in time. The impact of it threw me against the wall again, but at least I was standing. He clamped his hand around my throat and lifted me in the air until my feet were wiggling above the ground. I gagged, struggling for footing. They might be evil werewolves, but they were still men.

With that I delivered the hardest kick I could right in the nads. He released his hold on me as he hunched forward in pain.

I sucked in a deep gulp of air before reaching to retrieve my machete, which was conveniently still wedged in his person. He shrieked as I pulled it out and even more so when I jammed it back in. I was stuck between him and the alley wall so I didn't have the full range to reach his heart, but I ploughed it deep into his stomach. I had to let go of the blade handle to duck what would have been a killing blow from the mallet as the scarred man swung it over his companion's head. Pushing him backwards, I spun and delivered a roundhouse kick to his face. The mallet man stepped aside, allowing his pack member to fall to the ground as he advanced upon me with his hammer of death. Much to my relief it was then that Lorcan returned and blocked the path of the mallet with his sword.

He leapt into the battle with gusto. The scarred man was a lethal opponent and unsheathing one of my back-up short swords, I joined the fray. Lorcan was much closer to our foe in size than I was, which worked well because the man with the mallet couldn't be everywhere at once. I darted in and out of his range, delivering dozens of stab wounds. Lorcan kept him busy with the bigger blows as the sword and mallet were evenly matched. He was flawless, being everywhere he needed to be a second before he needed to be there and never breaking focus. It was the combination of our efforts that started to provide results when the mallet began to drop lower as the man grew tired and lost even more blood.

A wide swing gave Lorcan the opening he wanted and without hesitation he drove the sword straight through the throat and out the other side. I stepped back as the man dropped to his knees, only driving himself further along the length of the blade. The mallet fell to the ground. It was an incredible sight; the equivalent of someone being spiked on a rotisserie at their jugular. With a sharp pull backwards and a *swooshing* movement above his head Lorcan withdrew the sword before sending it back downwards to decapitate the man entirely. The headless body stayed upright for a few seconds before slumping to the side with a sound that was both heavy and wet. We were both panting. Lorcan looked up at me.

'Beheading them,' he said. 'It's the only way to be one hundred per cent sure with the Laignach Faelad, you understand?'

I nodded. It was suddenly very still in the alley. It wouldn't stay that way for long as I could hear police sirens in the distance. The commotion had the neighbourhood waking up around us. We needed to get gone.

'Baldy, where's baldy?' I said, looking around frantically.

'Who?'

'Baldy, the cat-faced boy! He had the machete sticking out of him.' I rushed to the place I had last seen him and followed a trail of blood with my eyes as it led away from the scene.

'He must have escaped when we were fighting him,' said Lo, nodding at the corpse.

'Bollocks!' I touched the wet substance and rubbed it between my fingers, sniffing.

'No,' said Lorcan, reading my mind.

'I can track him,' I said. 'He can't have got far with those injuries.'

'No, Tommi, we barely have enough time to get out of here on our own two feet.'

'Who said anything about two feet?'

'Can yo –'

Before he could even finish the question I was ripping my clothes off.

'I'll follow you as far as I can Tommi, but this could be an ambush.'

'He has to get back to the pack for it to be an ambush and he won't make it that far,' I said, unhooking my bra. 'And it will give us an idea of which direction their base is located.'

'I'll take care of these bodies and call the others,' he said. 'We'll be close behind. Howl if you get into trouble.'

I nodded and took off down the alleyway, butt naked. Holding the blood on my fingertips to my lips, I licked it and tried to get a taste for my prey. There was no time for the steady shift. If I was going to catch him I had to morph on the fly like at the warehouse. With one long, piercing scream my tread shifted from that of a woman to that of a werewolf. I shook my head and, still running, adjusted to my surrounds as I hunted down a member of the Laignach Faelad on the streets of Berlin.

Chapter 14

Sunlight had spilled over the horizon some twenty minutes ago. It was cold, grey light that promised a day of showers and clouds. I shivered and curled myself into a tighter ball, strengthening my grip on my arms. It was all I could do to stay warm. I had followed baldy right into the heart of the city when his injuries eventually caused him to slow pace. Either that or he thought he had made it clear of us. He hadn't.

He had been bleeding enough that I was able to follow the trail of blood right to him (that and his suffocating stench). I guessed this Laignach Faelad didn't have a lot of time to bathe, what between all the baby snatching and baby snacking. He reeked and maybe that cloaked my scent in part because he was unaware I was chasing him until I was almost on top of him.

He had been heading towards the Brandenburg Gate when he spotted me approaching at a ferocious pace. He sprinted into the Holocaust Memorial in an attempt to lose me. It was a maze in every sense of the definition. Thousands of grey concrete slabs spread out in all directions, with height and course undulating like swells in the ocean. Paths endlessly split off from each other towards places where the slabs could tower over you in height or be no taller than your waist. I didn't hesitate, diving into the labyrinth and frantically trying to keep sight and scent of him as he weaved through the memorial. If I thought the night sky was dark, down on the ground it was darker still as the tall slabs blocked outside light sources. A growl from behind spun me around and I took off after it. I caught a flash of someone here, no, a shadow. His scent again. Fuck, lost it. I was getting disorientated and losing my target, as had been his plan. This time the growl was mine as I ran my claws along the ground in frustration. Inspiration hit and I tensed my body briefly before launching into the air and landing on top of one of the tallest parts in the maze. I scanned every direction and spotted him limping towards an exit on the southern side. Practically flying over the top of the memorial, I leapt the open space between slabs and jumped from one to the other.

He was exhausted by the time he realised I was above him and by then it was too late. He managed to sprint to the entrance of a narrow lane, but I landed and went for the killing blow. In a surprising final burst of strength he managed to wrestle me off him and on to the ground. Before he had the opportunity to get into a defensive position I had already lunged, sliding low under his initial attack and raking my claws across his belly. He didn't even have time to roar in agony. I was back on baldy in an instant and with a resounding crack that echoed off the walls I broke his neck. His body went limp instantly as the life left him. Using the strength of my jaws, I tore his head off to be sure, just as Lorcan had said. There was blood, too much blood for me to disguise easily. I dragged his corpse deeper into the lane and did my best to cover it with whatever I could find lying around. There was nothing I could do about the gore. I placed discarded cardboard boxes and whatever litter I could find lying around over it. I knew that if anyone walked down here before Lo found me I was buggered.

So there I was: naked, bleeding and freezing my ass off. All I could do was wait.

Thankfully it was too early for people to be going to work and too late for people to be coming home, especially through a lane that several restaurants appeared to use as a dumping ground. I hadn't seen anyone since the pursuit began, but Berlin was Berlin. It wouldn't be long before the city started waking up. I was positioned next to a large dumpster at the mouth of the alley. Crouched down, I would be invisible to anyone walking past on their early morning commute. I had given myself two possible exit routes if I was discovered, but a bloodied naked woman would be about as conspicuous as a werewolf running through Pariser Platz. I shivered again.

'Hurry up you eejit,' I whispered. I had no idea how he intended to find me – only the faith that he would. I assumed he would use the Rogues to track my scent or the blood. I just prayed they would get here before some unsuspecting person came across a girl who looked an extra from *Carrie*.

The traffic frequency was beginning to increase and I tried not to panic. I looked down at my toes on the wet, grimy ground and wiggled them in an attempt to regain feeling. They were numb, like most of my extremities. I could see my breath billowing out in small clouds and I daydreamed about a shower so hot it would take the first layer of skin with it.

'Ah, the end of the line, I see.'

My head shot up in surprise at the sudden and silent arrival of the stranger. He appeared around the corner of the lane and my diminutive position on the ground only accentuated his height. He was tall: I guessed six foot six. Dark-blond hair fell to just below his ears and framed his face perfectly, as if didn't dare blow out of place. What I first thought was a trick of the changing light actually turned out to be a short beard the same colour as his hair. A heavy brow creased in a frown as he looked away from me and to the trash I had pulled over the body. He exposed what was left of baldy by nudging the pile with the tip of his foot and gave me a backward glance that revealed an amused smirk.

I didn't move from my spot on the ground (mainly because I had been crouched down for so long I wasn't sure if I could break free from the position the cold had moulded for me). While he examined the body I took a moment to check my laced arms accurately covered my boobs and that no other 'bits' were showing. I envied the grey trench coat he was wearing and wondered if it was worth exposing myself to try and steal it. I decided against, but noted the flash of a utility belt underneath that was equipped with all sorts of instruments. As he began walking towards me I took in the man's measured, confident gait. His strut matched the cocky expression on his face, which was still smirking. His eyes flicked over my delicate state in a way that made me certain he was very aware of my nudity.

'Aren't you curious who I am? Aren't you wondering why I haven't screamed for the police or tried to kill you?'

'You're from the Praetorian Guard,' I strangled out. My voice was almost robotic-sounding from the effort of preventing my teeth chattering. From the flash of surprise that crossed his features, I knew he heard me clearly. The cocky mask snapped back in place as he bent down to my eye height.

'And what makes you so sure, lass?'

'Please,' I said, rolling my eyes at him. 'From your outdated haircut to the sword hidden under your cloak, it was obvious who you were the second you appeared.'

He was about to ask me another question when the ear-piercing screech of car brakes broke the morning serenity. A navy-blue van skidded to a halt at the entrance to the alleyway and blocked the road's view of us. Lorcan rolled back the door and was out of the vehicle while it was still moving. 'Get away from her!'

The blond stranger didn't move. 'There's no need to over-react. We're merely having a little chat,' he replied, not taking his eyes from mine.

'He's from the PG, Lo.'

'I know exactly where he's from.'

The venom in Lorcan's voice was enough to make the man look up. Lorcan was striding towards us with a stance that I recognised from past experience as defensive. He was ready for a fight. The man stood, slowly, and took two steps back with his hands raised slightly in a peace gesture. The Rogues pack was now spilling out of the van and the man took a further step back. Lorcan gave him another menacing stare and then turned his back to him. If this guy was dangerous, that seemed like a strange thing to do. I kept my eyes trained on the blond as Lorcan's hands examined my body to assess the damage.

'Tommi, you're freezing. Are you alright? Tommi?'

I dragged my gaze to meet his. His green eyes were full of concern and genuine worry marked the lines in his face, which was now inches from my own. I nodded, relieved to finally be in his company. 'Aye, I'm just cold. And tired.'

His thumb traced a cut on my forehead and I gave him a reassuring smile. He reached behind to grab something and returned with a blanket, which he threw around my shoulders and adjusted so I could stand without flashing the small crowd gathered. I was unsteady at first and Lorcan placed a protective arm around my shoulder. Huddling into his warmth, I gratefully accepted the pieces of red licorice he handed me for a quick energy boost.

'That's quite the prodigy you've got there,' said the stranger.

Lorcan took a long time to say anything, choosing instead to stare down the blond while everyone else fidgeted nearby. At last, he spoke. 'What are you doing here, Heath?'

'I've been sent to assist, of course. Although it looks like you don't much need my help.' He gave the corpse a pointed look.

'They sent just one of you?' Gus spoke up. 'We're dealing with the whole Laignach Faelad here.'

'We've got the deaths of multiple children on our hands,' added Zillia.

'Fortunately for you then, they sent the best.' He grinned at the Rogues.

All of their faces were impassive as they tried to work between confusion and relief.

'We don't need your help,' spat Lorcan.

'Well, actually . . .' started Clay, reluctant to join the fray.

Heath laughed at that. 'Oh, no, I'd say *she* doesn't need my help. You took out how many Laignach Faelad members tonight by yourself, Tommi?'

'We – Lorcan and I – took out three together,' I clarified.

'Don't discount yourself. You took Ailbe out here all on your lonesome. That was a powerful thirty-year-old werewolf who survived on a diet of the richest, purest infant meat you could imagine.'

I grimaced at the description.

He chuckled. 'You shifted into full form without the assistance of the moon and without eating any citizens along the way. You achieved your objective with minimal harm to yourself. You're also still conscious now. I think Lorcan here has been underplaying your abilities.'

I tensed at that suggestion but Lorcan let out an amused breath of air. 'I'd be very surprised if you read my report, Heath. No, my guess is the opportunity to meddle was too much for you to resist. Even recruit, perhaps?'

'Don't be silly, old friend. Your feelings for your *first* ward are clouding your judgement. If the twins couldn't convince her to join our ranks then I doubt I could.'

'YOU got asked to join the Guard?!' screeched Dolly, incredulous. Many of the Rogues were looking at me with a variation of shock and awe. Yu was avoiding everyone's gaze.

'You didn't think the twins were in town for you, eh, Dolly?' Heath challenged her with the comment and she made a lunge for him. Gus and Yu held her back, despite her shouts and frustrated grunts.

'Everyone take a good look at Heath Darkiro. He's been here five minutes and already causing trouble. That's what he does,' said Lorcan. 'He brings nothing of any merit to anyone, only infecting the lives of others with trouble and trivial pursuits.'

'Trivial Pursuit did you say? Haven't had a game in decades. How about I get this body cleaned up and we go back to your abode for a round or two?' He clapped his hands together with boyish enthusiasm so sincere I had to search for the sarcasm. Lorcan gave him another long, weltering stare before pulling me in the direction of the van.

'You look after the body. You know where the club is,' he said over his shoulder.

'Captain, oh Captain,' said Heath with a grin. Lorcan stopped dead at that, the remark hitting an invisible nerve.

'Come on,' I said, tugging his jacket in the direction of our getaway.

He let it go. As the roller door to the van slid shut the last thing I saw was Heath, tall and golden, standing proudly in the space where we had left him. He caught my eye and winked.

We were thundering along the main road back towards Phases as Lorcan explained how he had debriefed the Rogues on what happened on the way to find me. Clay was driving and had Die Antwoord playing through the speakers to disguise the quiet that had now descended on the group. The van was your standard people mover and fitted all of us without much difficulty. Lorcan and I had the backseat to ourselves and I was absentmindedly chewing on yet another piece of red licorice.

'Who was that guy?' I asked him quietly. I shifted so I could look at his face. He had been staring off in the distance and he looked down at my question.

'Heath Darkiro's a member of the Praetorian Guard and a very capable warrior. He's also an unpredictable ally, deadly fighter, lothario and someone who cannot be trusted.'

I took all of that in. I'd never met someone that Lorcan had openly disliked as much he seemed to dislike this guy. 'Yes, but who is he to *you*?' I pressed.

Lorcan sighed. 'Do you remember the story I told you about the men who recruited me, the Pict and the Indian?'

'Aye.'

'Heath was the Pict.'

'T-that's the man who recruited you?'

He nodded.

'If he's a Pict, was a Pict, that's going to back to . . . the eighth, ninth century. Right? How old is he?'

'No one knows for sure: thousands of years old, certainly. His specific age is unclear.'

'Fuck. Me.' I just met a Pict. I just met a surviving member of the warrior clan that ruled Scotland for centuries. And I was butt naked. 'You guys have . . . history?' I stammered, still trying to get my head around the revelation.

'Yes, I was his star recruit for centuries. More than that, we were friends. He's a company man but he has reckless tendencies. I kept him out of trouble and he looked out for me. We fought side by side. We've saved each other's lives countless times.'

'What happened?' I couldn't imagine something that could destroy a friendship like the one Lorcan just described.

'Amos. We had both become friends with him over the years but I always thought Heath seemed somewhat jealous of our bond. When Amos died, Heath was different. Or I was different. Either way, Heath was furious with him for taking what he called "the easy way out". He barely grieved. He was simply ready to move on to our next station.'

'And you weren't.'

'No. He thought me wanting to leave the Guard was insanity: genuine insanity. When it was clear he couldn't change my mind he did everything he could to try and stop the transfer going through. He went to commanding officers, the Custodians, he tried every way he could to throw a spanner in the works. He considers my move spitting in the face of everything we've done together and everything he offered me in that tent centuries ago. I'm a waste of talent.'

I didn't know what to say. I had left most of my friends behind in Dundee when I came here – I'd left Poc and my grandparents. The good friends I had though, I kept for life. My heart panged as I inevitably thought of Mari and Kane. And Joss. Well, the duration of *their* lives, I thought with sick regret. I couldn't imagine all the friends you would collect being hundreds or thousands of years old, let alone the strength of emotion that would end a friendship that had been going that long. Lorcan felt betrayed, I could see it in the set of his forehead.

'You don't think Heath was assigned this?'

'I think that no matter what the case, he would have ended up in my path the first opportunity he got. He volunteered.'

'You're not worried about what he said, about noticing my abilities?'

He shook his head. 'We can't hide it any longer. At least there's a logical progression now. You've been working with a pack of advanced and highly skilled werewolves. Advancements were inevitable.'

His lack of concern soothed me.

'You though . . . you're going to be his greatest mystery,' he said.

'What do you mean?'

'Not only are you my first ward, but you turned down the Guard. He'll be fascinated by you.'

'Thanks for the warning,' I grumbled. Lorcan mightn't have noticed, but I certainly did as his grip on the back of the seat tightened subconsciously.

By the time we reached Phases, Clay had to carry me to the apartment while the others regrouped before Heath got there. I whined about being made to take a shower before crashing out, but Clay insisted I needed to get my cuts clean if they were to start healing properly. Also, dried blood upped the ick factor. I could barely stay conscious and Dolly waited with me in the bathroom to make sure I didn't pass out. Any sensitivity I might have had about nudity was gradually being chipped away the longer I was a werewolf and as I stumbled out, wet, I didn't even feel shy about showing my body in front of her. She made some comments about my injuries that I didn't register and with a knock on the door, Yu joined us and helped Dolly get me into a giant Batman bed shirt and undies. They helped me to my bed and I thought I'd never felt anything sweeter than the soft support of the mattress under my body. I lay there while Yu got ready to tend to whatever wounds needed a stitch or two. I was asleep before she even got started.

It wasn't until well after 8 p.m. that I woke. Even then, that was only because of raised voices coming from the hall. Lorcan. And Heath.

'You're even living together.'

'She's my ward, fool. I don't have a choice.'

'Lorcan, I'm impressed. This wolf has changed you. A bit young at twenty-three, but I suppose she can be taught plenty of tricks.'

'Yes, that's very insightful of you, Heath. You have no idea what you're talking about. I guess if a thousand years of living on this Earth couldn't mature you I don't know why I thought the past two years would.'

I had been tucked into the soft doona and I grunted as I sat up, feeling every muscle and every ache. And there were plenty of aches. I opened my mouth in a silent yell at the pain of simply getting up. I staggered with drowsiness as I ran my hands through my hair and made my way to the landing. The two were so caught up in their sniping they didn't even hear my approach.

When I opened the door both looked like they had been sprung. I blinked, taking in the sight. Lorcan had Heath by the collar of his coat and pressed against the wall. Heath, as usual, was smiling. I noted he had a nice grin. No doubt it had melted the hearts of thousands of women over the years. Unlike Lorcan, Heath was definitely not the 'walk the world alone' type.

'Lads,' I said.

Lorcan released Heath instantly as he stepped to me. 'You're up. How are you feeling?'

'Like I fought three fuck-off werewolves last night. You?' The deep bags under Lorcan's eyes hadn't gone unnoticed by me. 'Did you sleep at all?'

'A little,' he said, casting an annoyed look at Heath.

'I encouraged him to rest, but what can I say? He doesn't listen to me,' Heath added, adjusting his clothing.

Lorcan ignored him. 'We have a pack meeting downstairs in an hour.'

'Go sleep then,' I said. 'That's a solid fifty minutes you can get. I'll wake you.'

He looked from me to Heath. He didn't move. 'What are you going to do?'

'I'm going to have a little chat to your best frenemy here.'

Heath raised an eyebrow at the term, clearly fond of it.

Lorcan moved past me and closed the door behind him. I was certain he was listening on the other side.

Standing there with Heath, I was suddenly very aware of the fact I was in nothing but a thin T-shirt. A woman can make a potato sack look sensational as long as she wears it with confidence, I told myself. I drew myself up a little higher with that thought as I faced the ever-amused puss of Heath Darkiro.

'I don't have time for your bullshit,' I started. 'Lo seems to think that your sole purpose here is to cause trouble and from what I've seen of you so far, I'd have to agree.'

'He's told you about our history, has he?'

'Briefly. Heath, I don't have the patience for a personal vendetta from someone with a rejection complex. We're dealing with bigger shit than whatever unresolved issues you have over a failed bromance.'

His expression darkened as I spoke. 'You have no idea what you're talking about.'

'Oh, you don't like me trivialising your problems? Now you have an idea of how we feel about your response to the Laignach Faelad situation. Are they sending any more of you?'

'No.'

I bit my tongue with frustration. What were the Treize playing at? 'Fine. Then you're all we've got. Lorcan says you're good and coming from him that speaks volumes. We don't need another thorn in our side otherwise we're all going to end up dishes at the baby buffet. We need help. We need another soldier. We need your expertise.'

'You need me.'

'Yes,' I said, unashamed. 'You've been fighting evil for an inconceivable amount of time. I'd like to think you can stop being a bawbag and do so again.'

'Ah, but can he?'

I didn't rush an answer, instead I took a moment to think about it. For this? 'Yes. Lorcan can.'

Heath nodded, giving me an appreciative once over that I ignored. 'My main reason for being here is to wipe the Laignach Faelad from the face of the Earth.' There was a murderous gleam in his eye that confirmed the truth in his statement.

'Good.'

'Good.'

I made to leave, turning and reaching for the doorknob. I stopped at the last minute. Heath hadn't made to exit: he was watching me instead.

Meeting his gaze, I said firmly, 'Don't mistake my kindness for weakness, Heath. So you're a Pict? Big fucking deal. This is a building full of good people, good wolves, and if you get at them or get them hurt in any way . . . Well, you saw what I did to that man this morning. And that was quick.'

He smiled a wide grin that extended all the way to his eyes. There was a curiosity there, but also understanding. He nodded. 'You're a wolf in woman's clothing.'

'Aye, don't you forget it.'

Without another word I slipped inside the apartment, unsurprised to find Lorcan standing in the shadows of the kitchen.

'You hear all that?' I asked, walking towards my bed.

'Yes.' I heard a shake in his voice and I spun around to see him laughing.

'What?'

'I've never had anyone try to protect *me* before. And I could bet few people have stood up to Heath the way you did just now, especially women.'

'That's vaguely sexist,' I grumbled.

Lorcan shrugged. 'That's Heath.'

Chapter 15

We had some time to kill before joining the others in the meeting room, so I took to the bar at Phases and began knocking back whatever I could get my hands on. Zillia had called in the entire replacement staff so we had the night off to address our dire situation. And hey, what better way to face impending doom than getting blootered?

Across the opposite side of the bar I could see Zillia and Kirk sitting close together over what looked like a shared meal of chicken, fries and salad. It was clear she was upset, but attempting not to show it. Kirk had wisely picked up on the vibe and was doing his best to compensate, being overly affectionate and sweetly tucking a strand of hair behind her ear. I couldn't look away: for some reason the couple had me captivated and I wondered if that's because they had what I craved. Yet as soon as I thought about Lorcan, my stomach clenched. I downed the two shots of Jägermeister I had in front of me and started nursing a vodka and cranberry juice when I sensed someone's presence beside me. I could virtually sense their intentions as well, so I decided to tackle the issue before it got any further. Swivelling to the side on my stool, I whipped around.

'Listen, fuckboy –'

The next words died immediately as I realised my companion was Heath. He took a swig from his glass of Scotch while smirking.

'You were saying?'

'Ergh, it's just you.' I showed my appreciation for his company by taking a massive gulp from my glass.

'Hey, I said I'd play nice. There's no need to stoke the volcanic anger levels.'

'Sorry to snap.' I sighed. 'I'm not angry at you . . . right now.'

'And pray tell, who are you angry at?'

My fingers tightened around the glass and I could feel it weaken slightly under my grip. 'Everyone. Everything. When what happened back in Dundee happened, I was assured by your world that was an exception: horrible things like that weren't a regular occurrence, they were an anomaly. Now barely six months later there's fucking baby killers on the street, running around like it's October thirty-first.'

'You leave Halloween out of this,' he teased.

'My point is, all I've been told is how important the Treize and the PG and the Custodians and the Askari and whoever-the-hell-else are to maintaining law and order in this world. They're supposedly crucial to peace and protection.'

'You're not feeling very peaceful or protected?'

'Fookin' aye,' I scoffed. 'I feel like whatever job y'all are supposed to be doing, you're not doing it very bloody well.'

'If you're getting all your knowledge about this world from one source, I'm not surprised your information is inaccurate.'

'Ha, I'm not taking the bait there and throwing Lorcan under the bus.'

'You said his name, not me. And besides, if you're not satisfied with the job we're doing then why not become part of the solution?'

I raised a perfect, lone eyebrow at Heath as he casually threw the suggestion out there. His shoulders were shaking with a subtle kind of laughter as he caught my expression.

'You can't knock an immortal for trying,' he murmured, taking another sip of Scotch.

'The last time someone "tried" I was peeing blood for two days.'

'The situation with the twins was out of hand. But amusing.'

I said nothing, thinking of my sore face that was courtesy of the twins' negotiating tactics as I glanced out over the bar. He followed the path of my gaze until he too came to rest on Zillia and Kirk.

'Who's the suit?' he asked.

'Z's squeeze, Kirk Rennex. He's a billionaire but don't hold that against him. He's actually alright.'

Heath looked thoughtful, albeit disbelieving.

'What? I can make friends with the rich and well-to-do as well as gruff warriors.'

'Actually alright,' he repeated, shaking his head. 'Look at him, kissing her neck like that. What's he trying to prove, that he's not shagging the secretary?'

'Or the busboy,' I added, catching myself a second after the comment left my lips and feeling a little shocked. 'You bring out the worst in people.'

'No, I'd say he was pawing over Zillia long before I arrived.'

I was laughing when Kirk looked up, as if sensing we were talking about the two of them. Smiling politely, I offered a small wave from across the bar which he returned.

He whispered something in Zillia's ear and left her for a moment, weaving his way through the crowd towards us as a Kehlani jam played over the speakers.

'Here we go,' Heath grumbled as I elbowed him to shut the hell up.

'Tommi, great to see you again!'

'You too.' I nodded, not sure whether to shake his hand or offer a hug as neither seemed appropriate in the moment. He glanced at Heath, who had his back turned towards him as he continued to drink his Scotch. The blond giant made little attempt to acknowledge our new guest, but Kirk seemed undeterred.

'Hi there, I'm Kirk,' he said, offering a hand to shake.

'Congratulations,' Heath murmured, waving down the bartender for another drink.

I awkwardly shrugged, attempting to apologise for my companion's rudeness.

'Don't mind him, he's still mad the hairdresser gave him a Robin Hood haircut. I keep saying it will grow out in time but right now, the pain is still too fresh.'

'Ha, well, we've all been there. Listen, I've got to get back to Zillia but I just wanted to let you know there's a treat in the staff fridge for you.'

'A treat? For me?'

'Let's just say I know a chef who makes the best lemon meringue pie in Berlin.'

'What in the Joan Jett, really?'

'It's all yours. Maybe you can cheer your friend up with a slice,' he said, nodding at Heath.

Heath snorted. 'I'm diabetic.'

'Ah, well. Good to know for next time. I'll leave you to it.'

'Bye! Thanks! Have a good one!' I waved.

Heath gave me a disapproving stare. 'Oh, calm your calms will you, Wall Street just gave you a pie.'

'And all you've given me is a headache,' I replied, still smiling as Kirk left us.

'Aye, well, I'm about to give you some actual useful information now too,' he said, nodding towards the clock on the wall. 'We've got a meeting to take.'

Dolly and Yu were just passing by us and we fell in step behind them, with the others already having taken their seats in the boardroom when we arrived. We began by going through in detail what happened on the previous night's street sweep. From the quiet start to my push for action, we outlined it all. When we finished, it was silent for a long while before Zillia spoke up.

'What were you thinking, Tommi?'

I frowned, examining her reclining position at the head of the table. Her fingers were linked together and resting lightly against her lips. Fear saturated every inch of her face.

'WHAT WERE YOU THINKING?!'

Her scream made Sanjay, the closest to her, jump with shock. I leapt up from my position at the table until I was standing.

'I was thinking there was an opportunity to save a baby's life! I was thinking here's one family I can prevent from being ripped apart! I was thinking that maybe here's three less people we'll have to face in the end!'

Zillia was taken back by my anger and conviction. Her mouth hung open and I watched as it moved with the effort of trying to formulate thoughts. After our sudden outbursts silence penetrated the room like an uninvited guest. I settled slightly, flopping back into my chair as I continued.

'Have you forgotten why we originally decided to do something about this? It wasn't because we were scared or they were abominations. It was because they were *killing* innocent babies. They were murdering children. They were committing acts so evil it's difficult to even think about.'

'We had been given our instructions,' said Zillia. I could hear the strain in her voice as she tried to stay calm. 'If we could find them, observe. Do not interfere and do not let them know we're on to them. Don't engage.'

'You could have exposed all of us,' added Gus.

'I didn't though, did I? There was no "us" out there. It was just Lorcan and I because the rest of you thought street sweeps were stupid.' I heard a sound of indignation come from Clay and I quickly added, 'Excluding Clay and Sanjay, of course.'

'They saved a life and wiped out three of the enemy,' said Sanjay.

'That was not what we had been told to do,' Zillia resisted.

'When have we ever done what we're told?' asked Dolly in a voice so small I was uncertain whether it had come from her at all. It was only by making eye contact that I became sure. Yu was by her side and by the closeness of their arms I suspected they were holding hands under the table. 'Isn't that the whole reason we're here together, because we didn't want to be told how to be werewolves by a pack locked in archaic traditions?'

Heath was leaning back in a large office chair that somehow managed to incorporate his massive frame. He had been sharpening two thick, exotic-looking daggers and watching us with mild interest.

'We've got one of the PG here with us now.' I gestured to him. 'If I'm going to be slapped on the wrist it should be from the people calling the shots.'

Heath raised an eyebrow at being included and looked from me to the rest of the table. Everyone was looking at him with expectant expressions. He placed the daggers down on the surface of the table. 'What's done is done.' He shrugged.

Lorcan groaned. 'Heath really isn't the best person to be weighing in on this.'

'Why not?' Heath feigned offence.

'Because you're merciless,' said Yu. I realised she too had probably had some experience with him, given her PG past. This was turning into quite the reunion of sorts.

'His moral compass isn't exactly functional,' Lorcan added.

Heath picked a dagger back up and leaned back in his chair, looking thoughtful. 'Be that as it may,' he started, 'I'm the representative the Praetorian Guard sent. And since Yu traded immortality for the love of a good woman and Lorcan traded the sword for the zen life, I'm the only official figure from the Treize in present company.'

'And what do they have to say?' grumbled Gus.

Heath was examining the lethal curve in the dagger with intense curiosity. 'Nothing. They had nothing to say about it. My orders remain the same.'

'And those are?' asked Clay.

'To exterminate the Laignach Faelad by any means necessary.' The finality of his words spread around the room like an
invisible fume.

'When are the others from the Guard getting here?' Zillia
couldn't keep the terror out of her voice despite her best
efforts. There was a long pause before Heath replied. It was
the first time I had seen him uncertain, but his mask of confidence quickly hid it.

'They don't.'

'W-what do you mean they don't?' stammered Zillia. 'We
can't be expected to take the Laignach Faelad out on our
own?'

'You can and you will be,' he said. 'I'm all you've got and all
you're going to get, so you best make the most of it.'

'The twins are coming,' said Lorcan.

'Yes, ever the commander. The twins arrived in the city ten
minutes ago, thanks to your emergency beacon.'

'They were a few days away, at most. My only question is
why other fighters in Europe aren't being directed here too.'

Another long pause.

'You don't know, do you?'

Heath ignored Lorcan's question by stabbing a dagger into
the surface of the table. He smiled at me. 'Far as I'm concerned,
that's three less Laignach Faelad we have to worry about.
Although Tommi and Lorcan's actions here mean our timeline
will have to move forward considerably, which is a fitting
punishment in itself. The Faelad will be looking for their missing members. I cleaned the scene as best I could but that's no
match for werewolf senses. By now they'll know their men are
dead and they'll be looking for the culprits.'

'There were three witnesses and all three of them are dead,' said Yu. 'This isn't the only pack in Germany. This isn't even the only pack in Berlin city, not including all the rogues and passing supernaturals. There's nothing to link us to the dead Laignach Faelad straight away.'

'Bring the timeline forward,' Zillia whispered, still miles back in the conversation. 'And how are we supposed to do that? We're already stretched. Tommi, if you'd just followed orders we –'

'Zillia, within your first year of being an active werewolf were you able to change at will?' Heath's question was simple and he asked it in a playful manner.

'No. I have never been able to change at will. It's a rare gift.' She said the word 'gift' like it was toxic on her tongue.

'Right, a *gift* it takes powerful werewolves a great deal of time to control. Usually. Here –' he gestured to me '– is a wolf that was able to change at will, kill her target within a heavily populated area and shift back without harming a civilian.'

'You heard what happened,' said Lorcan, seemingly the only one who could talk sense into her. 'She fought in her own skin. She avoided the change until it was absolutely necessary.'

'Why couldn't you just let him get away?' She pleaded with me. 'You'd saved the child. You'd killed the others. Why couldn't you just leave him?'

I answered with complete confidence. 'Because he didn't deserve to live.'

She couldn't disagree with that. No one could.

'Hmm.' Heath's head was tilted as he examined me with a lazy smile.

'Zill,' started Yu, 'The Laignach Faelad's tracking abilities are uncanny. She couldn't risk him escaping or the chance that he could trace her back to somewhere they had both been.'

Zillia pulled her gaze away from me and looked at the wall opposite Yu. She nodded, slowly. 'You're right. I know you're right. It's just . . . I wish this had never been brought upon us.'

I understood how she felt. I understood her desire to protect her pack and her friends. Her anger wasn't directed at me specifically, it was merely an outlet to vent her frustration at the danger facing those she loved. Thinking back to Steven and everything I had gone through in Dundee, I could sympathise with that.

'What do you mean tracking back to somewhere we've both been? What does that involve?' I asked.

'They will find two scents at the scene: yours and Lorcan's,' explained Heath. 'It has been some centuries since Lorcan fought them and we don't know if we're facing survivors from the initial pack or something else. I'm leaning towards something else. Since Lorcan is essentially human, yours is the stronger of the two scents. A fellow werewolf is easier to find. They'll be coming for you.'

'Good! Use me as bait or something. At least if the surface danger is towards me, the Rogues aren't implicated.'

'Yet,' added Sanjay. 'It may take them a few days, but they will trace your scent back here. We already crossed paths with them once, remember?'

'Then we have a few days to make our move,' said Yu. 'Find their base and strike.'

'Oh, I know that one.' Heath raised his hand like an excited nerd in a high school maths class. 'It's on the outskirts of the city, naturally, an abandoned warehouse about ten kilometres from where Tommi and the gent were heading.'

'That's impossible,' said Dolly. 'We checked all derelict locations within the city limits. Some of them in person.'

'I know,' he replied sympathetically. 'An abandoned warehouse is just so generic. It's like the villains aren't even trying to be creative anymore. Personally I was hoping for more of a castle we could storm or something with a moat.'

I snorted. 'Ah, you realise this isn't the Middle Ages anymore, right?'

'Alas, who are we facing? A force of evil doers from the Middle Ages.'

He had me. I narrowed my eyes by way of defeat. 'One of them had a novelty mallet if that makes you feel better,' I muttered.

'Really?' Heath leaned forward on his seat at that, genuinely excited. This guy was unbelievable.

'You recognised one of them,' I said, suddenly remembering that Heath had called one by name. 'Ailbe.'

Lorcan looked at Heath sharply. 'You did?'

Heath nodded. 'Ailbe Jonkell, thirty-six, formerly of the Jonkell pack in Dublin. We were considering recruiting him for the Guard about a decade ago. We investigated him extensively and were close to making an offer, but deemed him unstable. It seems that's exactly what someone else was looking for.'

'Someone *made* these pricks? How exactly is that possible?' I asked.

'Which leads me to my next question,' Heath said, spinning on his chair to face Lorcan. 'You were there, you fought them in Ireland and you fought them today. Did this feel like the same foe?'

'No,' he murmured, biting the inside of his cheek as he thought. 'They had a lot of the hallmarks and the same motivations, but they felt different. Wrong, somehow.'

'Like someone hadn't got the recipe right?' Heath pushed.

The two men shared a significant look before Lo replied. 'Yes, exactly. But how? When we raided their base camp we wiped everyone out. Everyone. We destroyed everything. We made certain there were no survivors and no remnants of their existence. For a new pack of Laignach Faelad to be created it means someone has been researching Crom Cruach very thoroughly.'

'The bloodthirsty and all terrible god.' I let out a deep sigh. 'Tell me he doesn't exist.'

'He doesn't,' said Heath. 'But the mystical powers and rituals that bind the evil of his followers, however, is very real.'

'Crom Cruach isn't some Greek god personified in pop culture,' said Yu. 'This is an obscure, ancient, occult figure. You can't just dig up research on someone like that. It would take time, skilled personnel and a lot of resources.'

'The master of the new Faelad has all those, obviously,' said Gus. 'Or whatever they learned has at least been enough to create more of them.'

Heath turned to Lorcan. 'Would you say they were stronger or as strong as the previous Laignach Faelad?'

'Not as strong. Closer to the strength of a regular werewolf but just as wild as the original Faelad.'

'Interesting. I think there might be more dead children here than we realise. Or perhaps at the very least a fitting substitute.'

Yu shifted uncomfortably in her chair. 'That concerns me. The fact we missed their rundown hide-out too –'

'Uh-uh,' Heath interrupted. 'I said their base was abandoned not "rundown". I'd say the reason you missed it was because it's in impeccable working condition. There was even driveway jewellery.'

'What do you mean?' asked Sanjay.

'Driveway jewellery,' repeated Heath, as if Sanjay was deaf. 'A few expensive but unused cars parked on the premises, I expect to make it look like everything was normal.'

'No,' said Sanjay, 'what kind of working condition do you mean?'

'It's clean and state of the art. From the outside it's a shiny pinnacle of German industrialism. It's even owned by the Rennex Corporation.'

Zillia's head shot up at that. 'What? The building is owned by the Rennex Corporation? How is that possible? Wouldn't someone have noticed if a facility like that was being occupied by a pack of strange men?'

'Kirk,' said Dolly, making the connection. 'Your boyfriend's company owns the building?'

'His company would be perfect,' said Sanjay. 'It's one of the few big enough that you could slip something like under the books. With the Rennex Corp logo on the site no one would ask questions. It's the ideal mark.'

'Kirk . . .' Zillia still looked shocked. Clay reached out his hand and clenched Zillia's.

'Z,' I started, 'you know he has nothing to do with this. He doesn't even know about our world. The company has just been picked because it's massive.'

She nodded numbly, clearly concerned for her partner's safety. 'I don't want him anywhere near this. I don't need him finding out what I am, what we are,' muttered Zillia to Clay as he tried to soothe her worries.

I was still surprised that he didn't know; it would be hard to keep something that monumentous hidden in a relationship. The theory behind it made sense. You couldn't expose a human to our world, you just couldn't. Even your closest friends and family would be horrified by the truth. My mind snagged on something. I uncrossed my legs as I placed both elbows on the table.

'Our scents . . .'

Lorcan watched as I tried to finish off my thought process. 'The Laignach Faelad are incredible trackers,' he supplied.

'Aren't most werewolves?'

'They're different. More advanced. We're not sure if it was initially a way to locate infants of the targets they were set upon, but they can cross-reference scents.'

'Like a photographic memory,' Heath elaborated, 'they have an almost photographic sense of smell. If they identify a scent they can flip through their sensory memory to establish if they've come across that scent before, and where.'

My blood ran cold. All of my limbs froze in place. 'Joss,' I choked out.

Lorcan didn't understand, his eyebrows furrowing as he tried to gather my meaning.

I leapt up and heard my chair clutter to the ground with a hollow sound. 'The hospital, they stole their second victim from there. The maternity ward is just a few floors below the cancer ward and I've been there, what, five or six times before the kid was taken? My scent will be all over that place!'

Lorcan's mouth dropped open as I ran my hands through my tangled blue hair in a panic.

'JOSS!' I had barely finished screaming his name before I was running for the door.

My footfalls sounded like cannons firing in the night: they felt that loud as I tried to keep a steady pace walking through the hospital doors. There hadn't been any police cars out the front when we pulled up, so it was safe to assume the Laignach Faelad hadn't got here yet.

Yet.

Lorcan was keeping the car running in the parking lot while I went in to get Joss.

'Act normal. Remember: nothing is wrong,' Lorcan had said to me as I'd leapt out of the still-moving car.

It was integral that this seemed like a standard visit. I had a better chance of sneaking Joss out of Mechtilde General without raising any alarms that way. Stay calm. Act normal. Stay calm. Act normal. I repeated the words over and over to myself in my head as I stepped out of the elevator and into the oncology ward. I knew the floor layout by heart and I made a beeline straight for Joss' room. He wasn't expecting me and he looked up from his comic book with a surprised expression as I came in.

'Tommi,' he said, delight evident in his voice. I didn't smile at him as I shut the door behind me, locking it. He frowned slightly at my odd behaviour. I don't think I had greeted Joss without some sort of a smirk since I had known him – almost ten years.

'What's wrong?' he asked, taking in my mood.

'Listen, what I'm about to say to you is going to sound insane in the membrane. Joss, you're gonna have to trust me on this.'

'On what?'

'We need to pack up your stuff and get you out of here. Now.'

'What? Why? Wait, are they, like, harvesting organs here or something?' he whispered.

'I – wh . . . Joss, no.'

He appeared equally excited and terrified by the idea. I couldn't help but let out a quick laugh as I tried to reason with him. My smile faltered when I heard a yell from outside the door. It was followed by a gruff shout of another kind and then something crashing. It sounded like it was coming from the nurses' station at the beginning of the hallway. Joss' room was situated at the opposite end and I was grateful for that as a blood-curdling scream cut through the once-quiet hospital. My eyes widened in horror as I understood what was happening. I looked at Joss, who was staring at me with genuine fear now.

'Tommi, what was that?'

'They're here,' I breathed.

Another scream, this time further down the hall and closer to us, more things crashing and banging. There was a real commotion out there and I dreaded what was probably happening to the hospital staff and other patients as they searched for Joss. I couldn't worry about that now, I told myself as I heaved a massive wooden wardrobe over the entrance to the room.

'Jesus! How are you able to move that?!'

'Joss, we don't have time for this. Start unhooking yourself now and grab whatever meds you need, we've gotta go! These people are coming for you.'

I lifted a metallic desk that was resting against the wall and propped that against the wardrobe as well. It wasn't much. I knew it wouldn't stand against hungry, angry werewolves, but it would buy a few seconds.

'What people? Who? TOMMI!'

I paused as Joss yelled my name. He thought I was nuts, clearly, but I noted he was still removing himself from the various tubes and monitors he had been connected to. Searching the room quickly, I grabbed a canvas satchel at his bedside and threw in it his wallet, a change of clothes, shoes, his iPad, whatever medication I could see lying around and the doctor's chart. I left the phone, worried that it could be used to track us. At the last second I paused, looking at three pictures pinned next to his bed. The first was of Joss, Mari, Kane and me on the banks of the River Tay back in Scotland when Kane had been trying to teach us how to drive a dinghy. The photo was only about a year or two old.

The second image was of myself, Poc and his crew in front of the tribute to Mari and Kane that we had spray painted on a street wall. That image was less than six months old. The final image was of Joss and me at our old boxing gym. We were leaning against a wall adorned with posters and motivational slogans, sweaty and exhausted after a workout. I barely recognised a fifteen-year-old me, having just hit puberty and still sporting my naturally dark brown hair with only blue tips on the end. Joss looked the same to me: still a kid. My analysis took less than a second and I swiped all three photos with one movement, turning to meet the concerned stare of my best friend. The screams were more frequent now and it was clear something horrific was going on outside that door.

'Tommi,' he started, 'where are we gonna go?'

He gestured around the room, seeing no possible exit. He didn't see what I saw: the fourth side of the room, which was made up entirely of glass. The window gave a view of the Berlin streets below and I could see the Fernsehturm blinking in the background. Joss followed my gaze.

'No, there's no way. You'll never be able to break that window for starters and then how the heck are we supposed to get down eight storeys?'

I wasn't listening. I had already picked up the heavy metal chair that had been at his bedside. Ignoring his shouts, I ran at the window and whacked the chair against it. I didn't hurl it, I held on to it tightly, and after the initial impact I brought it back from the glass and struck the window again and again. It wasn't like a Hollywood action film where the hero punches through the glass on the first go: this took a solid ten blows before the glass finally caved. It fell apart in clumps, breaking away from the middle first and then the sides as I used the chair to smash out the remaining shards. Icy cold air blasted into the room and swept my hair back off my face. The wind made an eerie howling sound at this height and it whipped around the room, blowing up sheets and Joss' hospital gown. He wasn't wearing underpants. I returned my attention to our possible exit. Glass crunched under my feet as I put one foot out on the ledge and looked down. Fuck. It was a long way down and the grey concrete waiting for us at the bottom wasn't going to tickle. If we fell, it was done.

'Get some shoes on,' I said, scanning the side of the building for a pipe or something that we could use to scale the height. Nothing. A loud bang suddenly came from behind us and I jumped as I saw my makeshift barrier shudder with the impact. The desk screeched backwards with a second blow and I yelled at Joss to hurry up. He ran to the window and before he had a chance to look down, I held him back with my arm.

'Don't,' I said. 'Don't look.' I nodded to our left. 'We're going to follow that ledge away from your room and hopefully around to the other side of the building where we can find something to get down. You go first.'

'Me? Oh, very nice, make the cancer patient go first.'

'Joss,' I hissed, looking behind us as the door bucked again. 'I'm going.'

He brushed some glass off the ledge with his shoe first and then stepped out, back and palms flat against the side of the hospital.

'Just keep looking at the city lights,' I said, thanking God that the side of Mechtilde General was well-lit with spotlights placed every few metres. When Joss was ten metres along I took a deep breath and followed him out. It wasn't the cold that worried me (although it was freezing) – it was the strong wind. At times I felt certain the gale would send us right off the side of the building. I spared a thought for Joss, who had always been skinny but had dropped a bunch of weight since starting treatment again. He would be no more than a leaf caught in a current. I had to find a way to get us down from here, fast. I was surprised to find my werewolf claws had subconsciously extended and were now digging into the wall. Maybe, I could . . . no. But what if? What other choices did I have? I examined the drop once more. There wasn't much space on the ledge. The timing would have to be perfect.

'I thought you said not to look down,' said Joss, who had stopped moving and was watching me with trepidation.

Sliding the strap of Joss' canvas bag over my head, I held it out to him. 'Put this on.'

He took it and I used one hand to hold him against the side of the building as he struggled with it. Once on, he looked at me with a 'now what?' expression. I edged closer to him, until our sides were touching.

'I need you to trust me. And I don't mean trust as in "trust me about this new band" or "trust me that peanut butter and Nutella taste good together". I need you to trust me with your life.'

He was already pale. If possible it looked like Joss had gone two shades lighter since we stepped outside the window. A spotlight reflected off the smooth surface of his shiny bald-head. His eyes were full of a fear I had never seen in him. Even when doctors thought he'd been at the end, even when his parents had thought it, I'd never seen the kind of fear that was looking back at me now.

'I'm standing on the ledge of a hospital freezing my dick off because you told me to. I trust you, Tom.'

I nodded, feeling like I could cry with that declaration of faith. Now wasn't the time to get emotional. Now was the time to survive. 'I'm a werewolf, Joss.'

'What?'

'I can turn into a massive wolf at the flick of a switch. Lorcan is part of a supernatural organisation that has been helping me improve my powers and get them under control.'

I could tell he wanted to laugh, I could see it in the crinkle forming around his eyes. At the same time he could see the seriousness in my face, hear it in my tone.

'Okay, you're a werewolf,' he said, indulging me.

'I'm going to ask you to wrap your arms around my neck and not let go no matter what.'

I heard my barricade finally give way as the Laignach Faelad entered the room, shouting and tearing the place apart as they searched for us. We had mere seconds left.

'You let go and you're dead, Joss.'

'Okay.'

I gave my back to him, encouraging him to use both arms to grip around my neck.

'Tommi . . .'

'Shut up and hold tighter. Use the bag strap around my neck if you have to.'

He did and I stopped myself from telling him that I loved him. That's the last thing I had said to Mari, and look how that turned out.

'THERE!'

My head snapped in the direction of the yell to see the angry face of a pale man pointing out the window at us. Even from a distance I could see dozens of tiny white scars covering his face. I didn't need the second grizzled face that appeared beside him – one that I recognised from the encounter on the street with Sanjay – to confirm they were Laignach Faelad. The quickness with which they launched themselves on to the window ledge was enough to do that. I was quicker.

'Hold on tight!' I shouted before throwing us both off the side of Mechtilde General. I barely heard Joss' screams over my own as I began the shift, my clothes ripping off as the wind carried them away in strips. Urging the change to go faster, I was full-wolf in less than a painful second. My eyes widened when I realised what was happening: I was plummeting to the ground with a terrified man attached to my back. At least he was still attached. As I watched the ground rush up to meet us I extended my claws and felt them scrap along the side of the building. There was a reason I had tried to keep us falling close to the walls. I extended my claws again, wincing as they resisted against the friction. We had seconds to spare and with a growl I used everything I had to sink them into the concrete and grip as best I could. We slowed, not coming to a complete halt, but like a flailing deer down the side of a cliff we were sliding to meet the ground. It was only metres away now as we slid down the last storey, sparks flying from my claws. Before we made impact I pushed off from the building, leaping horizontally so we would land on the concrete on all fours. It worked and besides a stumble as I tried to regain my footing, it was perfect.

I let out a piercing howl into the night hoping Lorcan could use it to track me. My howl was returned by three others and without glancing behind me I knew the Laignach Faelad were mirroring my exit out of the building. I took off at a tremendous pace, ignoring the pain in my paws from the flesh that had been burned away as we slid down the hospital. The burst of speed must have taken Joss by surprise and I was glad to feel him tighten his grip on my fur as I increased my gait, sprinting across the courtyard towards the main road.

Just as I reached the asphalt a van swerved out in front of us, duck tailing as Lorcan tried to regain control after taking the corner at such speed. The side door was open and banged wildly as he accelerated. Neither of us could afford to slow down. I quickened my strides as I pounded towards the car, focusing on the empty interior where I needed to land. With a grunt I leapt forward, through the air, and when I was mere centimetres from the van I shifted back so both Joss and I could fit. Lorcan braked at exactly the right time and we fell into the back in a tangle of limbs. I tried to adjust to the shock of returning to human form as quickly as I could. The cold, metallic floor was like being doused in ice water and my body was thrown into the air as Lorcan took a traffic bump at speed. Joss and I both yelled as we hit, hard.

'Sorry,' Lorcan shouted from the driver's seat. Naked, I leaned forward and slammed the side door shut. The Laignach Faelad would have reached the hospital courtyard by now, but we were already gone. I couldn't even see the hospital through the mass of buildings lining the road back to the centre of the city. I wasn't looking away though. Locking the door, I kept my eyes trained on the road and space around us in case they managed to catch up or had others waiting to attack. The screech of another car made me leap in front of Joss, throwing my body protectively in front of his. Looking out the side window I met Yu's relieved expression from the passenger side of another vehicle. A mass of blond hair leaned forward to reveal Heath driving – and for once not grinning – as he gathered that we were okay and safely in Lorcan's hands.

'Back-up,' explained Lorcan.

'I gathered. Where are we going?'

'Where else? The club. They won't follow us back through the city. Actually, they might to determine exactly where we go, but they won't attack. Not with two of them. They'll go back to base and regroup.'

'Merry.'

I looked at Joss, giving him a quick once over to see if he had any serious injuries (only small scratches and cuts). When I peered up at him I got the biggest surprise of all. Shock was plastered on his face like foundation on a teenage girl. Yet his eyes revealed the most. They were looking at me as if he had finally seen what I was for the first time: a monster.

Chapter 16

Joss wasn't talking to me. I couldn't blame him. I wouldn't talk to me either if I learned that I had not only lied to him about the deaths of our best friends, but that I was also responsible for it. That was the main sticking point for him. The werewolf stuff – as unbelievable as it was – had been witnessed first-hand. There was no denying the blatant reality of the situation. Yet before he gave impenetrable silence though, he gave me screams. The second we were safely inside the apartment block and as far from the hospital as we could be, he let loose. What he had yelled at me about were the lies. I had lied to him about what happened in New Zealand, I had lied to him about Lorcan, I had lied to him about what I was going through. Joss and I had never had any secrets until now.

'It wasn't just you, Joss, I lied to everyone! I had to!'

'THAT DOESN'T MAKE IT BETTER, TOMMI!'

'I was trying to keep you safe.'

'And how safe do I look now, Tom? Here, in your apartment, and on the run from werewolves who eat *babies*. God damn babies!'

'I know,' I said, running my hands through my hair.

'No, you *know*. You know everything about this situation and everyone in it. You have all the power and you've taken it away from everyone else.'

He raged on for a while. I honestly couldn't recall him being this mad over anything before. In the end Lorcan had broken us up. He had been waiting outside the apartment while I told Joss everything, but after a good hour he intervened.

'Tom, this isn't helping,' he said, placing a hand on my shoulder. I looked at him with pain and frustration, not needing to say another word. 'I know. Give him some time, let him rest, and give him some space. I'll stay with him on watch.'

I nodded and silently made for the door.

The apartment complex was on lockdown. The club was closed and everyone was in the training room. When I walked through the door it became obvious why this had been chosen as the unofficial base for the meantime.

'I feel safest surrounded by weapons,' said Clay, unapologetically.

'Makes sense.' I joined his position leaning against the wall next to the daggers and propped myself against a pillow. He took in my appearance; I wasn't exactly at my best. I hadn't showered in a bid to get dressed quickly and start talking to Joss.

'Here.'

I sniffed and looked up to see Jenica holding out a steaming cup of coffee for me. From jumping off the side of a hospital to shifting on the fly – literally – a gesture of friendship from her had managed to be the most shocking event in a shocking night. Kind of.

'Er, thanks,' I said, cautiously taking the cup. She shrugged and went to join another Askari, who was in a deep conversation with Zillia across the room. I took a test sip of the beverage, which tasted bitter and hot. In other words: amazing.

'What was that about?' I whispered to Clay.

'She's trying to win you over,' he said with a huff, as if it was the most obvious thing in the world. 'She's after Lorcan baaad, girl. If I know her strategy right, she's trying to build a relationship with his best friend which will in turn make him like her more.'

I nearly choked on the coffee. 'I'm considered his best friend?'

'Tommi, I've known the guy for fifteen years, back when I was ten kilograms lighter and prettier. You and him have a special bond, it's easy to see.'

'He's a good . . . teacher,' I forced myself to say. 'And you're still pretty.'

'Mmm-hmm. In terms of playthings he could do worse than Jenica. She's just a bit –'

'Basic?' I offered.

He laughed, getting to his feet. 'For my taste, yes. But any port in a storm, you know?'

His presence was replaced by Yu, with Dolly giving me a nod but not sitting down to join us. We sat there in comfortable silence, watching the room bustle with activity. My mind was playing on the irony of my conversation with Joss. Hadn't I been the one begging Lorcan to stop holding back from me, begging him to quit keeping secrets while he claimed it was in my best interest? The tables had turned and I had a unique perspective on exactly how my best friend was feeling right now: betrayed.

'She feels sorry for you,' said Yu. I blinked and tried to drag myself to attention.

'Who does?'

'Dolly.'

I raised an eyebrow at her in disbelief.

'For having to tell your friend,' she explained. 'When she first experienced the change, she told her whole family. Mum, dad, six brothers and sisters. They completely disowned her and threw her out of home. She was fourteen.'

'Weren't they her pack?'

'Turns out she was adopted. They weren't her real family.'

'Fuck knuckles,' I said, truly saddened and surprised by the story. I was being given a fragment of understanding into the enigma that was Dolly.

'She would never admit this, but I know if she could do it all over again she wouldn't tell them.'

The 'big furry secret' wasn't an easy burden to bear. Heath entered with three claps of his hands, like a professional athlete psyching himself up for the big game. He looked around the room, taking in everyone's expressions and grabbing a blueberry bagel from a plate of pastries.

'Where's Lorcan?' he asked.

I pointed above me. 'Watching Joss.'

'How's that going?'

I looked down at the swirling black depths of my coffee and took a sip.

'That good, huh? Let's see what a few hours with the counsellor can do. He'll get him to do a Rorschach test and the kid will be right as rain ... besides the whole cancer thing.'

'What are we doing about that?' asked Zillia, walking over to join us.

'Aye, as much as we can from here,' I started. 'The only machines he was hooked up to at the hospital were a heart monitor and intravenous painkillers. We've got soft painkillers here, but I'll probably need to break into a pharmacy soon to get him something stronger. Otherwise he can last like this for a few weeks. He had another treatment two days ago, which is lucky for us because depending on the results from his surgery – due next week – it could be months before he needs another. Anecdotally the doctor said it went well, but it all comes down to the tests.'

'And what if the results aren't good?' asked Sanjay.

I didn't answer him, choosing instead to take another sip of coffee.

'He has to stay here with us until we take down the Laignach Faelad,' said Zillia. 'We have to make a move in the next day, two at most. As soon as it's over we'll be able to get him back to Mechtilde General.'

For the first time since I'd been living with the Rogues I thought Zillia actually sounded like a leader. Something had changed her, and I hoped this was the rational, action-driven woman we'd be dealing with from here on out.

'So. A plan then,' said Yu.

The brainstorming began.

Coffee or not, I had succumbed to exhaustion. After hours of planning and comparing strategies, I had fallen asleep on the training room floor. Surprisingly, it was Joss who woke me. His face was like being slapped with a fish: I woke with a start, rubbing my eyes to adjust to his sudden appearance. He sat down next to me and we remained like that for a long, silent while.

'I'm sorry,' he said.

I snorted. 'You don't need to apologise. I'm the one who should be apologising to you. All those things you said upstairs, you were right. I have been lying to you from the beginning. I did get Mari and Kane killed. I nearly got you killed last night.'

'None of that's your fault though,' he said. 'Not really.'

There was something about the way he spoke that sounded informed, knowledgeable even. I examined his face and he faltered under my gaze.

'Lorcan spoke to me. He spoke to me a lot actually, once I had a nap and could see things clearer. He told me the things you wouldn't.'

'Huh. Like what?'

'Like the people you've saved. Like how you tried to save Mari and Kane that night, how everything you've been doing has been to try and protect the people you love. He told me that you've saved people, that you saved a baby?'

'*We* saved a baby,' I corrected. 'And did he tell you that to save that baby I killed three people?'

Joss nodded. 'Yeah, and he told me how. You're a badass, Tommi.'

'No dude, I'm a murderer. Just because the people I've killed weren't innocent that doesn't change the fact I have a body count on me.'

'So does Wolverine. So does Dave Lisewski. So does Blade.'

I rolled my eyes at Joss' fictional heroes. 'Who's Dave Lisewski?'

'*Kick Ass.*'

This time I laughed outright. 'Those aren't real people, Joss. And they're all men.'

'How do you know? If werewolves and all this other stuff is real, how do you not know those stories aren't like all the biographies you read? And fine, how about She-Hulk then? Or Black Widow? Or Huntress? Or Xena?'

I sighed.

'I just wished you had told me the truth. I should have known about the real way Mari and Kane died.'

'I know,' I whispered. 'I'm sorry I lied to you. I just didn't want to expose you and –'

'Lose me?'

I nodded. 'I saw the way you looked at me in the van. I know I'm a monster, Joss.'

'That was bad timing. I had just fallen off the side of the hospital on the back of a werewolf formerly known as my best friend.'

'Fair call. I'm a gobshite.'

'From here on out though, no more secrets?' He held out his hand for me to shake. I took it.

'Deal.'

He winced as I gave his arm a solid shake. 'Now,' I said, getting to my feet, 'in this first chapter of honest best friend-ship, I'm off to break into a pharmacy to steal you some hardcore painkillers.'

Joss looked at me as if he wasn't sure I was joking or serious. 'Oxyies?'

'You got it.' I helped him to his feet. 'Your other medication okay? I grabbed everything I saw.'

'Yeah, it's all the daily stuff I'm supposed to take. There wasn't anything I was needed in hospital for anyway, waiting on test results and monitoring mostly. It's nice to have a change of scenery.'

I gave him a hug, trying to hide my horror at the bones that I could feel barely under the surface of his skin. 'You go rest, eat, whatever, and I'll go thieve. This place is well guarded and Sanjay's going to stay with you while I'm out. He's cool,' I added, seeing the reluctance cross Joss' face. 'He's a DJ.'

'Mad.'

That was all it took. Five minutes later I was trotting down the last flight of stairs with a mission to steal Oxycontins.

'Hey,' said Lorcan, appearing at the doorway as I opened it. He had agreed to come with me, thinking that we should all be in pairs as a safety measure.

'Hey back at you,' I said, giving him a tired smile. The full moon was pending and I could feel its presence in every cell of my body. We began walking towards the end of the alleyway, which was basking in orange sunlight despite the temperature being below 13 degrees Celsius. Berlin weather: weirder than Scotland.

'Heath explained the plan,' Lorcan said.

'Aye.' Given it was leading up to winter there was an unusually stunted full-moon cycle that lasted only two evenings. Heath wanted to strike once the second night was over, when the Laignach Faelad would be at their weakest and desperate to feed. The Rogues and I would also be disadvantaged, but we had Yu, Lorcan, Heath and the twins to stack our numbers. Fighting so close to the end of the full moon would force us all to remain in human form, which I thought was a clever strategic move given that we had proved better at hand-to-hand combat. So far.

'I think it's solid, with one exception,' he continued.

'And what's that?'

'You will be taking over Yu's position on the roof.'

'What?! Why? I have the most control. It makes sense for me to spearhead the charge.'

'You sound like Heath.'

'That's because he's right.'

'No, Yu said you're almost as good a shot as she is. We need you on the roof covering everyone.'

'On the roof and out of the action, right?'

'Tommi –'

He was cut off as a police car swerved into the alley leading to Phases, sirens blaring. It sped towards us at top speed, braking only at the last minute so it slid to a stop a few metres in front of us. Heath, Zillia, Gus and Clay peeled out of the apartment block's front door at the sound. Officer Dick Creuzinger stepped out of the driver's seat. I wasn't alarmed at the sight of him: that is until he raised his service weapon at me.

'Tommi Grayson, I need you to put your hands in the air and walk slowly towards me.'

Another officer stepped out of the car, thankfully gun free. I separated from Lorcan and did as he said, stepping in the direction of the car. 'Dick? What's this about?' I asked, still not taking the situation seriously.

'Just do as I say and keep walking towards me.'

'Officer,' came Heath's smooth and diplomatic tone from behind me, his German flawless, 'if you could be so kind as to tell us what's going on?'

'Sure,' said Dick, stepping out from behind the car door. In a flash he had my hands pinned behind my back as he slammed me down on to the bonnet of the car. Stars danced in front of my eyes at the harsh and unexpected nature of the impact.

'HEY!' I heard Lorcan shout. The sound of scuffled feet and grunts from behind me illustrated a struggle.

'Ouch,' I grumbled.

Dick demonstrated his compassion for my situation by lifting my head up and slamming it back down into the car again.

'Use your mentality. Cool down,' I said as my cheeks pressed up against the metal.

'You're under arrest, Miss Grayson.'

With that I felt the cold tingle of handcuffs as they clamped shut around my wrists. Fantastic. This was actually happening. I caught a glimpse of the others as Dick hauled me towards the back seat of the car. Lorcan looked furious and was being restrained by the powers of Heath and Gus combined. Heath was whispering madly in his ear as Lo continued to try and break free. I hoped it was something along the lines of 'beating a police officer to death will not help us. Or her'. I hoped.

'What are your grounds for arrest?' asked Zillia.

'You can find out the full details of that at the station. Good day.'

With that I was thrown in the car and driven down the alleyway to God knows where. Lorcan had finally managed to break free and took off after the car for three steps, before realising it was futile. He shouted something that I couldn't make out at first, given the thickness of the glass inside the windows of the vehicle.

'What did he say?' the other officer asked Dick.

'Full moon tonight,' he replied, shaking his head. 'Weird.'

'Very.'

My blood ran cold. 'Where are you taking me?'

Dick didn't even spare a look back as he answered. 'To LKA headquarters, where you're going to go through some extensive questioning.'

I gulped. Headquarters. A building full of live, breathing humans. A building that in a matter of hours would house a live werewolf. So much for secrets.

Chapter 17

'What's she in for?'

'Questioning.'

Officer Dieter Braun of Department 7 was peering through a small, glass window in the door to the interview room. His colleague Officer Dick Creuzinger had his back to the room as he flicked through a tiny notepad and examined his notes.

'Okay,' he said, turning to the older man, 'let's do this.'

'I don't exactly know what it is we're "doing" here, boss.'

'Just follow my lead.'

When they entered the room Tommi Grayson had a pair of heavy, black combat boots resting on the table at the centre of the room. She was leaning back in her chair, staring at the ceiling. Her head snapped in the direction of the two new occupants to the room, but she didn't change her position. Her sweater had been taken from her during processing in case it cloaked unseen weapons and she had her arms crossed over a tight, army green T-shirt with the words 'Not In This Lifetime' emblazoned across it in white print. The shirt was torn in places and splattered with paint in others. In the absence of an elastic she had twisted her long, blue hair back into a knot. Half of it had escaped the bind and was spilling around her face in strands.

Officer Creuzinger had been intrigued by her unusual appearance when they had initially met at the hospital. He wasn't distracted by her beauty this time. He saw what it was hiding underneath: a dangerous individual with dangerous secrets. He slapped a manila folder down on to the desk.

Tommi didn't flinch. She ignored the other officer as he sat down in the chair next to Dick. Instead, she kept her glare firmly focused on the man she had considered her friend. He returned the steely gaze as he spread his legs lazily in the chair. The room's blank, grey walls were as cold as the emotions of the individuals inside.

'How did you get those cuts?' started Officer Creuzinger.

She didn't even look at her hands and the dozens of scratches there, not to mention the faint bruising on her right hand. He also noted that she had a deep cut above her right eyebrow and several other serious ones that had been stitched up on her upper arms. What looked like a graze seemed to extend out from under her shirt and up her neck, finishing just below her chin.

'This may shock you,' she started, replying in Deutsch heavily affected by her Scottish accent, 'but I was arrested quite brutally by two Berlin detectives. Slammed on a car bonnet and all that. No rights read, no explanation.'

He snickered, seeming amused. 'Rights read? This isn't America.'

'You have no hope of saying we did all of this to you,' replied Officer Braun.

'No?' She removed her feet from the table and leaned forward. 'How about the bruising that's starting to form on my face here?'

Officer Creuzinger had the grace to look slightly embarrassed by this. It lasted only a second as his eyes returned to her hands. He noticed for the first time other scars, particularly two on her wrists that looked like identical bracelets. They were exactly where handcuffs would go.

'This isn't the first time you've been arrested,' he said.

She made a noise that sounded like a game show buzzer when a contestant was incorrect. 'Wrong, *Dick*. This is the first time I've been arrested. Shit, what's in that little folder of yours then? It's certainly not correct information on me.'

'Your wrists, those are scars from handcuffs.'

Her face darkened as she recalled the memory, before quietly replying. 'You didn't ask me whether I'd been in handcuffs before.'

He was confused, but her answer hinted at what he now suspected. She was involved in something bad. 'No, I didn't. But now I'd like to ask you where you were last night?'

'At Phases.'

'The whole night?'

'The whole night. Lorcan can testify to this.'

'You see, there was an incident at Mechtilde General. Do you know it?'

'You know I do. That's where we first met.'

'Yes, it's also where your "best friend" as you call him – Joss Jabour – was receiving treatment in the oncology ward. The same oncology ward that was destroyed last night in a violent rampage which left two nurses dead, one in a coma and several other staff and patients severely injured.'

She said nothing, continuing to stare at him blankly.

'Aren't you concerned about the fate of your friend? He was in that ward, after all.'

She said nothing.

'Perhaps it's because you already know what happened to him. Perhaps you already know who has him. Perhaps you know where he is.'

'And perhaps you'll get to the point sometime soon?' she retorted.

Officer Creuzinger slammed his hands on the desk and leaned forward, angry. 'His room was barricaded from the *inside*. Those men tore a whole ward apart to get in there. They destroyed the last week of security footage just to cover their tracks. They were after a seemingly innocent cancer patient who just so happens to be your pal. This is the second violent incident to happen in a hospital that has no history of anything like this happening before. Then you're found in the street right near where another child was reported missing just three hours after it happened. Burgermeister, my ass. I know that somehow you're at the centre of all this, Tommi.'

He was now standing over the table, looming down on the detainee as a vein pulsed in his forehead. His partner was looking at him with an expression of sincere concern. She spat her reply at the detective like venom.

'You know what I know, *Dick*? I know that I've been the victim of police brutality at the hands of you and your officer here. I know that I was brought in without any proper explanation and without an opportunity to call the lawyer I'm entitled to. I know that you're under a lot of pressure with your cases. Well, boo-fucking-hoo. I've been brought here on some bullshit hunches that you have no hope of backing up with any solid evidence and frankly? I'm done with you. I'm ready to be dismissed.'

'You're not going anywhere!'

'What the fuck can you possibly keep me here for?!' she shouted back. 'It's less than an hour until sunset and I shouldn't be here. I need to *not* be here!'

'Officer Creuzinger, can I have a word with you for a moment?' asked his colleague.

'WHAT?!'

'In private.'

He gave Tommi another piercing look, which she returned defiantly.

'Fine.'

The two detectives left the interview room as Tommi shouted behind them.

'LET ME GO! YOU CAN'T HOLD ME HERE, DICK!'

He didn't like the way she said his name: like she was using it as a curse. He was certain the word 'head' would follow every time she uttered it. Once out in the office, Dick stormed to his desk and threw himself into his chair. Frustrated, he dropped his head into his hands.

'What's going on in there, Dick?'

'I'm working on it, I just need –'

'Is this honestly all you have to go off? You can't drag some Scot in here like she's a career criminal over nothing. This is the damn girl we nearly shot on the street with the Indian guy the other night; you never even mentioned it was suspicious they were in the area until now. All you had to do was look at her face to realise she had no idea a kid had gone missing from there. Even if the parents are keeping it out of the press, she was as clueless as everyone else. C'mon, Dick, you know better than this. You *are* better than this. What's got a hold of you?'

The Child Protection Services Squad was positioned in a section of the LKAs that was separate from the rest of the building. It was small, yet it had its own interview room and another spare room with a couch, bed and TV to entertain young cases if they were brought in for a long period of time. It was the section of the station closest to the reception area, which was separated from it by a wall and a security door. That door burst open now as two men erupted into the room.

Officer Creuzinger and his colleague were the only members from the unit in the office, the others either having left for the day or being out in the field. The two men stormed into the empty space like they were ready to destroy an empire, which was a fitting description because they both looked like they were physically up for the task. Officer Creuzinger recognised the man at the front as Tommi's friend, Lorcan, who occasionally worked at Phases as a bouncer. The second man had tried to talk with him at the scene. If possible he was more intimidating than the other. While one was lean and muscular, this other was almost a hulking mass. He was a good two heads taller than Lorcan and the fabric of his coat seemed to defy physics as it resisted the stretch of the muscles underneath it. The other man's hair hovered just above his shoulders in thick strands tucked behind his ears.

'Officer Creuzinger, these are the two private detectives you wanted to meet with,' said Anne, the receptionist.

'Private detectives? We –'

'That's great, Anne, thank you,' Dick said, cutting off his colleague. She smiled and rushed out, leaving the group of four facing off against each other.

'You're from the club. You were with Tommi Grayson when we picked her up,' said Officer Braun. They gave no response.

'You're not private detectives. I know everyone licensed in this city. You used that to get back here.'

'Yes,' replied Lorcan. 'But since Tommi was arrested illegally we thought you'd prefer a visit from the two of us opposed to a visit from Kirk Rennex' legal team.'

'Kirk Rennex?'

'We have people in high places,' muttered the blond.

The officer gulped. Raising his hands in defeat as he turned to his boss, he said, 'Dick, I'm out. You're on your own on this one. I had nothing to do with this, okay?'

'Br–'

'I'm done for today.'

Backing away from the desk, he headed directly for the door that led to reception and ignored Dick's calls behind him. Officer Creuzinger was left alone with the two men in the squad room.

'Where is she?' asked Lorcan, the second they were alone. A muted crashing sound answered that question. It came from the interview room and the blond jogged over to the door, staring through the glass window.

'She hasn't changed yet,' he shouted over his shoulder. He frowned. 'It's dark outside. The moon is only minutes away, she should be beginning the shift.'

Lorcan let out a frustrated sigh. 'This is all your fault,' he said, poking the officer in the centre of his chest. Considerably shorter, he stumbled back, surprised.

'Hey, I'm a police officer, thank you very much. You don't lay a hand on me.'

'Like the way you laid a hand on Tommi? You *know* you're in the wrong now, just like you knew you were in the wrong the second you put handcuffs on her. Why else is it that we're standing here in your office without security called or a gun pulled?'

Officer Creuzinger had no response to that. Everything Lorcan had said was right. He was under incredible pressure to find out what happened to these children. He'd been working twenty-hour days and now it had led him to this. He'd drawn a connection between Tommi and the hospital, between Tommi and her missing friend. He'd read her file, or what little he could find on her courtesy of Dundee P.D. She had lost two good friends in a car accident several months earlier. Her mother too had perished in flash floods a year earlier. People close to her had a tendency to end up dead. Dick had a hunch. He knew she was hiding something and that she understood more than she was letting on. He knew she was involved in a part of this, if not all of it. His hunches had never led him astray before.

'I'll admit I haven't gone about this in the best way,' he started, 'but she has something to do with what happened at Mechtilde General last night. She knows what happened to the missing patient, Joss Jabour. And I don't know how but she knows what is happening to those kids.' As Lorcan stared at him, impassive, a realisation hit Dick. 'And you know too? Huh. Of course you do. There's probably nothing she doesn't tell you two about or get your help with. You know just as much about this case as she does, if not more.'

'Where's your proof, bacon?' called the giant from his position across the room.

'Heath,' Lorcan, scolded, shaking his head.

'What did you call me?'

'Listen, officer. We will help you in every way we can with your investigation and locating Joss Jabour. We will help you bring these people to justice. You have my word on that.'

Dick examined his face, resenting his control of the situation. He looked for all the usual tells he had catalogued in his years of experience interviewing criminals. Lorcan meant what he said.

'But right now,' he continued, 'we need to get Tommi out of here.'

'I can't let you just stroll out of here,' he growled. Yet even as he said it, Dick picked up on something: a sense of urgency both Tommi and Lorcan seemed to share. 'Why? What's going to happen "now" that you're so afraid of?'

'It's not us that should be afraid, Babe, it's you,' said Heath. The blond's eyes danced with humour, but his expression was dead serious.

'If you make one more swine re –' A woman's scream interrupted Dick. He looked at the door, which Heath was now blocking. 'What's going on in there? She's alone.'

'Like I said, we need to get out of here *now*, officer. Is there a back exit?'

'Ah, yes,' he said, distracted. 'You can take the fire exit but –' Another scream.

'She's demonstrating incredible control,' said Heath as he looked into the room again, this time like a scientist examining a fascinating experiment.

'I told you,' said Lorcan, stepping forwards. 'She had total recall from day one.'

'That's quite the foundation to build on. She should have shifted by now.'

Lorcan joined Heath at the viewing window, watching Tommi inside. 'She's holding it back.'

'Impossible.'

'Look at her, Heath. Look at what you're seeing.'

There was a long silence as his companion did so. Lorcan gestured to Dick to unlock the room and he did so all the while considering their curious conversation. Opening the door a few inches, Lorcan stuck his head into the room.

'Tommi?'

'Lo!'

Dick noticed her voice was strained, as if she was in pain and had been puffing.

'How you doing?'

'Barely holding on.'

'We're going to get you out of here. Heath is bringing the van around and it's reinforced but –'

'What?!'

'Can you hold on until the club?'

She grunted in frustration and let out a small cry. 'ARRRGGHH GOD DAMN BAMPOTS AR. Hergh, yup. I can. Hurry though.'

'I'll grab you in a few seconds.'

'S-s-sure.'

He popped his head out and closed the door. Heath had already disappeared to bring their vehicle around the back. The fire escape door had been propped open and when a honk sounded from outside, Lorcan checked to confirm it was his friend. He left the door unguarded and Dick took the opportunity to answer his own questions by peering into the interview room. What he saw was beyond his wildest nightmares.

The table was split in half, the chairs twisted, and across the other side of the room Tommi had her back to him and her hands placed on the wall in front of her. She was concentrating on her feet and appeared to be exaggerating her breathing as she gripped the wall. As he watched, her hands shifted from a normal woman's to an animal's. The colour of her skin – already dark – grew darker until it was almost black and hair began sprouting from her forearms. In width and length her arms grew as they transformed into monstrous limbs. Her fingers stretched out, growing like they were being pulled by some invisible force. The tips sharpened to reveal razor sharp claws that dug into the surface of the wall. And just as soon as it happened – it stopped. The process reversed and he watched the claws, the muscles, the fur, fade and shrink away until it revealed a normal arm again.

He was ripped away from the door as Lorcan returned to the room, tossing him aside. Lorcan was aghast: anger and fear radiated from him. It was now very clear to Dick that this is what they had been talking about. This is the 'thing' they had tried to avoid him seeing. Lorcan looked down at the officer, unsure of what to do. He considered him for a long moment, frowning with concentration.

'I can tell you what you've seen just now. To do so, you have to come with us. Bring your files and we can solve everything tonight.'

Dick, a slave to his own curiosity, was up and scooping his copies of the most valuable information into a box on his desk. He met Lorcan at the fire exit. Tommi was with him and she looked terrible. Despite the Berlin weather, sweat was pouring off her and her shirt was almost torn in half. Agony was etched across her face and she was gripping her own arms so tightly she was drawing blood. It snaked down her arms, mixing with the beads of sweat. She took one look at Dick and turned away, burying her face into Lorcan's chest. He had his arm around her as they moved outside to the van that was idling in the loading dock.

'Keep him away from me,' she said through gritted teeth. 'I'm afraid I'll rip him apart and that's something I'd rather do when I'm human.'

'Me too,' he replied.

As the door slid back Dick was suddenly unsure as to whether he would be joining Tommi and Lorcan in the back of the van.

'You're in the front with me, ham wallet,' called Heath from the driver's seat.

Hopping in the passenger side with the box balanced on his lap, Officer Dick Creuzinger felt like he was sinking in quicksand as they sped away from LKAs's headquarters. His hunch was right: she had been hiding something. Yet that 'something' was not only completely out of Dick's jurisdiction and area of expertise, but it was completely out of this world. He had always been an inquisitive man: you had to be in this line of work. He had always pushed and asked the tough questions. Now he was forcing himself to ask the toughest questions of all: what the hell had he gotten himself into? And, more importantly, would he live to see this night through? Glancing up at the throbbing full moon in the sky, for once he wasn't sure if he wanted to know the answers.

Chapter 18

'I killed him,' I said, swallowing a bite of lemon meringue pie and placing a finger on the photo of baldy.

'What?'

Officer Dick Creuzinger was beyond shocked. His mouth and eyes were mimicking a disbelieving expression.

'Whe –'

'Oh, and him,' I interrupted, spotting a picture of the ginger.

'*Unbelievable*,' he said, shaking his head. Heath was quietly laughing in the background.

'But look! That's the mallet guy, Lorcan killed that one.'

Lo seemed just as uncomfortable as the officer, who was giving him a considered stare.

'There's a trio to mark off the hit list,' said Heath, slapping his hands together. 'How shall we divvy the rest of them out?'

Sucking the last of the lemony goodness from the spoon dangling from my mouth, I felt the presence of the room forming at my back. We all stared at the members of the Laignach Faelad in front of us. The twins had arrived during the second night of the full moon and between them, the Rogues, a handful of Askari, Heath, Lorcan, Joss, and our makeshift ally in Dick the training room had amassed a significant posse. While the werewolves among us had spent half the day recovering, the daylight dwellers had made the most of their time. With our information and Dick's combined resources, we had pictures of the ten Laignach Faelad stuck up on the wall. Their stats – height, estimated weight, names that we knew – were on Post-it notes next to each image. Heath had Askari watching the warehouse 24/7 since he'd arrived and had gathered a handy portfolio of surveillance images that broke down the various entries and exits. He also had a blueprint of the property in case there were any hidden surprises we needed to look out for.

'Calling dibs on him.' Heath pressed his finger against the image of the biggest, toughest-looking guy. His height was listed as 6 foot 11 and weight somewhere around 120 kilograms.

'The sniper, Tommi, will be on the roof here,' said Yu, pointing at a building that sat next to the warehouse and slightly above it. 'Some of those windows could be open so you won't have to shoot through glass.'

'There are still obstacles. That's a distance of what, seven to eight hundred metres? At night?' asked Gus.

Yu and I shared a look. 'It can be done,' she said.

The details were coming together now, yet to say things had gotten off to a shaky start would be like comparing a volcanic eruption to a fart. I'd managed to control the shift until Lorcan and Heath were able to get me back to the club. Yet the second the door to my cell was locked, my wolf tore through my human body with an intensity I hadn't experienced since my first transformation in New Zealand.

Fighting the full moon made me aggressive and it had been a rough night as I paced the perimeter of my confines, growling and snarling as I waited for the hours to tick by. But my evening was nothing compared to what Officer Creuzinger experienced. He learned about our world first-hand. Everything he had believed in, everything he had based his reality on for the past thirty-eight years came crashing down around him as he was led into a den of werewolves.

Joss and Lorcan told me they had done most of the explaining under the guidance of Jenica the Askari who – I was shocked to learn – also made Dick sign a release form. In his own blood. Joss had been made to sign one too and essentially it guaranteed that if they were to talk of the Treize or the supernatural world to anyone, their lives would be forfeit. I had mixed feelings about this, given neither of them had willingly been exposed. It was through me, and knowing me, that they had been dragged into the midst.

Dick had surprised all of us though. He had adapted, he had asked questions and he had learned from what people were telling him. Sometimes you have to blow up the box and its complete annihilation had reinvigorated Dick. The Laignach Faelad had eluded his capture because they were something beyond this world: something superhuman. Now he had superhuman resources to combat them and I could see a manic sense of opportunity dancing behind his eyes. He could still bring them to justice and now he was better equipped to do it than ever before.

Dick didn't rest. He spent the night and most of the morning analsying the information we had. He disappeared around 9 a.m. and after a good five hours he returned with case files, maps, blueprints and victim information that was invaluable to bringing the Laignach Faelad down.

He felt guilty about my heavy-handed arrest, I could tell. At first he hadn't been sure how to handle that. Now that he knew what I was he didn't want to make me mad. He'd wisely stayed on the other side of the room, working with the Askari and casting nervous glances my way when he could spare them. It wasn't until I had eaten three raw steaks and drunk a litre of sugary soft drink that he dared approach me. Joss had been sitting with me while I ate and he discreetly left the table. Dick seemed hesitant to take his seat at first, but fought against his better instincts to run screaming from the room.

'You still mad at me?'

I gave a bitter smile as I wiped the remaining steak blood off my hands with a serviette. 'I don't get mad Dick, I get stabby.'

His eyes widened in horror. That is, right up until the moment I started laughing. 'I'm sorry,' I wheezed. 'I just couldn't help it. It was too easy.'

'Um, right,' he chuckled nervously, still unsure whether I was joking or not.

'Naw, seriously, it's all good, Dick. You acted like a complete and utter gobshite, but I'm going to look past that. We need you. We need your information and we need your resources. Plus, I've got to respect anyone who can take to all of this the way you have. It's no easy thing.'

He nodded, seeming more at ease. 'Thank you. And I do apologise for . . . you know.'

'Aye, I do.'

That was all it took. He didn't bring it up again and neither did I. We had bigger fish to fry.

'I'm still unsure how this whole thing works.' He sighed, gesturing around the room.

'Werewolfism?'

'No,' he said, laughing nervously. 'I saw that up close. What I meant was these Laignach Faelad creeps. From what I understand, someone *made* them. Or attempted to?'

'Basically, yes. It seems there was a type of profile this person or persons was after: young, lo-fi, psychotic men with a history of violence. My half-brother would have been an ideal candidate.'

'Would have?'

'He's dead.'

'Let me guess, you killed him?'

'It was self-defence.'

Dick let out a shaky breath of air. 'Alright then, have we started looking into politicians? See if there's any red flags?'

'I – huh? Politicians? They don't make great candidates, Dick. Too high-profile.'

'No,' he chuckled, 'not as Faelad: as the people pulling the strings.'

I blinked at him, still not sure I followed his logic.

'According to legend and the past experience your people have had with them, they fought for kings right?'

'Right,' I nodded.

'Kings don't exist now and neither do "ancient kingdoms". Who are they working for? The children are coming from within the Berlin city borders, so I think it's safe to say the "kingdom" now – well, it's Berlin. Whoever has struck a deal with them has interests deeply invested in this city.'

'Like what? No one is going to battle here, they're not fighting over land titles or a holy war. What could the Laignach Faelad offer them?'

'Exactly,' Dick said, clicking his fingers with excitement. I could practically see the thrill of the investigation pulsing through his veins. 'These aren't the same Faelad as before, they're modern and they're different. We have to think that way too: update what we know. Just because the price is the same, that doesn't mean what they can do for this mystery "king" is the same either.'

Heath had wandered over as we talked, looking thoughtful as Dick laid out his reasoning. He met my gaze and nodded while he rubbed his blond beard in what looked like a philosophical gesture. Joss too looked curious, joining in conversation with Dick.

There had been ten members to start with. Lorcan and I had killed three of them, which left seven for us to take down. With the addition of Heath and the twins, our numbers had gone up. Dick and the Askari were no match for the Laignach Faelad and would be staying at a distance while Lo, Gus, Dolly, Yu, Clay, Zillia, Heath, Jakea and Jaira headed into the warehouse for combat.

I wouldn't be joining them. Instead I would be situated on a cozy roof nearby with a CheyTac M200 and watching my friends' backs. My orders were simple: seconds before the Rogues would penetrate the premises, I was to start taking the Irish fucks down with shots to the head. Once they were inside, I was to provide back-up shots if necessary.

The plan had been conceived by all of us, but the part about me staying out of the action was all Lorcan. He had already talked everybody around to it before I was arrested.

The only person who seemed opposed to the idea was Heath, but he was outnumbered. I couldn't be sure of Lorcan's motivations and I couldn't get him alone to ask him outright. Sure, none of us had spare minutes alone in the lead up to the attack. Yet he was doing a very good job of staying busy. The only person who had any time alone was Zillia, who was occupied making preparations with fill-in staff to guarantee Phases was running and everything appeared normal on our night of the mission.

Joss, for the meantime, was remaining missing. Dick, Zillia and I had decided this was the best course of action until the Laignach Faelad were nothing but decapitated corpses. It was rough. Joss and I both knew his parents would be suffering by not knowing what had happened to him, but there wasn't another option. Medically we had everything vital – meds, painkillers that Dolly had slung, and a comfortable place for him to rest. We also had excitement. I hadn't seen Joss' spirits this high since before he had been re-diagnosed. He practically barnacled himself to the Askari as he tried to learn everything he could about the current situation. They had indulged him at first, but after a few days he was sharing ideas and contributing facts like a supernatural secretary. After a group analysis of the plan once more, I joined him on a beanbag as he pored over a stack of paperwork.

'Hey,' he said, not looking up.

'Hey. What's all this?'

'Victim profiles.'

'Oh?'

Joss lifted his head up from a newspaper article he was highlighting. 'I was thinking about what Dick said, about the Laignach Faelad.'

'He's said a lot about them in the past forty-eight hours. You'll have to be more specific.'

'*Specifically* about orders. According to tradition and experience with them in the past, they fight for a king who pays them with the flesh of babes from his kingdom.'

'You're speaking like a textbook.'

'Heath said in the meeting you brought up the question of who they could be fighting for now. Dick's following that same thread.'

'Aye, he's a good cop and it's a strong lead given that ancient kings and valuable territory aren't as easy to come by.'

'Right. And there's the question of who resurrected the ancient rituals to try and recreate the Faelad.'

'That too.'

'I think the answers are here, with the victims. They're connected, Tommi. The victims have to be connected somehow. They were selected.'

I couldn't entirely keep up with the leaps he was making, but I was along for the ride. 'You sure they weren't just like, "Hey! Baby! Dinner is served boys!"'

Joss gave me an exasperated look. 'Then why wouldn't they take more than one baby from the maternity ward? That's your baby buffet right there, but they take only Trshyna Croad.'

'Huh. You're right. That's the place you would be wrapping babies in napkins and shoving them into your metaphorical purse.'

'Here.' He pushed a stack of papers into my chest. 'We have an hour and a half before you have to start getting ready for the warehouse. I could use the extra set of eyes.'

'Homework? I dunno . . .'

I would have preferred to be practising with something sharp and pointy. One glare from my best friend was enough to silence me on the subject. I grabbed the papers without a word and began reading through the info. It wasn't gibberish, but it may as well have been. The babies were all different. They had different ages, different nationalities, different blood types. They were too young to have had enough time to develop similarities with another human – let alone a group of humans. I had a jolt when I reminded myself that these completely innocent, harmless children were all dead. Goosebumps ran down my arms as I considered their fate. It had nothing to do with the babies. If we were to find this pattern Joss thought existed, we would find it among the parents.

Placing the babies' information to the side, I began sorting through the tax records of one Jacob Tixo: a single dad whose daughter had been taken from the duplex I scouted. He was an accountant at a major firm and made serious coin. The next parents were a lesbian couple. One worked as a cleaner and the other as a schoolteacher. Then there was a stay-at-home father and his IT consultant wife. A property developer and a vintage boutique owner. A barista. A plumber and a taxi driver. My eye caught on the annual income of a corporate lawyer.

'Holy shit, Joss, you should see how much this woman gets paid a year.'

'Mmm-hmm.'

'I know the –'

My words ended abruptly. Paid. The Laignach Faelad didn't work for free: they couldn't. That's what Dick and Joss were repeating over and over: they were paid in babies from the kingdom of their employer. Joss was right. The victims weren't random: they were the children of people who were employed by the monster behind all this. Yet how could they be? We had cleaners and developers and lawyers and plumbers ... I frantically grabbed the papers I had dropped as I scanned through them and began scrutinising the figures again. Jacob Tixo handled two major accounts at his firm and one of them was the Rennex Corp. Flicking through the pages I stopped when I got to Nicollin Proverst, currently employed on an 18-month contract at ... the Rennex Corp. The plumber was employed by Wingar Industries, an offshoot of ... the Rennex Corp. The barista worked in an in-house café directly underneath the headquarters of ... the Rennex Corp. I didn't have to start digging into the employment addresses of the cleaner to know who the offices she cleaned belonged to: the Rennex Corp.

'There are no fucking coincidences,' I muttered.

'Uh-huh. Wait. What did you say?'

'You were right, Joss. The parents are the ones who are connected, even if it's not obvious at first.'

'You found something?!'

His excited tone drew the interest of three nearby Askari and the twins, who had been sharpening weapons nearby. They made their way over slowly, watching my facial expression. I imagined it was blank, because I was still slightly in shock. I never expected to know the person who was responsible for all this – let alone have had him within killing distance. Hell, he had given me *pie*. Kirk. Rennex. A man who had done remarkably well in the past few years, despite how much the rest of Europe was suffering amid the economic crisis. Now we knew why.

'The Rennex Corporation,' I said through gritted teeth. Anyone who hadn't been paying attention certainly was now as the room drew closer towards Joss and I. 'That's who everyone works for. It's all here, some six people so far. I guarantee if you start looking at the others, their wages will be coming directly from the Rennex Corp or a company under their umbrella. But it's them. It's all them. Or should I say, *him.*'

'Who?' asked Clay.

'Kirk Rennex,' Lorcan supplied.

Slowly, every head in the room turned towards Zillia. Her mouth had popped open in a small 'O' formation before she giggled. She did it again, placing a hand to her throat in surprise. 'I'm sorry, I just –' giggle – 'but Kirk? The Rennex Corp? You can't be serious.' The smile soon dropped from her face as she looked more closely at mine. The Askari had grabbed the documents and were consulting amongst each other. Joss was nodding slightly. 'No,' she said. 'Not a chance. Just because he owns the warehouse that's no reason to jump to conclusions.'

'It's not, but this might be.' Heath strutted into the room with such angry authority I was certain storm clouds would follow. He made a beeline straight for Zillia and shoved a leaflet at her so hard she stumbled backwards. Dolly caught her, giving Heath a venomous look.

'What's this?' she asked, still shocked by his aggressive actions.

'Read it,' he said. 'Out loud. So everyone can hear.'

She snatched the leaflet from him. 'Wicked Winter Warehouse Welcoming.'

'Go on.'

'With winter approaching, burn up the dancefloor with one final blow out. Free entry. First two drinks complimentary. Line-up includes Tissues For Issues, Risco, The Parrot DJs, Hemale and Skull Crossbones.'

'And the address?'

'The address is . . . it's –'

'WHERE IS IT?!' Heath screamed.

'It's at the warehouse.'

'That's right. *Tonight*. These are being handed out all over Berlin. Those are popular performers. Free entry. Free drinks. There's even a fucking hashtag. A great show by all accounts. It also means the warehouse we were supposed to attack tonight is going to be FULL OF FUCKING CIVILIANS, ZILLIA!'

She jumped. 'I . . . I . . .'

Yu was examining the leaflet. 'It says doors opened an hour ago.'

'It's brilliant,' I said. 'Incredibly evil, but brilliant. They're making a strategic gamble, betting that we won't go racing into battle when there are hundreds of innocent people in the crossfire.'

'Exactly,' nodded Heath. 'My question is, how did they know we were coming tonight? Hmm? Anything to contribute, Zillia?'

Silence.

'These went out two hours ago. Strangely, only an hour or so after you were on your own, downstairs at the club, finding staff. Or so you said.'

More silence.

'Zillia.' Lorcan's calm yet stern voice cut through the quiet. 'Have you spoken to Kirk?'

'He has nothing to do with this, I honestly thought –'

Lorcan cut off her barely audible tone with his own, harsher one. 'ZILL.'

'I spoke to him for five minutes,' she whispered. 'He called to come by the club and I tried to say I was busy but he wanted to see me and I wanted to see him and . . . and we were talking. And I was just so worried that there would be accusations and I wanted to clear it up so I asked him about the address and if he knew the people there and –'

'What did he say? "Yes, honey, that's where my army is. Sorry I didn't mention it sooner"?' hissed Heath.

'I didn't tell him they were werewolves, I just said they were bad people. He seemed shocked. He didn't know anything about it.'

'I'd say he knew they were werewolves given he employed them. Probably created them too,' said Dick.

'Fucking brilliant,' muttered Dolly.

We all jumped as a massive crashing sound rung out through the room. Heath had flipped the weapons table and everything that was on it halfway across the space.

Lorcan looked like he wasn't far off doing the same thing. Instead he said,

'You've blown it, you must know that? Any element of surprise we had or chance of sparing bystanders and future victims is gone now. We were already at a disadvantage numbers wise. They need those babies tonight. Who knows how many more, Zillia.'

Tears had begun streaming down her face and she clasped a

hand to the top of her forehead, equally horrified and still in shock. 'I . . .'

'We must go tonight,' said Jakea.

'Or they will only get stronger,' added Jaira.

'This is going to be a brutal and bloody fight,' I said.

'We can't risk putting people in danger like that,' urged Joss.

Sanjay was shaking his head. 'What's the alternative? Leave them undisturbed to go and kill more babies? It isn't a quick dea–'

'Okay! I get that, but we're talking hundreds of people in the crossfire. Possibly thousands given what a draw these DJs are and the Rennex guy's disposable income –'

'We must do this! End it tonight!' shouted Gus.

'Actually,' said Lorcan, 'this could work in our favour too. Yes, they know we're coming. And yes, they'll know we're in the building the second we enter. But those people provide us with cover as much as they will the Laignach Faelad. They want to disappear into a crowd? Well, so can we.'

The room fell quiet as we considered Lorcan's statement. I didn't know what to think. There had been so many revelations in the past flurry of hours that I was overwhelmed with information. I was anxious about what was to come. I was nervous about our best-laid plans falling apart. And I was filled with pity as I watched Zillia's world collapse on itself.

She had sunk down to her knees at the edge of the group, unnoticed and hugging herself as the rest of us tried to work out what to do. She had been betrayed by the man she loved. Worse, her faith in him was going to lead to a loss of life, no two ways about it. She had unknowingly enabled a monster and his monster posse.

I slowly got up from my spot on the beanbag and made my way over to her. Crouching down, she jumped as I slowly placed my hand on her shoulder. Her eyes were wide and glassy as they continued to fill with tears. I wrapped one arm around her and she leaned into me with relief.

'He's right,' said Yu after a long while. 'We need to attack tonight. It's the only way to stop them getting stronger and more children dying.'

'They won't expect it,' added Dick. 'We have that going for us. With such a last-minute shake-up I'm sure they'd expect anyone to wait. Regroup.'

'No,' said Lorcan. 'They'll expect us to come.'

Heath had cooled his raging and returned to the gang. He and Lorcan shared a look that I didn't understand until he spoke up.

'But we go anyway.'

Neither of them looked happy about it. A sense of reluctance was heavy in the room. It was overpowering. Clay had kneeled down beside me as we helped lift Zillia up and over to a couch. I watched as he eased her down on to the surface, placing a blanket over her shaking body. Tattoos snaked up his arms, but there was in one in particular that I was drawn to. On his forearm was a heart pierced with a dagger. A scroll was wrapped around the body of the weapon with three words boldly standing out against background: death before dishonour.

Chapter 19

I was invisible. Dressed head-to-toe in grey, even my blue hair was hidden from the world under a grey beanie. I matched the concrete of the rooftop I was lying on perfectly. My rifle was also spray-painted varying shades of grey. Even with werewolf eyes it would have been difficult – almost impossible – to spot me lying flat on my stomach, spread-eagle. I had been in this position for three hours, watching as the Laignach Faelad's warehouse filled up with hundreds of bodies. These people had no idea what they were walking into. I did. I had seen normal security guards and staff mingling with the were-wolves, clueless about what they were. I had also established my first targets: two of the Faelad who were positioned discreetly at opposite ends of the building. They were also the furthest away at some 900 m. Yet if I could take them out I could make the Rogues' entrance into the building a hell of a lot easier.

From this distance it would be like lobbing a round on their heads. There were going to be limbs flying apart and pieces everywhere. The least I could hope for was that it would disperse the crowd. I also had to be quick about it, picking which one to kill first and then moving to the second fast. Yu had taught me well and I had my mark – a blond, lanky were-wolf – in my scope. On a small notepad next to me I used the ABC to determine the exact distance and coordinates of my second target. The idea was I could re-aim and fire before he was alerted to the death of his colleague by the screams of witnesses. I dialled left for winds, I got my bearings, my Coriolis was correct with my latitude, I got my barometric pressure. I was ready to make the shot. Thankfully it was a still night, with only a slight breeze. Any humidity would have had to be taken into account also, but with the season that wasn't an issue.

'You need me to remove the muzzle break for you?'

Speaking of issues ... Heath had slipped on to the rooftop behind me. I knew I locked the stairwell door, yet locked doors weren't much of a barrier for someone like him. I had heard Heath the moment he began working his way up the building, so I didn't flinch at his sudden appearance. He also wasn't stupid. He kept low to the ground so as not to blow my cover and positioned himself against a massive air-filtering unit. I ignored his movements and kept my eyes focused on my targets.

'You only remove the muzzle break if you're trying to clean it. Otherwise you could fuck up the crown and that fucks up the barrel's flight and *that,* in turn, fucks up my flight,' I replied.

'Very good,' he said, sounding not at all surprised.

'You think Yu and Lorcan would have sent me up here with this kind weaponry if I wasn't capable? I don't need your little tests, Heath.'

'Okay, okay. Making conversation 's all.'

'Right.'

There was a long moment before we spoke again. I broke the silence. 'Don't you have somewhere to be?'

'I'll meet up with the others in a minute,' he said, not fazed. 'I came to give you these.'

I looked at the gift in his extended hand. 'Is that –'

'The 372 grain armour-piercing round that can punch through one inch of 500 Burnell at a hundred yards, pushing out at 3,150 feet per second? If that was your question then yes would be your answer. One shot, one kill. That's the motto of Marine snipers.'

My eyes were caught on the ammunition as I hesitated taking it. My CheyTac was presently loaded with a 419 grain round that was good. With a solid copper-nickel, it flew straight and it hit true. But the damage I could do with the 372 . . .

'Isn't it a little late in the game for an equipment swap?'

'And it's only getting later every second you waste thinking about whether or not to take these. Ask yourself, what's going to cause the most destruction? These aren't normal targets you're taking out.'

I gulped. He was right. 'Fine,' I conceded, snatching the ammunition and carefully loading it into the rifle.

'This is as close as you can get to a decapitation. Not as fun, but effective. Balance flight technology, baby.'

'Don't call me baby,' I muttered absent-mindedly as I readjusted my weapon and recalibrated my targets. I repeated Yu's words to myself. Think calm. Think sober. Wait for the right moment, then take your shot.

'I've been thinking about you lately.'

I snorted. 'Puhlease. You think about me as much as you do money in a birthday card. What do you want, Heath?'

'He's worried about you getting blood drunk.'

'What?'

'You're wondering why he's got you up here, away from the action, when you're one of the best fighters.'

' I . . .' I couldn't deny it. That's exactly what I had been thinking repeatedly, even more so now that I was up here and looking at the scene before us. 'It had crossed my mind.'

Heath took my admission as a sign to shift from his crouched position to sitting. 'Like I said, he's worried you'll get blood drunk.'

'What?'

'Personally, I think that can be a good thing. Besides, you're a long way off that.'

'What does that even mean, blood drunk? Lorcan has only ever been worried about me getting the standard kind of drunk. The Scottish kind of drunk.'

'It's an old term we used to throw around to describe someone who is overcome with the heat of battle. They'd get intoxicated by the killing.'

I let that sink in. 'How could he possibly think that? I've only killed people that had to be killed.'

'Wolves that *needed* to be killed, I agree. Lorcan has always had a faulty moral compass in my opinion.'

'Why? Because he defected to the Custodians instead of bro-ing out with you after Amos' death?'

'He didn't tell you everything.'

I gritted my teeth. 'I know what you're doing Heath, so stop trying to drive a wedge between Lorcan and me. You recruited him, he served you successfully for centuries, and now he doesn't want to anymore. You're taking this worse than a teenage break-up.'

Silence. There was nothing but silence for a lengthy period. I caught the faintest scent of tobacco on the air and I sniffed. My head snapped in Heath's direction. Sure enough, there he was rolling a cigarette. With the amount of people and smells coming from the warehouse below, there was no way he would blow my position with the scent. Instead I watched with envy as he meticulously prepared it. As he was running his tongue along the paper he looked up, catching my eye. I quickly looked away.

'Would you like me to roll you one as well?'

'No,' I said, trying to sound disinterested.

'Are you sure about that? Don't want to take the edge off?'

'I quit.'

'Ah, right. The friend with cancer currently sitting in a geta-way vehicle around the block.' Heath lit the cigarette. 'I won't tell if you don't?'

'No,' I replied firmly, ignoring his devilish grin. He consulted his watch before leaning back, cigarette between his lips.

'Why did you turn down the twins?' he asked.

'Simple: I don't want to live forever.'

'That's it?'

'And I don't do well following orders.'

'Especially in the context of an eternity. Shame.' He breathed out a cloud of smoke.

'Why do you care? You must know the only reason the PG wanted me is to trick Lorcan back into joining.'

His quiet chuckle confirmed my suspicions. 'You think that's the only reason the Praetorian Guard would want you? You mightn't be "blood drunk" but you're a killing machine, Tommi.'

'Stop it, you're turning me on,' I replied sarcastically.

'But there's a difference to being a killing machine and being able to see the bigger picture. You investigate as much as you annihilate, which is something far more valuable to the Guard than another mindless soldier.'

I considered him for a moment, judging the enthusiasm with which he was speaking. 'It was you, wasn't it?'

He just grinned bigger.

'You're the one who flagged me for recruitment.'

'Case and point,' Heath replied, winking.

'All those boys that maul the young cuties,' I muttered.

'What was that?'

'Nothing. You think you're so fucking charming, winking and grinning at how clever you are.'

'Aren't I though? The Lorcan factor was only one reason to recruit you, and not even a deciding one. Your skill set is considerable already, but it's the exponential growth of your abilities and control that got my attention. Lorcan can try and hide your talents all he wants, but the Praetorian Guard wants to give them their moment in the sun.'

'And utilise them for their own means?'

'Naturally.'

'The answer is still no.'

He opened his mouth to continue but the light on his watch flashed suddenly. He consulted it briefly, before stubbing out the cigarette on the concrete.

'We'll continue this chat later,' he said, crouching on all fours. 'And during that conversation I will tell you all about the Ihi pack's history, something I'm betting Lorcan has also failed to mention.'

I narrowed my eyes at him, examining his face in search of the lie. There was no lie there. He must have registered my own surprise as he paused when he reached the stairwell door. 'You should ask yourself, if a relationship is all about sharing secrets and bodily fluids, why are you receiving more of one than the other? I don't need to drive a wedge between you two. He seems to already be doing that himself with what he keeps *not* telling you. Question my motivations all you want, but maybe you should also be questioning his.'

He knew.

Heath *knew* about Lorcan and me.

There wasn't a sassy reply waiting on the tip of my tongue as I watched open-mouthed as Heath sprinted past the stairwell and to the opposite side of the roof. He leapt off the side of the building without a second look back. I was positive it hadn't been Lorcan who told him and since I hadn't said a word, Heath had deduced the true nature of our 'friendship' all on his own. The way he had dropped that knowledge bomb made me think he had known for a while, at least since he had been here with the Rogues. Yet no one else knew. Lo hadn't been reprimanded. No harsh consequences had been dealt out. Heath had kept quiet. What was he playing at?

There was too much to think about. And now wasn't the time to think about it. Shifting my focus back to the scene below, I tried to get my head back in the game. My targets were exactly where I had left them. In the distance a car horn tooted twice, then once, then twice again. In a night pulsing with background noise and calamity, those sounds distinctly stood out. That was the signal we had discussed. I took a deep breath, held it, and fired. My body jolted back slightly as the gun released its present.

It was a hit. I watched the chaos through the scope as the once blond and lanky werewolf exploded in a cloud of body parts and blood. Taking only a moment to check I was successful, I swivelled over to my next victim who was just beginning to realise something had happened. His head shot in the direction of the screams, and I knew he registered both the sound of the gun and the smell of blood in the air. His body tensed for action, but it never got any further than that as I unloaded a round. This shot wasn't as perfect as the first, as I missed the centre of his head by an inch or two. He was hit in the neck, which did the job just as well and I watched his twitching body separate entirely from its command centre.

I zoomed the scope in the direction of the entrances, catching only a glimpse of Gus and Dolly at the back of the Rogues as they swept into the building. People were running screaming in every direction and they were having a hard time moving against the sea of partiers. Once they were inside, I lost sight of them behind the walls of the warehouse. I moved from window to window, trying to catch a view of my friends heading into battle. What I saw instead was one of the Laignach Faelad picking up an axe as Yu moved towards him. He was in a clear line of sight and I set up the shot. I didn't have time to make calculations: I just went off instinct. The window shattered as the bullet punctured it and then the skull of the werewolf. Yu was splattered with blood as his body evaporated. She looked stunned for a moment, peering out the window. She couldn't see me, but she raised her hand in a mock salute before moving on to the next target. I had done everything I could. It was time for me to meet up with Joss and get the hell out of there. Packing my CheyTac and equipment into a shoulder case in a matter of seconds, I hit the stairwell running. Bursting out of the apartment block, I was caught up in the crowd of people rushing away from the venue as quickly as they could.

It went against all my better instincts to go with them, and I cast a nervous glance backwards as I was bustled along with the throng of bodies. It was the smallest of movements, but I saw a security guard rushing around the side of the building with a tiny, wriggling bundle wrapped in a blanket. The rasping of a child was all it took to have me knocking people aside as I pushed back to the warehouse. He didn't see me and I sprinted after him, frantically trying to dodge partygoers as I dived into the thrall after him. I was right on his heels, but I stumbled the second I was inside.

It was almost completely dark except for a pulsing blue light that danced over everything. I winced as a flashing strobe kicked into gear, obscuring my vision. Placing a hand over my eyes to block the obstruction, I stumbled in the general direction I thought he had gone. Unbelievably there were still humans inside, dancing and laughing and screaming along with the heavy doof-doof-doof of the dance music. As I weaved through the sea of moving bodies, I caught the back of the guard's head and made a beeline for him. He paused at a door, wrenching it open and sprinting down a flight of stairs. I was just about to follow him when I felt eyes on me and turned to see a tall, burly man smiling. His face flashed in and out of focus with the rhythm of the lights and I couldn't be sure if I was seeing fangs or normal teeth. I guessed I would find out, and I turned away, dashing after the guard. At the base of the stairs was a room that could be described as ordinary in every way except for one thing: it reeked with the unmistakable stench of death. I had exploded into the middle of the scene and the security guard spun around at the sound of my entrance.

'*Who are you?*'

'Uh . . .'

'WHO?!' came another voice, alerting me to the presence of a member of the Laignach Faelad huddled in the darkest corner of the room. He was covered in blood, his own, and clutching his stomach in a way that indicated he was trying to keep what was inside from spilling out. A normal human wouldn't have had long for this world, but this was no ordinary human. His eyes were desperate and feral as he looked up at me from behind strands of oily, black hair. Another series of cries from the wriggling bundle reminded all of us exactly what its purpose was in the room.

'Bring it to me,' he growled at the human guard, gesturing at him to come closer. 'And the others.'

I followed the movement of his eyes and gasped at two more bundles: one wriggling and one deathly still. A sigh of relief escaped me as the second one let out a piercing scream and began kicking furiously. Both had thin blankets covering them. Maybe it made them easier to eat, if you couldn't see their faces. We had been right: tonight was the night they were going out to get new victims. We just assumed they hadn't done it yet. The guard began towards his master, who was too weak to move.

'Nuh-uh, buddy. I'd stop right there,' I said, as I raised my

Glock and aimed it squarely at his head. He didn't need to understand what I was saying to understand what I intended.

'*Bring it to me! FAST!*' screamed his boss. He was torn between the two of us, eyeing my gun and the bleeding man with equal trepidation. I couldn't waste time letting him think about it. I lowered my gun and shot him in the kneecap. He screamed, lurching forward and tossing the crying baby. I dived forward and clumsily caught the child, not sure where its head or delicate areas were under the blanket.

'FUCKING BITCH!' he shouted, dropping to all fours. He clutched desperately at his gushing wound, shrinking away from me and closer to the injured werewolf. I wasn't paying attention as I fumbled through the layers of material to expose a very upset but otherwise healthy and safe baby boy. When I looked up I saw what was about to happen seconds before it did. The Laignach Faelad had slowly pushed himself off the wall and closer to the guard. The man was completely shocked when his boss launched himself upon him. Teeth ripping into his cheek, the werewolf began to tear his face off. I looked away, dumping my gun as I tucked the baby into the nook between my shoulder and breast. Throwing off the blankets of the other two children – also unharmed – I grabbed them as best I could, shoving their faces into my body and trying to protect their heads. Blocking out the horrible sounds of the guard being devoured by the Laignach Faelad was proving difficult, and I hoped the werewolf was weak enough that he would need to consume a fair amount of flesh and blood before he got his strength back (especially since it wasn't his meal of choice).

That was all I had going for me: the hope that it was a

timely process to eat another human being. I took that chance and ran with it as I awkwardly mounted the stairs balancing the three babies wiggling against me. I had no free hands, no access to weapons, and no ability to do anything but try and sprint from the building with my precious cargo. If I was attacked, I was screwed. I kicked the door to the basement free from its hinges and raced for the entrance. I used my shoulders to whack swaying partiers out the way, with only a few pausing to witness the strange sight of a woman cradling three crying babies. There was a cluster of people lingering at the entry and they all separated instantly as a terrifying roar rung out behind me. I didn't even turn to see who – or what – it was, but the metallic clash that followed indicated someone had engaged my pursuer.

Flying out the door, I leapt down the remaining steps and past the flashing lights of several police cars as they began pulling up at the warehouse. I briefly thought about offloading the babies to a police officer nearby, but the blood I was sprayed in would raise too many questions. There were so many people lingering about and fleeing the area, I was paid barely any attention as I diverted off the main road and down a narrow alleyway. I sprinted as fast as I could while trying not to jostle the three babies too much. Hitting a corner at incredible speed, my heaving chest experienced the slightest sense of relief as I spotted the Rogues van idling at the alley entrance.

'Joss!' I shouted as I ran, hoping he would see what I was carrying and have the passenger door open for me when I arrived. He did, and the van was already moving by the time I negotiated my way into the seat.

'What the –'

'Just go,' I hissed, sparing a second to glance at the shock on his face as he registered the screaming bundles in my arms. I needed to shut the car door and I needed hands, but I had zero free limbs. 'Shit shit shit.' Reluctantly I placed one baby on the car floor, trying to secure it between my two feet as we swerved on to the main road. I dumped the other in Joss' lap, juggling the third on to my other arm as I leaned across and finally shut the door, locking it, and doing up the seat belt.

'Ah! Tommi you dumped a baby on my lap! How am I supposed to drive with a baby on my lap!'

'I know, okay! There's a baby about to slide under the car seat as we speak, I'm doing the best I can!'

I snatched the child from Joss' lap – much to his relief – and tried to juggle one in each arm. They were both crying, loudly, and I tried to coo at them. Joss' face mirrored my own: I think we both would have preferred to take on a pack of werewolves than deal with three children under the age of nine months. The only person who seemed to be coping with the situation was the baby at my feet, who appeared somewhat amused as she bounced with the movement of the car. Either that or she was doing a poo (it was always hard to tell with babies). The important thing was that she had stopped crying.

'Ssshh, hush, please stop crying,' I pleaded at the babies in my arms. 'Oh God, why won't you stop crying?'

'I'd say they have plenty to cry about, given they were nearly werewolf food.'

'I'm not questioning their motivations, Joss, I just want them to stop. Why won't they freakin' stop? Look, your buddy there on the floor is having a grand ol' time. How lucky are you that you're in my arms?'

'What the fuck are we going to do?'

'We stick to the plan and get back to Phases, lock down in the training room and pray to God someone with more of a paternal instinct than the two of us rocks up soon.'

'Okay,' Joss nodded, sounding slightly calmer. 'Shite, okay.'

By the time we parked in the club's loading dock, one of the babies I was holding had fallen asleep. The other was turning a shade of beetroot with the effort of continued crying. I gave that one to Joss, arguing that if I had to carry two he could at least deal with the screamer. He relented. The 'floor baby' was still awake, but not crying or sleeping. It appeared to be taking in everything with a sense of profound confuddlement. Or it was still doing a poo. Floor baby was turning out to be my fast favourite. I swiped us into the training room, which was sitting in darkness save for the faint glow of one lamp at the opposite end of the room. It was also completely quiet, which should have been my second clue that something was off given the fact we had left two Askari and a sleeping Zillia here when we went to the warehouse.

'This one *really* doesn't want to stop crying, Tommi. I don't think I can handle it,' pleaded Joss.

'Dude, I have werewolf hearing. You have no idea how much worse this situation is for me right now.'

'You're n–'

The click of a safety switch being turned off cut Joss' sentence in half. We both froze in the position that we had been in, facing each other.

'I'm afraid to say the situation is only going to get worse, Miss Grayson. If I could get you to turn around now, slowly please.'

The voice was cold, but somehow it managed to sound entirely reasonable. Kirk Rennex was watching both of us as I slowly turned around to face him. He looked impeccable in a suede suit, complete with his signature sparkling cufflinks. The only flaw in his appearance was a small speck of blood that stood out on his white shirt. My eyes quickly glanced around the room and I spotted the motionless bodies of the Askari we'd left behind. They were dead, shot in the head by someone who knew how to wield a gun. When my eyes returned to his face he wasn't grinning or cackling manically: he was merely watching us very carefully.

'Now I would like the both of you to raise your hands above your head. Slowly, please, as I know you have a penchant for guns and sharp throwing objects, Miss Grayson.'

'We're kind of holding a bunch of babies at the moment so . . .' Joss said, stating the obvious.

'That's fine. Place them on the ground at your feet then continue to raise your hands in the air.'

'Soy cappuccino,' I growled, while doing as instructed. 'I should have known you were evil.'

I had left my shooting equipment in the car and I knew Joss didn't have a weapon on him. I had a small dagger tucked into the back of my jeans pocket, but there was no way I could get to it before Rennex would shoot one of us. I wasn't willing to risk it. The frustrating thing was, we were in a room with thousands of different kinds of weapons and we couldn't get to any of them. Our best chance was to keep him occupied until someone came home. I hadn't spotted Zillia's body anywhere, which could mean that she was still alive. Or it could mean she had sided with her boyfriend.

'What do you want?' asked Joss.

Rennex tilted his head as he considered the question. 'Want? What I want is of little importance now. What I need is for you to carefully back away from the children and press your noses against that wall.'

I frowned at his request. 'What do you need the babies for, Kirk? You're not a werewolf, they're of no use to you. And you must know that your soldiers are dead by now.'

'Some of my soldiers, Tommi, some.' He read the shock in my face and smirked. 'Surely you didn't think a businessman like me wouldn't have a back-up plan?'

'Where are they then?' said Joss, calling his bluff. Rennex' focus shifted to my friend.

'Where the true Laignach Faelad are born, son.'

'Ireland,' I said, registering his meaning. 'These guys were just the test batch. You have the real army in Ireland.'

'Correct. And they're days out from being ready. In fact, they're so close to perfect you and your little friends won't have time to stop them.'

'But what do you need the babies for?' asked Joss.

'To eat, obviously.'

Joss and I shared a look. 'But you're not . . . I mean, how can you when you're not a . . .'

'A werewolf,' I finished for Joss. We were both confused.

'No. My father was a historian and my mother a glorified librarian, yet both were werewolves. The gene skipped me entirely, which is ironic given how much more I could have done with it.'

'Like creating an evil posse of baby eaters?' I asked.

'Like creating a global empire!' he shouted, spit flying from his lips. 'The things I could have done if I had the gifts any of you had! And what have you done with them? NOTHING!'

'Listen to the Sith Lord over here,' whispered Joss.

'Choose a time when he hasn't got a gun aimed at our chest, will you?' I had been slowly lowering my arms as he raged, hoping I could get to the dagger. I was almost there when Rennex gestured madly with the gun.

'Stop right there, hands back up high, Tommi.'

I gulped as his finger twitched. I didn't know what his trigger discipline was like, but I didn't want to test it. 'Yessir.'

'How is eating the babies going to help you?' asked Joss, trying to get him distracted again. 'You said yourself the gene skipped you so –'

'You think I don't know these rituals better than anyone else? You think I invested millions in unearthing the legends of Crom Cruach just to create the Laignach Faelad? I didn't bribe my way into an ancient organisation for a one-time monetary gain. I plan to be one of *you*.'

'How is that going to work, exactly?' he asked, stringing the words together slowly.

'I eat the babies, alive, and then she bites me.'

My face wrinkled in disgust. 'Yeah, my mouth isn't going anywhere near you.'

'You will bite me, or I will kill him. Simple.'

'You mean you'll kill him after I bite you, as opposed to before. Once I bite you – which is not going to work Mister-I-Have-An-Expendable-Research-Fund – then you have no reason to keep either of us alive.'

'And also, I'm dying of cancer here. You'd just be accelerating the process.'

A vein in Rennex' forehead pulsed with frustration and I sensed we had pushed him too far. I dove for Joss a split second before he fired, knocking him out of the bullet's path. There was nowhere for us to take cover and I didn't waste a second going after the billionaire 'mastermind'. He might have been a good shot, but he wasn't used to being in high-stake situations. I was. Staying low and on all fours, I raced towards him, rolling once to the side to avoid a bullet as it made impact with the hardwood floor. He was frantic, firing shots wherever he could right up until I had a dagger placed at his throat. At this point it was almost instinct for me to follow through. I could have slit it right there. But what could he do? He wasn't a werewolf, he wasn't a supernatural assailant . . . he was barely a whole man. I reminded myself that this person was responsible for the horrific deaths of babies. He was willing to kill three more in this very room thanks to a deluded desire for power. He deserved death and then some. Yet I didn't need to deliver it. I broke his wrist, snapping the gun out of his hand and sending him whimpering to his knees. The gunfire had woken the sleeping baby, who had joined its crying counterpart with a fresh set of wails. I briefly reconsidered my decision not to kill him.

'Joss, grab me a pair of cuffs from that drawer over there,' I said, dagger still at Rennex' throat.

He stopped his pained panting to consider me. 'You're not going to kill me?'

'I'm not going to kill you. That's not to say you're not going to die – probably horribly – but it won't be at my hands.' I crouched down to whisper in his ear. 'You know, I hear the Treize have these prisons. Awful places, filled with every kind of nightmare creature. How do you think a lone human is going to go surviving in there?'

Horror spread over his face, but not as much as I would have liked. A small smile began to form and he let out a soft laugh. I frowned as I cuffed him, pissed that he wasn't more afraid.

'You think I'll get to prison?' he spat. 'You had one chance and you blew it. I'll get off and I'll be free before your next full moon. I've known what Zillia was from the moment I met her. It's the reason I could slip into this life and why it was so easy for me get into your monster police, the Treize.'

I leaned back from him, looking for the signs of a lie and finding none. His heartbeat was steady, his pulse even, he was telling the truth. He laughed harder as he watched me, hands locked behind his back. 'You don't think it's strange none of the Guard turned up to help besides a wayward general who makes up his own rules? You don't think he's not wondering why he doesn't have back-up from an organisation that fears a force like this? I'm *in*. I'm in so deep you don't have a chance at weeding me ou–'

Gun shots rung out, silencing Kirk Rennex forever as his chest filled with bullet holes. Blood splashed on to my face and I leapt back, shocked by the sudden explosion. Joss was behind me and I knocked him over too. He was gripping my arms with fear as we both looked up to see Zillia standing there with a smoking Ruger shaking in her hands. Thick rivers of black mascara had tracked down her face with the path of her tears. She let out a sob, dropping the gun to the floor and following it herself as she collapsed in a pile of heaving limbs.

'I . . . I went to my apartment to change when he came and killed them. I didn't know what to do, I didn't . . . believe,' she cried. 'I listened to it all. I couldn't even help you. I was . . . frozen.'

I crawled over to her, discreetly nudging the gun out of her path and towards Joss. 'It's okay,' I said, reaching out to touch her.

'It's not. He was right. I know him and if you let him live, he would have found a way to get off. I couldn't I just . . .'

Her speech descended into another fit of sobbing as I pulled her to me, hugging her tightly. I doubted it would be okay. My mind raced at the possibly of a Treize or PG official being bribed into inaction by someone like Rennex. I wasn't sure if I believed it, but my experience with these people was limited. He had certainly believed it and Zillia deemed it likely enough that he deserved to die at her hand. Then there was the matter of his back-up pack of Laignach Faelad . . .

'There, there,' I whispered, stroking her hair as she cried into my shoulder. 'It will all be okay.'

I met Joss' stare from across the room. Anything but the word 'okay' reflected in both our eyes.

Chapter 20

For once I thought I was awake before Lorcan, even though it was mid-afternoon. I was anxious to have the talk we'd needed to have since that night at the warehouse when numerous truth bombs had been dropped. If Heath knew about us and nothing had happened yet, maybe nothing would – maybe there would be no consequences. I didn't want to allow myself to hope and I wasn't foolish enough to think all the problems we had would be eradicated if we didn't have to hide anymore, but I couldn't shake the idea that maybe there was a chance for us. Fixing myself up in the bathroom first, I tiptoed upstairs only to find that Lorcan wasn't there. Frowning, I noted that his bed looked as if it hadn't been slept in.

The last time I had seen him was in the training room the night before, when everyone had returned and he . . . he had been comforting Jenica, who had broken down upon finding two of her colleagues dead. A low growl filled the room and I was shocked to find it was coming from my own mouth. Numb, I trotted down the stairs and tried to kill the thousand ugly possibilities that were filling my head. I slipped into a fitted pair of overalls, my favourite pair of kicks and grabbed a black coat as I dashed out of the apartment to go and visit Joss at Mechtilde General instead.

My best friend had returned there under police escort after Officer Dick Creuzinger advised the best solution would be turning himself into the LKAs. The official line was that when he'd heard the commotion – the screams, the destruction – he'd made a run for it. In a state of sheer panic he hadn't gone to the police or his parents, he'd come straight to Phases where he'd hid out with me. Dick had done more than his fair share post the final battle with the Laignach Faelad. He'd been ready to call in the warehouse incident the second we were clear of it, and he arrived on the scene with his officers in tow. There had been enough evidence at the makeshift club to determine that the murdered men found inside were the same people responsible for the child abductions. The security guards were accomplices and Kirk Rennex – who was still 'missing' – was being sought as a person of interest. Bones of the dead babies were also found within the premises and so far the media was passing it off as a bizarre series of cult murders that attracted the wrath of local crime lords. A bit of a stretch, but the Askari were helping fuel this theory by releasing new misinformation every few hours. It was going down as a particularly awful chapter in the country's modern history.

'You? Walking around before sunset? Did something bad happen? I expected you to be sleeping for another week!' I ignored Joss' comments as I strolled into his hospital room. His beaming grin proved his comments were the usual blend of light-hearted snark.

'Yes, something very bad happened,' I replied as I began wiggling free of my coat and sliding the gloves from my fingers.

'Winter has dropped on Berlin like Mr Freeze's balls. Have you seen the whitewash outside?'

Joss held his arms up in disgust, demonstrating the lines of cords that were ran from him to various medical machines. The doctors were taking his stint away from the clinic very seriously.

'Oh. Right,' I grimaced.

'There's not much freedom to make snowmen in the oncology ward.'

'Aye.' I took my spot at the end of his bed, sitting up on the mattress with my legs crossed.

'You just missed Dick – he came in to see me.'

'Really? If anyone should be sleeping for a week I'd expect it to be him.'

'You know, besides that time he arrested you under false pretences, I actually like him.'

'I nearly ate him for that, so I think we can consider it water under the bridge.'

'He handled the supernatural stuff a lot better than I did.'

I nodded. 'True. I think he's going to be a really useful contact here for the Rogues from now on. And hold up, you need to give yourself more credit. You took to the research side of things amazingly, Joss. You cracked the whole case open.'

'Thanks, man, that means a lot,' said Joss, genuinely pleased with the compliment. 'Once you get past the whole "werewolves are real and my best friend is one" then it's pretty much the coolest thing ever. I always wanted to be "The Chosen One" or some kind of kickass warrior. But I'm not. It's not my destiny. The people who read about that stuff and want it never are. It's always the unsuspecting that have power thrust upon them.'

'Joss –'

'No, I'm right, Tommi. Of course that person would be you. The awesome part is at least I get to come along for the ride as your faithful sidekick.'

'Who said you were my faithful sidekick?'

'That's the other thing: the protagonist never gets a say in who the sidekick is. The sidekick always appoints themselves.'

'Innit?' I said, raising an eyebrow at Joss.

'See! Exactly! That's why you were always going to be perfect for this! You're all cool and archy eyebrowing.'

'Uh-huh. Listen, hun, I'm glad this stuff is interesting to you and you haven't been terrified or horrified by me being a part of it. But I don't want you anywhere near this world. The humans involved? They tend to get hurt. Mortally. Look at what happened to Kane and Mari. I would die if anything happened to you.'

'Look where we are, Tom: we're in the bloody cancer ward. Things are happening to me and are going to continue to happen whether you like it or not. Mari and Kane had no awareness of this world and I'm not saying if they did that would have changed their fates but . . . don't shut me out. I know stuff. And the more stuff I know the more helpful I can be. This – the Treize, you, Lorcan, the PG – it's fascinating to me.'

Joss was a fervent believer in what he said. I could see the passion and sincerity oozing from him. I took it in. I judged the merit of it and fought with my desire to keep my best friend wrapped in a ball of cotton wool, conveniently placed high enough on a shelf where none of this could hurt him. Yet he hadn't been hurt so far. The most hurt he'd been was when he learned of my lies. Plus, it would nice to have someone to vent to about all this stuff. And who knew me better than Joss?

'Okay,' I said with a sigh.

'YES!'

I was bounced up and down on the edge of the bed as Joss jumped with excitement. 'Whoa, settle down. I'm not going to be able to get an Askari in here or anything like that. The best I can do is tell you what I know, which isn't going to be a whole bloody lot. But it's more than you know now.'

'That's pure *barry*. You're the best, Tom! And maybe Lorcan could come and tell me stuff too.'

I gave Joss a look.

'What?' he quizzed.

'Lo isn't exactly forthcoming with the secrets of this world. Even to me. Maybe especially to me.'

I avoided my best friend's measured gaze as I played with the edge of his blanket. 'Okaaaay then. How about we start now, take your mind off it?'

Meeting his cheeky grin with narrowed eyes, I couldn't play faux angry for long. 'Fine, ya bampot. Where do you want to begin?'

When I left Mechtilde General three hours later, I was surprised to find myself feeling somewhat lighter. I had just started to tell Joss everything I knew about this world, but I already felt better about having someone to share the load with. Talking with Joss might actually help me continue to come to terms with the reality as much as it might help quell Joss' insatiable desire to know everything *ever*. Of course, I would never tell him that. I was feeling pretty good about the whole situation right up until I stepped out of the hospital and was slapped in the face by a freezing wind. Like most Scots I preferred the cold over sweltering temperatures any day, yet this European winter had come on so quickly I was struggling to adjust.

'Fuck me,' I whispered through chattering teeth as I pulled my scarf over my nose. Yanking my coat tighter around me, I hopped on a tram and got back to Phases as quickly as I could. Shaking off in the stairwell, I enjoyed the warmth that circulated through my veins as I jogged up the flights of stairs. When I got to the top I found Dolly there, knocking on my apartment door.

'Oh hey,' she said, surprised by my arrival. 'I thought you were inside.'

'Visiting Joss at the hospital.'

'He's cool. I like the kid. How's he doing?'

I shrugged. 'Fine. We didn't majorly deplete his health bar or anything but the nurses are keeping a pretty close eye on him. He's got a taste for the outside now.'

'You make it sound like prison,' she laughed.

'Yeah, except you pay to go there and the food is slightly better.'

'Look, I know this is last minute but you know that band I was telling you about?'

'The Anna Thompsons?'

She grinned at me. 'Yeah. That showcase is on tonight and Yu and I wanted to see if you wanna come. With us.'

I mulled it over, weighing up the possibility of spending a night in bed compared to hanging out with a gaggle of cool lesbians.

'Clay and Sanjay and Gus have everything covered at the club while Zillia is off to her retreat with the Custodians,' she went on, 'so Yu and I were craving a free night, do something fun, especially with everything that has been happeni–'

'I'm in,' I said, cutting her off.

'Really?' she asked, surprised at my response.

'Fuck yes. There's nothing I'd rather do tonight than drink and rock out to good music with y'all.'

'Awesome, meet at our apartment in an hour?'

'See you then,' I said, unlocking my door and vowing to whip together an amazing outfit and face in record time.

Turns out, it wasn't the girls' night I had been craving. Heath had somehow intercepted the invitation and Yu – being politer than both Dolly and I combined – had invited him along. It made for a weird foursome as we trekked our way to the venue (which was too cool to have a name on the door and could only be found by regulars who knew exactly what side street to take and which stairwell to descend).

Once inside, Yu and Dolly collectively threw me to the wolves – the awkward journey there obviously being as much courtesy as they could handle. Dolly gave me an apologetic smile before she and her partner disappeared into the crowd and greeted a group of acquaintances. I did my best not to let out a disappointed sigh as I took off my jacket and cast a sideways look at Heath, who was doing the same. He was scanning the crowd with a frown and then did a double take when he looked at my ensemble.

'Don't,' I said, stopping him before whatever words he was forming on the tip of his tongue could escape his mouth.

'I was simply going to say, you look ferocious,' he replied giving me an appreciative once over.

I glared at him and after gathering that he wasn't actually taking the piss, said a begrudging 'thank you'.

Wearing a pair of wedged, black boots that crept up to midway along my thigh I felt taller than I usually would standing next to someone like Heath. The rest of me was covered in a tight, black mini-dress and left my two biggest assets sitting to attention in a push-up bra. I'd thrown a long-sleeved, see-through dress with sequin trim over the top of the whole thing but from the way the former Pict was looking at me it may as well have not been there at all. I'd also done something I rarely did: straightened my hair, which was brushing my tailbone as I spun around the room to find the nearest entry point to the bar.

'Booze!' I pointed, grabbing Heath's arm and dragging him along in the direction of alcohol. I was going to need a lot of it. I'd done two delicate braids at one side of my head to keep the hair off my face and I was glad as I bustled people out of the way and shouted orders for the both of us at the barkeep. To his credit, Heath downed the shot I handed him without question and graciously accepted the rum and coke that followed.

'Is it just me,' he said, taking a sip of the drink, 'or is this bar almost exclusively packed with women?'

'It's a gay bar,' I replied, grabbing my change from the tray and looking for a quiet spot.

Heath surveyed the room and nodded. 'That makes all of the sense. I assume we're watching k.d. Lang cover bands tonight?'

'Don't be an asshole,' I said, nodding in the direction of a clear space on a set of wooden stairs that went to nowhere. The crowd parted for us as we walked through, like we were a mini-Moses before the Red Sea.

'I don't know why everyone is looking at me,' muttered Heath as he digested some of the looks he was getting. 'I'm not the one wearing black lipstick and looking like something to eat.'

I snorted at the compliment in there. 'It's because you're almost aggressively heterosexual.'

There was just enough space for us to sit down and Heath folded into the opening as I settled in next to him. The stage was at the opposite side of the room and we'd have a pretty good view once the acts got going. The first up was a band called Abstract Random and the floor filled with bodies as people gathered closer the stage. The punters who had been sitting on the stairs with us left to join the fray and I nodded my head along to the beats.

'They kinda remind me of The Fugees meets early Black Eyed Peas,' I said to Heath, enjoying the bass-heavy tunes as the three women sung and rapped to the room.

'I'll take your word for it,' he replied, finishing the rest of his drink with a gulp. I was cradling mine and realised I had some catching up to do, now that I was in the company of a fellow Scot. He caught me looking at him and raised an eyebrow.

'I know what you want to know,' he said.

'Do you now,' I muttered, taking a casual sip. I redirected my gaze to the swaying bodies of the dancers as I felt his gaze penetrating me.

'You want to know why I haven't said anything to the Treize or the Guard about you and Lorcan.'

'Haven't you?' I asked, trying to play it coy.

'I haven't. The only person I've spoken to about it is you.'

I examined his expression closely to look for a lie, but couldn't find one. 'And why is that? You and Lorcan are far from friends now, you know that you could hurt him by sharing this information and win the feud once and for all. He'd be transferred and shamed and –'

'What makes you think I want to hurt Lorcan? Or even you for that matter? You've been endlessly useful so far.'

I said nothing, just took another sip.

'What has he told you about why we fell out? Not that we were ever – how does your generation say it – BFFs? We were good friends for centuries, yes, but the glue that held us together when we were at our closest was Amos.'

'He said that you felt betrayed by him leaving the PG after Amos killed himself,' I replied, crunching a piece of ice between my teeth. 'You were mad at him for wasting the opportunity you gave him and the centuries of experience he'd gained.'

Heath surprised me and laughed, loud and deep. It made me think that if the music hadn't been so loud it would have echoed off the walls. He kept laughing for a long while and finally wiped a small tear away from the corner of his eye.

'Aye,' he said, 'he would say that. But that's not the reason we fell out. Amos had always been . . . unstable? No, that's not the right word. He was a strong, forthright man who overcame a bad childhood. He was someone that should have always stayed very far away from alcohol. It took him to dark places he struggled to come back from. The night he died –'

'Just after he turned thirty?' I offered.

Heath nodded at the memory. 'It was early in the morning and he called Lorcan in a state. He was upset about something or everything. Lorcan and I were travelling in the car together at the time on our way to a raid. He told Lorcan that he was in pain. He said that everything was too much and that he couldn't do it anymore – live like a monster.'

I frowned and he held up his hand in a peace gesture.

'Hey, those were his words. I've seen enough monsters in my time to know werewolves barely rate on the evil scale.'

'So what happened?'

'Lorcan was tired, we both were, and he said some things that I don't think either of us expected Amos to act on at the time.'

'What things?'

'That he should do it. If life was too hard, if he was in too much pain, then end it.'

My mouth hung open. I took a big sip of my rum and coke, almost finishing it.

'I was in the car too,' Heath continued. 'I didn't stop Lorcan's words, I didn't call Amos back to see if he was alright and I didn't drive around to his house to make sure he didn't do anything stupid. We pushed on to the mission and afterwards it was too late.'

'Hmmm. That's why he blames himself,' I said.

'Bingo. That's also why ten Hail Marys weren't going to ease his Irish conscience. He joined the Custodians not because he thought it was the right thing to do or because he could help people, he joined because he wanted to make himself feel better. That's why we've had our . . . disagreements.'

I wasn't so certain about that. Sure, it was obvious Lorcan was haunted by his words to Amos but I didn't believe he joined the Custodians for purely selfish reasons. He wanted to find peace and he wanted to better himself, definitely, but I also believed that he truly wanted to help the lost, the alone, and those left with no other options – people who had been like me at the beginning.

'That doesn't explain why you haven't been screaming "Oy, they're boinking!" from the nearest rooftop,' I said.

'It does, actually. Contrary to whatever he thinks, I don't wish him ill. And that situation will sort itself out.'

'*Situation*?' I said, my voice raising in pitch. 'What does that mean?'

He jerked his head in a forward motion and I followed the direction to where Yu and Dolly were standing, swaying discreetly to the music with their arms draped around each other. Yu whispered something to her girlfriend and Dolly made a face before laughing. They were in love, even a blind man could see it.

'Lorcan isn't the only one to put his feelings before his duty,' Heath said, watching me with a smirk.

'But I thought Yu was in the PG wh–'

'She was a soldier on assignment when she met Dolly,' he said, batting a hand. 'Custodian and ward or Praetorian Guard and a mark, it doesn't really matter. The point is, she fell hard enough to risk everything for it: her reputation, her years of service, her immortality. She gave up everything for a shot at being with Dolly. And you can't tell me she would have done all that if they hadn't fucked first.'

My head jerked back at the comment, which was in such sharp contrast to the other vaguely romantic things he had been saying about the pair.

'What you're saying is Dolly's a vadgician?'

He laughed at my term. 'What I'm saying is, I want to give Lorcan that chance. I want to see how this plays out. Obviously you're both trying to do the "right thing" –' he made quotation marks in the air with hands – 'but if that doesn't work out, I don't want to be the person who shat on his chance at happiness. I'm not the heartless cretin everyone makes me out to be, Tommi. I understand he deserves that.'

'If he wants it,' I whispered.

Heath shrugged. 'There is that. One word of advice?'

'Fookin run me over with a mower,' I groaned, rubbing my head. 'Alright, what is it?'

'Someone who keeps that many secrets? They're never gonna give themselves over to you fully. And I'm saying that from experience.'

He left me alone then as he went in search of more alcohol. The Anna Thompsons had taken to the stage by this point and were singing a song about turning down a creep who hit on them at a club. I found myself chanting the chorus of 'fuck you' under my breath as Heath returned with a tray of drinks that would have satisfied eight people. At least.

'Are we expecting company?' I asked.

'We're Scottish, lass. Time we started acting like it.'

I laughed. It did cut out the hassle of going to the bar for another few hours.

'Heath Darkiro,' I said, stringing his name out and tasting the words on my lips. 'Was Heath a regular Pict name? Feels considerably nineteenth century if you ask me.'

'I didn't ask you, but I'll share. Because sharing is caring.'

I chuckled. 'I'm bracing my loins in anticipation.'

He gave me a suggestive look before pushing on. 'Heath is a derivative of Heathcliff, a traditionally English name for someone who lived near a moor.'

'How in the shite did a Scot end up with an English name?'

'I took it. My true name is Heif and Heath was the closest to it.'

'And Darkiro?'

'Made it up.'

'Ha, sorry you what?'

'I made it up. I went without a surname for a few centuries before deciding I wanted one. Darkiro sounded good, tough, you know? Metal.'

I was laughing so hard that I started to cough. Heath kept his eyes on the stage, but I saw a defined smirk playing on his face as he took a swig from his bottle. I wondered if that was actually the truth, yet given how much it amused me in the moment I didn't really care. Clutching my stomach with the pain of constant laughter, it took me a few solid minutes to settle myself down.

'You okay? You're not going to piss yourself?'

'Whoooo,' I said, letting out a gust of air. 'I haven't laughed like that in an age. Thank you.'

He did a mock bow just for the two of us.

'So,' I said, leaning closer, 'where is this prison that you keep all the supernatural baddies in?'

I grinned as he choked on the sip he was trying to take.

'Who told you about that?' He coughed. 'That's not common knowledge among the werewolves.'

'Well, you just confirmed it to me and I need to know where it is.'

He gave me a sly smile, as if impressed with my craftiness. 'I appreciate how much you just don't give a shit, asking what you want to know outright and luring answers out of people. You sure you still don't want to join the Praetorian Guard?'

'One hundred per cent positive, thank you. Now where is it?'

'Why do you want to know?'

'My half brother, Quaid Ihi, is locked up there. He's fourteen and got sentenced to *whatever* without so much as a trial or fair hearing. I want to visit him.'

'Figured,' said Heath, handing me a shot. We clinked glasses together and downed the fluid, which had a borderline toxic aftertaste.

'Ergh, what was that?' I gagged.

'Amaretto,' he said, unfazed.

'Sadist. Who takes that as a shot?' I shook my head. 'Right. Where is this prison?'

'Guess,' he replied, a massive grin spreading on his face. I frowned as I registered his weirdly excited expression. Why the hell would he think I could guess where . . . oh. Oh, it was that obvious.

'Scotland?' I asked.

He clapped his hands together. 'Aye, near your home town actually. You know the Cold War secret bunker in St Andrews?'

'Yeah, we had to visit it in high school history class. It's nothing more than a tourist attraction and a bleak one at that.'

'Do you remember how deep they said it goes?'

I strained my mind through the haze of booze and years. 'Uh . . . eighty feet or something?'

'Try eight hundred,' he said with a glint in his eye.

'Wait, you're saying the supernatural prison is *under* the secret bunker?'

'Has been for hundreds of years, which is why that location was originally chosen by a few well-placed members of the Treize inside the British government during the Cold War.'

'You reckon I can get in there to visit?'

'Extremely doubtful,' he said, sipping his Foster's.

'What a shame,' I said, smug. 'I guess I'll have to ask my mischief demon friend to get me in.'

For the second time that night I made an ancient warrior – a Pict – choke on his drink. I laughed with maniacal glee.

The four of us stumbled into Phases just before it closed for a nightcap. Dolly leapt the bar to grab us drinks and save the fill-in crew from having to serve us. We were all very drunk, so I'm sure they appreciated the kindness. Yu and Dolly's warming attitude to Heath had a direct correlation to how much alcohol was in their system. Suffice to say we were all merry comrades by then, with Heath and Yu engaged in a lighthearted argument about their favourite medieval weapon. I was laughing hysterically as Heath tried to point out the merits of something called a 'Holy water sprinkler' when I noticed Lorcan at the opposite end of the bar. The laughter died in my throat.

He was sitting there with Jenica, an empty bowl of fries between them. She was speaking to him as she held a glass full of red wine, but he wasn't looking at her. He was looking directly at me. She noticed his gaze and followed it until she saw us and smiled, waving discreetly.

Lorcan excused himself and started to make his way through the crowd towards our group. I abandoned my friends as I ducked into the throng of people too in a bid to meet him halfway. As a gang of bachelorettes cleared a space I ended up stumbling headfirst into Lorcan and he grabbed me to stop the sudden movement. Our bodies were pressed up against each other and I felt my heartbeat racing. His eyes were poring over me, taking in my outfit and my demeanour.

'Outside,' he said, attempting to drag me there.

I shook my head stubbornly and pulled him the other way. 'Too cold. The jungle hallway.'

He reluctantly agreed and we soon found ourselves alone in the hyper-coloured passageway of Phases.

'Are you and Heath on a double date with Yu and Slack?' he asked, the second we stopped moving. I couldn't breathe as I burst out laughing, my ribs aching with the gesture from previous wounds and the sheer force of my amusement.

'Oh my God no, what the fuck is wrong with you? He came with us to a gay bar to see some bands,' I said, when I could annunciate through the giggles.

'Why were you at a gay bar?' he quizzed.

'Why not? And enough with the grilling, it's me who has some questions to ask of you. What the hell is going on with you and Jenica?'

'Tommi, you know that we can't –'

'That's not what I'm asking. What is going on with *you* and *her*? Do you like her or is she an alibi?' Even as I said the words I could smell her on him, the sickly sweet perfume that made me want to kick the next hydrangea I saw. He was silent for an uncomfortable time.

'Have . . . have you slept with her?' I pushed.

'No. We've just . . . kissed.'

'Oh, God. *God.*'

'No one can find out about you and me, and I worried people were getting too close. A few comments Clay made here and there . . . I needed to shift the focus.'

'See, that's just the thing though – Heath does know about us. And he hasn't told anyone.'

Lorcan's mouth dropped open. 'How? How could he know?'

'I don't know Lo, he's known you for four hundred plus years so I assume you have a tell.'

'Why wouldn't he say anything? That doesn't make sense. He could –'

'Throw you under the bus?' I offered. 'He wanted to give you a chance to be happy, like Yu.'

'You've talked to him about this,' Lorcan stated, staring at me. 'He'll be using you for information. It's hard to understand, but girls your age –'

'Oh, fuck *you*,' I hissed. 'Girls your age? Fuck you. Fuck. You.'

'You can't trust him, Tommi.'

'Like the way I can trust you?'

Lorcan rested a hand on the wall with frustration, shaking his head as he looked down at his feet. 'Not this again.'

'Yes, this again,' I replied, hurt. 'He was being honest with me Lo, something that you're repeatedly choosing not to do. And it hurts, Christ it hurts. It pains me to learn that you kept Quaid's fate a secret from me, it pains me that you think I'm blood drunk and that you never told me the truth about Amos. Those are just a few things skimming the surface but the thing that *kills* me is to watch you sitting there with Jenica, flirting with her and kissing her when you've had another option all along.'

An expression of agony passed over his face as it crumpled for a moment, before he ran his hands over it. My chest was rising and falling with the emotion of the things I had just poured out. I felt a tear burn at the corner of my eye and I willed it to stay in place.

'You deserve the world, Tommi,' he said at last, slowly looking up at me. 'I'm just not sure if I'm the person to give it to you.'

The seconds blinked in front of me as I stood still, not breathing. At last I moved, walking past him and pushing open the door. I disappeared out into the crowd of people who were dancing ferociously as someone shouted the words 'last call' over the speaker system. I didn't even notice the people throwing their heads back as they moved to the rhythm of KRS One, I didn't see their faces, I just moved blindly through until I was slapped by the freezing air of outside. I closed my eyes as I took a deep breath. It was a relief and I relished in the temperature snap as I walked further and further out into the snow. I smelled tobacco and opened my eyes to see Heath standing there, sharing a cigarette with Sanjay who was bouncing up and down to get warm. He raised his head when he heard me approach and gave a grin that could only be described as positively cheery.

'Tommi!' Lorcan burst out of the door to Phases behind me and froze when he saw Sanjay and Heath there – the former waving merrily. With a cigarette dangling between his lips and a smile spreading on his face, under any other circumstances Heath's attitude would have been infectious.

'How are my favourite supernatural pair today?' he grinned at us.

Lorcan didn't answer. I avoided the question. 'Didn't anyone ever tell you cigarettes are bad for your health?'

He winked at me. 'Immortality, darlin'.'

The soft crunching of snow turned me around to see the twins slowly walking towards us. They were dressed in their usual black uniform, but this time their bald heads were covered from the cold with beanies. They didn't walk right up and join us: instead they stopped a few paces back. I frowned as I watched them standing there like silent soldiers, hands casually crossed. A harsh wind whipped my hair around my face and I turned back to face Heath. The look of confusion on Sanjay's face probably matched my own.

'What's going on?' I asked.

Heath didn't answer me at first, preferring to stomp the cigarette out with his foot instead. When his eyes finally met mine the mischief there was unmistakable. 'We're going on a little excursion.'

'Heath . . .' Lorcan warned.

By then it was too late. Lorcan pitched forward at the same time as Sanjay, both trying to grab something invisible at their necks. I barely had a moment to cry out before I too felt a sharp sting near my carotid artery. Instantly my legs began to go out from underneath me and the ground came rushing forward. Heath caught me seconds before I hit, and lowered me to the ground softly.

'Ssshh, ssshh, it's all right,' he whispered as we continued to fall. The last thing I remember was seeing the bodies of Lorcan and Sanjay lying motionless in the snow. Then came the blackout.

Chapter 21

By the time I came to, it was considerably warmer. Hot, even. My mind was still groggy and there were voices, I could hear them murmuring away and I waited patiently for my senses to bring them into focus. My vision was completely obscured by a blindfold, but I was surprised to find my limbs weren't restricted in any way. I had been drugged with something powerful enough to work through my werewolf immune system, so why wouldn't you tie me up as well?

'She is awake,' came Jakea's voice.

'You should help her up now,' added Jaira.

'Lorcan, would you like to do the honours?' Heath's tone was amused, as it always was.

'I can't believe we're here,' said Sanjay in hushed awe.

'*Esto es un problema.*' My ears pricked at that voice, as it belonged to Clay. What was he doing here? Wherever *here* was. Somebody began moving towards me and from the almost soundless pace I recognised Lorcan. His hands swept some of my hair from my face before moving to the back of my neck where he began untying the blindfold. I could feel his breath on the side of my neck and I took some relief in his closeness.

'Be calm, don't panic, and be careful what you say,' he whispered. He was leaning so close to me that his lips tickled my ear. His face was hovering inches from mine as he removed the blindfold. He remained in front of me so his face was the first thing I saw, specifically the deathly serious expression on it. He lingered for a few more seconds, holding eye contact so I understood just how important what he had said was. I nodded slightly to show him that I got it. The next thing surprised me, as he quickly ducked forward and kissed my forehead. Any feelings I had about that act were replaced immediately by white. All white everything. I squinted as I waited for my eyes to adjust to the sudden brightness. I was propped against a wall and Lorcan helped me as I slowly got to my feet. From the walls to the floor, everything in the windowless room was white except for the seven occupants in it. Heath's long legs were stretched out in front of him as he sprawled on an ivory couch, looking relaxed. The twins were both standing at attention to his right, while Sanjay sat on the arm of the couch and gazed around him. Clay was pacing the room in a skintight purple tuxedo with velvet lining the cuffs. He looked like Liberace, only with muscles. Not that I could talk, as I fixed up my dress and adjusted my boots while scanning the room. Clay was speaking entirely in his native tongue, which I didn't take as a good sign given the expression on his face.

'Are we in heaven?' I asked, running my hands through my hair as I waited for the warm flush to fade from being overheated for so long. Heath was chuckling at my question.

'Do you think we'd all be here if you were?' he asked.

'I'm technically an atheist but given the interior of this place . . .'

'Puhlease. I know what heaven is and considering there aren't any Italian men dancing in cages I feel confident in saying this is *not* it,' said Clay, still pacing. 'This is closer to hell. *El infierno el llamas*!'

'Clay . . .' Lorcan warned.

'We're in Romania, Lorcan! Don't even try to tell me this country isn't a hellhole.'

I was staggered by that fact. 'We're in . . . Romania? The country? How long have I been out?'

'The four of us,' Sanjay started, 'have been out for fourteen to fifteen hours.'

'What the hell did you pump us with?' I pointed angrily at Heath. Reeling on the twins, I gestured at them too. 'And don't think you're exempt just because you guys are all cute and stoic. What did you do us? You kidnapped us!'

Lorcan's hand rested on my shoulder as he whispered: 'Remember what I said about staying calm?'

Huffing, I took a few moments to do as he advised. One inhale. Two exhales. Three. 'Fine,' I said with a shuddering breath. 'I'm calm. Will someone please tell me why we're locked in a white box in Romania?'

'Gladly,' said Heath, not moving from his lazy position. 'We're at the Treize headquarters.'

I blinked. Everyone in the room was silent. They already knew this; I was just catching up. 'The Treize headquarters. In Romania,' I repeated, numb.

'Transylvania to be precise.'

My head snapped to face Heath. I examined his expression closely. The twins too were impassive and Lorcan gave the smallest of shrugs. I burst out laughing. The sound seemed to wake the room up and everyone looked at me as I clasped a hand over my mouth. I was just as surprised as they were and I tried to stop myself. That only made it worse and I laughed again, this time a loud and continuous flood of noise.

'Oh God, I'm sorry – I just –' I couldn't finish my sentence as I leaned back against the white wall. 'Fucking Transylvania?' I gasped through giggles. 'You have got to be kidding me.'

Lorcan didn't see the funny side. The twins looked confused. Sanjay was smirking slightly. Clay was still pacing. Heath was outright beaming.

'Transylvania man, that's a killer,' I said, wiping the tears from my eyes. 'Just don't say we're at Castle Dracula.'

'We're not at Castle Dracula,' Lorcan added.

'Good. I probably would have lost it if that was the case. Since I'm the last one awake, somebody want to explain why we're here?'

'And what's with the drugging?' added Sanjay.

'They can't have us know where their base is, obviously. We're not Askari, we're not Custodians, we're not part of the Praetorian Guard. We're not officials,' said Clay.

'But Lo, you've surely been here before? Why did they drug you?' asked Sanjay.

A simmering silence fell on the room as Lorcan shot daggers at Heath with his stare.

Flicking blond hair out of his eyes, Heath raised his hands in a truce gesture. 'Hey, don't look at me. It was the twins' idea.'

Lorcan appeared surprised at that as he turned to face them. They were unapologetic. 'We thought you'd fight when we took her down,' said Jaira.

'You were right,' whispered Lorcan. I watched him, watched how uncomfortable he was. He very clearly did not want to be here and he very clearly did not want me here either.

'That still doesn't answer the question as to why we're present,' I muttered.

A door I hadn't seen before opened across the opposite side of the room. It too was white (which is why I hadn't noticed it) and a spherical-looking man appeared from behind it. He was a stark contrast, dressed in a dark-green suit with a black tie. He quickly glanced at us, nodded, and in a heavily accented voice said: 'They are ready for you now.'

Heath and the twins seemed to know what this meant, Clay too, and they slowly made their way to follow the podgy British man.

'Perhaps it would have been nice if someone had brought me a change of clothes before I fronted the Treize,' Clay hissed at no one in particular.

Heath patted him on the bottom as he whispered, 'You look fabulous.'

'I always look fabulous,' Clay retorted.

The sheen of sweat on Sanjay's forehead and the look of fear in his eyes was making me feel just as nervous as he appeared. He gulped and made towards the door, while I quickly turned to face Lorcan. Placing my hands on his chest, I halted his movement forwards.

'What am I walking into, Lo?'

'We're going to stand before the Treize,' he said.

'Why?'

'I don't know,' he said, concern spreading over his features.

Suddenly I realised what I was wearing. I tugged at the hem of my dress but it only exposed my cleavage more (which did not help the situation any). I was drastically underdressed to present myself before the ruling supernatural body. A woman is only as confident as the skin she's in, I said to myself. It was a mantra of my mother's and repeating it internally I raised my head a little higher. It didn't matter that I was dressed in day-old clubbing clothes or a bunny rabbit onesie. Spinning on my heel, I headed out of the room with a steely expression on my face. Lorcan kept pace with me, and I felt his hand brush mine as we stepped into one of the grandest rooms I had ever seen.

Of course it was going to be grand, I wouldn't have expected anything else. I would have expected a medieval type hall with suits of armour lining the walls. What greeted me instead was a modern room. My boots clinked on the white ceramic tiles that lined the floor of this long, rectangular space. It was more of a hall, really. The walls too were white, but this didn't have the dentist's office feel to it like the previous room: mainly because of an exquisite collection of art that adorned the walls. I should have been looking forward, but I was distracted by the pieces that were both classic and contemporary. From a Jonathan Singleton Copley painting to the photographs of Julia Fullerton-Baten, I nearly walked into a sculpture I was so busy gawking at all the beautiful works. It was a curator's dream. Lorcan carefully guided me around a contorted steel version of the human form as we continued down the length of the room. A spiral staircase with black steps and a black railing stood at the end and split the space into halves. Sitting at a long desk that stood two steps higher than everything else in the room were thirteen people: the Treize. The desk was actually two items, with seven people sitting at the one on the left side and six sitting at the one on the right side. As I got closer to them, I realised there were carvings in the wood of the desk. They were incredibly detailed and I fought a desire to inch closer and examine them.

'They tell the history of the Treize,' said Lorcan, following my gaze. My mouth was hanging all the way open by this point. Up the staircase and sitting behind the Treize were several individuals who I assumed to be secretary types. Laptop screens were open in front of a few of them, and those without had their own tools. Some of them – a woman in a yellow hijab in particular – almost vibrated with supernatural energy. At the very back of the group was a familiar face: Chester Rangi. He caught my eye for a split second and winked, before looking back at a book he had open in his lap. I watched them watch us as the portly man stopped three metres from the Treize's platform. We had all been spaced out by about an arm's length while walking and I tore myself away from the spectators to examine the government of our world.

There were six men, six women and one for whom I couldn't identify a gender either way. Although I knew from Lorcan's teachings that they were all immortal, their ages were as varied as their cultures. Two of the women looked downright ancient, while another didn't seem real at all - he appeared that old. I was genuinely surprised when he demonstrated a sign of life by adjusting his glasses. There was a black man with African facial tattoos and another beautifully illustrated Maori man with half of his face covered in Tā moko, a plump woman with wildly curly red hair, a handsome man with an elaborate moustache, and a woman with skin so white I would have wondered if she was a ghost if not for her curtain of mahogany-coloured hair. Yet it was the eye of an Asian man with a high-collared grey shirt that caught mine. He was smiling ever so slightly at me.

'I see you enjoying our trappings, Miss Grayson,' he said.

'I . . . uh, yeah,' I floundered. I was startled at being addressed directly.

'I understand you're an art lover yourself.'

I cleared my throat in the hope of providing a better answer this time. 'Aye. Watson and the Shark caught my eye.'

'It is a classic,' said the elderly man with the glasses as he gazed at the painting behind me. His voice too was accentless, yet I could swear I caught the faintest French flavour on his lips. Was he one of the founding members the Treize was named after? Recalling Lorcan's warning from earlier, I stopped myself from continuing the conversation. Be careful what you say. Their interest in me didn't fade, however, despite the increasing silence. I grew uncomfortable under their gaze, but resisted the urge to fidget with my clothing.

'You must be wondering why you are here,' asked the pale woman with the long hair.

'It did cross my mind, once or thrice . . .'

She smiled at me briefly, while someone else on the Treize chuckled. I glanced at Lorcan, who was staring at his feet. Heath has his usual smirk plastered on his face while the twins looked alert. Clay and Sanjay both had a mix of fascination and terror on their faces.

'Bring in the prisoner,' said a tanned woman at the edge of the panel.

My eyebrows arched at this statement and I turned in the direction of shuffling feet. An exceptionally tall man was being dragged out by two escorts with matching expressions of severe dislike. He had been dressed in seemingly new clothes as the black garments didn't match the ragged state of the rest of his appearance. A cloth bag was placed over his head and his feet stumbled as he tried to get them to function properly.

He was thrown to his knees in the space between us and the seated Treize. A small gasp escaped him with the pain. I could see stains beginning to appear on his clothing and wounds were visible on his skin. Yet the freshest evidence of torture was the dead look in the man's eyes as the bag was removed. His eyes blinked as he correlated the surrounds. I felt Lorcan react next to me and I spared him a glance. He recognised this man.

The prisoner had been good-looking once. Now it seemed he had been through too much physical pain to retain much beauty. As he took in everything around him, a resignation settled into his features. He even held Lorcan's eye for a second, before looking away, ashamed.

'Monsieur Kirre, please introduce the prisoner,' stated a stout man at the desk.

'Certainly, sir. May I present to the Treize, guests and witnesses, former Deputy General of the Praetorian Guard Thaddeus Remellywn.'

There was a murmur from the upstairs court before a Treize member spoke up. 'You are found guilty on thirty-four accounts of treason, Thaddeus. You had served as a respectable member of the Praetorian Guard for one thousand six hundred and twenty-three years with a flawless record. Despite pleading guilty to all of the charges placed against you and answering our questions extensively, you have yet to provide an answer as to why you betrayed this organisation for the money of Kirk Rennex – a mere mortal.'

Silence.

'As well as exposing the organisation, your actions directly led to the deaths of our purest form of innocent – children – and the resurrection of a darkness we expended many resources to annihilate centuries earlier. You helped the spread of one of the blackest breeds of evil, something you had sworn to fight against repeatedly. And you have nothing to say about this?'

'There is not an answer that could change my fate. You will deliver *justice* as you see fit. Be done with it.'

The tanned woman raised her head a little higher at his defeated response. 'Very well,' she said, curt. 'The deaths are most severe and those counts are on your head. Yet it is the sabotage that intrigues me, Thaddeus. Perverting operations is the ultimate dishonour to members of the Guard – of which you were one of the most highly esteemed. And your only motivation for this is money, you say?'

He held her stare as she spoke, a smile raising slightly on one side of his face. 'Does wealth seem like such a little thing to you, Ashantii? Has money not been the carrot you dangled in front of worthy candidates for centuries?'

'It is one of many *gifts* offered,' she snapped.

'Then why is it so unlikely that I would be seeking a gift of my own, free of *strings*?' He grinned manically and his smile revealed several missing teeth that had clearly been removed recently.

'That is a pitiful excuse, Thaddeus, and one of the saddest things I have ever heard,' said one of the borderline ancient men at the panel. Quickly taking a glance at the other members of the Treize, he shared a silent message before he continued. 'Enough of this folly. You are sentenced to death.' He nodded at the portly gent, who waddled away and returned with a considerably muscular guard lugging the heaviest-looking sword I had ever seen. It was being carried horizontally between his two hands, and he moved slowly with it. Black and dark blue jewels glinted in the silver sheath, which was inscribed with French I could not recognise. The handle was almost as thick as my head. An ancient authority seemed to sing from it, like a soundless energy that carried through the whole room. This was a death dealer and I gulped as the guard paused in front of me with the enormous weapon. He looked at me expectantly. I glanced behind him to see the faces of the Treize watching me also, waiting.

'The honour is yours, Miss Grayson,' said the English aide.

'Heh?' I was sure he was mistaken. Shooting a sideways glance at Lorcan, he looked as surprised as I was.

'Surely you –'

'Is she not the one who uncovered this ploy, Lorcan? The one who spearheaded its downfall?' asked the redhead, cutting him off.

'It was more of a team effort,' I added hastily. 'I mean, we all contributed. I'd say it was Joss Jabour that did the hard yards research-wise –'

'The sickly mortal,' whispered the black-haired woman to her colleague.

– 'if anything I'd say this was Heath's operation so give the bloody thing to him.'

I took one look at Heath – standing still, eyes straight ahead, with a small smile playing on his lips – to know that there was no way he was taking the sword from me. He knew the ritual. He knew how this was going to play out. I had a sneaking suspicion that he was avoiding eye contact because he was about to burst out laughing. This was anything but funny. Clay and Sanjay were peering at me with anticipation, as if I would shrug my shoulders, grab the sword and get all medieval on his ass. Lorcan was staring at the Treize open-mouthed and his head jerked between them and me, before he took a step closer. The British man looked as if he was about to object, but Lo held up a hand in a halting gesture.

'Tommi,' he whispered. 'This is an ancient rite. Whoever they deem responsible for setting the wheels of justice in motion must also carry out the sentence.'

'Aye, I get it – but I don't think that person is me.'

'They can't bring a mortal here to do it. They would never allow it. Plus, Joss isn't the one who made the Rennex connection.'

'He also couldn't lift that thing,' I muttered, looking at the sword as it sparkled at me impatiently. I let out a deep breath. 'Okay. What do I do?'

'Kill him.'

'Right here? In front of everyone? Won't it be . . . messy?'

'That's very much the point.'

After another long moment, Lorcan stepped back to his previous position. Taking a deep breath, I glanced up at the waiting guard. He looked like he had just overheard a conversation between two crazy people. I gave him a begrudging smile and reached out to draw the sword. As my hands inched closer I felt a palpable power radiating from it. I paused, hovering over the object.

'You must do this,' said the Asian member of the Treize. 'If you do not carry out the sentence, he is free to go.'

I frowned at that. This was a pretty fucked-up legal system to say the least. I drew the sword in one swift go, using all of my strength to pull it wide and position it to the side of my body. It made a shrill, metallic sound as it split the air and both the aid and the guard drew back. Their departure revealed the prisoner, still kneeling in his original position. The awkward exchange in the lead-up to his execution had him grinning again. I hated his grin. It fell away quickly as he saw my face and the expression that had settled there. I had seen what the Laignach Faelad could do up close. I had seen the lives they had destroyed. I had seen their power in all its terrible glory. There was no grey about it: knowingly unleashing that kind of evil on the world was a monstrous crime. He was going to die and it was going to be me that ended his centuries of life. This fact dawned on him too and all hope, light and final resistance slowly faded from his eyes. He shut them, lifting his body as upright as he could from his position kneeling. I paused, not so much for dramatic effect as to make sure I would be able to decapitate him in one go.

'You think you know who they are? You think you know what I've done?' he whispered. His eyes were closed, but he was unmistakably talking to me. 'You think you know who you are? You think you know your history?'

'Enough of this, end it already,' someone from the Treize called. The prisoner's eyes flung open and he looked directly at me.

'You have no idea, blue wolf.'

With a final exhale, I took two steps towards him and threw

my hips into a swing that brought the blade down on the space between his shoulders. The metal sliced through his flesh like it was hardly there at all and his head landed with an unceremonious thud on the ground. I felt a warm spurt of blood spray my face and body as I turned away, not wanting to get any more on me. You'd think with my forward momentum he would go flying backwards, yet it was the reverse: Newton's law or equal and opposite. His body lingered in position for a few seconds before it slumped forward and hit the ground like a pile of old meat. And then I heard the strangest sound: a slow, soft clapping that started quietly and grew as more members of the surrounding parties joined in. Turning back to the corpse, I watched with a strange detachment as his blood spilled out on the tiles, pooling down the grouts in between each one and spreading further and further like a red grid. By the time I pulled my eyes away, the clapping had stopped. The Treize and members on the balcony above were all mostly grinning at me in a restrained manner. They were pleased. They were also creepy. Thaddeus deserved to die and I felt no remorse having killed him, but a chorus of people clapping for you after doing so was bizarre.

I numbly handed the sword back to the guard, who regarded the blood that decorated its blade with an eerie sense of wonderment. No one made a move to clear the body, and I stepped back to my position in the line. Keeping my head down, I felt my blue hair fall forward as I made to wipe the blood splatter from my face.

'That it?' I murmured, looking up at the Treize. They were regarding me with respect, which was almost as obtuse as the clapping.

'Not quite,' said the woman with long, brown hair. 'There is one other thing that we would ask of you.'

I very nearly snorted. 'Aye?'

She nodded casually in Heath's direction and he turned to me, arms wide as if he was ready to hug someone. 'We're assembling a team.'

'The Avengers?'

Heath snickered at me. 'Our battle with the Laignach Faelad might be over, but the war is not won. This is no football side we're putting together, Tommi. It's a hit squad.'

'A formal offer is being extended to Mr Sanjay Kehli, Mr Clayton Rodriguez, Mr Lorcan MacCarthy and Miss Tommi Grayson to fulfill a temporary contract with the Praetorian Guard,' said a Treize member.

'I already turned the Guard down once, and I'm flattered but I'm not joining.'

'That was for a full-time position, Tommi. Think of this as a part-time shift,' said Heath. 'We would employ you for a minimum of three months where a small team would head to Ireland to hunt down and exterminate the rest of the Laignach Faelad.'

'Three months?'

'Just enough time to finish them off for good.'

'You have skills that we've made no secret of wanting to utilise,' said the Asian gent. 'Although you might be hesitant about the conditions of the Praetorian Guard, this situation is one hundred per cent temporary. You would have every resource we could offer your disposal and once the mission is complete, you're free to return to life as you see fit.'

'With a substantial wage and us owing you a favour,' added the Maori man.

'Miss Yu Hingui and Miss Dolly Seetic have both declined the offer, and there are no hard feelings if you also would like to decline,' said the pale woman.

I mulled over their pitch, thinking about the complications of tying myself to this organisation and whether it would benefit or hinder my existence as a kathurungi: a rogue were-wolf. The words of the man I had just executed played on my mind. Then I mentally scolded myself as I thought about Berlin, about everything that happened over the past few months and all I had seen. If I didn't agree to this, I was quite sure Heath and co. would be capable enough to annihilate the Laignach Faelad. Quite sure, not certain. This enemy had been able to fester under the very feet of the ancient body of super-naturals I was standing before. What I was being given was an opportunity to personally make sure an evil like this would never again come to pass.

'I'll accept if I can ask that favour now,' I said.

'Very well,' said the moustachioed man. 'What's your request?'

'That my half-brother Quaid Ihi be released and returned to his family.'

There was a deep murmur around the room as people in the gallery discussed it and the Treize shared significant looks.

'That is a layered issue,' said the Asian man. 'He was serving time at Vankila initially for crimes committed against you, yet you want him freed?'

'Yes. He's fourteen. I know it's been a while since any of you were teenagers, but it's not the most productive time for deci-sion making.'

The red-headed lady laughed at that, nodding. 'You must understand, we won't release anyone that's dangerous back out into the public. Persons who go to Vankila don't come back.'

The Maori man met my eyes. 'We'll grant you visitation in six months. In another six months, upon revision of his crimes and demeanour, we'll look at permanent release. This has to be a gradual process as Vankila is . . . defining.'

'Deal,' I said, not bothering to argue with them. They and I both knew I had zero bargaining power here. If I said no to joining Heath's team, they would find someone else and move on. I had one shot at lobbying for Quaid and I had to take it.

'I'm in,' said Sanjay, breaking the silence that had fallen following my negotiation.

'Oh, *chico*. Adventure, danger, destruction. What else was I doing?' muttered Clay. 'Me too.'

'We can stop an encore performance,' Heath said quietly. Everyone in the room heard the words, yet I felt as if he was speaking directly to me. I glanced at Lorcan and saw all of my concerns reflected in his face. He was reluctant to become involved in PG matters again and I could see suspicion playing there also.

Turning to Heath I saw anticipation as he waited for me to make a decision. He was watching my face closely and his own began to transform into a mischievous smile. He could see my answer before I said it and I felt my own mouth curve into a grin. His mood was bloody infectious.

'I've never been to Ireland,' I started, twisting to face the Treize. 'Aye, let's finish it.'

Acknowledgements

This book wouldn't exist without the tireless support, hard work and brownies of the people at Little, Brown and Piatkus in London. They've supported the *Who's Afraid?* origin story and enabled it to continue as part of this weird, wacky and were-full paranormal world. Specifically the great editoress Anna Boatman – who squeals with joy and finds holes in equal measure – and Gemma Conley-Smith who named her first child after the characters in this book, right Gemma? RIGHT?! *stares hard*

These two extraordinary bebes went above and beyond what's required of them and straight up feel like family at this point. Also MERCI MERCI to the following – but not limited to – Ceara Elliot, my purple-haired publicist Nazia 'Agent' Khatun, Dominic Wakeford, Nick Castle, Kate Doran and the many more I've forgotten – sorry for that, but I had a stroke once so ¯_(ツ)_/¯. Kudos for making my first international book tour experience way less scary than it should've been.

Sam, who's so great he makes Samwise look like a shitty companion for Frodo. And yes, I realise that makes me Frodo but it's totally worth it if a Sam comes as part of this package. Eternal cheers for putting up with book-related talk, worry, stress, panic attacks and for not completely exploding with frustration when you tell me to 'take a break' and my response is 'nah'. Thank you for keeping me above the metaphorical fires of Mount Doom like a Great Eagle.

To my grandparents and my mother, for reading *Who's Afraid?* with such earnest excitement and not being horrified when they got to the end of it.

My agent Alex Adsett, always my agent Alex – a lady so grand she can simultaneously make *Who's Afraid?* tote bags while negotiating screen options like it ain't no thing. Every author should be lucky enough to have someone believe in them as much as Alex. And on that note Paul, here's hoping your predictions come true day-by-day.

To Wigtown warriors Steph and Carl at the Glaisnock Guest House and yes, that is a real place. Sorry I used it as the location for my characters to boink, but thank you for your years of support, thank you for welcoming a funny-sounding tourist in off the street with open arms, thank you letting me handle your farting twins, thank you for being the first people to ever ask for my autograph and thank you for the baking. Always the baking. Hey James!

To the IRL inspirations for the Rogues, the Berlin posse who showed me all the faces of one of my favourite cities while managing to avoid being arrested (mostly): Jak Skallywag, Emma Danger Bertoldi, Robert Dux, Karina, Hazle Nutts and the Meat Grinders crew.

Lexi Alexander for pursuing *Who's Afraid?* for the screen like Frank Castle would an organised crime syndicate and for just 'getting' what I was trying to do from the jump.

To my iwi sis Anna Gough, for improving my Te Reo Maori to the point I'm only mildly embarrassing now and being the best lady-on-point when it comes to representing our heritage. Kia whaia atu! And Sonja Hammer, for expanding my horizons and repping people of colour in horror and genre like no other.

To the wonderful team of people I work with on The Feed (weeknights at 7.30pm on SBS! Huzzah!) They didn't have anything specific to do with this book but they have every-thing to do with me waking up each day and frothing the thought of going to work on the best God damn half an hour of television on Australian screens. Yeah, I said it brah.

To my collective wolf pack: Bridie, Anna, Alice, Chris, Seamus and Philo Jabour, Candyke and Kylie, Cath fucking Webber who's the mentor Yoda wishes he could be, Denise Pirko, Rick Morton, the hairiest *Who's Afraid?* fan Harrison, Nicola Scott, Dr Nick Cocks, Yen, Mandy Spettigue and the whole extended UK fam, The Nerdy Bird herself Jill Pantozzi (hurry the fuck up and move to Australia mate), the Sydney and Melbourne Babe Collectives, Lou ya champion, Courtney, Bonnie, Georgia, India and the whole Hancock family (excluding your rat dogs), Red Cap, *Who's Afraid?* correspondent Rachel Junge, Chris Bath Vader, the first Tommi cosplayer I ever saw IRL Polly Meave, Gordy for a million reasons but especially for getting the book in Tarantino's hands you freakin babezilla, Rae Johnston, IRL Mari and Kane Hayley and Kieran – sozzles I murdered you, the whole Sultana family for being just the BEST, Ebs, Ineke, the Supanova Expo posse, Caris Bizzaca, four degrees of Dan Ilic, Cleo and Anna Waters-Massey, the growing Makepeace crew for years of support and kindness, Tassie Devils, Jamie Beloved and Martin Abel, J.Mo (for requesting every character be bisex-ual), MILF Leah Hallett and her growing she-pack, Glasgow dark sorceress Laura, the Centrelink of author pals Lynette 'IRL

Disney Princess' Noni, Marlee Jane Ward, Justin Woolley and Maria V. Snyder, Keri 'Kezzdawg' Arthur, Alison Goodman, Anne Bishop, Griffon Ramsey for being the first American fan (and the deadliest with a chainsaw), Tom Taylor, Alan Baxter, Bossy Love/Amandah Wilkinson, Blake and Sam, Daniel Radcliffe, Fanciful Fiction Auxiliary, the Australian Stroke Foundation, Eka Darville, Sydney Shadows, Cara and Ben, Kawaii Klaws, Fairchild my favourite Aussie ex-pats, John-Paul Langbroek, I Scream Nails, Anthony Calvert, Chewie Chan, the Gates family, human tornado Darynda Jones, Tricky Hickson, Kate Czerny, Kate Cuthbert, Laura and Louis, my-we-are-totally-not-cousins-cuz Manu Bennett, all my Twitter femmos and anyone else I have no doubt forgotten in my quest to thank everyone who somehow touched the *Who's Afraid?* collective in a positive way.

This is super important: to all the journalists and bloggers and reviewers and podcasters and vloggers who cared enough about my wee werewolf story the first time to give it space and attention – THANK YOU! I cannot tell you how hard it is to make a splash as a debut author so thank you x infinity for making that happen. A huge part of the interest and excitement in this book is due to you giving the *Who's Afraid?* universe inches.

Finally, to all of the readers and cosplayers I've met at signings and talks and book things across the world over the past twelve months – and to those I haven't who have sent me messages and emails and letters and fan art – one thing has been resoundingly clear and that's how hungry you were for book two. Now that it's here, I hope it does for you what *Blade II* did for me *cue Mos Def/Massive Attack slo-mo walk in*